FRANK MERCERLI

WAKE
TURBULANCE

AN ALCUBIERRE METRIC CONNECTION NOVEL

BOOKS BY FRANK MERCERET

First Verses
A poetry chapbook

CATSPAW
An Alcubierre Metric Connection Novel

WAKE
TURBULANCE

AN ALCUBIERRE METRIC CONNECTION NOVEL

by

Frank Merceret

ISBN: 978-1-7371858-2-6 (paperback)
ISBN: 978-1-7371858-3-3 (eBook)

TO MY FAMILY
Liz
Martin, Honor, Angela
August and Ida

TO MY MOST TREASURED TEACHERS
Professor Blair Kinsman
Professor JoLee Passerini

CONTENTS

PART I

THE WAKE

CHAPTER ONE

THE BEGINNING

AS THE FREIGHTER *Sensei Maru* steamed eastward in the Indian Ocean, about 140 nautical miles southwest of Adelaide enroute from the Middle East to Melbourne, optical and radio telescopes over that half of the globe reported strong signals at wavelengths ranging from radio waves through light and even up to gamma rays. At each instrument, the recorded signal looked like a single, large pulse that decayed quickly. Globally, these pulses occurred nearly simultaneously.

At the moment the telescopes were seeing the pulses, Captain Takahashi was on deck taking a smoke and catching the breeze. He was startled by a sudden, brilliant apparition in the sky. The collision of two aircraft? Should he report it to someone? He went to the bridge and contacted his company. After a short discussion with a company officer, he was told that they would notify Australian authorities and he should make a log entry describing what he'd seen.

At 4:45 PM Central Australian Standard Time, Takahashi entered the following:

15 September 0703 UTC – a bright flash of light appeared in the sky to starboard about ten degrees down from the zenith, almost due south of our position, which I estimate was 36.925 S, 137.04 E at the time. The event did not last long enough for any attempt to measure its altitude and azimuth with an instrument. The flash was followed by oppositely directed streaks propagating generally easterly and westerly from there. The streaks faded and vanished in seconds. There were no unusual sounds during or after the event. I could not identify the source, but some sort of incident involving aircraft seems possible.

He hoped that the Australian search and rescue services could locate any survivors.

As residents of Australia flooded the internet with visual reports and a few lucky photographs of the event, personnel of the armed forces in the United States, Russia, and China were examining military satellite data and ground observations. Something big had just happened, and they each suspected that one of the other nations may have accidentally or even deliberately detonated some sort of nuclear device in Earth orbit. The U.S. and Russia were alarmed over damage to imaging sensors on several of their reconnaissance birds, and one Russian orbital platform had simply vanished over the Indian Ocean at the moment of the event.

By 6 AM, at the Arlington Virginia headquarters of the Air Force Office of Scientific Research (AFOSR), Colonel Christopher Nilson had been called into the office of the director, a civilian with a doctorate in space physics. Nilson, the organization's deputy director, was himself a PhD physicist.

"Colonel Nilson, have a seat. I assume you have heard about the event over the Indian Ocean this morning?"

There were two chairs on the opposite side of the desk. Nilson took the one the director had indicated.

"Yes, ma'am."

She leaned toward him with her arms crossed. "We took damage to some of our recon birds and a few other assets I'm not authorized to mention, and half of the flag officers in the Pentagon are sure it was the Russians or the Chinese testing an anti-satellite weapon that, shall we say, over-performed. Our tracking network can't find one of the newer Kobalt-M series vehicles that was near the event when it occurred. Either the Russians were targeting their own or they're a victim, too. At 9 AM, the President will issue an executive order declaring a national emergency."

She sat back and clasped her hands on her stomach, awaiting his reaction.

"This isn't something we usually get involved with directly. What's different?" he asked.

She put her hands back on the desk. "The NSA and our own intelligence people have been looking at all of the data on the event, but also at the communications within and between other countries with capabilities similar to our own. They may be deliberately leaking false information, but the signals intelligence (SIGINT) folks don't think so. They're as stumped as we are as to how such a powerful explosion could have caught us all by surprise without there being any traces of a nuke— and, except for the Russian recon bird, no satellite anyone was tracking is gone. Our leadership wants us to have a look at the phenomenon and give them some options for what might have caused it."

Nilson tapped his fingers in front of him for a few seconds. "It sounds like something for the Physics Research area. I can have a statement of work ready for them in an hour or two."

The director raised her right hand and pointed at Nilson. "Chris, I want you to head this up personally. Set up a working group using whoever you need from as many of our research areas as you have to. I want answers that we can back up thoroughly, but I also want them fast. And this entire effort is classified."

"Secret?"

"Top Secret until we know more about what we're dealing with."

He stood up. "OK. I'll get right on it."

"You might want to include that Russian physicist the NSA keeps borrowing to hack into the Russian science databases. That might be a useful talent for this exercise."

"Irina Ivanova. Yes, good. Her technical background will fit in nicely, as well. Anything else?"

"Not at the moment. Just keep me informed."

Nilson nodded, and then he turned and closed the door behind him as he left.

Civilian science satellites and terrestrial telescopes had also seen the event. Optically, it had been about as bright as the sun. Astronomers and astrophysicists took immediate notice, but they weren't looking for an aircraft accident or the remains of an illicit space weapon. Their initial intuition was that their optical instruments had seen the visible light accompanying an extraordinary gamma ray burst from some super-massive cosmic eruption in the heavens. These infrequent bursts of high-energy radiation resulted from cataclysmic astronomical events which were not well understood. As reports appeared on the Transient Astronomy Network, several astronomical institutions asked the Laser Interferometer Gravitational Wave Observatory (LIGO) Scientific Consortium (LSC) to look for potential gravitational wave (GW) signals occurring at the same time as the event. If there were GW, they would assist in determining what kind of event had produced them. This event had been so powerful that it raised concerns about what dangers it presented and how likely another one like it might be. In this case, national security and scientific curiosity had a common goal—to find out what had happened, sooner rather than later.

∞

When the event erupted in the daytime sky over the Indian Ocean, it was dark in Louisiana. Lee Markson and Katty Clarke were sound asleep at Markson's home near the campus of the Louisiana Advanced Projects Institute (LAPI) in Baton Rouge. While they slept, software at the LIGO Livingston Observatory (LLO), 40 miles down Interstate 12 from their offices, detected a possible GW signal that lasted for several seconds beginning at 2:03 AM CDT. The automated, real-time quality control software flagged it for additional examination. As research professors in the LAPI Department of Physics and Astronomy, it wouldn't be long before Markson and Clarke would find out that they'd slept through what could become the most important event of their professional lives.

Markson and Clarke's personal and professional lives had become entwined like the horizontal and vertical threads in a woven tapestry—without both, the picture would fall apart. They'd met forty months earlier at a conference at Queen Mary University in London, which had been sponsored by the UK Institute of Physics' Gravitational Physics Group. At the time, Clarke had been a postdoctoral fellow at Virgo and had presented a paper that could have application to Markson's work, specifically when it came to identifying GW signals in the raw data from the LIGO instruments. At the end of the session in which she'd given her talk, he'd introduced himself, attracted to both her work and her person. Just a few years younger than him, she'd been someone he'd found most attractive from the start.

"Where do you work?" she'd asked.

When he'd replied that he was a physics professor at LAPI, she'd given him a quizzical look and had asked, "What's an LAPI?"

He'd told her 'LAPI' stood for the Louisiana Advanced Projects Institute, a graduate research university in Louisiana with a mission to do basic research with the long-term goal of eventual practical applications.

She'd raised her eyebrows and tilted her head a bit. "You look awfully young to be a full professor."

"Associate professor," he'd said with a laugh. "I should have been more specific. But I do have tenure!"

She'd nodded in appreciation. The day's lunch break had come next, so they'd decided to eat together while discussing his interest in her paper, and she'd not objected when it became clear, though unspoken, that he'd also developed an interest in her. His light complexion and pale blue eyes—suggesting Irish descent—were qualities she found attractive. His straight, reddish-brown hair with the half-hearted part on the right struck her as pleasantly whimsical.

Now, forty months later, she was his colleague at LAPI, and they often slept together.

When they got to their offices that morning, they were each greeted by messages from the LSC alerting them that both LIGO and Virgo had recorded candidate signals overnight. They also saw messages from astronomers requesting immediate examination of any such signals coinciding with radio, optical, x-ray, and gamma ray emissions originating somewhere above the Indian Ocean near Australia at about the same time.

LIGO and Virgo had been built to observe gravitational waves. These observatories provided new capabilities for the human species and opened up a new field of astronomy based on gravitation rather than the electromagnetic radiation used by optical and radio telescopes. When combined with traditional optical and radio observations, the GW information created yet another new field called "multi-messenger astronomy." The event near Australia was already beginning to look like a practical, "real-world" application for these emerging areas of research.

Markson was about ten minutes into reading his correspondence when Jorge Aguillero stuck his head in the door. "Good morning, Lee. You've seen the news?"

In addition to his position at the institute as their department chairman, Aguillero was a consultant to the LLO. Markson and Clarke were his primary resources when he needed assistance with any task for the observatory. Like Aguillero, Markson was a physics and engineering expert involved in the observation of gravitational waves.

"Good morning, Jorge. Yes, I'm reading the mail now."

"What do you think?"

"I don't know yet. I just got here a few minutes ago, but it definitely looks like something worth exploring."

Aguillero stepped into the room and closed the door. "You know, the President just declared a national emergency. There may be some Defense Department money available for this."

"I hadn't heard that. Seems like an overreaction."

"He said some of our military assets were damaged and the Russians and Chinese have put their forces on high alert."

Markson took a deep breath and let it out with an audible sigh. "Scary. I guess we should give it our full attention."

Aguillero nodded. "Good. I agree. Keep close tabs on it. I may have some work for you, depending on what we find out in the next week or two."

Markson noted that his boss hadn't mentioned Clarke even though she had skills which could be important to any investigation they might undertake. "If there's really a GW signal there, I'd like to have Katty take a look at it. I think we should work together on this if we get into it."

Clarke was the department's resident guru when it came to digital signal processing and algorithms for gravitational wave detection and analysis. Before joining LAPI, she'd completed her postdoctoral fellowship at Virgo under Aberto Giordano, who was one of the world's best in the field.

Aguillero scoffed. "If you think you need her, it's OK with me, but I doubt it will be necessary."

Aguillero had hired Clarke based on Markson's recommendation and a glowing letter of reference from Giordano; Aguillero and Giordano were about the same age and had known each other for decades, during which they'd attended conferences together and cited each other's papers in their own journal articles. Aguillero respected and trusted Giordano, and the letter had convinced him to accept Markson's recommendation—but he didn't take Clarke seriously as a colleague.

For his part, Markson resented Aguillero's visible lack of respect for Clarke. It was the blatant openness of Aguillero's attitude that most concerned him. His boss didn't fully accept women as equals in the workplace, but he usually concealed it well since the dean, his boss, was female.

"Why won't it be necessary?" Markson pressed. "You suspect the candidate GW signals aren't real?"

"No, they're probably real, but if they are, they're large enough that we won't need any fancy special signal processing to characterize them."

"OK, Jorge. I'll let you know as soon as I get a better feel for what part, if any, we'll have to play in this."

Aguillero and Markson had a difficult relationship that predated Aguillero's hiring him at LAPI forty-four months earlier. Markson wondered if perhaps some of the ill will permeating their relationship was generating friction between Aguillero and Clarke, too, because he had been the one who'd talked him into hiring her sixteen months earlier.

As Markson's PhD thesis advisor at LSU nearly a decade earlier, Aguillero had told his protégé that his proposed thesis topic was unacceptable. Markson had wanted to write a paper demonstrating the theoretical possibility of a device that could send information back a few milliseconds in time in a manner consistent with Einstein's field equations. When Markson had enrolled at LSU, Aguillero had promised him he could select his topic without any restrictions, and so when Markson had accused him of welching on the promise, Aguillero had taken it as a personal attack on his integrity.

Aguillero kept his promise, but warned Markson that a thesis proposing a "time-machine" would be considered junk science and make him unemployable as a physicist. That turned out to be an accurate prediction. Despite his anger at his protégé's disrespect, Aguillero gave him a post-doctoral fellowship to tide him over for a few months and so that he could complete some work they'd been doing for LIGO. Halfway through his postdoc, though, Markson got a job offer from a Wall Street investment firm, Catalano Automated Trading (CAT), which he accepted. As a result, he left LSU before completing his assignment. His mentor considered that a breach of trust and couldn't forgive him, even though Markson had completed the work remotely while working for his new employer.

Later, when Aguillero hadn't gotten an expected promotion to serve as Dean of the College of Sciences at LSU, he'd blamed it on the negative reaction to his work with Markson.

Thinking that having been Markson's thesis advisor may have negatively impacted his own professional reputation, he'd left LSU to accept the position he now held at LAPI. Aguillero had never dreamed that Markson would become famously successful in building a working prototype of his time machine that made CAT, and Markson, a fortune. He'd also never imagined the nightmarish eventuality that his boss at LAPI—Joanne Simpson, Dean of the College of Physical Sciences—would coerce him into hiring his disrespectful, untrustworthy former student as a tenured associate professor in his own department.

As Markson reflected on all this history, the pieces assembled themselves into a picture. Dean Simpson had supported his request that his contract include a provision ensuring that he'd be consulted on the hiring of a junior faculty member with expertise related to their gravitational wave research. So, it probably wasn't just Giordano's glowing letter of recommendation that had induced Aguillero to hire Clarke at his recommendation. He realized now that their boss may have felt coerced. It was more than Clarke being a woman that bothered the man: Aguillero probably saw her as being a woman who'd been forced on him by Markson, whose preference had itself been backed up by that other annoying woman he had to humor because she was his supervisor—the dean.

The gravitational wave event at LLO was also detected by LLO's twin, the LIGO Hanford Observatory (LHO) in Hanford, Washington. At the same time, software at Virgo in Pisa also set flags. It was 9:03 AM there, and Clarke's Virgo mentor was wide awake.

Giordano was one of those wizard mathematician/physicists who'd developed ways of reliably separating the true signal of a gravitational wave from the attendant natural background and sensor system noise. This signal got his attention immediately—it was huge and unfamiliar. If it was real, something spectacular had just happened in the sky near Australia. If it was not real, then some powerful source of interference manifesting itself as apparent gravitational waves had suddenly appeared worldwide and just happened to coincide with the optical observations over the Indian Ocean. Either way, it was going to be an interesting day.

Originally predicted by Einstein's general theory of relativity, gravitational waves are ripples in the structure of space and time that occur when things as massive as large stars orbit around each other or collide. To observe them, LIGO, Virgo, and their Japanese counterpart KAGRA (which had been offline for a planned upgrade at the time of the event) were built.

Gravitational waves change the shape of space as they pass, and they are fiendishly difficult to detect. GW detectors like LIGO measure changes in the distance between special mirrors kept several kilometers apart in a vacuum as these waves pass. The fractional change is called the "strain," and it is unimaginably small. The length change occurring on Earth due to the collision of a pair of black holes, typically more than a billion light years away, amounts to less than the diameter of a proton in 4 kilometers. This makes even the tiniest of thermal or electrical vibrations in the mirrors appear as noise in the mirror position data. This noise can be similar in amplitude to the size of genuine gravitational wave signals, and it's often difficult to determine whether a candidate astrophysical GW signal is real or just an artifact of the noise.

The difficulty involved in examining a GW signal was why specialists in finding ways of recognizing, diagnosing, and reducing sources of noise—people like Aguillero and Markson—were important assets to LIGO and its companion programs elsewhere in the world.

Until LIGO had detected the collision of two black holes that had been orbiting each other as a binary pair in 2015, many doubted it would be possible. That original detection, and several more which followed it over the next two years, excited the astrophysics community so that top priority was then given to verifying the results. Verification methods were refined and largely automated in the years afterward, but it still took time before a candidate signal could be considered an observation of a real event rather than just random noise. A major ingredient in assessing the reality of a signal was matching its characteristics to the predicted characteristics of known astrophysical phenomena that produce gravitational waves. These predictions, called templates, formed part of the quality control process for verifying LIGO and Virgo data. Unverified candidate GW detections didn't carry as much urgency as they once had because valid waves were being seen on a regular basis. And although it had not been officially verified yet, Giordano knew because of its strength and unusual characteristics that this one was different—even though it didn't match any of the templates.

This was where Giordano and Clarke excelled. Although Giordano's first research with Virgo had been in the same area as Aguillero's, he'd found that the challenge of identifying signals excited him more than improving the noise reduction efforts and had eventually become the European Gravitational Observatory's resident expert in the area. That was why Clarke had chosen to work for him for her postdoc. With his blessing, she'd undertaken to develop techniques meant to extract the time series of a GW for which there was no template, and cleanse it of any noise remaining after the initial processing and filtering so that the true shape of the wave, the waveform, could be determined. That would allow others to explore what possible phenomena might generate such a waveform, thereby identifying likely sources. Her addition to the LAPI faculty had strengthened its limited experience in that area and, combined with Aguillero and Markson's commanding expertise in noise identification and reduction, it had made the LAPI team one of the best in the field.

∞

As speculations regarding possible sources of the phenomenon ramped up on physics and astronomy websites, Markson and Clarke were intrigued by the variety of possibilities being suggested, as well as the differing weights individual investigators were giving to various pieces of the evidence. One item in particular caught their attention: four days after the event, Aguillero posted a link to a journal article he'd published several years before. He claimed it supported the speculation that a new kind of astrophysical event was responsible for the signals, and postulated a specific phenomenon—an exploding star called a hypernova in a star cluster a few thousand light years from Earth, in the constellation Norma.

Markson knocked on Clark's open office door. "Got a minute?"

"Sure. Come on in."

He closed the door behind him and locked it before pulling the chair near the door to the front of her desk and sitting down. "Did you see the paper Jorge posted this morning?"

"I just read his commentary. That seemed sufficient for now. Anything worth reading?"

Markson had his arms folded and was scowling. "Did he mention anything to you about it before he posted it, or send you a copy?"

"No. You?"

"No. Pisses me off. I've been bending over backwards to

make things right with him after what happened when we were at LSU, but he still can't seem to treat me as a trustworthy colleague."

"So, that's why you locked the door? So that you could come in here and bitch about him without taking the chance that he might walk in on us?"

Markson's face relaxed into a small smile. "Sure. Why the hell not?"

She laughed. "No reason. Bitch away!"

He took a deep breath and let it out with a sigh. "I'm good. All bitched out now."

"You didn't answer my question. Anything in it I should read?"

"I didn't read it either. Like you said, his summary on the reflector was enough for now."

A few days later, the pair went to Markson's office in order to hash out the merits of the various opinions being presented online. A week of analysis by different research teams had provoked conflicting responses. The pair had chosen Markson's office for this day's effort because it was larger than Clarke's and had a worktable that was comfortable for informal discussions. They sat catty-corner, with him at the end and her sitting next to him on one side so that there was nothing between them and they could easily face each other.

"Let's see if we can make some preliminary sense out of this. Jorge's probably going to want us to do something with it, and I'd like to get a little ahead of the game," Markson said.

"OK, but the problem I have is that we haven't even decided what class of phenomenon we're dealing with, so it's hard to know where to start narrowing down to specifics."

"What do you mean?"

She got up, went to the whiteboard at the front of the room, and wrote a list of possibilities:

The candidate GW signals coincident with the visual event were just noise, so the phenomenon was only an electromagnetic one.

A mishap involving a secret satellite somehow generated GW in addition to its electromagnetic effects.

It was a routine astrophysical event, but much closer than ever observed before.

It was a unique, cataclysmic astrophysical event at a typical cosmological distance.

It was a new kind of astrophysical event and much closer than previously observed events—perhaps Jorge's hypernova?

She then turned back to face her colleague. "Here are the main contenders. Did I miss any?"

Markson leaned forward. "I think we can eliminate two of them right away. First, I have no doubt that the GW signals were real, not noise."

All of the correspondence on the internet acknowledged that there'd definitely been candidate signals at Virgo and both LIGO sites which had been well-correlated with each other, and most thought noise was an unlikely source. Correlation meant that these signals at all three locations had looked similar while they'd lasted. Noise was generally random, so no two noise sources were likely to remain similar for as long as these signals had persisted, but some correspondents insisted that it couldn't be totally ruled out yet. Markson didn't agree.

"They were too strong above the background level and too well-correlated among the three different sites at LIGO and Virgo. When I was a research assistant working on noise reduction systems at LLO as a grad student, the systems were good enough not to pass anything that big unless it was real. And now, of course, they're even better. The quality of these signals looks like it might even be good enough for us to use the time differences that produce maximum correlations as a consistency check on the direction of the source in comparison with the EM observations."

"But the electromagnetic pulse was huge. Couldn't some of that energy have gotten through the screening?"

Markson shook his head and frowned. "Not a chance. Each of the GW detectors has thousands of probes measuring electromagnetic radiation; they'd detect any radio, optical, or high-energy radiation strong enough to cause interference. The system isn't perfect, but it would take a major failure to permit this level of contamination to go undetected. Besides, the optical source was below the horizon at all three sites. The whole Earth was shielding the GW sensors from electromagnetic radiation. It's not a reasonable hypothesis."

After a few seconds, Clarke turned to the board and put an X through the number 1. Then, she turned to Markson and said, "OK, so what's the other one that gets the axe?"

Markson laughed. "That satellite thing. An exploding satellite would have to have the mass of a planet to produce any gravitational waves we could hope to detect. Not even the Death Star explosion in *Star Wars* would do it."

"That's not so funny. There are accusations and threats all over the news. One mistake, and modern civilization—including us—can be vaporized in a thousand thermonuclear fires."

That thought sobered Markson as he recalled the President's declaration of a national emergency. It struck him that this was much more than an interesting scientific exercise. It could have serious, and even deadly consequences if it wasn't resolved shortly. He was confident that the explanation would eliminate any possibility that the event had been caused by an orbital weapon.

He shook his head. "The politicians and military types are too self-interested to blow away the social structure that makes them rich and powerful. As soon as the GW are confirmed to have been caused by the event, the war hysteria will fade away, except for a few nutcases that were already rattling their rockets before it happened, anyway."

She sighed, crossed out the number 2, and returned to the table. With her elbows in front of her and her hands on her cheeks, Clarke sat for a few moments before she looked up and said, "The other three are all astrophysical. It doesn't look like collisions of binary black holes or neutron stars or anything?"

Some of the internet correspondents had emphasized that the signal didn't match the expected waveform for any known astrophysical event. The LSC had a large library of computer calculations, the templates, that used Einstein's field equations to predict what GW from known types of sources like black hole collisions would look like when they reached Earth.

"The LSC ran the data through its standard quality control for potential GW detections, which includes the part that compares candidate signals with the templates. No matches."

"They compared all of them?"

"Yep. That's why the data failed the QC run that followed the initial quick look. It didn't match any of them. Not colliding neutron stars, not a collision of black holes, nothing. The templates for these known sources simply didn't look like the data from the event, and the template library is pretty complete. Whatever this is, we haven't seen it before, but the strain is too large and the correlations are too great to let the failure to match a template be the end of the analysis."

"What about the other two? I don't give much credibility to an explosion at cosmological distances being large enough to produce the optical effects. Something that gargantuan would have messed up space in its vicinity big-time, but none of the post-event astronomical observations show any such thing."

Markson agreed. She cocked her head to the side for a moment and then asked, "Was there a template for Jorge's hypernova?"

Markson startled. "I hadn't thought of that. Let's check."

A few participants in the online discussions had agreed with Aguillero's proposal that a previously unconsidered astrophysical event was the most likely source of both the GW and the optical observations. A few others had offered similar proposals of their own, though they were generally less specific than his. Most didn't accept the concept because they thought the two streaks racing away from the flash had been too fast and the whole thing had faded too quickly.

Markson accessed the online documentation from the LSC. "It doesn't look like they took Jorge's paper seriously enough to make a template for it."

She nodded. "So, maybe Jorge's unlikely hypernova isn't so unlikely after all? It does have some supporters. Definitely interesting. I think it's time to get us a copy of his complete paper."

"Yeah... If it turns out to be a serious possibility, it could make our lives easier. I'd like to be on Jorge's side for once."

One morning after another week had passed, Markson leaned into Clarke's office in Wigner Hall. It was just down the second-floor hall from his own, but smaller—a junior faculty office that reminded him of the one he'd had as a postdoc at LSU. Clarke's desk faced the door, and she sat behind it in a comfortable, ergonomic swivel chair. A small table with another big monitor abutted the desk to her right. There were a couple of bookcases behind her and two chairs that she kept by the door, as well as two large whiteboards, one on the wall by the door and the other on the opposite wall.

She didn't look up, so he watched her writing for a few seconds before he knocked. He could look at Katty Clarke all day—tall, only an inch shorter than he was, and muscular, she had a charismatic attractiveness and complexion. Her thick, blonde hair hung past her shoulders and down onto her ample breasts. She could easily have been a movie star rather than an astrophysicist. She was deep into concentrating on something, so he knocked lightly on the doorframe.

She raised her head, appearing irritated until she saw who it was, at which point she smiled. "What brings you around so early in the morning?"

"Actually, I wasn't expecting you to be here yet, but Jorge wanted to see me about that odd event we've been discussing the last two weeks, so I thought I'd stop by and check. You might have something to contribute."

She picked up the large leather purse from the table by her desk and headed for the door. She pointed for him to lead the way. "After you."

When they arrived at the anteroom to Aguillero's office, his secretary escorted them through a rear door to the right of her desk that opened into Aguillero's inner office. Against one wall, the department chairman kept a small table with a Keurig Machine, a hot plate, and supplies for making and flavoring coffee and tea. He still retained his Argentinian family tradition of formal hospitality, despite decades spent working in the more casual U.S.

Directly across from the entry, an exterior wall boasted two sets of double-width windows with about four feet between them. A tall bookcase took up the space between the windows. In the corner to the right, Aguillero had placed a triangular credenza and oriented his desk parallel to it, putting his desk at a 45-degree angle to the walls and about four feet in front of the credenza, his chair between the two pieces of furniture. From the corner with the credenza, the room extended twenty feet to the left to another corner where there was an exit to the building's second-floor hallway. This part of his office constituted a conference area with space for another large bookcase, a rectangular conference table, and six chairs. The right wall of the secretary's anteroom separated the conference area from the anteroom. The placement of the desk ensured that every corner of the office was visible to its occupant.

Aguillero had coffee waiting for Markson, and he insisted on making Clarke a cup of Earl Grey, her favorite tea, before talking business.

Clarke hadn't known him long. She found him to be an enigma. In Europe and the U.S., academics were generally informal in their dress and mannerisms. The ones from Latin America who she had gotten to know in the UK, at Virgo, and at LAPI—except for Aguillero—had more or less adapted to their new milieu. But Aguillero always wore a dark suit and a matching tie, not the sport shirt and casual slacks which Markson preferred or the jeans worn by some of the faculty and most of the students. Like a few of the other academics around, he sported a full beard. Unlike theirs, his beard was always neatly trimmed. Not a free spirit's beard. More like that of a cleric. Eastern or Greek Orthodox, perhaps. And his fashionable shoes had probably cost more than she paid for a month's rent and utilities.

Aguillero's reaction to Clarke was equally equivocal. Her clothes were always stylish. He appreciated that she took the time and expense to find and buy quality apparel, but he found her fondness for blouses that emphasized her cleavage to be unprofessional and provocative, just like her short skirts and tight-fitting pants that showed off the curves of her posterior. That day, her blouse was one that didn't offend him too much, but her skirt ended halfway between her knees and her hips, and was a deep maroon. He thought it belonged in a nightclub rather than a graduate school faculty member's office.

"Thank you for the tea," she said with a nod.

"You're welcome, Dr. Clarke," he said with a nod of his own as he gestured for her and Markson to join him at the nearby table where most of their meetings with their boss were held.

The chair nearest the secretary's office was clearly at the head of the table. Aguillero always sat there beneath the large whiteboard, which hung on the wall separating his office from his secretary's. He seated others depending on how he perceived their importance. The higher one ranked, the closer one sat to him. He pointed Markson to the seat next to him on the right, and suggested Clarke bring up the chair from the other end of the table in order to sit next to her colleague. The chair on the left side, which was closer to the head of the table, remained vacant. She didn't notice the slight, but Markson had known their boss too long to miss it.

Once everyone was seated around the worktable, mugs in hand, Aguillero asked Markson to lead an investigation into the source of the signals from the September 15th gravitational wave event. He had a hypothesis he wanted them to verify...

"I think the electromagnetic and gravitational wave phenomena are together consistent with a cosmologically nearby, high-energy stellar explosion."

Markson leaned forward. "Cosmologically nearby?"

"Yes. All the sources for gravitational waves which we have detected so far have been billions of light years distant. I'm thinking of a source within a few thousand. I wrote a paper on such a possibility about two years after you quit science to go make money on Wall Street. Nobody would take me seriously because of my association with your unorthodox dissertation. Well, you proved them wrong about your dissertation. I think this will give us a chance to prove they were wrong about my paper, too."

"Mmmm." Clarke frowned as she spread her hands on the table in front of her.

"You have a question, Dr. Clarke?"

She looked up. "Perhaps we have the wrong paper. When I followed the link you posted, the paper it downloaded was co-authored with Professor Jelani. Since you didn't mention her name online or just now, I was wondering. Do I have the correct paper?"

"Yes, of course. She did some of the relativistic calculations, but the concept and the astrophysical aspects were entirely mine."

"Alright then, what sort of thing would we be looking for?"

"I was about to ask that myself," Markson said.

Aguillero brightened, obviously believing them both to be interested in his idea. "The most likely candidate is a hypernova, one of those supernovas that eject excessive mass and produce abnormally long gamma ray bursts. I think this event was a hypernova in the open stellar cluster NGC 6067 in the constellation Norma. It's in the right direction and at a reasonable distance from Earth. I tossed the idea out to the community that's been following our discussions, but it hasn't generated much enthusiasm yet."

Markson grimaced. "We've followed the discussion rather closely and kicked it around ourselves. I know it fits the initial visible and gravitational wave intensities, and there are certainly a few who agree with you, but many have posed objections. What's your rationale?"

Aguillero nodded. "We have a powerful burst of electromagnetic energy at wavelengths from radio waves through gamma rays, as well as coincident gravitational waves, right?"

Markson and Clarke agreed.

"And nothing we know of can produce GW strong enough to be detected with current technology unless at least stellar masses are involved, right?"

"As far as we know," Markson said.

"But we don't know everything," Clarke added.

"Perhaps not, but we can certainly assume that anything of less than stellar mass that produced GW of that size couldn't have been a billion light years away. Those we have detected have all been black holes with combined masses of ten suns or more. This had to be closer, just based on the strength of the GW signature, unless it was at least that massive."

Clarke nodded.

"But if it was big and far away, it would look like all the others do, right? This one was too bright. Hundreds of thousands of times more energetic throughout the EM spectrum. That means it couldn't have been much more than a few thousand light years away."

Markson and Clarke looked at each other. Aguillero did have some valid arguments.

"And it certainly couldn't have been as close as a hundred light years or we'd have been incinerated, yes?"

"That had occurred to us," Markson said, smiling.

Clarke waved her hands to interrupt. "Wait a minute. I don't believe you've eliminated something of, say, planetary mass that is much closer. Smaller explosion, smaller distance; both the GW and the radiation have large amplitudes despite the small mass because it's so much closer."

Aguillero shook his head. "Dr. Clarke...." He paused, sighed, and shook his head again. "Colliding planetary mass objects wouldn't produce that much EM radiation on Earth unless they were inside our solar system, and even if they were black as soot, they would have been sensed long before this event by numerous observing systems. Their gravitational effects on the orbits of the other things in the solar system would have been notorious, and that would have occurred even if they'd been made out of dark matter—whatever that turns out to be, *if* it actually exists. That's not a credible possibility."

It wasn't what he'd said that offended her. He was probably even right. It was the unmistakable air of disrespect with which he'd said it. She folded her arms, sat back, and glared at him.

Then she looked to Markson, who appeared to be deep in thought. He couldn't see anything good happening if he spoke up now since what their boss had said was technically true. Aguillero's contemptuous, condescending tone troubled him, as well, but this wasn't the time or place to address it—not if they didn't want their fragile relationship to be immediately damaged beyond recovery. He'd later have to consider whether to address Aguillero's attitude toward Clarke in private.

For the moment, he looked back at her with a frown and raised his eyebrows as if to say, *"I don't know what his problem is."*

Turning back to Aguillero, he said, "Interesting. What would you like us to do?"

The department chairman directed him to re-examine the GW and electromagnetic data using analytical tools not yet applied by the LSC to demonstrate that the strength of both the electromagnetic signals, from radio to gamma ray frequencies, and the gravitational wave signals fit the concept of a hypernova explosion at a distance of a few thousand light years.

"For that, I'm going to need Katty," Markson said, nodding toward her.

"Of course. I was just about to suggest that. She can help us make the case," Aguillero replied.

Clarke folded her arms across her chest. She and Markson had found some of the online objections to be serious, and she was still steaming from Aguillero's earlier putdown of her case for a smaller, nearer phenomenon. "Suppose we find out that the data don't support your case?"

"That won't happen. Work with Lee. He's got a lot of experience with both optical and GW sensors."

Markson smiled at the compliment. The old wounds from his long, complicated relationship with Aguillero were still on the mend. As time passed, he'd become ever more frustrated that Aguillero still didn't fully trust or respect him, so despite his concern about Aguillero's attitude toward Clarke, he was delighted that his boss was giving him an opportunity to mentor his colleague.

Clarke broke Markson's reverie as she responded to Aguillero. "It sounded to me like you were telling us what the right answer has to be. I'm not comfortable with that. I want to keep an open mind."

"Just follow the data. That's all I'm asking," Aguillero assured her. "You'll see. Nothing else makes sense."

He assigned Markson to coordinate their efforts and assemble a formal report before sending them back to their offices to get started. "I'd like to have something to present to the LSC as soon as possible so they don't waste any more time chasing some wild goose idea."

"No problem. We'll follow where the data leads us," Markson said.

"How long do you think you'll need?"

"Right now, you've got me working on our recommendations for the next LIGO noise reduction upgrade, and Kat's working on developing methods for improved generic signal identification without templates. How important is this? Do you want us to put those projects on hold and work full-time on this or what?"

Aguillero thought for a moment. "The whole world is talking about this. Even the politicians are asking what it was and where it was, and whether it represents a threat. I want you full-time on this. If there's DOD money to be had eventually, I want us to be first in line. Put the other stuff aside. I think Dr. Clarke's current research may already be applicable to this, too, so she can also work on it full-time."

Markson looked at Clarke. "At least a month?"

She frowned as she shook her head. "More than that, I think."

Markson turned to Aguillero. "Give us five weeks."

"I was hoping for something quicker than that. See if you can simplify the work and give me your best effort. Certainly no more than five weeks."

"Will do," Markson said.

∞

When Markson and Clarke returned to his office, she was still frowning. "Even five weeks sounds awfully optimistic to me."

Markson sat down at his desk, took out a pad of paper, and motioned to her to pull up a chair across from him. "Let's put together a schedule. Remember, he's not expecting a rigorous, detailed analysis at this point. The goal is to see if his hypernova is a reasonable hypothesis and, if not, what the other plausible candidates are."

"We still have to get most of the data from the obvious archives and do the quality control, formatting, and synchronization needed to turn it all into a usable database. That alone could take a month."

"I don't think so. We've already downloaded some of it just out of curiosity, and if an archive is *obvious*, as you say, it's going to be one that's already been identified in the email and online media discussions. We can collect the URLs in as little as a day and download the files in a few more days. I think we only need a week to identify and collect all of the raw data we'll need for this little project of Jorge's."

"O...K. Suppose I buy into that. We need to unpack each of those files, extract the metadata describing how they were processed, and QC the files. That's another month if we do it right. There are thousands of files."

"Kat, you're making too much of this. We don't need to use them all. If we have three sets of observations from the same general location with similar instruments, for this exercise, we pick the best set and use it, setting the other two aside. We'll actually use a few hundred files at most, and many of those will have common formats, which means we'll only need a few software packages to extract and reformat the information. We can write scripts to run them automatically 24/7."

Clarke took a deep breath and let it out with a sigh. "To 'pick the best' sets of observations, we have to extract enough data from each one to be able to compare them. Even if you can do your down-selection in a week, doing the QC is not something that can be done in a few days."

Markson looked down at his desk. Deep inside, he knew she was probably right, but they had to try to meet the commitment he'd made to Aguillero. He looked up. "I understand your concern. I'm confident we can get all the data in a week. During week two, we'll eliminate any data that isn't in a standard format unless it's essential to this preliminary analysis. We already have software to parse most of the standard formats, and many of those have automated QC built in. We can grab any additional software we need online. If it isn't available, we'll avoid using the files that require it. Let's give ourselves another two weeks to unpack, QC, and reformat the files into a common database."

"I hope you know what you're doing. What *we're* doing. But even if this fantastic riot of productivity happens, it only leaves us two weeks to examine the data and draw conclusions. I presume you're also assuming that the data will all be consistent and the answer obvious?"

Markson broke into laughter. "I love that about you, Kat. An arrow right in the heart! Yes, actually, that is my hope! If the data are not consistently pointing to an answer, then that will be our answer, and we'll tell the boss that a more thorough—and thus lengthy—analysis is necessary to solve the mystery."

Again, Clarke breathed deep and let it out with a sigh. "So how do we divide up the work?"

Markson's background in electronics, optics, and the LIGO hardware made him the data guru. In addition to the GW, visible, and microwave data they already had covering an hour on either side of the event, he went to data distribution sites posted on the internet and downloaded additional electromagnetic data for the same interval at wavelengths from shortwave radio through gamma rays.

"DC to daylight and beyond," he called it.

To determine whether the GW and EM data were consistent with each other and with their boss's theory, they'd need to review the signal processing. That was Clarke's bailiwick. She located detailed descriptions of the software used to collect, process, and distribute the data that Markson downloaded. Even to build a database with the limited accuracy and precision they needed would require complete descriptions of how the data had been prepared and stored. In many cases, information about the observations they obtained was stored in the files with the data. This so-called metadata was critical to the quality of their ultimate database.

Department of Defense (DOD) data was in unfamiliar formats and most of the metadata was unavailable, so they didn't bother downloading it. If it was needed later, they could get the remaining data and documentation from the DOD. This followed in line with their plan of keeping the data gathering and validation efforts manageable.

Still, assembling the database took longer than the three weeks they'd allotted for it. Four weeks into the project, Markson and Clarke sat in the LSU Student Union, which was a pleasant half-hour walk from their offices. It was across the street from Nicholson Hall, where Markson had had his office as a graduate student and postdoctoral fellow. They'd wanted a relaxed, easy lunch and he liked the familiar, tasty food there. Kat grabbed a poke bowl upstairs at ON-THE-GEAUX and he got a turkey wrap, and they adjourned to a common space on the first floor.

"I expected things to be in different units with differing sampling intervals," Markson said, "but I didn't expect our QC screening to pick up serious inconsistencies between two sets of measurements of the same thing from similar sensors at nearby locations."

"Like what?"

"The latest one I found this morning. Some microwave pulse observations from India that differ in timing from similar observations on the north coast of Australia by about 10.4 seconds."

Clarke frowned. "So, at least one of their clocks was way off."

"Obviously. But is it just one? Maybe it's both. And if it's one, which one? If both, how much is each one off? We don't have time to figure all that out. I hate to throw away the data, but bad data is worse than no data. The microwave travel time between them is twenty-one milliseconds. To use the pulse timing to make a useful estimate of the location of the source, the time has to be accurate to within better than about one percent of that, or two hundred microseconds. We could probably develop a correction to either or both clocks using known radio sources picked up by the systems near the same time, but we don't have the time it would take. I wish everyone would adopt GPS timing. It isn't that damned expensive."

"Things like that make automated quality control all the more important, but I'm worried about the metadata I need to do it. Not only are the formats different, but they don't seem to contain the same information in a way that allows them to be compared. I can't write generic, automated QC routines using the metadata to validate the observational data because each metadata package is unique. They're not as standardized as you had suggested," Clarke grumbled.

"Give me an example."

"We have quite a few radio and optical datasets archived with the data time-stamped every tenth of a second—like 07:03:27.2, 07:03:27.3, and so forth. But the metadata only tells me whether the value is an instantaneous value or an average, and sometimes not even that. For the kind of sub-millisecond precision you're asking for, I need to be able to determine whether an average is *centered* on the time stamp or *ends there.* If the sample is 'instantaneous', I need to know the response time of the instrument, and many data systems don't put that in the metadata. They expect you to look it up in online documentation, which isn't always readily available. Do we really need absolute time accuracy in microseconds?" she asked.

"Two hundred microseconds equates to 60 kilometers. That not only throws off position estimates based on the timing, but assuming the emissions from this thing behaved even a little like the shock wave from a nuclear explosion, then being off by 60 kilometers could mean you're looking at a different part of the wave than you think you are. It will throw off your understanding of what the data mean."

"Everything is so damned interdependent. When I was working on algorithms in the abstract, I felt comfortable because I was in control. Here, with real data, I have to react to what somebody else did or didn't do. I don't like being dependent on other people's competence and judgment, especially when they obviously aren't all on the same page."

Markson laughed in sympathy. "All we can do is keep putting one foot in front of another as quickly as we can. I think we should be ready to crank out some numbers for Jorge in another couple of weeks if we get back to work."

"Is that a hint?"

He nodded and stood up to take their trash to the receptacle. She joined him for the mile-and-a-half hike back to the LAPI campus.

Six weeks into the project, while acrimonious debates raged on astrophysics websites, Aguillero raged in his office in his formal, understated way.

Markson stood in front of Aguillero's desk, disappointed that he hadn't been offered the usual cup of coffee. He felt like a second lieutenant on the carpet in front of his battalion commander rather than a tenured professor being addressed by his department chairman. The Argentinian flag and some of the pictures on the wall behind the desk certainly didn't diminish the illusion. Strategically placed among pictures of Aguillero's family, his revered German Shepherd, and his two prize-winning Golden Retrievers, photos of him in uniform were prominent. The credenza behind him had some dog-show trophies and awards for church and civic accomplishments, but the place of honor at the center of its tabletop was occupied by a stand holding a shadow box with his military medals and the insignia of a naval lieutenant.

"I gave this exercise to you two because you're supposed to be experts," Aguillero was saying. "You told me five weeks. Download the data and look at it. Draw the obvious conclusion. How hard can that be?" He had not raised his voice, but his complexion, more ruddy than usual, disclosed the unseemly frustration and nascent anger he was doing his best to conceal.

Markson tried to be firm rather than rude. "You've been in this business a lot longer than I have. You know better than that. You based your hypothesis partly on the simultaneity of the signals. To assess that, the synchronization between observations has to be within two hundred microseconds or better. Not everything is documented to that level of precision."

"You just told me you finished that a few days ago. So, what's the hold-up now?"

Markson took a deep breath. "There isn't any hold-up, Jorge. I'm looking at the data, and Katty is about halfway through the huge pile of software specifications she has to catalog in order to examine the signal processing. By the time I know what the potential signal processing issues are, she'll be ready to address them."

Aguillero raised his eyebrows. "And when will that be, Dr. Markson?"

"Couple of weeks, probably."

Aguillero shook his head and frowned. Then, he waved Markson to the door. "Get back to work and see what you can do to hurry it up."

"Yes, sir," Markson said as he left. He resisted the temptation to salute.

Two weeks later, ten weeks after the event had occurred, Markson commandeered the department's small conference room so that he and Clarke could spread their work out and compare notes. The room was well-lit with two large triple-windows dominating the wall opposite the entrance from the hallway. The rectangular conference table, its longer dimension running parallel to the windows, had a faux-wood top balanced on two circular, stainless-steel pedestals. On the wall to the right of the door was a large-screen monitor that could be accessed via Wi-Fi as well as by ethernet, HDMI, or VGA connectors on the table. The table also had AC power and USB charging outlets. The other end of the room boasted a large whiteboard and a mechanical scanner that, with the push of a button, could make a digital copy of whatever was drawn on the board. At each side of the table were three black, five-wheeled chairs.

Markson and Clarke pushed four of the chairs back against the walls so they could roam freely around the table, keeping just the remaining pair near one end. There, a black leatherette briefcase and cup of black coffee in front of one chair marked it as Markson's while a steaming cup of Earl Gray and a dark blue backpack identified the other chair as Clarke's. When they got tired of standing, they could sit and discuss what it all meant.

"OK, let's see what you've got," she said.

"I've got a lot. Let's take the simple stuff first. I have optical telescopes and a few microwave observations that give us the source's general visual and radio frequency appearance."

He projected a graph of the intensity of the light observed from a telescope in Australia superimposed on the intensity observed from another telescope in India. The chart had a time scale running from left to right at the bottom, beginning at 07:02 UTC and ending at 07:05 UTC on September 15th. He'd already normalized the graphs for comparison. That meant the

Australian graph and the Indian graph had separate vertical scales, such that for each one, the largest value during the three minutes exactly reached the top of the chart.

"Are those the ones you had the timing problem with?" she asked.

Markson shook his head. "No. These folks got it right. GPS timing."

"Cool."

With a laser pointer, Markson traced the line representing the brightness of the light beginning at the left at time 07:02 where it was near the bottom of the chart representing the normal sky illumination before the flash occurred. He continued along the line until, at 07:03, the line jumped straight up to the top of the graph and then descended smoothly until it returned to the baseline, which happened well before the end of the chart at 07:05. He narrated as the laser pointer followed the progress of the line.

"Notice that the onset is sudden, but the intensity decreases less rapidly with time."

"I assume they're all like that?"

"Yes."

"Observations from space? Gamma rays? X-rays?"

"All the same," he said.

"So, that's consistent with Jorge's idea so far, yes?"

Markson put up a graph with the same data as he'd presented in his first chart, but with the time scale expanded to show only the first half-second in which both signals appeared.

"Actually, no. You can't see it in the other chart because the differences are too small, but when I expand the scale, the onset times differ a bit."

"But you'd expect that since the Earth is round and the telescopes are at different altitudes. Their distances from Jorge's hypernova differ so the time of arrival of the light from the explosion differs, right?"

"Absolutely right!"

"Sooo... what's the problem?"

Markson smiled as he opened a new file on the screen. "In addition to recording the light intensity as a function of time, the observatories always record the viewing angles in order to locate the exact spot in the sky where the target being viewed appeared."

With more than one telescope looking at the same thing at the same time, you draw imaginary lines from each telescope to the target. Where the lines cross is where the target is located. If Jorge was right, the lines from these observations would all appear to point in the same direction, to the exact same spot in the sky, however infinitely far away it was. There would be no observable parallax. No parallax meant the lines would not cross because the differences in the angles from two places on Earth to something several thousand light years away were much too small to measure.

"And they all converged on a single location?" Clarke pressed.

"About 50,000 kilometers—give or take 10,000 kilometers—above the Indian Ocean near Australia."

"Uh oh!"

Markson laughed as he switched back to his second chart. "And the differences in the times of arrival at the various sensors are consistent with the near-Earth source location, but not with the deep space location proposed by our boss. Without the high precision timing you were grumbling about, I couldn't have determined that."

"It's too bad the gravitational wave observations don't provide enough directional precision to verify the location from the electromagnetic measurements," she said.

"Yeah, but they sort of do."

"How? You don't have enough sensors to do a time-of-arrival position calculation. You need at least four, and you only have the two LIGO sensors and Virgo."

"I correlated the signals at the three GW observatories with each other as a function of possible time differences between the site and the source of the signal. That gave me three sets of correlations: LIGO Livingston with LIGO Hanford, and each of the two LIGO sites with Virgo. The largest correlation in each case was the one with the time difference consistent with a near-Earth source positioned at the location derived from the electromagnetic observations."

"Did the time differences you tried include ones that would be consistent with Jorge's hypernova speculation?"

"Yep. All three correlations were much lower. All of the measurements tell the same tale, and it's not the story Jorge wants to hear."

Clarke put her hands over her face and took a deep breath. Then, she looked up and clasped her hands in front of her on the table. "I don't suppose I should tell him 'I told you so.' What else you got?"

"Well, there is a small bit of good news for Jorge. The strength of the GW signals and the initial strength of the EM signals are consistent with a hypernova at his proposed distance."

"*Initial* strength?"

Markson laughed again. "You caught that, huh? Yeah. The intensity dies off too fast. It starts out looking like a hypernova, but the light dims and the radio signals fade in a few seconds rather than in the hours or days you'd expect—or even longer, depending on what parts of the spectrum you were looking at in a hypernova."

A spectrum described how much energy was at each frequency or wavelength of electromagnetic radiation, such as radio waves, light, and gamma rays. If you compared the relative brightness of each color in a rainbow, you were assessing its spectrum.

"In addition to the timing, a hypernova spectrum would have bright and dark lines at different wavelengths, those corresponding to the synthesis and decay of elements like silicon and nickel in the explosion," she said. "Did it look like that?"

"It's smooth and has the characteristics of a thermal spectrum, not an elemental one. If it is thermal, the rapid change in brightness shows that the source cooled quickly or was relatively close and moving away from us fast. Either way, this thing was much smaller than a star or even a planet, but damned hot."

A thermal spectrum varied smoothly in a particular way that depended only on the temperature of the thing emitting it, and its brightness depended only on the temperature and the distance from the observer. The hotter the emitter, the wider its range of frequencies and the brighter its glow. If you could measure these characteristics, you could calculate the emitter's temperature.

"How hot?" Clarke asked.

"I don't know yet. Things changed fast and the decay rates seem to be wavelength-dependent. The shorter wavelengths die off more quickly. I'm not sure yet whether that's physical, or a result of the instruments' responses or the signal processing, but my gut reaction is that it's physical. That's one thing we might want to look at."

"Isn't that what you'd expect from a rapidly cooling thermal emitter?"

"Yes. We just need time to pull all of the pieces together quantitatively."

Clarke pored over the graphics piled on the table and asked questions until she felt comfortable with what the EM data appeared to be showing. She made some notes relating to signal processing concerns that she'd investigate next. Then, she asked if Markson had found anything else of interest in the GW data.

He began to push the EM graphics aside to make some room and spread out another packet from his briefcase, but there were too many sheets of paper in the pile. Clarke tried to catch the ones falling off the edge of the table with only partial success.

"Oops!" he said as he stopped pushing and began stacking the EM charts neatly on one corner.

She gathered the ones that had fallen to the floor and added them to the stack while Markson began spreading out the information from the gravitational wave observatories.

These graphs were designed in the same way as the previous ones. They depicted the time evolution of the quantity called "strain," which was a measure of the intensity of a gravitational wave. The data were from the LIGO Livingston Observatory about 40 miles down the interstate from LAPI, its twin in Washington state called the LIGO Hanford Observatory (LHO), and Virgo, the European equivalent in Pisa, Italy.

"I think you can flip through these yourself if I tell you what to look for," he said.

The charts confirmed what he'd said earlier—that, like the EM signals, the onset was sudden, and the time difference was consistent with their geographical locations if the source was at the location that best fit the EM data. Additionally, when the time difference was accounted for, the GW waveforms were well-correlated with each other. This rarely happened unless an astrophysical signal was being detected, but the automated quality control process didn't match the data to any type of astrophysical phenomenon for which the behavior of the associated GW waves had been calculated.

"The GW waveforms certainly don't look familiar," Clarke commented. "Every GW signature I've ever seen begins rising slowly out of the noise and increases in both amplitude and frequency until it reaches its peak strength, and then it rapidly fades out. This bunch appears suddenly at the peak value and then decreases in both amplitude and frequency until it decays into the noise. It's bass-ackwards. What should they look like if the source was Jorge's hypernova?"

He nodded. "That's something we need to calculate, unless Jorge has that on file somewhere."

"Jorge said his co-author did the relativistic calculations for the paper. Maybe I should go talk to her."

"Good idea. Meanwhile, we're going to want to look at the data in detail ourselves. If Jorge is wrong, then we're going to have a mystery to solve, and these waveforms may be the critical clue."

"And what we have so far doesn't seem to fit his theory."

"No."

"One more thing. I almost forgot—" she said.

He cocked his head to the side, inviting her to continue.

"What about those streaks the ship captain saw? Did you do anything with those?"

"Not really, but those are certainly near Earth. The angular velocity was on the order of degrees per second. Something at a distance of thousands of light years like Jorge is proposing, even something moving at the speed of light, would require a century to move a degree in our sky."

"Then, no matter what the GW waveform looks like, he can't be right. He isn't going to like this."

Markson shook his head and grimaced. "No, he's not." He didn't look forward to another confrontation with his boss, but someone had to tell Aguillero what they'd found so far, and that was Markson's responsibility. "I think the best thing would be for me to bring him down here to the conference room now and show him what we've got."

"I can't wait."

Markson hesitated for a moment. "It would be better if I handled this one-on-one, if you don't mind."

"I do mind, Lee! I'm as much a part of this as you are. Besides, I want to see his face when you tell him."

Markson looked down and drummed his fingers on the table for a few seconds. "I may have mentioned that Jorge and I have had some issues in the past. I've been trying to rebuild our relationship. I think I have a better chance of getting through to him here without losing any progress I've made if we don't have an audience—especially one of his junior faculty members. No offense meant. That's just the reality of the human ego, and Jorge's ego is... well, huge *and* fragile."

Clarke made a face, then stuck out her tongue. "Crumbs!" She turned to go, and then faced Markson again before taking another step. "Take notes. I want a full report!" she said, shaking her finger at him before she headed out the door.

Markson smiled. He shared Clarke's contempt for politics and bureaucracy. And he liked that she was usually reasonable and didn't take things personally, but if somebody gave her a hard time, she'd fight their bark with her snark. She usually won the battle.

Aguillero was meeting with someone when Markson called.

At Markson's request, the department secretary took a handwritten message in to the chairman. Aguillero glanced at it as if preparing to put it aside for later, but the word "results" caught his eye. He read it more carefully.

"Professor Markson would like to show you some results if you are available to come to the small conference room."

"Something urgent has come up," Aguillero said as he excused himself, leaving his secretary to dispose of his guest.

"I'm sure it must be extremely important," she told the perplexed visitor. "He's never done that before."

Aguillero didn't knock. He banged open the conference room door and rushed in, creating a gust of wind that blew several of the working papers off the table. "You've got confirmation, right? When do we write the paper?"

"Good afternoon, Jorge," Markson said as he stooped to retrieve the documents that had drifted to the floor. "I'm glad you're in a good mood. We're not ready for a paper yet, but I do have something interesting to show you. Sit down. Have a look." He gestured toward the chair where Clarke had been sitting.

"My paper nailed it, didn't it? I knew it!" Aguillero shook his fist in the air.

Markson waved his hand harder in the direction of the chair. "Have a seat, Jorge. You tell me."

Markson showed his boss what he'd presented to Clarke without mentioning what they themselves had concluded. He explained how the data had been selected and what the graphs portrayed, expecting that Aguillero would draw the same conclusions they had.

The department chairman picked up the gamma ray charts and then the ones for the longer wavelengths before looking at the gravitational wave plots, and finally he compared them with each other.

"Excellent! I think this confirms our GW signals are from a hypernova in the vicinity of Norma. Don't you agree?"

Markson was too stunned to speak. He and Clarke had shown in their charts that the initial brightness of the event was the only aspect consistent with Jorge's hypernova hypothesis. What was the man thinking?

"Well?" Jorge pressed.

"I'm sorry. I don't see it."

"The amplitudes are just what I predicted!"

So, he'd locked in on that initial brightness to the exclusion of everything else.

"Yes, but the timing..."

"What about it?"

"Jorge, the radiation faded out in seconds across the whole spectrum, from microwaves to gamma rays. A hypernova would glow for anywhere from minutes to months depending on the wavelength."

Aguillero threw his hands in the air and stared at Markson for a moment before composing himself. "There is no delay between the GW and EM onset other than propagation time. That means the source has to be astrophysically close. And at those distances, it couldn't be anything as massive as a black hole merger or even a neutron star collision. Right? Q.E.D., if that rapid decay is real, it's an opportunity to explore whatever new physics is driving it."

Markson scratched the back of his neck as he groped for the right words. "The timing isn't the only problem. The optical data are of excellent quality, and they have enough parallax that the location can't be at an astrophysical distance. The correlations between the GW sites are largest when the data are processed with a time lag that's consistent with a distance determined from the parallax."

"Were some of the observations you used made near the horizon? Perhaps they could be contaminated by atmospheric refraction. Did you check that?"

"Not yet," Markson admitted.

"Have you made position estimates from the GW data? Have you checked all of the metadata?"

"Coarsely, yes. Not in detail."

"Do you understand that, even close in, any sort of astro-nomical event energetic enough to produce detectable GW signals would have been *so intense* that its radiation would have killed all of your observers?"

Reluctantly, Markson agreed that Jorge's suggestion was not an unreasonable conclusion.

"You called me out of an important meeting to look at half-finished work that neither of you apparently understands!" Jorge exploded. "Next time, please wait until you know what you're talking about!"

Markson stepped back. "Of course. Sorry... I thought you'd want to see these as soon as they were available."

"I expect you to have a full and detailed analysis of these signals and the correct physical interpretations on my desk in two weeks. Is that clear?" Then, without waiting for a response, Aguillero stormed out.

Markson threw away the beverage cups and collected papers as he pulled together his thoughts, preparing to go to Clarke's office and give her the report she had only half tongue-in-cheek demanded.

When he got there, the door stood open and she was sitting behind her desk, so he walked in without knocking. He hauled over one of the two old chairs stored by the door so that he could sit facing her, and then he took a deep breath. "I had hoped for better."

"Uh oh. Hold that thought. Sounds like this is going to

require more tea." She took a pod of Earl Gray from the box on the smaller of her two bookcases and popped it into the Keurig on the table to her right. When she'd put her Virgo souvenir mug on the machine's platform, she turned her attention back to Markson. "I was expecting good news. What happened? You promised to give me all the details. Now would be a good time."

Markson watched as she removed her cup and the empty pod from the coffee maker. He started to get up. "I left my coffee back in the office."

"Sit! You're not escaping that easily." She reached behind her and grabbed a pod of breakfast blend from the box next to the Earl Gray, then turned and took a foam plastic cup from the stack next to the brewer. In less than ninety seconds, she handed him a cup of hot coffee, three packets of sugar, a packet of creamer, and a plastic spoon. "Now, where were we?"

Markson shook his head and smiled. *Beautiful? Yes. Smart as a whip? Yes. Stubborn? Damned stubborn.* He took another deep breath as he assembled the ingredients in the cup and stirred. *Here goes.*

Without further delay, he recounted his exchange with their boss, and how Aguillero had focused on the weaknesses of their preliminary analysis while refusing to admit or accept its strengths. He told her that they had been ordered to fill in all of the gaps Jorge had identified and present a report within two weeks.

"He's expecting the report to support his theory," Markson said when he'd finished.

Clarke was flummoxed. "I was afraid of that from the beginning, given the way he was talking. Why's he being so unreasonable? I haven't gotten to know him well yet, but Shanta says he's a good physicist and a decent administrator. It's balderdash."

"Shanta Jelani, his co-author?"

"Yeah. We do yoga together at the LSU rec center and play a little golf sometimes. She's known him for several years. Her only complaint is that he's something of a sexist, but then, most men are. She told me he didn't want her name to appear on their paper as an author and the dean had to intervene."

Markson folded his arms and frowned. "I'm not going to get into a discussion about his attitude toward women, but I agree he's a more than competent physicist—or at least he used to be. On the other hand, he was never open-minded. And maybe it's just me, but he seems especially perturbed whenever I dare disagree with him. He still hasn't forgiven me for CATSPAW."

She stood and put her hands on her hips. "What? You insisted it would go better if you presented our findings by yourself!" She shook her head, laughed, and sat back down. "So much for that! What's his big beef with CATSPAW, anyway? Is he jealous that you're richer than he is?" she asked with a dismissive wave of her right arm.

Markson turned away from her. "There's more to it than that, Kat."

He hated being reminded of how he'd disrespected Aguillero when the academic had objected to his thesis topic, or how angry Aguillero had been when Markson had left to join CAT before finishing the work he'd committed to as a postdoc.

When he turned to face her again, he just shook his head. "Look, I'm not comfortable with us talking about him like this behind his back."

"We need to talk about him, Lee. He's trying to force us to a conclusion we know is wrong. It's bad science and, frankly, unethical. If I'm going to have to put up with this shit, I'm entitled to know why."

"You think our work is shit? I think it's damned interesting!"

"It isn't the work that's shit. It's being told what the answer has to be by our boss. It's his obsession with his hypernova that's the turd in the punch bowl."

Markson sat back down in front of Clarke's desk, folded his arms across his chest again, and took a deep breath, but still sat looking down at his lap.

She waited half a minute. "Tell me what you're thinking."

He lifted his head. "I understand where you're coming from, but I'm trying to put my relationship with Jorge back together... and I can't do that if I'm telling stories about him to one of his employees. Can we focus on the event for now and talk about the past later?"

"Don't mind me!" she snarled, and reached for her keyboard.

She'd generated a three-dimensional map of the Earth that included the continents and the location of the point south of

Australia where the data suggested the event had occurred. Now, she superimposed a great circle onto it, separating the half of the Earth from which the event would have been visible and the other half where it would have been below the horizon. She turned the laptop so Markson could see the image.

"I wish you'd had this to show him. The optical and radio observations came from all over the hemisphere where the event was visible. Atmospheric refraction was not an issue for most of them."

"This is getting scary," Markson said after a few seconds. "Jorge was right about one thing—anything massive enough to generate these gravitational wave signals should have been spectacular. We should have seen global tidal waves as large as seismic tsunamis in the oceans, and the EM radiation should have fried everything in orbit and most of what's on the surface of half the Earth. Why is everything still here?"

CHAPTER TWO

STIRRING UP TROUBLE

ALTHOUGH THEY WOULD NEVER SAY so to his face, their main motivation for identifying the source of the event was no longer to satisfy Jorge Aguillero. The event raised huge questions about both fundamental physics and planetary security. Finding the answer outranked who was asking the question.

"The ball's in your court now," Markson told Clarke as she sat with him at the table in his office.

"You mean I have the honor?"

"What?"

"You used a tennis metaphor. I prefer golf."

Markson scoffed. "Golf." He shook his head in disgust.

She stuck her tongue out at him before asking, "So, what do you want from me?"

"You're the signal processing guru, and you'll need to be at the top of your game. To learn more about the source, we'll need GW and EM waveforms from which noise and distortions have been removed. The source is probably moving, and nobody has firm information on how fast or in what direction."

"Hmph. Is that all?"

"No. The satellite sensors are also moving. As a result, every measurement is Doppler shifted by an amount unique to that sensor's location and velocity."

She paused to ponder the complication for a moment. "That's still not too bad. It just means that when the source is moving toward the sensor, the signals will appear to be at a higher frequency than what was emitted and signals from a source moving away from the sensor will appear at a lower frequency. That's a correction I can make as soon as I have all of the motion data. Anything else?"

Markson nodded. "There is one additional complication. Some instruments couldn't follow the rapidly changing parts of the signal while others responded strongly to them. In addition to the Doppler shift, these instrument response characteristics distorted the waveform readings."

"I can handle it."

"I believe you, but it will be a challenge, Kat. You'll have to limit your search for the true EM and GW waveforms to data from sensors whose position, velocity, and response characteristics are available so that you can apply the appropriate corrections. We'll stick with the quality-controlled database we already have, but still, the data selection effort may be harder than the actual calculations."

She liked a challenge, and her smile reflected that. "I'm on it!"

In the two weeks Aguillero had allotted them, they selected EM measurements for detailed analysis and corrected most of the data for their instrument responses and sensor motions. The GW observations didn't require any additional processing for instrument response beyond what had already been performed by the LSC. They would still have to apply a Doppler correction for the motion of the source to both the EM and GW signals, however.

While Clarke was untangling the signal processing, Markson took a crack at estimating the track of the source. But unless the answer he kept getting was clearly wrong, it would give the department chairman a seizure. He needed a second opinion from his partner, so he took Clarke into the small conference room and projected his charts on the monitor.

He had two ways—triangulation and time of arrival (TOA)—to estimate the position of the source over time, from which he could derive its speed and direction. Triangulation required the target's altitude in degrees above the horizon and its azimuth in degrees clockwise from North, as recorded simultaneously by at least three different optical or radio telescopes. He showed Clarke how he'd done it, beginning with a picture of a cloudless Earth seen from space, directly above the Indian Ocean.

"I've marked the locations of three of the optical telescopes from which we have pictures of the event. They're all small aperture telescopes associated with optical lightning detection and location systems. Two are in Australia and one is in India—as you can see. They're associated with some commercial time of arrival systems used to track thunderstorms. We'll talk about those in a few minutes. When the TOA detects and locates a thunderstorm, the automated telescope turns toward the direction of the storm in order to attempt to photograph the recurring lightning. The altitude and azimuth angles at which the scope is pointed are recorded along with the GPS time for every image."

"'Turns toward the direction'? How fast can they move?"

"Over 300 degrees per second, but that wouldn't have been fast enough. There are several dozens of these things in India and Australia, as well as some in New Zealand, and we got lucky. These three and two others happened to have been observing a storm over the Indian Ocean the night before the event and were already pointed in the general direction of it. They're relatively wide-field instruments. They caught the flash before the instrument began to slew."

Clarke nodded, and Markson clicked to bring up the next chart. It was the same as the first one, except that he had added three yellow lines, one originating at each site, that intersected at a single point in space.

"These lines are drawn in the direction determined by the azimuth and elevation angles of the centerline provided by each telescope at the same instant, with adjustments for the position of the center of the flash in the image. Each one is aimed right at the event. Where they intersect is where the event occurred. Right there...." He pointed to where the three lines crossed at a point in space above the Earth.

"Nice cartoon. Have you got any real pictures?"

Markson laughed and put up the next slide. "You want pictures? Here's pictures. All of these images show a flash at 07:03:27 UTC that appears to separate into two oppositely directed pieces traveling rapidly, roughly ten degrees North of East and South of West."

"Can you get speed and direction from these?"

"Yes. Just track the positions of the leading edges of the two streaks. If the telescopes hadn't begun to move, it would have been easy, but the centerline-pointing angles began changing and I had to correct for that."

She lifted her head and crossed her arms. "OK, but these are consistent with the ship observations and rough estimates by manual triangulation. Nothing really new. You called a big meeting, so what's the big news? The TOA data? Are the TOA positions consistent with the images?"

TOA used timing rather than angles. A common application was locating lightning from the radio pulses generated by each flash as it traveled through the sky. When pulses were detected by sensors at four or more locations, the differences in the time the pulses arrived at each detection site could be used to calculate the position and time for the source of the pulse. The timing had to be accurate to a few nanoseconds.

"I looked at the TOA," Markson replied. "In addition to the data from the little lightning location units, I found high-quality observations from true radio telescopes in Australia, India, and New Zealand. They weren't pointed at the event, but the signals were so strong that, even working against the directivity of the antennas, I could get precise timing. The TOA-derived position of the flash agrees with the optical position. There are continuing signals that appear to be associated with the streaks, but getting speeds from them will take some additional effort."

"So, nothing new yet from the TOA data, either. Can I go get a cup of tea now?"

"Triangulation indicated that the streaks were moving really fast, Kat. I'm going to need all of your signal processing genius to confirm that from the TOA data."

"Now I know how the audience felt when I did a slow strip. Why is this so important? Stop teasing me and show me what you've got."

Markson didn't much mind Clarke's past as an exotic dancer from when she'd been a student, but he wished she wasn't so open about it—even with him. Nonetheless, he couldn't help thinking, *I'll show you mine if you'll show me yours.*

Instead, he asked, "What more do you want?"

"Stop nattering! Give me the numbers. Quantify *fast.*"

"Oh, that," he said with an ear-to-ear grin. "Faster than light."

$$\infty$$

"Are we going to keep working through the Christmas break, or are we going to have some fun?" Markson asked as they sat sipping coffee in the Student Union.

"*We* are not doing either, love. *I'm* going home to see my dad and mum with a stopover on the way back in Pisa to see Aberto. I made the reservations yesterday. I was going to tell you this evening."

"From the way you phrased that, I gather you weren't planning to tell me you reserved two seats on the flight."

She reached across the table and took his hand. "Not this time, my love. Dad's not been well, and Mum's been taking care of him. She needs some help, but she won't ask for it. She and I have a relationship sort of like you and Jorge do. I need to repair it as much as I can and take some of the stress off of both of them. Besides, I need to get away from you and Jorge to take some of the stress off of *me*. Your constant battles are wearing."

Markson sat back, but didn't release her hand. "You never told me much about your mother, but I know you always speak well of your father. If you don't mind my asking, what caused the relationships to be so different?"

"Nothing complicated. Dad always encouraged me to use both sides of my brain—all of my abilities. He supported me when I wanted to enter beauty pageants and when I signed up for *Odyssey of the Mind*. When necessary, he interceded with my schools to allow me to take both dance courses and STEM courses whenever the counselors insisted I had to 'make up my mind,' as they phrased it. When I set my eyes on a career in physics, he was overjoyed, and when I told him I'd applied to appear on the reality show *How to Look Good Naked*, he congratulated me for having the courage to explore my feelings about my body. Mum didn't like much of any of that, and she constantly reminded me how *good girls* should behave. Science and math? Those were for men. Dancing? That was for *loose women*. Public nudity? Well, that was the end. Only whores did that."

Markson laughed.

"You think that's funny?"

"I'm sorry. No, it's not funny. Your dad sounds like he's wonderful. It's just that the way you've described your mom's responses to your goals and values sounds like the way Jorge responds to mine. You said your relationship with her was similar. That seems so accurate, and what struck me as funny was the image of Jorge as my mom."

Clarke laughed. "You're forgiven." Her smile faded, and she added, "I just hope Dad's not too ill to appreciate the visit."

"How serious is it?

Clarke withdrew her hand. "I don't know for sure. That's one of the things I need to find out. Mum says he's doing fine, but if he's doing fine, why doesn't he tell me that himself? He isn't answering my texts anymore."

"Hmm. Not good."

"No."

"Are you sure you couldn't use some assistance? I mean, if he's really sick..."

"Fortunately, we live in the UK. If he's really sick, the healthcare system will provide all the help we need at no cost. I'm amazed you yanks still haven't figured that out."

Markson shook his head and grimaced. "I'm still not completely sold on the idea of socialized medicine, but OK. Still, if you find you need help, call me. I'll catch the first available flight."

"I'll keep that in mind."

"When does your flight leave?"

"Day after tomorrow."

"Thursday. Can I at least drive you to the airport?"

"You know I'm flying out of New Orleans, right?"

"Gives me an extra ninety minutes with you," he said.

When Markson got back from dropping her off at the terminal, he settled in his office. With only one more day until the campus closed for Christmas break, he hadn't fully reprogrammed his subconscious to the unexpected departure of Clarke and he wasn't sure what to do with himself.

A knock at the open door broke his contemplation. When he looked up, he was surprised to see Aguillero standing at the threshold.

"May I come in?"

"Of course."

The department chairman closed the door and motioned for Markson to join him as he took a seat at Markson's worktable. Markson nodded and took the chair across from his boss.

Aguillero looked down at the table before raising his eyes to Markson's. "Lee, I may have been a bit curt with you about your analysis a few weeks ago. When you weren't ready to support my hypernova proposal, I let my disappointment get the better of me. I'd like to make it up to you. Teresa and I would like you to share dinner with us next week. If I remember correctly, you enjoyed her cooking the last time and we enjoyed your company. It's been too long. Perhaps it might..."

As Aguillero silently completed his sentence by spreading his arms palms up, Markson smiled. "I agree, Jorge. I'd like that. Thank you, and please thank Teresa for me. Will the rest of the family be there?"

"The children won't be coming until after Christmas, I'm afraid, but you'll get to meet Max."

"Your German Shepherd—the one in the pictures in your office?"

"That's him. Replaced the Golden Retrievers you got acquainted with in your student days. What day would be best for you?"

"Tell Teresa I'm at her service. Since she has to do most of the work, she should pick whatever works for her."

Aguillero took a tone of mock offense in replying, "I'll have you know, young man, that *I* have quite a few contributions to make to this get-together." He'd turned lighthearted, but then continued, "Nonetheless, I will ask her. It will probably be Tuesday, and I think we'll get together sometime in the afternoon and then eat around six. I'll let you know for sure tomorrow."

As his former teacher and mentor disappeared down the hall, Markson nodded his appreciation for the fact that, like Katty, he would also have a special opportunity to mend his fences over the holidays.

He took out his phone to text her the news, but laid it on the table instead. *She'll be in the air for hours more*, he thought. *Given her need to get away from me and Jorge, maybe it wouldn't be such a good idea for the first thing she sees when she lands to be a text about us. And suppose it all goes bad next week?* He put the phone away. *It can wait.*

The drive from Markson's house in Highland Park to Aguillero's in Brownfields, northeast of the airport, was a bit more than 20 miles and went through the populous urban area adjacent to LSU and the institute. Even though many of the students had gone home for the winter break, the 3 PM Tuesday traffic wasn't light. Perhaps people were doing their last-minute Christmas shopping. The drive took Markson nearly an hour.

The residences in the area had large lots and were set back as much as a hundred feet from the road. Many didn't have visible house numbers. Fortunately, Markson had been to

Jorge's before, and his GPS got him close enough to recognize the place. He immediately noticed one major change; the last time he'd visited, the driveway had been a tree-lined dirt road. Now, on the right, the trees in front of the house had been removed and the large lawn was manicured like the fairway of a championship golf course, albeit without the bunkers. The soil and gravel right-of-way had been replaced with concrete running all the way from the street, past the trees still standing on the left, to electronically operated gates that limited access to the parking area behind the left side of the house. Aguillero must have been on the lookout for him, though, because the gates opened as Markson approached. Not a minute after he'd parked, his host was there to greet him and escort him inside.

As they walked to the back door, Markson could see smoke coming from the backyard. "Parrilla?"

Aguillero smiled. "You remember it—good! You expressed your concern that my poor Teresa might be over-worked, so I thought I might ease her burden by making my exquisite, barbecued steak. I hope you didn't have your sights set on her turkey."

Markson laughed. "My apologies to the cook. I'll admit to fantasizing about having Teresa's turkey again, but the parrilla you brought to the faculty picnic was magnificent, so I doubt I'll be disappointed. Yours was so much better than what's available at the Argentinean restaurant in town."

"That's because they marinate their meat in the sauce for a day before cooking it. They have to because they cut the meat too thick. I cut it thin, cook it on the grill, and then let it soak in the sauce on the serving plate. That way, the sauce doesn't get burned. My family has always done it that way."

They went straight to the kitchen, where Teresa was preparing the side dishes and desserts. She hadn't aged much in the nearly nine years since Markson had last visited. Her short, dark hair was showing a bit of gray and she appeared several pounds heavier than he remembered, but she looked youthful for someone in her mid-sixties.

As they entered, she looked up. "Lee, welcome. It's so nice that you can share part of your holiday with us."

She picked up a tray of pionono and brought it to them. "Here's something you two can munch on in the living room while I make the sauce, salad, and empanadas. Then, Jorge can do the barbecue. I think I should be ready in another hour and a half maybe?"

The men thanked her for the snack and accepted her offer of glasses of iced tea.

"Will we be eating outside?" Markson asked as he and Aguillero made their way down the hallway and past the dining room to the large, elongated living room.

"No. It's only 55 degrees out, and with the clouds and breeze, it would not be comfortable. I'll make the parrilla and bring it to the dining room. If you'd like to assist, we can continue our conversation while we cook."

Markson was now certain he had interpreted the invitation correctly. Aguillero, like himself, wanted to repair their relationship and was willing to risk opening some old and some not-so-old wounds if that's what was necessary. The holiday season, informal venue, and Teresa's presence reduced the likelihood of things blowing up in their faces. *Well done, Jorge.*

The living room featured a real, wood-burning fireplace centered at the bottom of a true brick wall. The bricks were various shades of brown, running from almost black to a light tan. Markson laughed as they sat down next to a low, seven-foot-long wooden table facing the fireplace and supported by columns of the same bricks at each end. He'd just realized that the eighty-pound German Shepherd dozing in front of the fireplace was almost invisible among the décor.

He pointed at the dog. "Max, I presume?"

"Named him after Maximilian, the Holy Roman Emperor."

"Almost missed him. He's the same color as the bricks. Great camouflage."

Aguillero pointed to a trophy on the left side of the mantelpiece above the fireplace. "He's a conqueror just like his namesake. That's for 'Best in Breed' at the Louisiana Kennel Club competition last year."

"I saw some certificates in your office. You must be quite a trainer. And your wife's a vet, right?"

"She keeps him in good shape with a beautiful coat and conformation. I teach him how to follow commands. He has everything a champion needs."

Markson walked over to inspect the mantel up close. He wanted to see the smaller plaques on the other side. "I see you and Teresa have some public service awards from something called the 'Legion of Decency.' What is that?"

"Our parish is trying to revive it. We're leading a national effort to reduce the explosion of nudity, explicit sex, and other forms of pornography that are pervading the internet and even televised, so-called entertainment these days. The legion was a well-respected Catholic organization that reviewed and rated motion pictures from the 1930s until it changed its name in the 1960s and finally went out of business in 1980. American cultural standards have gotten worse for lack of an organization like that, and we want to rebuild it with a broader scope than just movies. Teresa and I have volunteered our time and taken leadership positions in the movement."

"Hmm," Markson said. His pulse rose as he contemplated how it might affect Clarke's career if Aguillero found out about her history in the adult entertainment business.

They placed their drinks on the table with the pionono between them. Aguillero had positioned two of his most comfortable armchairs a few feet apart—mostly facing the fireplace, but at enough of an angle that they could make easy eye contact without having to turn their heads, yet avoid it with a small motion if necessary.

"I'm thankful you took the initiative in this, Jorge. We've got too much in common not to be friends as well as colleagues. I'm glad you hired me, but I don't feel like I'm really a full member of the team right now. I always feel like I'm walking on eggshells. It's gotten worse since that event happened. I'm afraid to tell you what I think if it isn't what you're looking for. As scientists, we should be more open to the truth than that."

Aguillero scowled and took a swig of iced tea. "You speak the truth. I didn't intend to start so abruptly, but let's begin with that. *I didn't* hire you. Dean Simpson hired you over my strong objections. All I did was minimize the damage to the department as best I could and sign the papers like I was told to."

Markson hadn't expected such a negative response. This man had invited him to his home and carefully prepared an environment conducive to reconciliation. What was happening?

"But you took me aside. You told her that we would have to work it out between us, and we did—"

"The only thing we worked out was how to be civil to each other over the long time it was going to take to repair the damage."

"But you compromised and negotiated an agreement to bring me on. I was there the whole time. I didn't hear her force you to do anything."

"She made it clear that you were going to be hired. If I had simply refused, she'd have found a way, at my expense. Do you realize how much that infernal crackpot thesis of yours has cost me?"

A disappointing revelation. Markson had always assumed that, except for his own admitted rudeness to his mentor during the selection of his thesis topic, their estrangement had been about the scientific merit of his work. Now, it appeared there was more to it, and the chasm was deeper than he had known.

"Jorge, I was disrespectful and ungrateful. I said you lacked integrity when you didn't support my choice of a thesis topic. That was cruel to you and unworthy of me. I admitted it and have tried to apologize more than once, but the work... the work was good physics. Ground-breaking physics. I've never understood why you aren't able to acknowledge that, even now."

"You ruined my career, Lee. I was passed over for dean and had difficulty getting grants and being published. And for what? To build a gadget that's little more than a parlor trick and use it to fleece investors?"

"Jorge, you're not making sense. I certainly didn't ruin your career! And the gadget you so easily dismiss is a functioning time machine. I built a damned time machine, Jorge, and it worked! I was your student. I thought you'd be proud."

Aguillero picked up his tea and took another sip.

When his boss didn't respond with anything more than that simple motion, Markson became uncomfortable. To break up the awkwardness, he picked up his glass, but the rattle of the ice cubes seemed almost disrespectful and made him feel worse. He was relieved when Aguillero spoke again.

"When I published my hypernova paper, there were snide comments about how much faith one could put in a paper by someone who'd been the thesis advisor for a dissertation that didn't even comply with the basic laws of physics. And after you showed that it worked, I was criticized for encouraging you to sell out to Wall Street."

"You didn't encourage me. You should have, but you didn't."

"Didn't encourage you? Perhaps not in the way you wanted, but even with your disloyalty and personal attacks on my character, I gave you a postdoc when you couldn't even get a job teaching elementary school. And my reward? You ran away to New York with zero notice before the work I'd hired you to do was even finished."

"Ken didn't give me any choice, Jorge, and I did finish the work. I just did it remotely from New York."

"Oh, yeah. A month late."

Markson looked away and picked up a piece of pionono. He took another sip of tea and then turned to face Aguillero directly. "So, it all comes back to my disrespect, not to anything tangible and certainly not to the merits of the work. What can I do to make amends? I acted badly. I agree. How can I fix it.?"

"I was next in line to be dean of the LSU College of Science. The controversy generated by your paper killed that. Did you know that?"

"Why do you say that?"

"The provost told me. Not that he'd admit it, of course."

"That wasn't right," Markson agreed.

"Nothing *right* has happened since you submitted that contemptible piece of junk science for publication, and then compounded it by using it to transfer millions of dollars from unsuspecting innocent people into the pockets of you and that coven of thieves you worked for. You apologized for being disrespectful. OK, I accept your apology for that, but when are you going to admit that what you did in New York was unworthy of you? If you can bring yourself to apologize for that, I think we'll be getting somewhere."

For the first time during their conversation, Markson felt angry. Until now, he'd been surprised by the scope of Aguillero's grievances, disappointed by their depth, and irritated that they hadn't surfaced earlier so that they could have been addressed before. Now, he felt that his friends from CAT and his personal character was being assailed. Not his science or his perceived disrespectful behavior. Now, it was his friends and his character. Now, he was pissed off.

He leaned forward and pointed his finger in the other man's face. "That's unfair and beneath your dignity, Jorge. Those people at CAT committed no fraud and broke no laws. They may have been Wall Street sharks—a species I don't generally appreciate, either—but they weren't thieves, and these particular sharks were good, decent people!"

"And yet you and they have lots of other people's money in your bank accounts. Whose? A school district's retirement fund? An AARP investment club? Some family's college tuition fund for their children?"

Markson took a deep breath as he struggled to hold his temper. He wasn't yet ready to abandon all hope of eventual reconciliation. Not yet. Not even now.

"Jorge, if CATSPAW could transport people rather than just photons, and for years rather than a few nanoseconds, I'd hop into it and go back and undo the things I did wrong—but it doesn't, and I can't. And building a working prototype of the device described in my dissertation wasn't one of the things I did wrong. Until I did that, nobody would accept the validity of my work. It hurts me that you still don't appreciate it. I was hoping we could get past this, but apparently not yet."

Aguillero sat silently with his arms folded, as if waiting for Markson to continue, but the younger man had said all that he had to say for the moment.

After some awkward seconds, Markson nodded at his host. " Maybe we could make more progress if we went out and cooked some parrilla. I promise to follow your instructions without question."

Aguillero shook his head and scoffed. He rose and gestured for Markson to remain seated, then walked toward the kitchen. He returned shortly. "Teresa says we can start heating the meat. Follow me."

A large charcoal grill sat on the concrete patio in the fenced-in portion of the yard. In it, a nearly uniform bed of coals and ash glowed faintly red as the breeze fanned the flame and cleared the smoke. Adjacent to the grill was a masonry table with attached benches that the Argentinian had built from leftover fireplace bricks. The tabletop and the surfaces of the benches were concrete, sealed with a thin epoxy coating to keep them smooth and easy to clean. At the end of the table nearest the grill, Aguillero gave Markson a large chunk of beef and a sharp, serrated knife.

"You cut; I'll cook. Have you done this before?"

Markson nodded. "Usually with fish rather than beef, but the idea is the same. Thin slices heat through more uniformly, so there's less risk of burning the outside while the inside remains raw. About an inch wide and an eighth thick?"

"You *have* done this. Take your time. We're in no hurry. If there's much fat, trim it off unless you like it that way. Teresa and I prefer it lean."

Markson wielded the knife in a delicate but firm sawing motion, and handed Aguillero two pieces about an inch wide and a foot long. Aguillero nodded approvingly, but returned them to his guest.

"Perfect, except now cut them in thirds. Four inches is about as long as will fit on the bread without folding."

Markson put the pieces on the cutting board and resized them as directed, and then Aguillero tossed them onto the grill. "Keep 'em coming," he said.

As Markson sliced the remaining steak, Aguillero asked, "What's Dr. Clarke doing over the holidays?"

One of the unspoken things about their relationship that irritated Markson was Aguillero's habit of talking down to Clarke and treating her more like a student assistant than a faculty member. He wondered whether Aguillero really cared.

"Her dad's sick and her mother is taking care of him, so she flew back to England to lend a hand."

"Is she coming back?"

"Of course, Jorge! Why would you ask that?"

"Well, family takes priority. Especially for a woman."

Markson couldn't help himself. "Is that why you're so condescending toward her? Because she's a woman?"

The older man turned his attention from the grill to his guest. "If I don't give her the respect you think she's due, it's because she doesn't deserve it. Her dress is unprofessional, and she curses like a sailor. She shows little respect for any form of authority. She should stay home and take care of her father so that he can recover and teach her how to behave like a lady."

Markson was stunned. All he could say was, "Really?"

"She struts around with that exaggerated British accent, telling everyone what's wrong with the United States. If she doesn't like it here, she can stay there!"

"Jorge, her accent is as real as Teresa's—"

"How dare you bring my wife into this! She's a loyal Argentinian-American, not one of those murdering Brits!"

Aguillero had stepped toward him, and Markson stepped back. He raised his hands in surrender. "I'm sorry—you're right. Teresa has nothing to do with this and I shouldn't have mentioned her. But I never thought you would have such strong antagonism against someone because of their nationality, especially when we're talking about an American ally like England."

Aguillero stepped forward again. "That so-called ally killed two members of my family during the Malvinas War. Satan can have the lot of them."

In the decade and more that Markson had known him, his boss had never mentioned this. Markson began to realize that their conflict wasn't about physics. The physics was being held hostage to the feelings of two emotionally wounded people, one of whom was himself, and he wasn't handling that very well at the moment.

"I'm sorry," he said.

Aguillero turned back to the grill. Without looking at his guest, he asked Markson to bring the large ceramic platter over and take the grilled meat into the dining room. Markson said nothing as he obeyed.

Aguillero went to the kitchen and brought out one plate of empanadas and another with homemade bread while his wife brought out a large bowl of tomato and onion salad as well as a pitcher of chimichurri sauce. He put the empanadas and bread by the steak in the middle of the table. She set the salad next to them and then poured the sauce over the steak before taking the pitcher back to the kitchen as the men sat down.

Teresa was clearly puzzled when she returned several minutes later and took her seat. The men sat in silence. Each had taken a healthy serving of salad and several empanadas, but they both just picked at the food with their forks. Neither made an attempt to build a sandwich from the barbecue and her fresh-baked bread.

"You don't like my food? Did I do something wrong?" she demanded.

"The food is good. I'm just not hungry right now," her husband said.

"I think we may have inhaled some smoke at the grill," Markson added.

Aguillero looked toward Markson and nodded his appreciation of Markson's attempt to cover for them.

After half an hour, and with some scraps still remaining on their plates, Teresa told the pair that if they weren't hungry enough to eat their dinner, then they were too full to have dessert. "I'm sorry you won't be having what I spent all morning making. Since it's frozen, perhaps it will keep for another time."

Both men looked up at her, then at each other. Markson spoke first. "Your helado? Your wonderful helado?"

"Sí. My helado. But, of course, you have no appetite for it today, I see."

Markson looked at Aguillero and then applied his fork to the remains of his meal.

Aguillero sighed. "I also cannot resist your helado, Teresa. Please give us a few minutes."

This time, it was Markson who nodded to his host in appreciation. Markson was an ice cream connoisseur. Her homemade, Argentinian helado combined the best of ice cream as Americans knew it with additional ingredients from Italian gelato and her unique blend of flavorings. It was among the best he had ever eaten.

With a satisfied smile, Teresa folded her arms. "I'll wait."

After dessert, as Teresa got up to clear the table and do the dishes, Markson offered to help. When she declined, he looked to Jorge and suggested that perhaps he should be going.

Teresa responded first. "No, Lee. Why so soon? I'm sure you and Jorge have more to talk about. Perhaps I'll come and join you as soon as I clean up the kitchen?"

Aguillero shook his head. "Teresa, I'm sure Dr. Markson has things he needs to do. I don't think we have anything more to discuss this evening, do you, Lee?"

Markson sighed. "No, I'm afraid not. Thank you for your hospitality, Teresa. The food was wonderful as always, and the helado was spectacular. Jorge, I'll see you at work after the break."

In his formal department chairman's voice, Aguillero said, "Of course."

∞

Markson picked up Clarke at the airport in New Orleans the evening before LAPI reopened in early January. As they waited for her luggage in the baggage claim area, he asked about her father.

"Well, it's not good, but it could be worse. I'll tell you about it when we get in the car. Just don't ask me about how it went with my mother. The only thing I said that she approved of was that I'm not dancing anymore, and even that blew up."

"That's too bad. What happened?"

"I said, *don't ask*. I don't want to discuss it. But, on a happier note, Aberto sends his regards to you and Jorge. He's looking forward to anything we can contribute to figuring out what *the event* was. It seems that even in Europe, everyone is calling it that."

"I hope you didn't mention the phrase 'faster than light.' That's a bag of worms I don't want to have associated with my name until we examine the evidence a lot more rigorously."

"No. I just told him we might have some interesting things to consider in a few weeks. What were you up to while I was gone?"

Markson hesitated. He still hadn't decided how much to tell her about his dinner with the Aguilleros. He needed time to think. Even a few more minutes might help. "We can talk about it in the car."

On the ride home, Markson kept Clarke talking as long as he could. "About your dad. You said things are bad, but could be worse? I'd like to hear the details. Why hasn't he been returning your texts? Is he going to be OK?"

"It turns out Dad had a stroke. I don't know why my mum didn't just tell me. I had to get the details from the doctor. It affects his language capability. He can understand what you're saying, but can't respond either verbally or in writing. It's like a computer where the keyboard and microphone are working, but the speaker and screen have gone bad. Data can go in, but the responses can't get out."

"Sounds pretty bad to me. Is there any hope he can recover?"

Clarke described what her father's neurologist had said, and Markson asked a series of questions before he summarized what he thought he'd heard: "So, in as many as a quarter of cases like this, the patients eventually recover most of their ability to converse, and in as many as half, they recover enough to have an acceptable quality of life... have I got that right?"

She agreed that he had it right. He'd also managed to avoid having any time left for them to discuss his little misadventure before they pulled into her housing complex. Being tired from the long transatlantic flight, as soon as they got her things up to the apartment, Clarke suggested that they get some sleep separately and reconvene the next day over breakfast at the Student Union. He kissed her goodnight and went home.

∞

"So, while I was beating my head against the wall with my mum, what were you up to?"

The pair had bought "back to school" breakfast specials and large cups of coffee, which they brought to an out-of-the-way table for two.

"I caught up on the pile of reading material that was beginning to clutter up my office at home, and I also worked a little on the data," Markson said.

"Boring. Did you do anything interesting? Anything?"

Markson took a deep breath, sighed, and decided she'd eventually find out anyway. "I had dinner at Jorge's house with him and his wife."

"And...?"

"*And*, the food was delicious. Jorge and I made barbecue, and Teresa made some snacks, a big salad, and some great empanadas. She even hand-made an Argentinian ice cream called helado that's marvelous."

"And...?"

"And what?"

"And, what did you talk about?"

Markson hadn't recovered from the strain of their emotional collision, and wasn't ready to talk about it with anyone yet. "I won't ask you about your meeting with your mother if you don't ask me about my discussions with Jorge."

She startled. "That bad?" When she got no visible or verbal response, she said simply, "O...K," and waited for the stilted silence thereafter to evaporate.

Finally, she stood and picked up her tray.

"Shall we get to work?" she asked aloud.

He picked up his tray. "Sounds like a plan."

When they'd stopped for the holidays, they'd been examining evidence that the event appeared to be a manifestation of something traveling faster than light. Now, Markson was relieved to get back to doing physics. They would need overwhelming evidence before going public with such a claim.

When they got back to this office, Markson showed Clarke the detailed data and calculations he'd summarized for her in December. She agreed that they appeared to show a track at superluminal speeds over part of the observed trajectories. If true, and if they could prove it, there could be fame in their futures.

"How should we handle this?" he asked.

She laughed and slapped the table. "You're the one who made a fortune and pissed off Jorge and most of the physics establishment with a time machine! The paper you based your physics on said it's possible to make a warp bubble that can go faster than light. How do *you* think we should handle it?"

He admitted the irony, but wasn't eager to go there yet. "That's what destroyed my friendship with Jorge, remember?" he asked.

She cocked her head and raised her eyebrows. "You aren't going to wimp out on me, are you, dearie?"

"No, but not a hint of this to Jorge until we've either dismissed it or demonstrated it beyond all reasonable doubt, as the lawyers say. I guarantee you we will be on trial here."

Markson paused. They had both images and time series data. The time series were lists of numbers representing measurements of things like EM field strength and GW strain as a function of time at regular intervals, these ranging from a few milliseconds to seconds depending on the observing system. The images needed Doppler correction because, otherwise, the colors in the images would look bluer if the object was moving toward the camera or redder if moving away, but the true spectral characteristics of the light given off by the targets could be important in divining their nature and composition. The time series required both correction and signal processing in order to be useful for identifying the exact shape, the waveform, of the signal.

When Markson spoke, he said, "Alright. Here's how I think we should approach it. We're going to need compelling evidence detailing the characteristics of the event both electro-magnetically and gravitationally. That means a more thorough and rigorous analysis of both the images and the time series. That's our short-term goal. To get started, let's divide up the labor. You're the signal processing guru, so you take the time series. I've already been looking at the imagery, so I'll handle that end of things."

Clarke nodded. "Sounds like a plan."

The images were easier to analyze, and the results could help with the analysis of the time series, so he began with the few videos they had from telescopes in the region, as well as the visual observation recorded by the captain of the *Sensei Maru*. The images agreed with the captain's logbook: after the flash, there'd been two of whatever it was, traveling in opposite directions. That was complicated enough, but things got worse when they put numbers on the observations. Quantitative estimates derived from the few available video images showed that the two objects had been traveling at different speeds at any particular time.

Having two objects traveling at different speeds wouldn't seriously impede Doppler correction of the images where the two could be seen individually and thus individually corrected. This simple strategy wouldn't work with the time series which were just sets of time-stamped numbers, however. The signal strength was available as a function of time, but it was a mixture of the signal from the eastbound target, Doppler shifted by its velocity, and the one from the westbound target which had been Doppler shifted by its different velocity. What they needed was the time history of the eastbound and westbound fields separately, and without the Doppler shifts. Unless they could isolate the true, individual unshifted signals, the data would remain gibberish, like words on a Scrabble board that had been shaken back into the bag. Recovering this information would resemble the process of unscrambling eggs, and Katty Clarke would have to invent the unscrambler.

"I'm going to need to make an assumption," she told Markson.

"Why? The more assumptions we make, the less compelling our findings will be."

"Because I have too many variables. For each variable I want to model, I need measurements of the eastbound and westbound values, but all we have is their time-delayed, weighted sum... and we don't even know what the time delays or the weights are. That's not enough information for me to develop unique equations. There'd be an infinite number of possibilities, and since we can't manufacture more data, we have to cut down on the number of variables."

"OK. So, what's the assumption?"

"I'm going to start with the simplest assumption and see where it leads. I don't see any compelling reason that one track should be significantly different from the other. I'll assume that the true time series for the emitted radiation from both tracks is the same, and that any differences are due to Doppler shifts and relativistic effects caused by their high speeds. We have enough information to compute those speeds."

He agreed. "Go for it. We have to start somewhere. If we can't figure out the details of these waveforms, we aren't going to figure out what they came from."

She returned to her office and re-examined the EM time series charts. Each of the signals began with a huge pulse, followed by a rapid and sometimes oscillating fade-out. She would need an algorithm built to uniquely describe waveforms using mathematical tools that were tailored to that kind of signal. It would have to produce equations that could account for most observed waveforms, assuming the waveforms would be the same for both tracks when corrected for time differences, relativistic effects, and the Doppler shift.

Three weeks later, when Markson finished his analysis of the imaging data, he asked her if she was ready to discuss their results. She wasn't.

"You've had the advantage of not having to invent your signal processing methodology," she explained, "and your imaging data set is much smaller than my time series. I'm still developing my algorithm."

She was finding the challenge more daunting than she'd expected. The algorithm had to work on GW data and EM signals ranging from microwaves to gamma rays, and there was no guarantee that a "one size fits all" procedure existed. Even if the variables could be handled, every individual instrument responded to the data it was measuring in a different way, again casting doubt on the practicality of a single, all-encompassing algorithm. It was going to take time to get it right.

Twice more, she declined to meet and examine Markson's results. She was making good progress by trying ideas out on selected samples of data and including only those that worked best in later versions of her code. It was important not to allow Markson's findings to subconsciously bias her work—it was supposed to be independent. Instead, Markson began documenting what they'd accomplished in preparation for submitting a paper to a scientific journal.

Six weeks later, Clarke was ready. She collected Markson and took over the conference room, where she turned on the big monitor and connected her laptop to the ethernet outlet on the table. With a scowl, she discarded two paper cups and a filthy napkin that had been left behind by the previous users of the room, and also removed their leftover presentation packages; these, she put on one of the chairs, which she then shoved out of the way against the wall.

She asked Markson to project his imaging results first because some of them were charts showing how the signal strength varied with wavelength. These could be compared to her waveforms in order to see if the contributions from various wavelengths in the signal were consistent between the two approaches.

The spectrograms confirmed that the peak energy at every wavelength occurred at the time of the initial flash, and that the energy in both tracks decayed with time. The rate of decay was more rapid at the shorter wavelengths. Both results were consistent with Clarke's calculations. More importantly, they supported Markson's initial assessment that the source was a small, nearby, rapidly moving object that was very hot, and not the explosion of a star-sized object at an astronomical distance as had been suggested by Aguillero.

When Markson finished, Clarke cleared the table and handed him a printed deck of PowerPoint charts, before spreading out a collection of EM and GW graphs. "I'd put these on the screen, but this way, you can shuffle through them and compare as you see fit."

She'd developed the algorithm using wavelets and something called *EOFs*, and now began to describe how it worked, but as soon as she used the phrase "wavelet analysis," Markson interrupted her.

"What's a wavelet, and why are you using them?"

"Sheesh. You could have at least let me finish my sentence. You know what a sine wave is, right?"

"My freshman double-E book said it's a pure oscillation back and forth at a constant frequency and amplitude."

"And a Gaussian?" she continued.

"We all took statistics. I'm familiar with sine waves and the bell-shaped curve. What do they have to do with wavelets?"

"Roughly, a wavelet is a sine wave that grows from nothing to a peak and then dies out again. It looks like a sine wave multiplied by a Gaussian."

"OK. And what's the advantage of using them rather than simple sine waves?"

"Because wavelets often work well with pulse-like signals, which is what we're dealing with. Can I tell you the other half of the story before getting to the details? When you have the whole picture, maybe things will gel a bit."

He laughed. "Sure. Sorry."

Sorry or not, Markson interrupted again just a minute or so later when she mentioned EOFs.

"Another new term. What's an EOF and why are you using them?" he asked.

She hesitated for a minute before responding.

"The acronym stands for Empirical Orthogonal Functions. I use them because EOFs are powerful tools for signals that have regularities not captured by standard mathematical functions."

"What do they do? How do they work?"

She hesitated again. "They find patterns in the data rather than imposing pre-selected patterns on the data. I know how to use them, but I don't know how to explain them, and all you need to know is what they do. I hope we don't have to get down in the weeds about this?"

"No, I was just curious. I can look it up if I want to know more. Tell me about the analysis."

She next explained how she'd applied the algorithm she had developed to isolate and characterize the GW signals from the event. Markson asked a few more questions, but he was impressed with her thoroughness and rigor.

"Let's see 'em," he said when she asked if he was ready to look at some waveforms.

"When you handed Jorge our graphs the last time, the shit hit the fan. Have a look at these and tell me whether we should duck."

Her derived EM waveforms behaved in the same manner as Markson's images. The signals were most energetic at the onset and then faded with time. It took more than an hour to go through data from nearly six dozen sensors at various wavelengths and compare the derived functional forms from the different instruments. At the end of their examination, they'd determined that her waveforms had the same spectral and temporal properties as his images at each wavelength. They also felt confident that they'd identified the waveform and could proceed from there to look for possible physical causes.

All that was left was the GW data. There were only three sensors—LLO, LHO, and Virgo—and she'd used the same algorithm as she had for the EM data to unscramble the east-bound and westbound signals. She skipped the signal process-ing details and asked Markson to start with the summary before she got into the individual waveforms. He didn't. He sat motionless, except for flipping several pages of processed waveforms back and forth, back and forth, back and forth.

"What's the matter?" she finally asked.

"If this is what I think it is, we should duck."

∞

The GW waveforms seemed familiar to Markson the instant he saw them, but it took a minute or so more before he recognized what they resembled. He looked up at Clarke. "Does the name Alcubierre mean anything to you?"

Miguel Alcubierre was a Mexican physicist who'd published a paper showing that faster than light travel was theoretically possible. The paper described locally warped, superluminal regions of spacetime—"warp bubbles"—'consistent with Einstein's general theory of relativity. A "warpship" could ride inside one of these bubbles.

"CATSPAW!"

Markson grinned. "Right! Alcubierre's paper was the inspiration behind CATSPAW." He was pleased she remembered the connection so immediately. For his PhD thesis, Markson had modified Alcubierre's work to find a related way for a signal to be propagated backward in time. Eventually, he'd built a working prototype of the device called CATSPAW, which had made him quite wealthy.

"I learned the mathematics for CATSPAW by doing exercises with Einstein's field equations. I thought a faster-than-light ship might have a gravitational equivalent of a supersonic aircraft's bow shock, which causes its sonic boom, so I ran those calculations. Your Doppler-corrected waveforms look very much like the ones in my exercise."

"Yes!" She raised her arms raised in triumph.

Markson smiled and raised his eyebrows. "Yes?"

"Yes!" She stood up and walked around the table, contemplating the possibilities this discovery opened up.

Markson was amused to see her mouth moving, although she said nothing aloud. He could almost follow the conversation in her gestures, but he asked anyway: "What are you thinking?"

Clarke put her hand up, shook her head "no," and kept walking. Even when she spoke silently to herself, her hands and arms sometimes got involved. She put her hand to her mouth and then held it out and pointed into the air like she was emphasizing something to an invisible companion.

"Please tell me what you're thinking," he said again.

She stopped, folded her arms, and then unfolded them and went to the whiteboard, where she looked up as if recovering from a trance before she turned from the board to Markson: "I'm glad we're getting prepared to write a paper. I can smell a Nobel Prize."

"Whoa!" he said. "I've been down that path before, and it's paved with broken glass. If this is real, we're just getting started."

Any claim by Markson and Clarke that faster than light travel could be a reality would be met with extreme skepticism in the physics community. As employees of LAPI, they would need the permission of the Department of Physics and Astronomy to submit such a paper for publication in a journal. That effectively meant that Jorge Aguillero had a veto. The old professor was not an out-of-the-box thinker, and Markson couldn't see getting his approval without overwhelming evidence.

Even if LAPI approved submitting their paper to a journal, their work would have to get through a professional journal's peer review process, during which the legitimacy of the entire concept would once again be challenged. Markson and Clarke needed a plan of action.

Markson had a suggestion. "There are some things we obviously need to do, and you're better qualified for some of them while I am for others—"

"So, I'll do what I'm best at, and you'll do what you're best at. I get it. Next," she said, cutting him off.

He crossed his arms and frowned. "No."

"Excuse me?" she asked, eyebrows raised.

He unfolded his arms. "If you'd let me finish, that's not what I was going to say. At LSU, I worked up the Alcubierre calculations I told you about, and I still have them. You've already processed the observed EM and GW waveforms. Suppose one of us made a mistake? We need to cross-check. What I'm proposing is that we make a list of what additional GW and EM analyses we need, and then you do the theoretical GW calculations and I work on calculating possible EM signatures."

Clarke looked toward the ceiling and then at Markson. "I can see your point, but won't that slow us down?"

He nodded. "Some, at first, but once we have the results, we'll both be familiar with the whole package. That should speed up the process of bringing the information into a single, coherent picture we can take to Jorge."

It would be Clarke's challenge to compute what the gravitational equivalent of a sonic boom from a superluminal Alcubierre warpship would look like from the perspective of the three GW observatories for various warp bubble sizes, speeds, and distances from the Earth. Markson would develop estimates of what the EM signature of such a vessel would look like at wavelengths ranging from microwaves to gamma rays. These analyses would be essential to any justification for claiming that the mysterious event involved a faster than light alien spacecraft.

Unless there was overwhelming confirmation of the observable consequences of their hypothesis, it would never be accepted by the scientific establishment. If confirmed, though, the impact on physics—and also on philosophy, literature, biology, and eventually engineering and exploration—would be profound. They had to take the time to get this right.

Professor Jelani had previously told Clarke she might be able to recover the GW waveforms that would be produced by Aguillero's hypernova from the calculations she'd made for their paper, but it would take more work than she wanted to contribute unless it was essential. But the calculation would be difficult and subject to error if Clarke had to do it herself, even with Jelani's help. So, while Clarke expected the department chairman would demand it be done, she decided to wait until she had the Alcubierre results before going to her colleague in the Mathematics Department.

In December, just before Christmas break, Aguillero had given them just two additional weeks to complete their analysis. In late January, he demanded a final progress report, but they weren't even close to having the level of proof they'd need to deal with his insistence that the only acceptable answer was that the GW signal had been produced by a hypernova a few thousand light years distant. Thus, his growing impatience required some deception.

Markson and Clarke reported computer malfunctions to the IT department. IT couldn't find anything wrong. Markson told Aguillero that both he and Clarke had to redo some of their work because of these computer errors. Meanwhile, it took several months of difficult mathematics for Clarke to develop the code to perform simulations of the GW wake of a passing Alcubierre warp bubble, and then debug the code and run the necessary simulations. It was worth the effort since the results matched the observed GW signature, as she showed Markson when the calculations had been completed. The match was so good, in fact, that she felt optimistic that perhaps Aguillero would accept them, and she wouldn't need to take Jelani up on her offer to go back through her calculations.

The math for Markson's work was easier, but the physics was speculative at best. There were no Maxwell's equations for things that were superluminal. What he'd accomplished by the time Clarke was done was for the most part not rigorous, but it was consistent with the observations, and he decided to go with it so that they could get something to the boss. It was early May when they were ready to meet in the usual conference room.

Clarke went directly to the whiteboard without waiting for Markson to load their charts into the projector. She wrote a three-foot tall number '7' with a red marker.

Markson looked up. "Seven?"

"Seven."

"What is that seven telling me?"

"Warp seven, Mr. Sulu. Seven times the speed of light."

"Inconsistent data. The *Star Trek* warp scale is non-linear. Warp seven is faster than seven times the speed of light," Markson said, laughing.

"I get to make the rules here, Dr. Markson. I say warp seven is seven times the speed of light, and our little UFO was going warp seven."

"Damn!" Markson said.

To estimate the size, speed, and direction of travel of the hypothesized Alcubierre warp bubble, Clarke had tried various combinations of assumed warpship size and mass, along with trial altitude, speed, and direction values centered on the image-based estimates after correcting them for relativistic effects.

Only one combination of these variables was consistent with the LIGO and Virgo signals, but with those values, the calculated signature matched the observations within the errors of measurement—except that the calculated speeds for the two trails varied from the observations more than she would have liked.

Markson was still impressed. Both the process and the mathematics were rigorous, and the results were compelling. He was also somewhat chagrined.

"Kat, I'm jealous. I'm amazed that you mastered those calculations so quickly. What's your secret?"

"I'm cute and smart!" she said, wiggling her hips suggestively while pointing to her head.

"Smart ass," Markson said. "Nice ass, too, but neither one of those simplifies tensor calculus in a four-dimensional Riemannian space. I'll bet your old mentor Dr. Giordano gave you a hand. Good for him!"

"How much do you want to bet?"

"Dinner at Mansurs."

"Shanta Jelani."

Now, Markson felt foolish. The reason Jelani held a joint appointment as a professor in the Department of Physics as well as her home Department of Mathematics was that she was an expert in the mathematical foundations of general relativity.

"A gift from Shanta Claus! I wish she'd been here when I was doing my dissertation."

"Actually, she gave me three gifts."

"Oh? What were the other two?"

"Well, I'd been wondering... if the warpship was emitting gravitational waves, wouldn't it be using up huge amounts of energy uselessly that way? Shanta told me to examine the metric farther away from the warp bubble. It goes flat quickly. The bubble doesn't radiate waves—it just carries a distortion of the metric along with it. It was the local distortion of space-time sweeping by with the ship that our GW observatories saw. That's why the signature wasn't wavelike."

Markson cracked a huge smile. "Damn! I was worried about that. The Alcubierre metric's symmetry would make it a weak emitter, but over interstellar distances, any emissions would be a serious drain and would limit their range. Our GW signals are what electrical engineers call 'the near field' when talking about EM radiation. It looks like the same thing applies to gravitational radiation. Nice! So, what's the third gift?"

"It's the flip side. The hypernova waveforms aren't similar to what was observed. She was able to determine that from some work she did for Jorge as part of their paper."

"Well, she's been a gold mine. Thank her for me."

Now it was his turn.

"Most of my work is more speculative than yours, but I do have one rigorous result that I think you'll appreciate." Markson brought up his charts on the projector.

He'd assumed that, in addition to a GW wake, a warpship would have an EM bow wave, an optical sonic boom. The ship would collect matter and radiation in front of the bubble because neither could move fast enough to get out of the way. The matter would soon be heated to temperatures high enough to decompose into elementary particles and more radiation, which would propagate out from the trajectory at or near the speed of light and result in something like the vee shape of supersonic shock waves. He'd calculated how it might look to someone on Earth as the ship passed by. The answer explained a lot.

"I calculated this for various distances, from 50,000 to 200,000 kilometers from the center of the Earth, and at speeds from less than light to warp nine—to use your terminology. At speeds much above warp one, the result is counterintuitive. The light from the point of closest approach arrives before any of the other light, including light from the incoming path. The first thing you see is a flash as the bow wave's leading edge arrives from the point of closest approach."

"So, what about the light from the approach trajectory?"

Markson put up a diagram showing light from the approach trajectory reaching the ground after the initial flash, with the light from the closest parts of the approach path arriving before the light from farther away. This made it appear from the ground like a flash followed by something traveling up the approach path in the opposite direction.

"And the light from the departure path looks normal?"

"Yes."

"Just like the observations."

"Right, but the speeds calculated for both the approach and departure paths from images or TOA are *not* correct because of the relativistic effects," he said.

"So, this explains the flash followed by oppositely directed trails."

"Yep!"

"And why my trajectory calculations in the vehicle's frame of reference don't match the speeds observed in Earth's frame of reference."

"Exactly." He grinned as he waited for her to ask the obvious follow-up.

"OK. I assume one of your models gave a best match to the observations?"

"60,000 kilometers from the Earth's center at warp"—he hesitated for effect just a fraction of a second before completing the sentence—"seven."

To evaluate the consistency of the EM data with a warpship's hypothesized EM wake, Markson had made some assumptions. Although, until now, there'd been no data on anything traveling faster than light in a vacuum, light traveled more slowly in matter, and it was possible for subatomic particles passing through water, for example, to be going faster than light in that medium. When they did so, they were observed to give off light called Cherenkov radiation that had certain well-defined characteristics, including a conical wavefront like the acoustic "Mach cone" around a supersonic missile, this being what caused its sonic boom. The luminal shock wave would be very hot, producing a plasma like that which surrounded conventional spacecraft as they reentered Earth's atmosphere. Interactions between electrons and heavier particles in a hot plasma generated another well-defined form of radiation called Bremsstrahlung. Markson assumed this would also be present. By weighing these contributions based on some additional assumptions, he'd gotten a decent agreement with most of the EM observations.

Markson concluded with a summary: "This analysis shows that if a spaceship going faster than light by riding in a warp bubble is possible, then what everybody saw and measured was consistent with what the ship with its bubble would look like as it flew by. The details of the appearance of our mysterious event look like the wake of an Alcubierre warpship."

"Doesn't the EM radiation drain energy from the system just like GW radiation would?" she asked.

"Yes, but at a much lower rate. A lot of the light show is due to concentration and rearrangement of the energy already in the environment. A ship with enough mass to sustain a warp bubble can afford to spend a bit of it on the EM wake accompanying it."

"OK. So, let's invite the boss to the party!" Clarke said brightly.

PART II

THE TURBULENCE

CHAPTER THREE

ACTION

WHEN MARKSON AND CLARKE ARRIVED for the meeting they'd requested with the department chairman, he looked happy. "Your favorite dark roast, Lee, and Earl Gray for you, Dr. Clarke. Have a seat and give me the good news." He was smiling as he rushed them to the table.

They'd prepared their pitch to ease into the conclusions, doing so in the hope that it would give their boss an opportunity to get used to the idea before he realized its full impact. They even tried to set the stage psychologically.

Clarke raised her cup in salute to Aguillero as she sat down. She'd chosen conservative attire, which Aguillero had once complimented—long, black, loose-fitting trousers and a white blouse buttoned to just below the neck with a ruffled collar and ruffled sleeves. She thought she looked a bit frumpy, but it could be worth it if it kept him in a good mood.

"Thank you very much," Markson said, also smiling as he took his seat.

Although he hadn't worn a jacket, Markson had on a dark blue tie that matched one of his dressier sport shirts, a light pastel blue one, and he'd pulled it almost tight around his neck. Like Clarke, he wore black trousers, clean and freshly pressed. At least their appearances wouldn't count against them.

Markson took a deep breath and exchanged glances with Clarke. Both of them were relieved that Aguillero seemed upbeat.

Markson faced Aguillero as he began. "I hope you're going to find this to be good news. We believe we know the source of the GW signals, but it isn't exactly what you were expecting," he said, deliberately trying to maintain a positive tone and facial expression.

Aguillero sat up straighter than usual, paused, and leaned in. "Oh? Then, what was it?" His tone had turned cold.

Shit, Markson thought. In his mind, Aguillero had taken on the aura of a snake looking for an opportunity to strike. He glanced over at Clarke and raised his eyebrows, indicating, 'duck,' and then looked Aguillero in the eye. "The data suggests that although the EM and GW signals have a common source, it was near Earth rather than light years away." He paused to see what reaction he'd get from denying the validity of Aguillero's hypothesis without yet having mentioned the Alcubierre metric.

"I was hoping you weren't going to try to sell me that story. OK, make your case. What was it?"

Markson let out an audible sigh after taking a deep breath. Clarke gave him a quizzical look as if to say, *"Get on with it."*

"We have strong evidence that, at about 07:03 UTC on September 15th, an Alcubierre warp bubble traveling at seven times the speed of light passed the Earth over the Indian Ocean, south of Australia at an altitude near 60,000 kilometers above the center of the Earth at closest approach. The EM and GW signals were produced by the bow wave of the superluminal bubble."

Aguillero put his right hand to his face and slumped in his chair. "Madre de Dios." He sat motionless for several seconds before slowly sitting up with a grimace. Shaking his head from side to side, he spread his arms with his hands facing Markson. "Here we go again."

"Here we go again?" Markson couldn't stop himself from saying, "I was *right* last time, remember?"

"You can't let it go, can you? Just because a quantum freak of nature let you send a few pitiful photons back a few milliseconds to grab other people's money doesn't mean some little green men have found a way to violate the laws of physics and engineering by sending some imagined starship hurtling through cislunar space."

Can't let it go? Markson thought. *Can't let it go? He's the one who's wrapped himself around the axle about the past.* Although he felt like hitting someone, Markson limited himself to kicking back from the table and raising his voice.

"Get over it, Jorge! I don't know whether they are green or fuchsia, male or female or robotic, but it looks like somebody zipped by here throwing out a gravitational wake that has an Alcubierre signature."

"I was hoping you'd grow out of that fantasy once you had a responsible position." Aguillero sighed.

Markson scowled, picked up the bulging briefcase he had placed on the floor by his chair when he'd come in, and pointed to it. "Don't you at least want to see the evidence?"

Aguillero threw up his hands. "I don't have time for science fiction! Your conclusion is physically impossible. You already know why, but you're wasting my time with it anyway. I'll just have to find someone who's competent to do the analysis."

Markson's heart was in his throat. "Jorge, that's not fair. I'm willing to admit that there are serious issues with our hypothesis. By the same token, you wouldn't have hired us if you didn't believe we're among the best in the field. We're not claiming that a warship flew through the solar system. It's too early for that. We *are* saying that the data's more consistent with that hypothesis than any other proposed so far, including yours. At least it warrants further investigation. Let us show you what we have, and you can tell us where we went wrong."

Aguillero scowled and folded his arms as he looked Markson in the eye. "OK, show me." The *"I dare you"* remained unspoken.

Markson handed Aguillero a package of graphs, charts, and computations summarizing the work he and Clarke had done with the EM data. The department chairman spread it all out on the table and challenged almost every page. He dismissed the methodology as inadequate, the models as simplistic, and the conclusions as preordained by the assumptions used in deriving them.

"Look, you admit that the location in the sky is consistent with an event in Norma," Aguillero argued, "and that given that distance, both the optical brightness and the gravitational wave intensity are what would be produced by a hypernova like my paper described. You're chasing zebras instead of horses."

Markson looked down and shook his head, not knowing whether it was worth continuing to try to convince his boss of the problems with the hypernova paper. He took a deep breath and let it out with a sigh. "You know the parallax and times of arrival require the source to be in the neighborhood of 60,000 kilometers from the center of the Earth. The spectral characteristics look like a small, hot black body, not an exploding star. And your hypothesis provides no explanation at all for the streaks receding from the flash."

"Blah, blah, blah. You've said all that before, but I still haven't seen a convincing error analysis. Have you got anything new? No."

"Actually, we have. They're both astrophysical. In the first place, you were so insistent that I asked NASA if they had anything available to check what's going on now in Norma.

There's no afterglow, Jorge. Any sort of nova, and especially a hypernova, has an afterglow from the residual decay of unstable isotopes created in the explosion. There is no afterglow where your hypernova is supposed to have been."

Aguillero's jaw dropped. "NASA? You went over my head to NASA? Requests like that are supposed to go through institute channels!"

"The request was informal, Jorge. I have a friend there. The data were already on file since NASA is interested in this, too. All he gave me was a link to the data. The bigger deal is this— the GW waveforms *don't match* those Kat got from calculations of the phenomenon presented in your paper. They match the warpship."

Aguillero scowled. "I wrote that damned paper, and I don't want the opinion of a signal processing expert whose experience with serious relativistic calculations is minimal. If I want an opinion on that, I'll ask Jelani."

Clarke started to speak, but Markson touched her arm and spoke over her. "Why don't you do that, Jorge? Ask Jelani."

Clarke shook her head and laughed in disgust. "OK by me."

Markson continued, "Jorge, nothing supports your interpretation but the signal intensities. Everything else says you're wrong."

Aguillero raised his voice again and leaned forward, coming as close to his former student as the table between them would permit. "At least I have something. All you have is an interesting set of coincidences. You are not the first person to examine the Alcubierre metric. There are three insurmountable objections to such a thing, and we discussed them back when you first got interested in this pseudoscience. Do you remember them?"

Markson nodded. "How could I forget? You were quite emphatic. Energy, radiation, and GNC."

"I wasn't part of that conversation. Would you mind enlightening me?" Clarke asked.

"Do you want to tell her, or should I?"

"I've got it," Markson said as he turned to face Clarke. "To create an Alcubierre warp bubble, you need negative energy, which implies exotic matter with negative mass. There's no known physical process that can generate exotic matter in large quantities, and the amount needed to transport a warpship would range from the mass of a small mountain to that of a large planet—depending on whose calculations you accept."

Clarke put her hand to her mouth and frowned. "But you built a working time machine that used a modified form of the Alcubierre metric. Didn't that require negative energy?"

"Yes, but only in microscopic quantities. One of the oddities of quantum mechanics is that it allows for the local production of small quantities of negative energy in the vacuum between two closely spaced metal surfaces. It's called the Casimir effect. You can look it up. The 'C' in CATSPAW stands for Casimir. That's where I got my negative energy, but the amount necessary was tiny because my payload was only photons, not a spaceship."

"Hmph. OK. Now, tell me about radiation. What's the problem there?"

Markson thought for a moment about how to explain this part. "Remember we discussed how a supersonic airplane makes a sonic boom?"

"Sure. It's going so fast that the air molecules can't get out of the way. They pile up in front of it, and the increased pressure and density create a bow wave that travels with it and propagates outward at the speed of sound. When the pressure wave hits your ear, it sounds like a boom."

"Exactly. Now, imagine our warp bubble tooling along at several times the speed of light in the reference frame of some matter. The matter can't get out of the way, and it collects at the leading edge of the bubble in the same way. Just like the acoustic case, the pressure and density rise—except that the energies involved are so much greater that the matter becomes a superheated plasma. The bow wave follows the bubble and propagates outward at about the speed of light because, rather than sound, it consists of electromagnetic radiation and relativistic particles. If the bubble slows down to sub-light speed, the plasma collected at the bow will be released from the bubble and continue forward on its own inertia. Calculations suggest that the intensity of this radiation would be enough to fry anything or anybody encountering it close-up. As the ship made its final approach to its landing place, the radiation would incinerate it."

Clarke crossed her arms and looked down before gazing at Aguillero and then Markson. "I can see where that would be a problem."

Aguillero focused back on Markson for a moment. When Markson didn't speak, he pressed, "Don't you plan to tell her about the other half of the radiation problem?"

Markson glared back at Aguillero. "That's the one piece we disagree on, Jorge. But I'll tell her." He turned back to Clarke. "There are some physicists who've looked at the Alcubierre warp bubble's internal structure and concluded that the bubble would also be filled with radiation, and at a temperature too high for life to survive. Jorge accepts these speculations at face value. I don't. They depend on quantum mechanical calculations of Hawking radiation that haven't been verified in the real world. That's something else you can look up for yourself. Until we have a viable theory of quantum gravity, I'm not going to blindly accept that quantum theory works perfectly in highly curved spacetimes."

"I'm familiar with Hawking radiation," she said. "It seems to solve a lot of conceptual problems relating to black holes, but I don't see how it applies to the interior of warp bubbles. I'll look it up. Now, tell me about GNC. I thought 'GNC' was a vitamin store. What's it have to do with our little ET?"

"Guidance, Navigation, and Control. To pilot your spacecraft, you need to be able to change its direction and speed so that it will follow the desired course. In the case of a warp bubble, that means you need to be able to change the shape of the bubble the spacecraft is riding in."

"So, what's the problem?"

Markson folded his arms, cocked his head to one side, and smiled. "How do they do it? Putting aside the possibility that changing the bubble's shape could make it unstable and destroy it, how do they get their instructions to the bubble?"

"Just reconfigure the exotic matter, no?"

Markson shook his head. "No. Let's assume they have some way of redistributing that stuff, whatever it is. The effect of the redistribution doesn't propagate to all parts of the bubble instantaneously. It propagates at exactly the speed of light with respect to the local inertial frame of reference at each point along its path, which is not its speed as observed by the crew in the flat spacetime in the interior of the bubble where their ship is."

He explained that the warped spacetime of an Alcubierre warp field contained a horizon similar to the event horizon of a black hole, somewhere behind the leading edge of the bubble. Although the two weren't exactly the same, the results were equivalent. To the distant observer—meaning one in a flat space—an object approaching a black hole appeared to fall more slowly until it effectively came to a stop without ever reaching the horizon. From the crew's point of view, their commands could never reach the horizon or any part of the bubble beyond it in a finite time. They could not "cause" anything to happen there, whatever they did.

"Damn! If even one of these objections is valid, our interpretation can't be right," she said. After a pause, during which Aguillero stood watching her silently with his eyebrows raised over a triumphant smile, she asked Markson, "Have you got answers to any of them?"

Markson was forced to admit that they hadn't addressed these issues, but countered that the match with the observations was too good to be ignored. Aguillero responded by challenging the sufficiency of the observations. He asked if the proposed Alcubierre signature was unique, and particularly stressed the importance of observations missing from Markson's package of documents.

"What did you find in the very high-energy gamma ray region? As you yourself said, at seven times the speed of light, that wake should be loaded with extremely energetic photons. Did the satellites see any?"

Markson and Clarke hadn't downloaded the high-energy data because most of it would have to come from the DOD satellites that didn't meet their selection criteria for documentation. They would need to get that data in order to answer this concern, though. Meanwhile, Markson wanted to pacify Aguillero without having him terminate the project. He believed part of the man's reaction was personal, and attempted to use that to gain them time to continue working on the problem.

"Jorge, you make a good point. We haven't really done all of our homework—"

"Speak for yourself," Clarke interrupted.

Markson turned to her with his back to Aguillero and put his finger to his lip.

She put her hands on her hips. "Don't shush me!"

"Please, Kat..."

She waved him off and made a sour face as he continued addressing their boss.

"I would like to get the high-energy data you've suggested and have another look at the literature regarding those big three objections. If we're wrong, we're wrong, and I'll be the first to admit it. Can we revisit this in a few weeks?"

"Another few weeks? You're already a couple of months past due!"

"Jorge, you know that's unfair. The assignment gets bigger every time we meet. You don't like the conclusions we reach, so you ask for more data and more analysis." Aguillero started to say something, but Markson raised his hand. "Let me finish. Nothing you've asked for is unreasonable—" Clarke started to interrupt, but Markson raised his hand again. "Please let me finish. More data and more analysis can only strengthen the eventual credibility and value of whatever result we come to, but each new set of data has to be acquired and quality-controlled before analysis can even begin, and the analysis has to be tailored to the type of data and characteristics of the measuring instrument."

Aguillero scowled and turned away for a second or two before he faced them again. "Alright, a few more weeks. But try to get it right this time."

Clarke rolled her eyes. "Oh, please!"

"You have something to add, Dr. Clarke?" Aguillero asked.

Markson put his hand on her arm. "We were just about to leave."

She shook her head and mumbled something inaudible as Aguillero pointed them toward the door, saying, "I assume you can find your own way out."

$$\infty$$

Markson and Clarke went back to her office, where she slammed the door behind them, grabbed a chair from beside the door, and slammed it down in front of her desk.

"Enough! Sit!" she said, grabbing Markson by the arm and nearly throwing him into the chair.

"Geez, Kat, chill! What's gotten into you?"

She yanked her own chair back from her desk so hard that it bumped one of the bookcases behind the desk, and then plopped down into it and rolled forward as close as she could get to Markson with the desk between them, at which point she leaned over face to face with him.

"I know you and Jorge have a past that's got something to do with your thesis and that company you worked for on Wall Street. You have constantly refused to share it with me even though we're sleeping together and acting almost like we're married. I've let you get away with that. I've respected your precious privacy and haven't cross-examined you about it, but now it seems to be affecting our research and my career, and you're going to tell me what the fuck is going on!"

Markson realized he couldn't hold out any longer. He took off his tie and sat back. His working relationship with

Clarke and his personal relationship with her, if he was going to continue to have one, required candor—which meant he'd have to accept his discomfort and open up completely.

He took a deep breath and let it out audibly. "OK. Fair enough, but it's a long story, and you'll need to hear the whole thing from the beginning if you want to make sense of it."

"I enjoy stories and have an extended span of attention, so please proceed."

He took another deep breath. "I chose LSU for my PhD studies because LSU was big into gravitational waves and close to LIGO. With undergraduate and master's degrees in electronics and optics, I thought I could get an assistantship with LIGO without needing to take out any loans. Aguillero was there, and I thought he'd be a good mentor."

"Why Aguillero?"

"Aguillero's field was general relativity with specializations in gravitational waves and astrophysics. He was a pioneer in multi-messenger astronomy, which used simultaneous gravitational wave and electromagnetic observations of astrophysical events. It was a new field and that was exciting. He also had a joint appointment with LIGO, so he was a natural fit as my advisor."

"So, you got accepted. Then what?"

"Before they accepted me, Jorge interviewed me. He liked my background, and not only accepted me as his doctoral student, but got me a position as an instrumentation engineering technician at LLO."

"You got along OK?"

"Yeah. We both enjoyed mixing theory and experiment rather than being purists. He was good with the astrophysical applications of LIGO, and I was good with the engineering aspects. We admired and learned from each other. He even had me over to his home for parties and, once in a while, dinner with his family. I was the only one of his students to have that honor, as far as I know."

"You'd never know that from the way he behaved today."

"Tell me about it. It all went to hell when I selected my thesis topic."

"And where'd that come from?" she asked.

Markson rubbed the back of his neck and looked down at his lap.

"Would you like some coffee?" Clarke offered.

He shook his head and sighed. "No. Thanks." He looked up. "No. I just hate thinking about it and I need to get on with it."

"I'm listening."

Markson nodded. "I read Miguel Alcubierre's paper as an undergraduate. As a *Star Trek* fan, I was tantalized by the prospect of a warp drive. As soon as I could do enough of that impenetrable tensor calculus, I played around with Alcubierre's solution to Einstein's field equations. I derived a similar solution that might enable another impossible phenomenon: time travel. Since time travel and faster-than-light travel are closely related in general relativity, I thought it was a natural extension of Alcubierre's work. I proposed a doctoral dissertation about the use of this variation on the Alcubierre equations as a method of sending information back in time on a laser beam in a fiber optic waveguide. It was an intriguing mix of physics and opto-electronic engineering. I thought Jorge would love it."

She scoffed. "I gather he didn't."

"He hated it. He insisted that everyone knew time travel was impossible. He insisted it was for crackpots and science fiction writers—'not that there's any difference between them,' he said."

Markson paused.

"And...?"

He folded his arms across his chest and sighed again. "We argued for weeks. He told me my thesis topic wasn't acceptable to the department. He explained why. It was all of the standard stuff—temporal paradoxes and violation of the causality—and it wasn't completely unreasonable or frivolous. The problem is that during our interview before I was accepted, one of the things I asked him was what liberty I would have to choose my own dissertation research. He promised me that I could pick my own topic without interference from the department. I kept throwing that back in his face."

"And he didn't like that?"

"No, he didn't, but I'm the one who finally blew the whole thing up irreparably."

She looked surprised. "How so?"

"I got so wrapped up in the brilliance of my hypothesis and its potential that I couldn't accept being denied the opportunity to explore it for my thesis project. I finally accused Jorge of being dishonorable for breaking his promise. I used that word. *Dishonorable.* Aguillero comes from an old, aristocratic family in Argentina. Honor is among his highest values. When I made that accusation, he reluctantly relented and let me have my topic, but another of his values is loyalty. He called me an ungrateful fool who would be ostracized by the physics community when my thesis was finished. We rarely spoke again after that, except when required to do so by our academic obligations."

Clarke mulled that over for a few moments before speaking. "I'm gobsmacked. You were right. You actually built a prototype of your time machine. It worked. I would think he'd have been proud of you."

Again, Markson considered how much to say before speaking. He'd bottled it up for long enough and had to get it off his chest to someone he could trust. He trusted Katty Clarke.

Markson explained how he had published a summary of his thesis in *Physical Review Letters* and posted the full dissertation on *arXiv*, a website for professional scientific papers. The professional recognition he'd gotten wasn't the kind he'd expected.

"I couldn't get a job in physics," Markson told her. "Jorge was right about that part. I was a joke or a fraud, depending on who you asked. Jorge gave me a postdoc at LSU to finish a project I'd been working on for him, but he also made it clear the position wouldn't be renewed. I was looking at serious poverty when I got a job offer from Ken Huntsman to come to a company called Catalano Automated Trading (CAT) in New York and build a prototype of my device. The salary was more than Aguillero was making, and CAT would cover all of the costs of designing, building, and testing the prototype. Huntsman said he thought I'd be willing to sell my soul for that opportunity, and, in a sense, I did."

"How do you mean?"

"CAT is a Wall Street firm that makes millions doing high-speed automated securities trading. They use computers to buy and sell stock. No human beings involved. The software reads the trades being made on the stock exchanges and computes what to buy and what to sell in a fraction of a second, all day every day, while the exchanges are open. Huntsman led a group that developed the algorithms they use. He's a physicist himself and he read my thesis after I posted it on *arXiv*. He saw the potential to make billions by sending buy-and-sell orders back a few milliseconds. He talked his boss, Henry Catalano, into an applied research project named Casimir Alcubierre Temporal Signal Propagation Anomaly Waveguide—what we called CATSPAW. He talked me into leading it."

Markson then related how it had been four years before CATSPAW had gone operational, but then in a quick few months, CAT had made billions. CAT employees who'd led the project, including Huntsman and Markson, had made hundreds of millions. The Securities and Exchange Commission had threatened criminal charges and then backed off because there'd been no law against using a time machine to buy or sell securities. Congress had quickly fixed that in an emergency session, at which point the project had been permanently shut down.

"It worked, I got famous, and we all got filthy rich as a result. That's the bottom line," Markson concluded.

For a few seconds, she contemplated what he'd said.

"So, CATSPAW used your modification of Alcubierre's equations and negative energy from the Casimir effect to propagate a signal backward in time, a temporal anomaly, in an optical waveguide. Have I got that right?"

"Perfect."

"And how did our fearless leader react when it worked?"

Markson told her that Aguillero had been revolted. He'd been raised to believe that only inherited money was respectable. Family money. His own family had cut him off from their wealth when he'd left Argentina to pursue his physics career in the U.S. He'd been frustrated and envious that Markson had been able to use his knowledge of physics to make a fortune in what Aguillero considered a morally reprehensible manner.

"So, why did he hire you after that?"

"The institute pressured him. They thought my fame might attract privately funded research and maybe even a few donors. He resents that, too!"

"Shit. And we're supposed to overcome that with a bit more satellite data?"

"Welcome to my world," he said.

Clarke stood up. "I think that deserves a trip to the loo. Excuse me."

When she returned, Markson rose and they stood facing each other. "Have I answered your questions sufficiently?"

"Just two more things. Let's start with this: exactly how much money did you make at CAT?" Clarke stood with her arms folded. "Even with all the publicity, you seem to have kept that well-hidden."

Markson looked down at his shoes and said nothing.

She put her hands on her hips. "Are you ashamed of it? Don't think you got your fair share?" She cocked her head to one side and folded her arms again. "You certainly don't act like you're filthy rich."

Markson finally looked her square in the face. "They paid me four hundred million dollars, Kat, and if it was anybody but you asking, I'd tell them to go fuck themselves."

She gasped and took a half-dozen deep breaths. "Four hundred million? Four hundred million dollars? You have *four hundred million fucking dollars* and you put up with this petty shit from Jorge? What the fuck is wrong with you?"

"In the first place, I don't have near that much. After state and federal taxes, I only have about half that—"

"Oh, poor baby! Reduced to penury—"

"Let me finish!" he said, waving his hand above his shoulder and lowering his eyebrows. "You asked the question, so now let me answer it!"

She stepped back, and then with a big sweeping bow, said, "Excuse me, Baron Markson, please proceed."

He grimaced. "That's exactly why I've kept this information to myself. Your attitude's no different than Jorge's. Somehow, there's something unsavory about being wealthy. Well, I earned every damned cent of it."

"Then, why not use it? Why put up with being an associate professor who's subordinate to Professor Arsehole? Why—"

"Kat, stop! I'm trying to tell you why if you'll just shut up and listen."

"Don't you tell me to shut up! I stood by you at great risk to my professional future, and I'm damned well not going to shut up!"

Markson raised his hands to shoulder height, palms out in surrender, and took a deep breath. "Look, I'm sorry, but please let me explain what you asked me to explain. Then, you can tell me why everything I've done is wrong."

She nodded. "Maybe we should sit down." She turned the chair Markson had been sitting in toward them and then placed the one remaining by the door to face it. "Nothing between us, Lee. Just you and me. This isn't a business meeting or a scientific discussion. Just you and me. I'll shut up and listen, just like you said. Until I hear bullshit. Then, we'll have nothing more to talk about." She stood with her arms folded across her chest, still glowering at him.

Markson sat down and motioned for her to do the same. She unfolded her arms to sit, but then folded them again and sat back at an angle, cocking her head as if to say, *"I dare you to justify your behavior."*

Markson shook his head. He took a deep breath, sighed, and said what he needed to. What she would make of it would have to be up to her.

"I didn't take the job at CAT to make money, and certainly not to get rich. If I had any ulterior motive beyond proving my thesis correct, it was to get even with all of the nay-sayers and with Jorge. When CATSPAW worked, I was on top of the world. After a few weeks of news media interviews and responding to congratulatory emails, the social media attacks began and the physics got lost. I began to ask the obvious question—what would I do next? The answer wasn't to become a Wall Street quantitative analyst, not even at CAT." He stopped. "May I have a bottle of water?"

She nodded toward the bookcase behind the desk, where she kept bottled waters with the coffee and tea.

He got up, got a bottle, and returned to his seat. After taking a few sips, he continued. "I wanted desperately to get back to doing physics. Part of it was purely selfish. I thought the work was worthy of a Nobel Prize, but controversial stock market traders don't get nominated for the prize in physics. Actually, the other part of it was also selfish—I love physics, Kat. It's been my life for a reason. I had to get back to it."

"But why LAPI, especially with Jorge as the department chairman? You could have gone anywhere. You could have funded your own research laboratory!"

"At the time I left CAT, I had no idea Henry Catalano was going to set my bonus at almost half a billion dollars. I was expecting maybe a million, which these days is just enough for a comfortable retirement. I'd already accepted Jorge's offer when I got word about the bonus from Henry."

"But what made you accept LAPI's offer?"

"In addition to an associate professorship with tenure, despite my having zero academic experience since my post-doc, it was the same things that brought me to LSU as a grad-uate student. The department had a close association with LIGO Livingston and research interests that dovetailed exactly with mine, and Jorge was still one of the leaders in the field. The institute's mission statement centers on interdisciplin-ary research in engineering and science aimed at ultimately achieving practical results. Most academic institutions are still built on disciplinary boxes and give less emphasis to useful end products. Also, I have to admit I still felt guilty about my behavior toward Jorge when we'd been at LSU. I wanted an opportunity to make it right, and then, even once I heard about the bonus I'd be getting, I certainly didn't want to break another commitment to him by withdrawing after having accepted the position here."

Clarke leaned back and snorted. "Seems to me, love, that Jorge's the one who ought to have been feeling guilty."

"He probably should have, but that doesn't excuse my disrespect and rudeness, Kat. He was trying to save me from making what he saw as a huge, career-ending mistake. He was wrong, but his intentions were good. And even after I challenged his honor and ignored his well-intentioned guidance, he still gave me a postdoc to tide me over for a while as I looked for a job. He could have shown me the door before the ink on my diploma was dry. And I used that opportunity to take a job on Wall Street. That was the final ingratitude. The final disrespect."

She let that sink in for twenty seconds before continuing, "So, tell me again why he made you an offer if, as you say, he had some justification for how he felt about you?"

"I didn't realize it at the time, but Dean Simpson didn't give him much choice. The institute liked that I'd turned a speculative theoretical idea into a functioning piece of equipment. They also thought my presence might attract some interest from donors or private sector investors hoping to pursue additional applications of the CATSPAW technology."

"Have they asked you to do any fundraising?"

"Only once. I told the dean that I came back to an academic environment in order to get out of the money world, but had no objection to her using my presence on campus as a resource—for whatever that was worth. She was willing to let it go at that."

Clarke thought for a few seconds. "May I ask one more question?"

"Why not? You said you had two," he said with a trace of fatigue.

"Actually, you already answered my second, which was why you accepted Jorge's offer, but now I'd like to know what you're going to do with the money. You're obviously not spending it on a lavish lifestyle."

"I'm saving it for a rainy day."

"Really?"

"I've invested it in a good conservative portfolio with some guidance from a financial advisor Ken recommended. I'll keep growing it until I find something that I feel strongly enough about to get heavily involved in, and then I'll have something to bring to the table."

∞

A few days later, Clarke was worried. "Lee, you got a minute?"

Markson looked up from his desk as Clarke stepped into his office, which was larger than hers. In addition to the furnishings she had, he had room for a rectangular table and two additional chairs so that he and colleagues could hold meetings or spread out documents while collaborating on a project. One of the privileges of being a tenured, higher-ranking faculty member.

He stood and gestured for her to sit at the table. He found it more convivial than sitting across the desk from someone. "Sure. What's up?"

"I can't find the gamma ray data. It's gone." She punctuated the word "gone" with her hands, as if throwing a pile of confetti in the air.

Clarke needed the data to satisfy Aguillero's demand that they look at the high-energy part of the EM spectrum, and she watched as Markson went online and searched everywhere that the data had been or was likely to be. He couldn't find it, either.

"Are you sure it was there before?" she asked.

"Yes. There were observations from some DOD satellites, three civilian satellites, and three ground stations I thought we could download later. I'll look into it."

"I'll make some inquiries, too. I got to know some of the Virgo people rather well when I did my postdoc there."

After several more days, Markson still had nothing useful. The points of contact for the missing data sources hadn't responded to his emails, and nothing was posted on the LSC or astronomical websites or bulletin boards.

That being the case, Clarke had his full attention when she strolled into his office, closed the door, held her finger up a few inches in front of her lips, and said quietly, "Something strange is going on. I don't like it."

"Why are you whispering? What's happening?"

She looked sheepish and dropped her arms to her sides. "I don't know, but I'm frightened. Somebody's deliberately suppressing the data." She told him that she'd asked Aberto Giordano, her supervisor and mentor at Virgo, if he knew what had happened to the gamma ray data in the archive. The answer had not been what she'd expected.

Aberto had told her that he didn't know why the data had been removed. He'd said he was hoping she could tell him. What disturbed him most was what he'd heard from an Italian astronomer who'd downloaded the data when it had first been posted.

The security police had confiscated his hard drive. They'd promised to return it the next day, and they'd kept their promise, but when he'd checked the contents, all of the data that was missing from the archive had been deleted from his disk, as well.

Markson whistled. "Wow! What are we getting ourselves into here?"

"Your pal Ken Huntsman—you said he's a big deal at NASA now?"

"Yeah—Associate Administrator for the Science Mission Directorate. What have you got in mind?" He dropped his hand to his desk.

"Well, two of the three civilian satellites we need belong to NASA. Maybe he can at least tell you what's going on. Best case, maybe we could get a peek at the data?"

Markson sent multiple messages to Huntsman's NASA email address. After several days spent getting no responses, he tried his personal email. Huntsman called him at home the same evening, and while Markson was glad to hear from his old mentor and friend, the news wasn't good.

"I shouldn't be talking to you at all, so keep this to yourself," Huntsman began. "If it gets out that I discussed it with you, I could lose my job or worse."

"Worse?"

"The DOD classified the data and directed us to remove it from the archive, and then imposed a national security gag order on us. I could face federal charges for having a conversation like this one—which, by the way, never took place."

Huntsman wouldn't say anything more about the DOD action or his agency's response to it. He made it clear that Markson would have to get the data from the DOD if he was going to get it at all.

"OK. I surrender," Markson agreed. "I won't push you any further. I only wish I'd taken a look at the data when I had a chance."

"Yeah," Huntsman said. "It was pretty interesting."

Markson raised his eyebrows as he spoke. "Really? How?"

"Forget I said that. I wasn't paying attention to what I was saying, and I've said too much already."

"Crap. I understand. I don't want to get you in trouble, so I'll let you go. Thanks for returning my call." He was about to hang up when he had a final thought. "Oh, Ken, wait a second. Since you saw it before it was classified, can you just tell me this—at the highest energies, was the gamma ray signal abnormally strong?"

Huntsman hesitated before answering, "You did not hear this from me. My impression of the unclassified data was that it was *intense*."

Bingo! Markson thought. "Thanks, Ken," he said as he ended the call.

Before telling Clarke what Huntsman had said, Markson needed to assure himself that she would keep it just between the two of them, no matter what. He didn't want to put Huntsman at any risk. Given Clarke's dislike of government secrecy, though, Markson decided to hold off on that conversation until they got up the next morning.

While they were eating breakfast at Denny's, Clarke asked, "Any news?"

"Actually, there is."

"And the news is?"

"We'll need a more private place to talk. Let's wait until we get to the office."

"Interesting! Let's do it in mine for a change."

"My table would be more comfortable."

"Humor me."

He laughed and offered a slight bow of the head, hands folded below his chin in a prayer mudra. "As you wish, my love."

Back at Wigner Hall, she rolled her chair from behind her desk so that they sat facing each other in front of it. "Comfy enough?"

"Delightful!" he said with mock sarcasm.

"So, what's going on?"

Markson's look turned serious. "Before I say anything, I need to have your word on something. I need you to take this seriously, Kat."

"OK, I'm listening."

Markson explained that he had spoken with Huntsman and that what he'd said might place Huntsman at risk if it was ever disclosed.

"So, you want me to agree to keep this between us, regardless of the consequences. Is that what you're saying?"

"I'm saying that I expect you to trust me enough to make that commitment. There's nothing he told me that we could ever use in public, and I won't have his career and possibly his freedom put at risk over it. I hate to be that way, Kat, but anything less would be dishonorable on my part."

She looked startled. "His freedom?"

"Possibly, Kat."

She took a deep breath, frowned, and looked down while she pondered her choice. Shortly, she shook her head from side to side and looked up. "OK. I won't snitch on your pal Huntsman. What'd he say?"

Markson told her about the gamma ray data. Her response was predictable.

"You mean that the gamma ray data does exactly what Jorge said it would do if we were right?" She sat with her eyes wide, mouth open slightly and eyebrows raised.

"Yep," he agreed.

She put her arms on the table, hands flat and palm down. "It confirms our analysis, yes?"

"Absolutely."

"But we can't get access to it."

He shook his head. "Nope."

"And we can't even admit we know what it shows."

"You have correctly assessed the situation."

"That's shitty," she said, folding her arms across her chest.

"No shit," he replied.

They were becoming as interested in what was motivating the DOD as they were in responding to Aguillero, but Markson had another idea. He called Henry Catalano, the founder and CEO of CAT. Catalano had been Huntsman's boss when Huntsman had hired Markson to develop CATSPAW, and he and Markson had gotten along well. It was a long shot, but Markson thought Catalano might have an inside track to the DOD. He was a retired Air Force colonel who'd still been active in the reserves when Markson had left CAT.

Catalano took the call immediately, which was a good sign. "Lee, glad to hear from you! What have you been up to lately?"

The warmth of the conversation evaporated as soon as Markson explained what he wanted to talk about.

"Lee, you're a good man and I'd like to help you out, but even if I knew anything, which I don't, I wouldn't risk jail time by discussing classified information with an unauthorized civilian."

"I understand, Henry. I don't want to cause any trouble. Thanks for returning my call."

"Can I give you a piece of advice?"

Markson smiled into the phone. "You always have."

"Drop it."

"Excuse me?"

"Don't mess with DARPA. Find something safer to do, like skydiving or bullfighting."

"DARPA?"

Catalano ended the conversation with "Bye, Lee."

"DARPA?" Clarke asked when Markson told her what Catalano had said.

The Defense Advanced Research Projects Agency was the DOD agency specifically chartered for cutting-edge technology development. They'd invented the internet. The implication of Henry's warning was that DARPA was somehow involved in research and development that involved gamma rays, and the embargoed data must reveal something about that project which the DOD didn't want anyone to know about.

"You're telling me the Air Force built an Alcubierre warp-ship?" It sounded like a question, but her hands on her hips and incredulous expression suggested otherwise.

Markson let out a big belly laugh.

"What's so damned funny?" This time, she *was* asking.

"Can you imagine how Jorge would react if he found out that a prototype of the *Starship Enterprise* was sitting in a hangar in Area 51?"

Clarke cracked up.

When they'd regained their composure, they had to accept that they couldn't address Aguillero's gamma ray spectrum concern because they couldn't get the data. However, if they could get around the other three issues Jorge had raised, they had a good justification for not addressing the spectrum question. Those issues were theoretical, and addressing them shouldn't draw the attention of the DOD. The biggest obstacle now was Aguillero's vested emotional interest in having Markson admit he was wrong.

"Let me know if you get any brilliant ideas," Markson said about that.

∞

Markson recognized the extension on his caller ID before he picked up the phone and found out that Clarke had a proposition to discuss. "Your office or mine?" he asked.

"Yours. Your table is more comfortable than my desk. I'll be right down."

Since they both knew that, no matter what the final result was, their analysis of the event would be worth documenting in a peer-reviewed scientific journal, Clarke proposed that it would be more efficient and effective for them to use the first draft of their paper to convince Aguillero of the merits of their hypothesis rather than work on the two things separately.

He wanted to know why.

"Kills two birds," she said.

The first task was to marshal a convincing case for their boss and the second was to organize their material persuasively for the journal referees. These were complimentary goals. Peer reviewed publication was essential. A resume with a lengthy bibliography of oft-cited papers was the ticket to promotion and recognition.

"Journal editors and referees are natural skeptics," Clarke reminded him. "If our paper is going to be good enough to get past them, it ought to be good enough to satisfy Jorge's scientific objections."

"Maybe. But remember, his reaction to our idea is as much emotional as it is scientific. Putting our approach to him in the form of a paper may aggravate the emotional issue."

She thought for a moment. "Mmmm. Look, we have to get permission from the department to submit our paper to a journal. If we approach Aguillero with the whole thing as a package, it will boost his ego. Tell him how much we value his comments. Show him how we've backed off from making any firm claims. Hell, tell him he can write a critical comment against our paper for the journal!"

"That might work. I like it. Besides, the departmental approval requires that it be submitted to a faculty panel for review. He won't be able to reject it unilaterally."

They couldn't avoid answering Aguillero's objections regarding energy, GNC, and radiation. Although each point involved cutting-edge theoretical physics, the issues were, at their root, engineering objections. Even if a warpship was mathematically possible, it couldn't be powered. If it could be powered, it couldn't be controlled. If it could be controlled, it couldn't safely approach its destination. They didn't have to solve these problems themselves, but they did have to amass enough evidence to make a convincing case that someone else had solved them to build the warpship they were claiming was the cause of the event.

Markson confirmed Clarke's assumption that Aguillero's concern with the gamma ray spectrum was tied to the radiation problem. An Alcubierre wake would be rich in high-energy radiation. If these intense gamma rays were detected, it would support their hypothesis while also, paradoxically, supporting the radiation objection to it.

Clarke leaned over and pretended to bang her head on the table. "I shouldn't have given up dancing. You can't win at this."

Markson smiled. "There isn't a Nobel Prize for burlesque. Besides, this is one I think we can work our way around."

She kept her head low to the table as she looked up. "Oh?"

"I've been thinking about this ever since Jorge raised the issue when we were debating the merits of my thesis proposal. The radiation issue was always one of his big three—but suppose we slow our warp bubble to sub-light speed, keeping it a safe distance from our destination, and let the bow shock dissipate?"

She cocked her head to one side, looking up with her mouth slightly open for a moment, and then turned her attention back to him. "And then coast in?" she asked.

He nodded.

"Cool!" she said. "How close can we get?"

He waved his hand. "I haven't done the calculation yet, but if we can't get the warpship close enough, it can carry a shuttlecraft that uses conventional propulsion."

Clarke gave Markson a high-five. "Sold! What's next?"

"That leaves energy and GNC."

They'd reduced three problems to two, but those remaining issues were severe challenges. If they couldn't deal with them both, their potentially Nobel Prize-winning discovery could remain nothing more than an unpublished speculation.

The energy problem would require new physics, but they hoped an operational workaround like they'd found for the radiation problem could answer the GNC objection.

They didn't find their answer in their offices. Instead, they found it at Fox and Hound English Pub & Grill. The space between the bar and the entrance was dominated by six professional-sized billiard tables which were well-maintained except for a few ineradicable stains, the origin of which Markson didn't want to know. The bar ran the length of the back wall and parallel to it so that the bartender could watch people as they entered or left by the front door. The entrance was centered in the front wall with two tall windows on each side, and booths along both side walls provided places for people to sit, talk, and drink if they weren't using the tables or sitting at the bar.

Markson watched Clarke run the table at 8-ball a couple of times. She was always a pleasure to look at, and he admired her performance, too. Everything she did was done with skill and elegance. Physics or pool, no difference. Well, maybe there was some difference... She enjoyed using her looks to seduce macho men, especially graduate students and cocky young faculty members, into challenging her to a game of pool at a couple of bucks a point. It delighted Markson to know that he'd be sharing both her winnings and her bed later that evening.

When she'd finished playing, she ordered drinks to celebrate and led him to a pair of stools at the bar. The insight that had been gnawing at him subconsciously while she played came to the surface as they talked.

"That pool table's like space," he said.

"You mean it's rectangular, flat, and green?"

"No, dear. The balls travel in a straight line until they hit something. Then, they change speed or direction."

"True."

"And yet, you can make them go wherever you want if you're good enough."

"Actually, if you're good enough, you can make them curve. It's called English."

"And you're obviously good enough," he said, pointing at the wad of bills she'd placed on the bar in front of her.

"That's because I'm also English!"

"But if you couldn't spin the ball—no English—you could still pocket the ball using caroms off the other balls and the rails, right?"

"Want to try me?"

"Just answer the question, please."

"Sure. Why?"

"Because that's how our warpship can navigate."

The next day, they examined star charts and exoplanet lists for solar systems within twenty light years of Earth that might have been the source or destination of their warpship. That would be about three years of travel one-way at warp seven. When Clarke suggested the limit, Markson asked why three years.

"We have to cut our search off somewhere. Four centuries ago, my ancestors would set out on a voyage of exploration expected to take up to half a decade, but nobody wanted to sign onto an expedition with the expectation of being away much longer. Six years round-trip seemed reasonable for our ET."

"What makes you think our alien is English?"

"Have you got a better number?"

Markson hesitated for a moment, and then shrugged his agreement.

In addition to candidate solar systems, they also examined stars without regard to accompanying planets so that they could identify those with a large mass which had close-enough proximity to reasonable trajectories that the stars could be focal points for gravity-assist maneuvers for such a spacecraft as they'd envisioned. These estimates were rough because all of the stars and the vehicle were moving at different speeds in different directions. The equations were actually simple, but not analytically solvable. To get answers to whether such a navigation strategy was feasible, they needed to run mathematical simulations on the department's fastest computer.

The simulations demonstrated the possibility that some flights between their candidate star systems wouldn't require turns, except for those that could be accomplished using the gravitational fields of stars along the flight path. For interstellar travel, faster-than-light technology was essential and would be worth the effort and expense. Once in the destination star system, more conventional propulsion without the GNC problem could suffice.

"So, how do we start and stop the damned thing? We don't have a cue stick or pockets," Markson said. "Maybe we could use a 'gravitational slingshot' like NASA does with some of its planetary probes in order to accelerate at departure and decelerate on arrival?"

Unable to answer that question, they also considered two other options: pre-programming the acceleration and deceleration, or commanding it from the outside. Both possibilities were problematic, but each was worth further evaluation. They put the arguments for and against both options into a short "white paper."

Now, they could no longer avoid the energy problem. Several days of brainstorming had brought them no closer to a solution.

"Is there any way we can present the gravitational wave data as simply being a set of observations worthy of further study? That way, we avoid all of the controversy surrounding the Alcubierre metric," Clarke wondered aloud.

"I don't think so. The LSC has already done that. If we don't include some interpretation, the referees won't consider our findings worth publishing. They'd have a valid point. LIGO and Virgo are always seeing things that look like signals and then turn out to be noise. They only write them up when they match a template or otherwise connect to some known phenomenon."

Markson paused as Clarke shook her head in frustration. Then, he laughed. "Our problem isn't that we can't match the waveform to a phenomenon. The *real problem* is that the physics establishment doesn't believe the phenomenon to which we've matched it is possible."

"But that dragon's biting its own tail."

He chuckled. "If you mean their argument is circular, I agree. What we're up against is, 'Your waveform can't be used to prove that a warp drive exists because a warp drive is impossible, so it couldn't cause that waveform.' There's no way to rebut that argument. It's a self-contained, closed loop."

"Blimey! Maybe that's the rebuttal."

"How do you mean?"

Clarke proposed that they present the waveforms and show that the signals weren't seriously degraded by noise at any of the sites. She'd then show the analysis tying the waveform to an Alcubierre wake and admit that there were serious objections to that interpretation. They could recommend further analysis and study on the grounds that simply denying the interpretation as impossible was circular, and hence not an adequate way of addressing the issue.

"Send him a googly," she said.

"A googly?"

"Yes, a... a curveball, I think, is the Yank equivalent."

Markson thought for a moment. "In other words, we don't claim that the objections are wrong, but that they're inadequate, and further investigation is needed?"

"Yes. Aguillero shouldn't get his knickers in a knot about that. We're agreeing that he might even be right and suggesting that more study is required. It would give us grounds for seeking additional grant money from the NSF or NASA, too."

"Let's do it," Markson said.

She gave him an approving fist-pump.

They crafted the paper to showcase the quality of the observations and the high correlation of the waveforms at the various locations of measurement. He wrote the sections on the observations with her suggestions and edits. She led the preparation of their mathematical analysis of the waveforms that supported the Alcubierre interpretation of the data. From time to time, they compared notes in one of their offices or commandeered the small conference room when they really needed to spread out. The time differences between the signals at each of the GW sensors were consistent with the differences in their locations and the distances from the object as it traveled. The GW data lacked the precision to allow the trajectory and the speed of the object to be determined precisely, but was consistent with the more exact location and velocity determined from the EM data.

Following the presentation of the data and their analysis of one interpretation consistent with the data, they listed the standard objections and responded to them as Clarke had suggested. Their closing summary left open the question of what the data "really" meant, but argued that answering the question was important to relativistic physics no matter what the answer turned out to be.

Markson attached the manuscript to a formal request for permission to submit it to a peer-reviewed physics journal of their choosing. The request went to Professor Aguillero, since he was the Chairman of the Department of Physics and Astronomy.

CHAPTER FOUR

REACTION

AS CHAIRMAN of the Physics Department, Aguillero convened a review committee in his inner office. He selected four additional faculty members to consider whether or not the department should give Markson and Clarke permission to submit their paper for publication in a scientific journal. This was standard procedure; it protected the department and authors from embarrassment by catching errors or significant omissions before they reached a journal's referees.

Markson and Clarke's paper involved several specialties in physics and engineering. Its core was the Alcubierre solution to the equations of general relativity, and the institute's expert in this area was Shanta Jelani, who held joint appointments in the departments of physics and mathematics. Her specialty was differential geometry, the mathematics on which general relativity was based. Given Aguillero's well-known bias against the Markson-Clarke hypothesis, he needed Jelani on the panel to assure that it would be seen as having an independent expert on the subject.

The authors had suggested the possibility of eventual quantum mechanical solutions to the energy and GNC problems, so Aguillero included his department's authority on quantum mechanics, Dr. Zhao Ming. Meanwhile, the engineering aspects of the paper prompted him to appoint his only engineering physicist, Dr. Daniel Lambert, along with Dr. Loren Haley, an observational cosmologist who was familiar with both electromagnetic and gravitational wave observations.

Aguillero welcomed them each with their own favorite flavor of coffee. He rolled the chair from his desk to the table, where he joined the other four experts already seated there. His seat was nearest the whiteboard. He wore his "chairman's uniform"—a complete three-piece suit, pleated dress shirt, and a tie carefully selected to complement both.

Haley had earned his doctorate in astrophysics and gravitation at Georgia Tech. He dressed comfortably, but not so laid-back as to offend Aguillero, whose penchant for formality was well-known.

Lambert had earned his doctorate in applied physics at Caltech. He had on an open-collared cotton sport shirt and jeans. He and Aguillero would not have been a good combination, except that they often thought alike. As much as Aguillero liked formality, he liked intellectual compatibility better.

Zhao Ming had gotten his doctorate in the People's Republic of China. He'd come to the U.S. on a postdoctoral fellowship at the Kavli Institute for Theoretical Physics and stayed to accept a tenure-track faculty position at Stanford. Now, he was a full professor leading LAPI's program in quantum gravity. He sat back in his seat, obviously at ease.

Professor Jelani stood out, though not because of her age. Mid-40s was about average for academic mathematicians entering the upper echelons of their careers. Her height, weight, and build were also unremarkable... but she was the only woman in the room. Aguillero was more traditional, so to speak, when it came to a woman's "proper place" in the learned professions than was truly acceptable these days, at least in public. She was also the only person of color. Her mother was from India, and her father was African-American. She had a lovely light brown complexion that often passed for "white" among people who had trouble grasping the concept of a non-white female being a full professor of mathematics at a major American educational institution. She wore a loose, flowing garment that was brightly colored and décorated, as if to say, *"I will not allow you to deny my ancestry."*

Prior to the meeting, Aguillero had given each member a copy of the drafted Markson-Clarke manuscript and directed them to review it beforehand. He'd also included a copy of the hypernova paper which he and Jelani had published previously, with the suggestion that they consider it as an alternative interpretation of the phenomenon.

He opened the meeting by explaining what he wanted to accomplish.

"Alright. We have a paper in which the authors present simultaneous electromagnetic and gravitational wave observations that occurred during an event which is still not understood. It gives some interesting analyses and comparisons of the data that may be of some value to the astrophysics community in eventually determining the origins of the event. We're not going to find anything controversial there. For this, we just need to make sure the work is correct and assure the analysis is of sufficient interest to be worth presenting to a journal."

He paused for a moment. Hearing no disagreement, he continued.

"The concern I have is the authors' assertion that the observations are consistent with the passage of some faster-than-light spaceship and that the Alcubierre metric justifies taking such speculations seriously. The Alcubierre metric has been shown to have fatal flaws—which the authors acknowledge, but persist in disregarding. I'd like to know if any of you see any redeeming merit in this nonsense that could possibly justify submitting the paper from our department, especially since there's a more conventional possibility proposed in the paper by myself and Professor Jelani."

"May I say something?" Jelani asked before Aguillero could go any further.

"Of course, Professor Jelani. What is it?"

"I discussed your alternative interpretation of the observations with Professor Clarke. Unless there's more to the story, our paper is consistent only with the amplitudes of the observations, not with their timing or the observationally derived source location. Additionally, the electromagnetic signals have the wrong spectral characteristics and decay much too rapidly. Also, the GW signatures don't match. That means the hypernova isn't a viable option. Their hypothesis at least fits the data. What did I miss?"

Aguillero tossed the papers onto the table. "Their EM work in that regard was sloppy and incomplete. I don't trust their GW waveforms, either. Clarke did those computations, and she's a signal processor, not really a cosmologist. Who knows whether she's up to such complex calculations?"

Jelani gave Aguillero a cold stare. "She got those calculations from me, Jorge. In case you have forgotten, I did them while we were working on our paper."

"There was nothing like that in our paper. At least our interpretation, whatever its weaknesses, is physically possible."

"It is *our paper*, Professor Aguillero, but this particular hypernova hypothesis based upon it is *your* interpretation. Unless you can explain the discrepancies I've already mentioned, plus at least two others, I see no value in muddying the waters of a discussion of their paper with an untenable proposition based on ours."

"What other discrepancies?" Lambert asked in a doubtful tone.

Jelani hesitated for a second before answering. "OK, I didn't want to engage in overkill, but the two bright streaks heading away from the flash are not consistent with our paper and must be local since their angular velocity is much too high for anything sub-light beyond near-Earth space. And the *coup de grâce* is that there's no afterglow in Norma, where the supposed hypernova took place. No afterglow means no hypernova."

Lambert looked up at Aguillero. "Is that right, Jorge?"

Aguillero picked up his papers with a sigh. With his co-author against him, he couldn't make his case. "Perhaps Professor Jelani has a point. Let's take the Markson-Clarke paper for what it is and not worry about other possibilities at this juncture. The question then remains, do any of you see any merit in this nonsense that could possibly justify submitting this paper from our department?"

Lambert immediately spoke up. "The energy problem is insurmountable even in principle. I don't need to go any further. Unless they take the faster-than-light stuff out of the paper, it should never see the light of day."

Aguillero nodded his approval, but Jelani asked what made them so sure.

Lambert looked at her with condescension. "It's about the physics, not the math. The Alcubierre metric requires copious amounts of negative energy... *huge amounts*. Planetary mass amounts, except that the mass must be negative—so-called exotic matter. There's no way to create it even in minute quantities." He looked toward Professor Ming. "That's correct,

Zhao, right? The standard model of particle physics won't support it."

Ming frowned. "I feel like I'm being pressured into supporting an argument against publishing an interesting idea that's supported by both data and theory."

Aguillero could see Jelani's gaze focused on Ming as she awaited his answer.

Ming took a deep breath and continued, "At the present state of our knowledge, you are certainly correct, but I'm sure you are also aware that the present state of knowledge doesn't cover interactions between quantum mechanics and general relativity in strongly curved spacetimes. The two theories are fundamentally incompatible, and at least one of them has to be wrong even though both have passed every observational test so far. That's why the search for a quantum theory of gravity is so important."

Haley agreed with Lambert and Aguillero that the idea of a faster-than-light spacecraft violated physical law as it was known, but he was unwilling to challenge Zhao Ming in his field of specialty when it came to whether or not current knowledge was sufficient to be dogmatic about it.

Having no consensus on the energy objection, Aguillero took up GNC—Guidance, Navigation, and Control. "Even if there is some magical loophole that quantum gravity or string theory or some such thing can wiggle through to make the energetics possible, you still couldn't control such a vehicle. You couldn't get it to superluminal speeds, and *if* you could, *then* you couldn't steer it or stop it because there would be a horizon between the interior cabin and the front of the warp bubble. There's no causal connection between the pilot and the business end of the spacecraft."

Lambert nodded his approval and asked if anyone could see any plausible way around this.

"Quantum gravity or some version of string theory might make that problem disappear, or redefine it in a way that it could be solved," Ming observed.

Jelani sat up, her face alight with a big smile as she realized the importance of her colleague's comment. "That's especially true if the physics takes place in more than four dimensions! The analog is a wall on the surface of the Earth. In two spatial dimensions, you have the equivalent of a horizon. You can't get past it. But with three dimensions, you can fly over it without having to invent some magical method of punching through it," she said.

"Horizons arise in classical computations," Ming added. "They raise similar issues relating to black holes and the Big Bang. Unless you're talking about superluminal flight, everyone seems comfortable with pushing the can down the road by invoking new physics like the quantum gravity and string theory Jorge mentioned. Why not in this case?"

Lambert shook his head. "Professor Jelani, I think your friendship with Professor Clarke has clouded your judgment. Dr. Ming, I don't know what your problem is, but this is junk science."

This time, Haley sided with Jelani and Ming.

Aguillero saw they weren't making any progress on this issue, either, so he ended the discussion on GNC and moved forward. "We have one more major objection to take up before we decide whether or not to permit submission of this paper. Unlike their discussions of the energy and GNC problems, where Markson and Clarke admitted that no solution was possible without new physics, they claim that they can avoid the radiation problem at the destination by staying far enough away from it and using some sort of conventionally powered, short-range vehicle to cover the remaining distance. It strikes me as improbable. Does anybody think this strategy is acceptable?"

Jelani immediately spoke up. "I certainly don't see anything wrong with it, Jorge. What's so improbable about it?"

Aguillero deflected her question to Lambert, who had been in lockstep with him thus far. Lambert thought for a moment before answering. "This is not a physics problem. You can calculate the required stand-off distance. The only concerns are engineering and financial. How big does the landing craft have to be, and how much will it cost to carry the crew and cargo the necessary distance? I couldn't justify rejecting the paper on those grounds."

"But wouldn't horizons inside the bubble emit Hawking radiation into the spacecraft, making it lethal to the crew?" Aguillero persisted.

Haley sided with Ming and Jelani that any physics which resolved the navigation and control problems with the horizons would necessarily solve the Hawking radiation problem, if it existed.

Aguillero, finding himself a minority of one on the radiation issue, conceded the point and proceeded to ask for a binary "yes" or "no" vote on the primary question: "Should the department approve the Markson-Clarke manuscript for submission to a peer-reviewed journal?"

Lambert voted first: "No."

Jelani next: "Yes."

Ming: "Yes."

Now, it was Haley's turn. At this point, everyone knew that Aguillero would vote no, so Haley's vote would be the tiebreaker.

"Dr. Haley?" Aguillero said, but Haley didn't respond. He sat looking down at his hands folded together on the table. "Dr. Haley, please don't embarrass our department by letting this piece of pseudoscience be submitted to a journal with our name on it! How do you vote?"

Haley put his hands in his lap and looked up. "I'm sorry, Dr. Aguillero. I don't believe I am qualified to make that decision. I see both sides. I don't think such a thing can be done, but the observations and analysis are sound. The proposal for new physics, however, seems contrary to everything we know about quantum mechanics and relativity—"

"If that's what you believe, vote no," Aguillero interrupted him.

"Please let me finish. I think Shanta and Zhao have made a good point in saying that we don't know everything. I am reluctant to endorse such a paper, but equally reluctant to suppress it. I abstain."

After brief but vigorous prodding by both sides, Haley convinced them that he wasn't going to change his mind.

Aguillero shook his head. "I vote no," he said. Then, he stood for a moment looking out the window, before turning back toward the table.

"The vote is a tie," Jelani said. "We should give them the benefit of the doubt."

Aguillero looked at her intensely. "Dr. Jelani, your appointment with our department is only half-time, and while as a mathematician you are a valuable asset to our program in general relativity, I don't believe I should weigh your vote equally with the rest of us who are full-time physicists. There is no tie. If there were, the result would be the same; as chairman of the faculty review committee, I have the authority to break ties. I find that the committee declines to approve submission of this paper to a journal."

Jelani glared at him. "That's not right, Jorge! I was appointed to this committee by you as a member of *this* department, and I am wielding my vote as a Department of Physics faculty member. The vote is a *tie*," Jelani said, tapping the edge of the table with her hand at the word "tie."

Aguillero stared at her. He did not appreciate her challenging him. "Even if that were true, Professor Jelani, as department chairman, I have the authority to break ties. I will notify the authors."

Hearing no support from any of the others, including Professor Ming, Jelani let the matter drop.

∞

Markson stuck his head into Clarke's office, where she was sitting behind her desk. "Kat, come with me. Jorge said the committee has reviewed our paper and he wants to give us their recommendations."

"Is that good or bad?" She stood and put on her sweater. Aguillero always kept his office cold.

"Let's find out."

When the pair entered his office, Aguillero pointed to the big, multi-cup Keurig machine. "Dr. Markson, would you like some coffee? Dr. Clark, some tea?"

"No, thanks, Jorge, we're fine. Are we good to go?" Markson asked.

Aguillero indicated their usual places at the table.

As they were about to be seated, though, Clarke said, "Actually, if you don't mind, a cup of hot tea would be quite nice. Thank you for asking."

Markson stared at her as Aguillero went to brew some Earl Grey.

She grinned, leaned over, and whispered, "It's the only warm thing in the room."

He laughed.

"Did I miss something?" Aguillero asked as he returned

with a full cup on a saucer and a small plate with containers of milk and sugar.

"It amuses me to watch you make tea. You were always a coffee person," Markson said.

Aguillero smiled. "Actually, I make a good cup of either, don't you think?"

Clarke raised her cup in salute. The cordiality of the conversation seemed incompatible with calling them in to announce the rejection of their work.

She was wrong.

Aguillero thought he was being diplomatic and even generous when he phrased the decision this way: "Your paper is not something the department feels comfortable submitting to a journal. We appreciate your recognition of the difficulties of the Alcubierre interpretation of the gravitational wave signature, and it is to your credit that you openly discuss them in the manuscript. Unfortunately, your discussion leads to the same conclusion that I suggested before. The Alcubierre interpretation is untenable. You can't make that hypothesis publishable by admitting that it is impossible."

Clarke rose and stood staring at Aguillero wordlessly, her mouth open.

Markson raised his voice as he argued, and pointed at his boss. "You don't understand the key point we're making! You can't prove something is impossible by assuming it to be impossible! We don't understand all of the necessary physics, and neither do you. The point is to publish the paper and let the whole physics community take a shot at it."

Clarke sat down, and the argument went around and around, but Aguillero wouldn't budge. He felt sure he was right, and that was that.

"When you can make a case that this doesn't violate the laws of physics rather than the case you've made that it does," he told them, "then you'll have something." The department chairman did not appreciate it when the conversation dwindled to Markson and Clarke sullenly glaring at him. "Your tea is getting cold," he told her.

"So am I," she replied. Then, she turned to Markson and waved her right fist thumb-up like a hitchhiker. "Let's go."

They stood up. Before turning to leave, Markson asked Aguillero, "Was the committee's recommendation unanimous?"

Aguillero sniffed. "If you were willing to carry your weight on faculty committees, Dr. Markson, you'd know that these deliberations are confidential."

Back in Markson's office, the co-authors vented for a while. When they'd run out of unpleasant words to describe Aguillero, they recycled some of them for use on the physics establishment in general, and their fellow faculty members who'd failed to back them up, in particular.

"Fuck it. There's a nice Irish place on Third Street. Let's go eat," Clarke finally suggested.

Markson thought Happy's Irish Pub overdid the green. The outside of the building was painted a textured, camouflage-like olive drab. The separators between the panes in the big glass windows looked like jail-house bars running horizontally and vertically, and were the same color as the walls. The interior tiles were a glossy dark green. The ones on the floor matched the ones on the front of the bar which also matched the ones on the bar top and tabletops. Of course, the logos on the cups, mugs, plates, and napkins were also green, but couldn't they at least have picked a different shade?

Clarke turned sarcastic as he continued to critique the surroundings while waiting for their orders to be served. She made a sour face and said, "I didn't know you were an interior décorator."

It wasn't her sarcasm that silenced him. When the food and drinks arrived, he found them as delicious as the décor was disappointing. "I guess next time I won't judge a pub by its color," he said as they ordered dessert and an after-dinner drink.

With a full meal and a medicinal dose of Irish whiskey under their belts, they decided to revisit the issue.

"My place or yours?" he asked.

She leaned over the table and took his hand in hers. "Let's do it here and give the drinks a chance to settle."

"I'm OK, but here is good."

She sat back and tossed him a kiss, and then put her hands on the table in front of her. "If we can't submit it to a journal, can we send copies out for comments and suggestions?"

He cocked his head a little to one side. "What do you have in mind?"

"Well, for starters, I'd like to know what Aberto and his group at Virgo would think, now that we've done a thorough analysis."

Markson nodded in agreement. "I'd like to get some input from some of the quantum physics folks about the energy problem, as well as the bow shock."

"Let's make a distribution list and send it out to a dozen or so people."

He frowned. "Why don't we just post a summary of it for comment on the Transient Astronomy Network? That way, we can reach a broader range of experts."

"Why not the full article?"

"That's not really what TAN is for. Besides, if we focus on the observations and ask the network for any additional coincident optical data they may have, we can avoid the whole fracas about our interpretation."

She frowned. "But isn't it our interpretation that we want people to review?"

Markson sighed. After some additional give and take, he agreed to posting the paper on a less restrictive site for professional physicists—but with a caveat: "We'll add a paragraph at the end stating that the paper is speculative at this stage and only a preliminary draft awaiting departmental approval. That should keep us out of trouble with the department."

She agreed.

The next morning before leaving for work, Markson drafted the disclaimer notices and posted the package on a website usually accessed only by professional physicists. The post instantly attracted an avalanche of comments, some of them vicious and personal. These were followed several days later by an invitation for Markson to appear on a popular television interview show where he'd appeared five years earlier to discuss CATSPAW when it had been big news.

∞

Markson sat on a well-worn sofa in the cramped green room in the backstage area of the studio watching a barrage of commercials on a small monitor.

The technician who came in to install a pair of wireless microphones on his shirt instructed him, "Give me a little chatter in your normal voice."

"Mary had a little duck living in a garbage truck. One... two..." Markson said.

The tech cut him off, "That's good. Follow me."

He was told to wait in the wings at stage left until he heard the host introduce him, and then come in and cross the stage to a seat on the guest couch to the audience's left of the host's desk.

As usual, the program began with the host's opening lines: "Welcome to *The Willard Manchester Show*! Tonight, we have a special guest. He's a noted and sometimes controversial physicist whom you may remember as the one who made a fortune in the stock market with the infamous CATSPAW project. Please welcome Doctor Lee Markson!"

Markson entered as directed, squinting slightly as his eyes got accustomed to the bright lighting. He waved to the applauding audience as he crossed the stage to the guest couch. In the time since he'd last appeared on the show, the host, who was now in his late fifties, hadn't changed much. His reddish-brown hair had gotten just a bit grayer over the ears, and he still looked just like he did on TV—except shorter.

Those heavy brown eyeglass frames look a little geeky for a big-name TV star, Markson thought with amusement.

"Thank you for joining us tonight, Dr. Markson," Manchester said as the physicist took his seat.

Markson sat up straight, his gaze angled so that he could maintain eye contact with the camera and the host as well as the audience. He made a conscious and effective effort to appear eager. "Thanks for having me."

Manchester had once commented in an op-ed piece that many of the academic guests he interviewed chose not to dress up in any way for the show. He found that a disappointing sign of a loss of civility in the country. Breaking that trend, Markson had worn a jacket and tie. Nothing especially fashionable or expensive, but respectful. Manchester had smiled in response when he'd seen Markson come through the curtains.

When his guest was seated, Manchester sat with his arms folded in front of him on the desk as he faced Markson and asked his opening question: "You haven't granted many interviews in the last few years, have you?"

Markson turned to face the host rather than the camera. "No. I used to do a lot of them, but I got fed up with interviewers who had an axe to grind or hadn't done their homework—or both."

"So, what's different this time?"

"I posted a first draft of a potential paper on a closed professional physics website a few days ago. Somebody seems to have taken offense because things were leaked to the public, and now there's a concerted campaign attacking me on social media. It makes me look like a greedy egomaniac who's only concerned with acquiring fame and fortune. A lot of it is pure fiction, and the rest is distorted and out of context. I wanted to set the record straight."

Manchester nodded and pointed at his guest. "Fair enough. I'm going to ask about your paper in a few minutes, but why do this here on my show?"

"I've watched most of the popular interview programs. You still make the effort to get your facts straight and let your guests answer your questions without talking over them. The last time I came, you were courteous and professional—qualities that are sadly rare."

Manchester turned to the camera and smiled. "Honest, folks, I did not pay for that endorsement!" Turning back to Markson, Manchester asked, "What is your biggest complaint about the commentary? You don't expect to be immune from criticism, do you?"

"Willard, these are personal attacks, not criticisms of the

science they are purporting to critique. They make me out to be something I'm not. Something nasty and selfish."

Manchester leaned forward and raised his head a bit. "Give me an example."

"Well, they focus on CATSPAW. They rehash those accusations that I took the job at CAT—"

"Catalano Automated Trading?" Manchester interrupted.

"Yes. They make it look like I took that job because the salary of a physicist wasn't enough for greedy young Lee Markson. In fact, I was very reluctant to even return Ken Huntsman's call when he approached me. I hated Wall Street. I understand it a bit better now, but I'm still not fond of it."

"Then, why did you take the job?"

"That's the thing. I returned the phone call because nobody else would hire me, and I needed to put food on the table. The physics establishment said my thesis on a practical time reversal device was junk science. Because of that, I had to consider employment anywhere I could find it. I at least wanted to hear what Huntsman was offering, since it was the only offer on the table."

The host turned his hands face-up, fingers spread. "So, you did take it for the money, right?"

"No! The money was nice, but it was not the driving factor. CAT offered to fund the construction and testing of a prototype of the device in my thesis. Nobody could have offered me enough money to refuse that. If it worked like I thought it would, I could shove it in the face of those self-righteous know-it-alls who'd refused to admit that my math was right, and that the theory—which was Einstein's, not mine, by the way—was correct. Taking that job was about rehabilitating my reputation as a physicist so that I could work in the field. It wasn't about money."

Manchester turned toward the camera. "OK. We'll be back with more questions for Dr. Lee Markson right after these messages."

During the commercial break, Markson asked for some water, and Manchester took a bottle from a small refrigerator under his desk.

"First a time machine, and now a faster-than-light spaceship. It must be a thrill to play with such futuristic toys," Manchester said as he handed the bottle to Markson.

"Actually, Willard, your automated cameras and computer-programmed lighting systems are higher tech and certainly more visually impressive than our offices. We sit in front of computers crunching numbers and symbols just like accountants at a bank. The excitement comes from what the numbers mean, not the tools we use to crunch them."

"CATSPAW was a heck of a lot more than that," Manchester countered.

"That's true, but that's in the past. And even CATSPAW just looked like an oversized vacuum bottle laid on its side, which is what it mostly was, in fact. The actual time shifters were inside the structure and invisible from the outside."

The two men talked quickly about Markson's current

relations with the other people at CAT. When the director gave the ten-second warning, Manchester turned back toward the camera, and when the red light came on, the show resumed.

"Welcome back to *The Willard Manchester Show*. Our guest tonight is Dr. Lee Markson. Dr. Markson, looking back on your days at CAT, do you have any regrets?"

"Actually, I do, Willard, but it's probably not what you'd expect. As much as I dislike the whole Wall Street environment, I wish I'd defended CAT and CATSPAW more vigorously when they were being attacked in the media after the project was shut down. The people at CAT were decent, ethical, and productive. They didn't deserve to be pilloried for thinking outside of the box, developing and applying a radical new technology, and getting rich while doing it. I walked off into the academic world and let them take more of the heat than they deserved. I could have helped more."

"Let's talk about that. You left CAT as soon as you had the opportunity and joined LAPI as a professor, right?"

"Right. And, just to be clear, I joined as a tenured associate professor."

"But now your work there has become just as controversial as your work at CAT. Is that what the new paper you mentioned earlier is about? Tell us about that."

Markson frowned and hesitated. "I wanted to talk about the personal attacks rather than the paper, but it's a fair question. Gravitational waves are extremely weak. Even with today's advanced technology, the signals from these waves are accompanied by a great deal of noise. The gravitational wave signals are identified by comparing their shape with *signatures* computed from Einstein's field equations in order to match them to specific phenomena like colliding black holes or binary neutron stars."

"Could you tell our audience what you mean by *signatures*?"

Markson felt sheepish that he hadn't seen that question coming. "Sure. Each astrophysical event that generates gravitational waves produces a pattern of waves that can be predicted using Einstein's field equations. That pattern is what we mean by its signature. The calculations are complex, but given enough time on a powerful computer, the pattern can be generated and stored. We used the stored signatures as templates for comparison with our observations."

"And your paper is based on these signatures?"

"In part," Markson replied. "There was a signal on the 15th of September that didn't match any of our templates. My colleague Katty Clarke and I performed some calculations to demonstrate that the signal matched the signature calculated for the wake of a warpship."

"A warpship?" Manchester asked, his chin lowered and his eyebrows raised.

"Yes. A spaceship traveling faster than light."

"I thought that was impossible."

Markson gave a fist-pump, and with a grin like a man who'd struck gold, he said, "Exactly! We also thought that was impossible, but apparently not. That's what's so exciting about it."

"So, Einstein was wrong?" Manchester asked.

"Not at all! His famous field equations actually permit it if you can assemble a certain configuration of negative energy."

"Then, if it's OK with Einstein, why is this work so controversial?"

"It's the negative energy thing, Willard. I also think part of the physics establishment sees a chance for revenge over CATSPAW. The mathematics behind the two things are the same. Since the math is correct, they use the negative energy problem to attack the engineering as being physically impossible. Nobody, including me, can see how the negative energy issue can be overcome."

"Negative energy? Is that like antimatter? They use that in science fiction to power spaceships. Is that it?"

Markson laughed. "I wish it were that easy. Antimatter exists, and we know how to make it. Our only problem would be storing it. The energy in antimatter is the same as what you find in regular matter. What we need is an exotic substance that most physicists believe cannot even exist—except in infinitesimal quantities—due to quantum mechanical effects in microscopic spaces like those I used in building CATSPAW."

"What's the difference between this exotic matter and regular matter?"

"Exotic matter has negative mass and negative energy. Electric or magnetic forces on it would accelerate it in exactly the opposite direction as normal matter having the same electrical properties and charge would move, for example."

"Well now, that would be interesting! So, why are you convinced you're right?"

"Because I don't believe in pounding the table with assertions that something is impossible while someone is doing it in plain sight. That's why I've been hoping that some of the quantum physics folks would be motivated to work on the negative energy problem. I'm an expert in general relativity. The quantum stuff is out of my field."

Manchester threw up his hands a bit. "But why do you care? Isn't that just an ego thing, like the trolls are saying?"

Markson leaned toward Manchester. "Since *Star Trek* first hit the airwaves in the 1960s, science fiction fans have dreamed of traveling the universe using spaceships powered by warp drives. We know now that it can actually be done, and somebody out there is doing it—because we're seeing their wake. Throughout all of human history, the biggest inhibition to technological progress has been getting past the conventional opinion that something new couldn't be done. It frustrates me that the physics and engineering communities are so trapped in their little intellectual boxes that they'd pass on the opportunity to make those dreams a reality."

"Dr. Markson, thank you for sharing your thoughts with us today," the host said before turning to the camera placed between the set and the audience and announcing the commercial break: "I'm Willard Manchester, and we'll be right back."

Both men stood up as the director motioned to Markson to leave the stage the same way he'd entered. Separately,

Manchester and Markson both took note as the audience erupted into roaring, raucous applause. The men acknowledged the response.

As the clamor subsided, Manchester extended his hand and his guest took it. "I hope you'll come back and join us again sometime. You're entertaining and informative. My audience likes that."

"I may do that. Especially if there's more scurrilous commentary about me," Markson replied with a wink as he turned to leave the stage.

Once again, the audience erupted, and most remained standing until the physicist vanished behind the curtain.

A week after their paper was posted and two days after the interview, Markson was surprised to be summoned to the office of Dean Joanne Simpson late in the afternoon. The dean's secretary ushered him into the College of Science's administrative conference room, where his surprise turned to alarm.

Simpson stood at the head of the large, old-fashioned wooden table that dominated the interior of the room. She was flanked by Physics and Astronomy Department Chairman Aguillero as well as three others, one of whom Markson recognized, but couldn't place. The remaining two, he hadn't met before. Nobody else was present. The lectern in the corner was unoccupied, and the ten-foot by six-foot projection screen on the wall by the lectern was dark.

This wasn't going to be a technical or budgetary briefing.

Markson rarely paid attention to people's appearances, but he found it disquieting that Simpson's jet-black hair streamed past the onyx of her eyeglass frames and blended seamlessly into the charcoal wool of her open jacket. The only relief from the depressing darkness was a pattern of white dots on the black cotton of her blouse, as if she'd been caught in a storm of small, circular snowflakes. He couldn't get the image of her in a pointed black hat seated on an antique broom out of his mind.

She indicated the chair at the opposite end of the table, which would put as much space between them as possible—as if he had a communicable disease. "Professor Markson," she greeted him formally, "please be seated. Of course, you know Professor Aguillero, and this is Vice Provost Mark Connor from the Office of Academic Affairs." As she spoke, she waved toward the people sitting along the table to her left. Turning to the right, she introduced representatives from the school's Office of the General Counsel and Human Resources.

Markson's pulse rate rose when he noticed that his boss was wearing a vest again. He raised his voice to ask, "What's this about? What's going on?"

Dean Simpson sat down, leaned forward, and picked up a letter-sized folder that appeared not to have much in it. She looked at Markson as she opened it. "Professor Markson, it seems that you have disobeyed direct and specific instructions not to publish a paper that was reviewed by your department and found to be without merit, as well as potentially embarrassing to the institute. Such behavior by you and your co-author will not be tolerated. I am seriously considering recommending that your employment with LAPI be terminated."

Markson's jaw dropped and he stood up. "We didn't publish *anything*. What are you talking about? What have you got there?" he asked as he started to come around the table toward the dean.

"Please sit down, Dr. Markson," she said with a withering stare.

He paused in place for a moment and then shuffled back to his seat before reacting any further. "We did *not publish* that paper. The department told us not to submit it to a journal, and we didn't! I still think the department made a mistake, but we've followed their instructions and plan on continuing to do so."

Dean Simpson took several pages from the open folder and handed them to Professor Aguillero so that he could pass them down the table to Markson. "Then, perhaps you can explain where these came from," she said. "They were posted on three different sensationalist fringe science sites within the last several hours."

Markson grabbed for the papers the instant they were within reach. They were printouts of postings describing and citing what he had put on the physics website. He tossed the sheets on the table in front of him.

"This isn't publication! If I was going to publish our paper on the web, I'd send it to *arXiv*. Nobody said we weren't allowed to discuss our work with other physicists. As you said, the department's direction was specific. It said we could not *publish*. It did not prohibit discussion."

"You not only posted it on a publicly accessible website, but you then gave a major TV interview defending it!" Dean Simpson responded. "The reputation of the institute is at risk whenever junk science is publicly advocated by one of our faculty members, and your department chairman assures me that this is junk science. You were fully aware of the concern that led to the instructions which you and Dr. Clarke were given, and you two ignored it."

"That interview was in response to personal attacks on my character as relating to CATSPAW. Any connection to LAPI was coincidental. The paper was barely mentioned. As far as posting the paper goes, Professor Clarke didn't ignore anything. *I* posted it," Markson said, tapping himself on the chest with his index finger. "I deliberately picked a site that is mostly visited by specialists, and I explicitly noted that the work was not to be forwarded or otherwise distributed. That certainly does not constitute publication. I even admitted that my own department disapproved of it." He waved his hand in the air in their general direction. "That should be enough to cover your asses, don't you think?"

"Dr. Markson, if that's the way you talk to senior institute officials, this obsession of yours with imagined spaceships is not your only problem," Dr. Connor interjected.

Markson looked over at the Vice Provost and took a deep

breath. "I'm sorry, Dr. Connor. I let my frustration get out of hand. I apologize."

Connor nodded his acceptance.

Simpson turned to Professor Aguillero. "What does the department want to do about this, now that you've heard Professor Markson's explanation?"

Aguillero looked toward Markson rather than at Simpson. "First, I want that paper taken off the internet as soon as he leaves this room. Second, I want his resignation. I'm tired of his insubordination. He thinks that because he's rich, he doesn't have to follow the rules."

Markson rose to speak, but Simpson was faster. "That's enough, Professor Aguillero. Another thing we won't tolerate is personal attacks on our faculty members. Lee, please accept Dr. Aguillero's apology. You are offering one, of course, Jorge?"

Aguillero looked from Dean Simpson to Markson, and then back to the dean before he nodded. "Of course. I regret speaking discourteously in response to Dr. Markson's misconduct." He turned to Markson as the younger man appeared to be about to rise and make a reply. "Please excuse my rudeness, Dr. Markson. It was beneath me."

Markson reluctantly resumed his seat.

"Will you take the paper down?" Simpson asked Markson.

Markson scowled and shook his head. "Sure."

"And you will do no more public interviews on the subject, and will follow the instructions of your department chairman regarding your research priorities?"

Markson objected, citing the institute's stated policies relating to academic freedom for tenured faculty, but Simpson remained adamant.

"Academic freedom isn't unlimited, Professor Markson. We have academic standards," the dean continued, "and they apply to you, just like anyone else. You crossed the line when you posted your speculations where they were accessible to the public, and then you doubled down when you went on a prime-time television talk show to defend them. I want your assurance that you will continue to be an asset to the department, not a liability."

Markson didn't see any upside to further resistance at the moment. He breathed out a sigh and looked toward Aguillero. "You're the boss, Jorge."

"See that you don't forget that again," Aguillero said.

As the meeting with the dean ended, Aguillero took Markson aside and told him to cease all work on the September 15th event. "Go back and finish what you were working on before I made the mistake of assigning you this project. Before you got derailed, you said you were working on an idea for improving the LIGO signal-to-noise ratio for broadband gravitational wave signals at the next upgrade. I'd like to see it as soon as you can have it ready. If you just can't let this thing go, then find out how the two of you can use your highly active imaginations to identify a physically reasonable astrophysical origin for the observed signals. I have proposed one. You don't like it, fine—find a better one that doesn't involve spaceships."

A week later, Markson was notified that, based on the recommendations of the department and the college, he would be formally censured. Censure was sometimes the first step toward revoking a faculty member's tenure, which meant he would have to be careful.

When Markson informed Clarke of his censure, she wasn't surprised. Not only had she been removed from their project, but Aguillero had told her, "It was a shame you wasted such talent on such nonsense." He had directed her to apply her algorithms to some as-yet-unverified candidate GW detections by LIGO in which the gamma-ray-burst researchers were interested. He'd also called her into a meeting with the dean.

"They told me that they were overlooking my behavior this time because I was under your 'nefarious influence,'" she relayed to Markson. "They warned me that if I get involved with your 'fantasy' any further, I'll have to suffer the consequences, as well."

Markson resolved to see that that never happened.

Markson steamed for days. He told Clarke that he was keeping his promise to drop any further work on the Alcubierre hypothesis, but it was a lie. He wanted to ensure that she returned to working on what she'd been doing prior to the September 15th event. He wasn't going to let his protégée and lover lose her job just because of his stubbornness. Meanwhile, he kept digging.

His hard, after-hours work hadn't yet paid off when he was handed a gift. Russia introduced a resolution in the UN which condemned the U.S. for violating the Outer Space Treaty banning nuclear weapons in space. Russia charged that the September 15th incident had been caused by the malfunction and explosion of a U.S. space-based nuclear weapons satellite. To bolster their claim, they posted a hefty data archive for the time immediately surrounding the event; it was sourced from the Russian equivalents of the U.S. DOD's nuclear test monitoring satellites and posted on a public website. They also included data from the U.S., which they had downloaded from American sites before the DOD had classified and removed it. Russia was encouraging the delegates to have their own country's scientists examine it.

Markson saw the charges reported on CNN when he got home from work. Within an hour, he'd accessed the site and downloaded most of the data. Then, after a quick trip to the electronics discount store for another terabyte of storage, he copied the remainder of the data that evening.

He didn't yet accept the new data as reliable. It wasn't beyond any major power to fake information in order to support a propaganda campaign. Markson made a detailed comparison of the part of the Russian data corresponding with unclassified data he'd loaded into his home copy of the LAPI database. In cases where the same quantities had been measured, the different measurements agreed closely, and the small differences were of the kind expected due to differing locations and the characteristics of the instrumentation.

He needed access to the institute's supercomputer in addition to his home database so that he could do more sophisticated calculations in a reasonable time. He accessed the system from home in order to copy the Russian data to the LAPI server. For the next several weeks, he devoted every waking hour at home and more than a few hours in his office to applying the Doppler corrections and Clarke's signal processing algorithms to the optical, X-ray, and gamma ray data which the Russians had provided. If their data was fake, it was a damned good fake, or a cleverly altered copy. He decided that if all of the wavelengths for which he had his own measurements matched the Russian data, then the missing high-energy observations should also be close to what he would have had if he'd downloaded those when they'd been available.

Honest measurements or clever copies, either way, now he could talk about what the extreme gamma ray spectrum showed. And it showed what Huntsman had said it did—the shortest wavelengths were bright. Outrageously bright. *Take that, Jorge Aguillero!*

While eating lunch in his office nearly a month after his censure, Markson got inspired to run TOA trajectory calculations with the Russian data. If they'd faked or copied the data, they may have overlooked this subtle timing issue. Only if the trajectories matched within reasonable margins of error would he accept the data as genuine.

He was engrossed in reading the results when he looked up and was startled to see Katty Clarke standing by his chair. How long had she been there? He hadn't wanted her to be fired from her job since Aguillero had ordered them to stop work on the wake signature. For the last several weeks, he'd gone out of his way to convince her he wasn't working on the event any longer so that she wouldn't be tempted to break the rules, as well. He hoped she hadn't seen what was on his desk.

"Just wondering what you're up to this afternoon. I missed you at lunch."

"I've been looking at old event candidates with weaker signatures that the new signal processing algorithm you developed is picking up. Several of them may be of cosmological or astronomical interest." He took a graph from a pile on the credenza behind him, placed it on top of the printouts on the desk, and pointed at it. "Here, look at this."

She leaned over as if to inspect the graph, but instead grabbed several of the underlying documents and stepped back before he could react.

He stared. "Hey! What do you think you're doing?"

"I'm trying to find out what you're doing. I don't believe for a minute that you've caved in to Aguillero on the warp signature. We used to be partners, Lee. Now, you're shutting me out."

"I'm just following orders so I don't get fired," he argued. "Maybe I can go back to the wake signature when Jorge cools down in a couple of months."

Clarke didn't respond. The papers in her hand had her full attention. Markson stood to retrieve them, but she stepped farther back.

"Sit down, you lying bastard. I've already seen enough to know what these are," she said, waving the papers. Then, she turned her index finger to him. "You want to take all of the credit for yourself? Well, I'm keeping these until I've had time to read them in detail! I can't believe you'd do this to me."

Markson sighed, but then he opened the lower right-hand drawer of his desk as she turned to leave. "Kat, wait. You might also want to look at these." He held up several folders full of observations and analysis.

"Why?" she asked as she reached for them.

"Why am I giving them to you now, or why didn't I tell you about them before?"

"Either. Both."

Markson got up, walked to the door, and closed it so that they could have some privacy.

"What?" she said as he returned and rolled his chair from behind his desk so they could sit together with nothing between them.

When she sat down, he reached over and touched her hand. "Kat, I'm rich. It will hurt me professionally, but I can afford to be fired. You can't. Besides the money, you're in the States on a work visa. You getting fired could even put that at risk. If Jorge finds out either of us is still working on this, that person is toast. I didn't want to put you at risk until the case was so compelling that writing a paper on it would be an asset to your career, not a liability."

Clarke scoffed and folded her arms tightly across her chest.

"I don't know whether you're lying to me or insulting me, but either way, I don't like it."

"Insulting you?" he echoed.

She brought her hands to a prayer position in front of her, adopting a sad face and pathetic tone as she replied, "Poor little girl. Has to be protected from the cruel world by the heroic, self-sacrificing male! Can't be allowed to decide for herself what risks to take. The man knows better."

Markson scowled and raised his voice. "That's bullshit."

She raised her eyebrows, placed her hands on her legs, and leaned back. "Is it? Then, if you are telling me the truth, why didn't you just ask me from the start how I wanted to handle our dear boss's edict?"

Markson sat back in silence, his arms on the arms of his chair as he contemplated her question for half a minute before continuing. "I'm sorry. I wasn't being macho. I was being selfish—"

"Selfish?" she interrupted.

He nodded. "I'm the one who didn't want to take the risk. I didn't want to lose you." He paused, and then asked, "Where do we go from here?"

She looked incredulous. "Lose me? I'm not your possession to lose."

Markson lowered his eyes. "I know, Kat. I know. I'm sorry."

She looked down at the papers in her hand. "Let me read through these and think about it. Then, we'll talk."

∞

The next day, Clarke was back in Markson's office with some additional analysis. She sat down across from him at his desk and handed him several graphs.

"I decided to use the electromagnetic waveforms we already developed and map the Russian data onto them in position and time. Copies wouldn't match because there'd be phase differences in the wavelets making up the EOFs. Fake data wouldn't match unless they had copies of our empirical functions, which they didn't because we didn't include them in the material we put online. Their stuff is real."

Markson didn't look as happy as she'd expected after hearing the news. He tossed the graphs aside, sat with his arms crossed, and glowered at her.

"Lee, you look like you just chugged a glass of pickle juice. Did I say something wrong?"

Markson shook his head. "You lied to me and I fell for it. I even let you get away with calling me a 'lying bastard.' There's no way you could have done those calculations from home in one evening. You've been moonlighting on this just as much as I have! I apologized to you, and rightfully so. I shouldn't have kept you in the dark, but that works both ways. You mean a lot to me, Kat, and it hurts that you deliberately tried to make me look like an ass when you were doing exactly the same thing."

Clarke blinked several times, and then she pushed her chair back. She'd been sincere the day before when she'd expressed her offense at being treated as less than an equal by a male, especially when it came to the male she was sleeping with. Considering his words, she stood up and turned away from him, taking a few steps before turning back to face him again.

She'd gotten used to always seeing such things in a gender context, and her automatic pilot had kicked in. Her subconscious had assumed that Markson's attempt to protect her had just been another put-down of a woman presumed to be incapable of taking care of herself. It hadn't occurred to her that her partner, who happened to be male, was truly concerned about her financial well-being, as a friend, and not behaving that way because she was 'just' a woman.

She hesitated before she returned to her seat, looking down at the table and then looking up at Markson. "I'm sorry, Lee. You're right. I was miffed about being left out, but complaining about it was hypocritical—and the name-calling was totally unwarranted, in any case. We need each other, and I wasn't helping. Can I start making it up to you by taking you to dinner tonight?"

Thinking about how much strain Aguillero had put them under, Markson regretted that they'd both responded poorly. Three big egos don't make a harmonious trio.

He lightened up and nodded. "If you'll let me take you to lunch. That way, we'll be even."

"Deal," she said, giving him a thumbs-up. "By the way, there's more."

"More what?" He looked worried, as though another confession might be forthcoming and ruin the truce they'd just negotiated.

"You asked Jorge whether the committee vote was unanimous. It wasn't."

Markson asked how she knew, and Clarke told him Shanta had been on the committee; the woman had revealed that she and one of the other members had voted to permit a revised version of the paper to be submitted to a journal.

Clarke made her hands in the shape of a "T" and said, "In fact, the vote was technically a tie since one member abstained."

Markson just shook his head.

The two of them decided to keep any further conversation on the subject of the September event out of the office, and in an abundance of caution, they removed all related paperwork, as well. What they were going to do would put their careers in jeopardy, and so there was no margin for error.

They would rewrite the rejected paper on their own time so as not to violate their promises to the dean and Aguillero. They'd include the high-energy gamma ray measurements posted by the Russians along with the new TOA calculations and the EOF analysis as verification of its fidelity, and resubmit the paper to the department—making it clear that the revision hadn't been done on the job. If the department rejected it again, then they would submit it to a journal as unaffiliated individuals. They thought the department couldn't prevent that.

"Aguillero has the persistence of a brick wall, but we have the persistence of a jackhammer," Markson said.

Clarke laughed. "Actually, he has the persistence of a jackass."

"Then, we're going to hammer his ass," Markson replied, smiling and pounding the desk.

Clarke reached over and caught Markson's coffee cup just as it was about to slide off onto the floor. She nodded and winked. "Sounds like a plan!"

CHAPTER FIVE

INTERACTION

"DO WE START FROM SCRATCH or revise the old paper to add the new data?" Clarke asked Markson as she sat across from him at the table in his office. He'd cleared it except for a writing tablet, a red pen, a blue pen, and a black pen which were poised in front of him and ready for service.

"From a labor standpoint, it would be faster and more efficient to rewrite the old piece, but I think we have a better chance of getting it approved if we start over."

"Why?"

"The committee has an emotional investment in their rejection of the other paper," Markson pointed out. "I don't want them to see this one as a simple extension of it. I suggest we take a different approach in organization and language, and maybe they can look at it with fresh eyes."

"How do we do that? The LIGO and Virgo data are what they are, and they've seen it all before. The first time the word 'Alcubierre' appears, Aguillero's blood pressure's going to go up twenty points no matter how the rest of it is worded."

Markson sat thinking while Clarke awaited an answer.

Finally, he said, "Let's start with the title. Suppose we call it something like 'Broadband Electromagnetic Signals Coincident with a Gravitational Wave Signature Event.' That avoids even the mention of our controversial interpretation of the signature. It's standard, bland physics journal-speak."

Clarke chuckled, shook her head, and folded her arms as she leaned back. "I defy you to play that game with the abstract."

Clarke had limited experience as a journal author, but she knew reviewers would require the abstract to summarize all of the significant findings of the paper. She and Markson couldn't expect to keep the 'A' word out of it.

Still, Markson agreed to take up the challenge. "Give me an hour."

She stood up. "Come down when you're ready. I'm going back to get some work done in the meantime."

About forty-five minutes later, Markson strolled into Clarke's office, smiling like a pickpocket who'd just lifted a bigwig's wallet. He tossed a piece of paper onto the desk in front of her without a word, and she grabbed it before it had stopped moving.

It took her less than a minute to read over his work. "Not bad, I have to admit. Wishy-washy, but maybe that's what we need."

The proposed abstract, in its entirety, read:

"Satellite and ground-based observations of a unique, localized emission of electromagnetic radiation from the microwave to the gamma ray portion of the spectrum coincident with a gravitational wave signature, as detected by LIGO and Virgo, are presented in this paper. The onset timing, rate of decay, and calculated trajectory of the source of the EM observations are consistent with the same characteristics of the GW measurements. Calculated EM and GW wakes produced by an object moving faster than light, using an Alcubierre metric, are shown to be consistent with all of the data."

Even if drafting an abstract had taken only forty-five minutes, just roughing out the first draft of the full manuscript took over 45 days. That wasn't unusual. The importance of formal publication in the professional literature and the rigor of the peer review process made it worthwhile to be thorough.

They put the electromagnetic data first. The LAPI reviewers probably wouldn't be biased against it; it was traditional physics based on traditional sources and would start them off on a positive note. The LIGO and Virgo data came in next, as though they were confirming the EM data rather than the converse.

As they sat in Markson's office working on the manuscript one day, he quipped, "A lot of the EM data comes from NASA. Maybe some of the good will toward the space program will rub off on us."

Clarke looked over at her colleague. "Maybe this is going to work after all. With what we've done so far, the reviewers ought to be convinced that all of the data are valid and mutually consistent, and their sensitivities won't have been jarred by any heretical interpretation of what the source of these signals was."

Markson nodded. "Agreed. I think we can minimize the shock by presenting the Alcubierre interpretation as one possible hypothesis without asserting that it's actually true."

Clarke wasn't buying that part of the plan. She got up from the table where they'd been working and walked over toward Markson's whiteboard as though she was about to write something on it, but then turned back to face the table where Markson remained seated. "Lee, do you believe that what we've seen is a warpship wake?"

"Of course."

"Of course? *Of course!* If that's your answer, then why be such a"—she hesitated, circling her hands in front of her as she searched for exactly the right word—"...then, why be such a wimp? You're saying it's one possible hypothesis? Is there any other plausible hypothesis?"

"No, but I've been through this before. I don't want to have to build a damned starship in order to have our work accepted by the community. I don't want to rub it in their faces."

"Well, I do!" Clarke countered. "They may be dicks, but they're scientists, not bureaucrats. The data speaks for itself. Why not let it sing for them?"

They argued at length. Then, tired and frustrated, they settled on a compromise that neither liked, but both could accept. They would present their conclusion as the only known process consistent with the data, while expressly leaving the question of currently unknown processes open.

By the time they had finished writing, revising, and editing the paper, it had taken them three months of intense effort, but the manuscript they submitted for faculty review showed it. It was powerful, polished, and, they hoped, persuasive.

When he received the new manuscript, Aguillero was frustrated and angry that the matter hadn't been put to rest. That his employees continued to work on their crackpot idea on their own time seemed to be a sign of fanaticism rather than professionally acceptable persistence. Nonetheless, the academic custom was to treat such submissions by faculty members no differently than if they'd been written in their official capacity.

Once again, he called a departmental review committee meeting in his office. It was a replay of the earlier meeting, except that Aguillero now included the Russian claim of an exploding U.S. space weapon as another alternative. Jelani remarked that such a satellite wouldn't have had enough mass to generate detectable gravitational waves. Her rebuttal was accepted by everyone except Aguillero and, again, the committee could not agree on whether to approve submission of the revised manuscript. The members voted or abstained exactly as they had during the first go-round and, once again, Aguillero announced that the majority's failure to agree to approve submitting the paper constituted disapproval—and he would act accordingly. He did not expect what came next.

"That's not right."

Aguillero turned toward the speaker. "Is that the Math Department's position, Professor Jelani?"

"No, Professor Aguillero, it's my position, and just like the last time we went through this charade, I am a member of *this* department and a voting member of this committee."

"And I am the chairman of this department. I get to break ties in my committees."

Jelani took a copy of the 220-page Faculty Handbook from her well-worn leather briefcase and opened it to a page she had bookmarked. "Actually, Jorge, you don't. That would be the equivalent of you voting twice. The Faculty Handbook gives each member of a committee exactly one vote, and there is no provision for *anyone* to be a tiebreaker." She handed the highlighted page to Aguillero, not requiring any additional gestures to make her point.

Aguillero threw his arms up in the air and then let them drop. He put his elbows on the table and rested his face in his hands for a moment. Then he looked up, straightened his suit, and demanded, "What would you have me do? I know you want to give them the benefit of the doubt, but even you must admit that what they are proposing is not accepted science. We have to make a decision, and I'm not going to let them embarrass this department or me by submitting *this* paper to a journal with our attribution."

Zhao Ming, who supported approving the submission, turned to Lambert and Haley; Lambert opposed submission, and Haley had consistently refused to take a position. "Look, guys, I understand why you don't agree with the paper. I don't understand why you object to Markson and Clarke merely submitting it to a journal. If it is as bad as you say, it will be rejected, and no harm will be done. If a respectable journal accepts it, perhaps it's not as bad as you've been led to think. Especially you, Loren. If you aren't convinced enough by Jorge's argument to vote no, then you owe it to your fellow faculty members to give them a chance to have outside reviewers look at it."

Lambert sat back and waved his hand. "This isn't a physics paper, Zhao. It's about as scientific as creationism or flat-Earth fantasies. At a minimum, the editor of a scientific journal and at least two referees will be telling their colleagues about the piece of trash submitted by two faculty members in our department, and that it came with our approval. No way."

Ming looked back at Loren Haley.

"Hey, don't look at me. I'm giving them the benefit of the doubt by not voting no," the man protested. "I still think they're wrong, but because I don't understand the quantum mechanical stuff and you so strongly support them, Dr. Ming, I've been willing to withhold my no vote. That's as good as it's going to get."

To break the deadlock, Aguillero suggested asking for review of the paper by the School of Engineering, with special consideration of the objections relating to energy, radiation hazards and control of such a vehicle. The committee agreed, but the Dean of Engineering reminded Aguillero that LAPI's experts in most of those areas were in Aguillero's own department. He recommended using outside reviewers if Aguillero's people couldn't handle it.

The Dean of Engineering and Aguillero negotiated with the Rhode Island State University for a team of two relativistic physicists and a space vehicle engineer who would prepare an evaluation report. The report was submitted sixty days later with three sections: Theoretical Analysis, Engineering Aspects, and Cosmological Alternatives.

The theoretical analysis found no errors in the paper's physics and mathematics, but noted that the Alcubierre metric was still controversial. They suggested that, rather than seeking publication in a top-tier journal, the authors should submit their manuscript to a lesser-ranked journal that would be more appropriate for somewhat speculative work.

The engineering section focused on Aguillero's three issues and came to the same conclusions that he had. They saw no value in submitting the paper for publication.

The section that examined cosmological alternatives to the Markson-Clarke hypothesis recommended that the paper be submitted after a few revisions. It found no natural phenomena that were consistent with the observations and noted the theoretical analysis section's inability to find any physical or mathematical flaw in the manuscript's reasoning. Although the report's authors wouldn't say that the Alcubierre interpretation of the data was correct, they observed that the interpretation would stimulate productive discussions that by themselves would warrant the paper's publication if it survived the peer-review process.

The report could have been interpreted several different ways, but Aguillero saw it as strongly negative since it did not conclude that any of his objections were frivolous. He disapproved publication, citing the RISU report, and notified the dean and the department's review committee members.

Aguillero called Markson and Clarke to his office to remind them that although their new manuscript may have been written at home, it had incorporated observations from LAPI databases and some of the work had been performed on LAPI information processing systems. Unless they deleted those parts of the paper which had been based on the LAPI-derived data and analyses, they could not simply publish it as individuals. The only LAPI-based material they could use without permission was that which was available to the general public—and much of the paper depended on information that hadn't yet been released.

He also issued a formal written directive ordering them to terminate use of institute assets for any further work relating to the faster-than-light hypothesis.

∞

Soon after he got the latest word from Aguillero, Markson sat slumped behind his desk.

"Back to routine astrophysics, I guess," he said to Clarke, who'd joined him after she'd received the instructions from Aguillero.

"I'm not going to just give up. Are you?" she asked.

Markson blew out a long breath. "No. I guess we'll just have to do it on our own. How 'bout coming over for dinner? I have a couple of steaks I need to get rid of."

Clarke grinned as she stood up. "That's the spirit! See you about six?"

"Done."

As soon as she left his office, Markson put his notes on the now-forbidden work in his briefcase and headed home.

When Markson had joined the faculty at LAPI, he'd had a quality home built in an upscale development with shopping and other amenities. Unlike in his student days at LSU, he didn't need to be within walking distance from the campus; he had a comfortable car and didn't mind a short commute every day.

He'd selected one of the one-story models with an attached two-car garage in a community in the Highland Park area, about 10 miles southeast of his office. The house had just over 2,700 square feet under air, and while the modifications he'd ordered hadn't affected the floor plan, they'd improved his access to power and communications. In every room, there were extra outlets, a cable TV connection, and an ethernet connection. The ethernet was fed by a separate router from a different internet service provider than the one that provided his Wi-Fi, and he had enough solar panels installed on the roof to power the entire house if the electric service failed. He could afford the reliability and security that redundancy provided.

Markson was on the terrace cooking the steaks on a gas grill when he heard the front door open and close. "That you, Kat?" he called.

"You expecting someone else?" She put a bottle of Merlot on the kitchen table and crossed through the family room to the terrace. She pointed to the grill. "Are you planning to eat out here or are we going to bring those inside?"

Markson leaned over and kissed her. "Whatever you'd like, my love."

She laughed.

He was bewildered. "Did I say something funny?"

She kissed him back. "Not at all. It's just that I don't often see you in jeans and a T-shirt, and especially one that says, 'Why yes, I am a rocket scientist.'"

Markson bowed toward her.

"It's getting dark soon," she said. "The light will be better inside. I'll go rustle up a couple of ears of corn and some chips. We can eat in the breakfast nook," she said, pointing and still smiling.

The breakfast nook adjoined the terrace at the back of the house and the kitchen, which stood between the nook and the dining room at the front. It was comfortable and informal, and easy to clean.

Two steaks, four ears of corn, a pile of French fries, and a bottle of wine later, they'd solved world hunger and established Jorge Aguillero's simian ancestry, but failed to determine what they could do to make their paper acceptable to the LAPI faculty.

Markson thought it best to set that problem aside and eat dessert. He never passed up an excuse for ice cream, and he had a new flavor he wanted to try out with Kat.

"Cinnamon oatmeal cookie?" she asked. "What prompted that? You usually favor something with at least a few chocolate chips! You have fifty different flavors in that freezer. Why cinnamon oatmeal cookie?"

"You're always giving me a hard time because I don't eat enough healthy food. You said yourself that both oatmeal and cinnamon are healthy. Enjoy!"

Clarke laughed, took a bite, and then admitted that it tasted better than she'd expected.

"Actually, it needs some chocolate," he said.

When their dishes were empty, Clarke began to place the soiled china in the dishwasher piece by piece.

Markson tapped her on the shoulder. "For now, just pile it all in the sink. I'd like to get some feedback from other experts in the field who don't have their egos wrapped up in the discussion. Let's do that first while I'm still awake."

That evening, after planning the effort carefully, they posted their paper online. There would be no repetition of the release of their work by sensationalist fringe websites. To avoid recurrence of their online posting becoming public, they used an access-limited email reflector for gravitational wave physicists. It required an account with a password. Only recognized professionals from established institutions had accounts.

They attached the paper to a post that said:

"We have submitted the attached draft manuscript for faculty review. Although several members of the review committee recommended publication, others recommended against it. The department chairman decided that it was not ready for publication. We would appreciate comments directed at identifying errors and opportunities for improvement. We would also appreciate identification of additional data or analysis to reinforce or refute our interpretation of the data. Please treat this as restricted and not to be copied, forwarded, or otherwise divulged to anyone not on this reflector."

Then, Markson turned Clarke loose to load the dishwasher in her meticulous fashion, after which they went to bed— hoping that the morning would bring some useful comments.

∞

While they slept, responses trickled in. By the time they began reading them over breakfast in the morning, the trickle had become a torrent that they had trouble following.

Some were short, simple, and binary: "Great job!" or "Total nonsense!" Others were complex, nuanced critiques worth more time than they were able to give to preparing replies at the moment. Long or short, simple or complex, binary or nuanced, by the end of the day, the now all-too-familiar pattern emerged— there were two camps of responses: Nobel Prize and junk science.

Clarke clapped her hands. "I think we're gaining ground."

Markson scoffed. "How's that? Thirty percent of our colleagues seem to be suggesting our PhDs should be rescinded."

"Killjoy. That used to be sixty percent."

Later in the week, Markson was happier and Clarke was ecstatic. Several influential elders of the "physics establishment" had opined that the paper should have been approved for publication so that the community could formally consider its merits and weaknesses. Responses to those opinions had been largely favorable. Even a few of the "junk science" contingent had expressed disappointment that they'd not had the opportunity to confront the Markson-Clarke hypothesis in peer-reviewed literature.

Clarke pointed in the direction of the administrative offices. "Let's take this to the dean. She can overrule Aguillero."

"Before we do that, I'd like to give Jorge the courtesy of running these comments by him. I don't want to go behind his back or back him into a corner unless we have to," Markson said. "I'll send him links to some of the comments that focus on the desirability of publication rather than on the merits of our work."

Aguillero didn't respond immediately. It was Monday of the following week when Markson and Clarke were summoned to Aguillero's office by his secretary. When they stepped into Aguillero's outer office, the secretary warned them the department chairman was furious, although she didn't know why.

"What now?" Clarke asked as they sat waiting on the small sofa by the door to the inner office.

After a few minutes, Aguillero buzzed the secretary on the intercom, and she gestured for them to go on in—softly wishing them good luck.

"You almost had me," Aguillero said as soon as Markson passed through the door. He was sitting behind his desk, in front of which two chairs had been positioned. He didn't even wait until Clarke made it into the room to say, "Sit down, both of you."

The two looked at each other, but did as they'd been told without comment. Aguillero's face was flushed. The secretary hadn't exaggerated.

Aguillero bit off every word as he spoke. "Based on the links you provided and my own research, I thought you were playing by the rules. I was seriously reconsidering whether to let you submit your paper to a journal. Then, I got *this*," he said as he held up a scan of the front page of the latest edition of *Inside Enlightenment*, a Baltimore supermarket tabloid. A banner headline read: *"Louisiana Physicists Detect Alien Spacecraft."*

Markson grabbed it out of Aguillero's hand and read it. The article was a hyped exaggeration of their proposed article, along with an accusation that LAPI was suppressing their work as part of some unspecified conspiracy undertaken by industry or the government. He stiffened and threw the page to Clarke. There was enough force behind the throw that it fluttered and she had to lunge for it.

"Where the fuck did *that* come from, Jorge?" he demanded.

"I see that Dr. Clarke's foul mouth is beginning to rub off on you."

Clarke started to speak, but the chairman cut her off with an intensity that Markson had never seen in him. Markson began to apologize but was also cut off.

"Be quiet, both of you! A colleague from the University of Maryland emailed it to me an hour ago. I can't believe your utter lack of integrity!"

"Jorge, it's obvious! Someone got access to the reflector," Markson said. "Look—the only quotations in the story are word-for-word from comments posted there."

"I know that reflector, and it's secure. The press doesn't have access to it. You or one of your stooges had to have given it to them."

"If I had given it to them, they wouldn't have botched it up so badly," Markson insisted.

"*Inside Enlightenment* botches up everything it touches that's related to science. Everyone who works there must be a creationist or climate change denier, but I suppose you knew that when you had someone send them the link."

Clarke opened her mouth, but Markson took her arm before she got a word out. "That's beneath you, Jorge. We're going to ask Dean Simpson for permission to publish. Feel free to take your best shot," he said.

By the time they met with the dean after spring break, both the physics community and the public had been battering LAPI for weeks.

CHAPTER SIX

NUCLEAR REACTION

LAPI'S PUBLIC RELATIONS OFFICE received thousands of inquiries about the Markson-Clarke paper from news media and other organizations worldwide. Their limit on incoming email message storage was briefly exceeded, and envelopes piled up in the secretary's postal inbox. They had to request permission to hire temporary staff. Suddenly, money was involved, and that caught the attention of LAPI's top management.

Institute President Warren Burke asked the Dean of Engineering to re-evaluate the report from Rhode Island State University in order to assist the Department of Physics and

Astronomy in reconsidering their refusal to approve submission of the paper to a journal. The dean noted that two of the three authors of the RISU report had recommended publication of the paper even though they'd disagreed with its faster-than-light (FTL) hypothesis, and concluded that Aguillero had misinterpreted the report. With the weight of the institute's administration favoring publication, the scales tipped.

At the request of Dean Simpson, Aguillero convened an all-hands meeting of his faculty to reconsider the department's position on submitting the controversial paper to a journal. The authors recused themselves from the discussion, but called it to the attention of Professor Jelani—whom the department chairman had neglected to invite.

When Aguillero noticed Jelani's presence, he thought it best to act as though her attendance had been expected. He opened the meeting by referring to the media commotion as an "ill-informed public fascination with baseless speculation" and then presented his case against the paper, including his interpretation of the RISU report.

When he asked if anyone had anything to say in defense of the paper, Jelani and Ming each presented their now-familiar rationales for encouraging submission of the paper: *Professors Markson and Clarke have presented a coherent but controversial interpretation of the event, and it should be discussed in the peer-reviewed literature rather than just on the internet.*

Several faculty members who'd previously played no role in the conflict over the paper asked Aguillero what harm would be done if the department approved its submission to a journal. If the paper was as worthless as he insisted, then it would be rejected, and no harm done.

Aguillero responded by suggesting that its publication could hurt the department's reputation with funding agencies and impair their ability to compete for grant money. He said this could especially impact the careers of junior faculty for whom promotion was dependent on externally funded research.

"Are you threatening our faculty members with reprisals if they vote against you, Jorge?" Jelani demanded.

Aguillero looked astonished. "No! Of course not! I just wanted to make them aware of the possible collateral consequences that are outside of our control."

When the vote was taken, the members of the Physics and Astronomy Department almost unanimously recommended publication.

Aguillero appeared to have no choice but to accept his department's vote to permit submission of the paper for publication, but thought perhaps he could still put a stop to it. He went back to his office, turned on his laptop, and sat staring in disgust at a British reality show available on the internet through a link which he'd received early that morning in a message from an alumnus.

The message, which also had a video file attached, said only, *I don't think this is what President Burke meant a few weeks ago when he said, "Our faculty should try to get more public exposure."*

Aguillero had clicked on the link when he'd first read the message, but turned off the show as soon as he'd discovered its content. But the circumstances had changed. *I can't fight the administration and my own faculty, but if I don't do something drastic, the institute and the department and I will end up with reputations as havens for crackpots.*

He remembered how his own reputation had been tainted just for being Markson's "time-travel" thesis advisor. He remained sure that that was why he hadn't been promoted to Dean of Sciences at LSU. He had even heard that much of the skepticism about his paper on gravitational waves from hypernovas had resulted from the perception that he'd condoned pseudoscience. Now, it seemed that Markson and Clarke were conspiring to keep him from vindicating his work.

I have to do something.

The program he had downloaded to his laptop had appeared on UK Channel 4. It was called *How to Look Good Naked*. Nearly every episode going back to the beginning of the series was available online. This particular episode featured an undergraduate physics major named Katty Clarke. By the time it ended, it had been true to its title.

He shook his head sadly and sat back with a sick feeling. *If this was broadcast to the general public on regular television, I can't imagine what's in the attached video file.* But he needed to find out, and then decide how it could be used to get rid of Clarke—and Markson, as well.

He saved the attachment from the email to his computer,

and then he ran it. The five-minute video began with a brief title screen that faded into an image of a theater stage on which a man in a colorful suit stood holding a microphone.

The image came to life as the man with the microphone announced, "And now, a special treat! The cutest cosmologist in all of the UK. A super-smart scientist by day, and a super-sexy entertainer by night! Please welcome our neighbor returned from across the Atlantic, Cheshire Kat!"

As Katty Clarke stepped into view from stage right, she wore a one-piece bathing suit with a three-foot tail attached to its rear, a scarf that was attached to long sleeves, and thigh-high boots, all made of shiny black vinyl. Stage lights reflected from every piece of her costume except the small pair of fuzzy black ears on her head.

She struck a seductive pose. "Meow," she purred in a slow, sultry voice.

A second later, the theater erupted with the pulsating rhythm of Motley Crue's "Girls, Girls, Girls." Clarke stepped smartly across to downstage left, where she turned her back to a full house and wagged her tail in synchronization with the song's beat.

Watching, Aguillero was breathing heavily—from anger, not arousal. *This is what I've been fighting for decades. It's evil. I will not tolerate it from one of my faculty members*, he thought as she began removing her costume slowly, piece by piece.

Three minutes into the show, she had taken off her boots, scarf and gloves, and had just discarded her one-piece to reveal the black lace bra and black lace panties she'd been wearing underneath.

Aguillero clicked "pause." He was ashamed of her and ashamed of himself for watching her. He was also furious with Markson for bringing her into his department and into his life. The fury outweighed the shame. He clicked "play."

I have to know everything that's in this file so I know what I have to work with.

In the last two minutes, Cheshire Kat gyrated in synch with the music as she removed her bra, tossed it behind her, and danced her way out of her panties until all she wore was a tiny black thong held up with a bow. Then, she pranced back to the end of the curtain stage left where she untied the bow and swung the thong around her head before throwing it at her feet. She turned, placing a hand on the curtain as she looked over her shoulder at the crowd and said a sultry "meow" while the lights faded to black.

"A whore and her pimp. That's who I have working for me—a whore and her pimp!" he shouted to the walls of his office.

The material from the message would give him some leverage, he was sure, but how to use it? He took out a pad and began a list of options. He wrote the number 1, then sat back and folded his arms while he evaluated his options.

If I take this to the dean, she'll fire her in order to keep the politicians off her back, but then the whole thing will end up in court. The court will probably let them submit the paper while the suit takes forever to go through the system, and in the meantime, the two of them will get a sympathetic following on social media—and, of course, I'll be the bad guy.

He pushed the pad aside, got up, and walked to the window. "I need something more subtle," he whispered to himself. He stood there, arms folded, staring at the quadrangle below for twenty seconds or so until an idea clicked.

She's the weak link and Markson's Achilles heel. If this gets out, her reputation as a serious scientist is ruined. She won't be able to find work when they fire her, so she'll lose her green card. Markson will lose his lover, and he won't let that happen. They're going to realize the flaws in their hypothesis and remove the Alcubierre nonsense from the paper or withdraw it entirely.

He summoned Markson to his office. There was no coffee, as he planned to get right to the point. After all, that was the preferred style in this God-forsaken country, even if something inside him still rebelled and he skated around it.

"Against my recommendation," Aguillero began, "the department voted to allow you to submit your paper to a journal. So be it. I just hope your submission of it doesn't damage our reputation any more than you already have."

Markson spread his arms, hands facing upward. "No, Jorge, it's going to build our reputation! The work is sound and groundbreaking! Don't you realize how important it is? It will put LAPI at the forefront of research into a brand new field—the practical application of general relativity to not just measure, but manipulate the geometry of spacetime!"

"It won't do any such thing. I highly doubt any reputable journal will accept it."

"I guess we'll just have to wait and see."

The old Argentinian sat back in his chair, arms folded and head down, and sighed. "I'm afraid not, Lee. You're going to take the Alcubierre fantasy out of the paper or withdraw it entirely."

Markson startled. Wide-eyed, with his eyebrows raised, he demanded, "And why would I want to do that?"

"I'll show you."

Aguillero leaned back in his chair, and his demeanor changed—as though someone had thrown a switch. He looked more relaxed; the anger in him seemed to have dissipated.

That's odd, Markson thought. But it was what the old professor said next that threw Markson for a loop.

"When you recommended that I hire her, were you aware that Dr. Clarke had appeared nude on British television?"

Markson didn't know quite what to say, but he finally asked, "Are you talking about that British reality show she was on as an undergraduate? What's that got to do with publishing our paper?"

Aguillero opened a browser and clicked on the link he had saved, but paused it immediately. He turned the laptop around so that Markson could see it. "UK Channel 4. *How to Look Good Naked*. I'll step out while you run it. You may recognize the young woman. I was going to say 'young lady,' but as you will see for yourself, there is nothing lady-like about her."

Markson took a deep breath and focused back on his boss. "I know all about this, Jorge. I've seen it. She showed it to me, but that was a long time ago. I repeat—she was just an undergraduate when she was on the show. What has this got to do with our paper?"

"And you didn't think that might have been worth mentioning when you recommended that we hire her?"

"No, sir, I didn't. It wasn't pornographic or anything. It was a reality show about building one's self-image, and all perfectly legal and aboveboard."

"Well, that's an image of one of our professors, thanks to you, and legal or not, it is a poor reflection on our faculty."

Markson stood up again and raised his voice. "That happened in another country at another time. I'll ask you for the third time: What's this about?"

"Sit down. It's about respect, Dr. Markson. She has no self-respect, and neither of you seem to have any respect for authority in general or me in particular. I'm tired of being sassed by a two-bit stripper and a spoiled, rich-kid publicity hound masquerading as physicists in my department."

Markson placed his hands far enough apart on the front of Aguillero's big oak desk to lean over into the chairman's face.

"Well, Jorge, if we're going to let it all hang out, Katty and I are both tired of your arrogant and ignorant disregard for the evidence, as well as your disrespect for us. You can't refute our science, so you order us to drop the investigation! We're not soldiers, and you're no commander. All three of us are faculty members of this institute—something which you seem to forget. And if you impugn Katty's character again, I'll tell her exactly what you said and testify on her behalf in her slander suit against you."

To Markson's renewed surprise, Aguillero smiled. "Do you know she's still doing it?" he asked.

"Doing what?" Markson asked, his hands on his hips.

"I'm glad you asked. The alumnus who sent me the link I just mentioned also sent me a video. He thought I might benefit from a different perspective on one of his former research professors. You should have a look."

Aguillero did not turn the laptop so that Markson could see it. Instead, he switched on the sixty-inch, high-definition television on the wall to the right of the whiteboard, and clicked an icon, again pausing the video immediately.

He directed Markson's attention to the screen. "Cheshire Kat, she calls herself. At least, she could have called herself Schrödinger's Kat, don't you think? A quantum superposition of a respectable physics professor and a cheap, shameless, no-account stripper? Decide for yourself. I'll be in the outer office. Let me know when you're done watching. Then we can talk." He turned the laptop around for Markson to use and left the room.

As the door closed, Markson was reluctant to play whatever game Aguillero was up to, but he was curious about what had gotten his boss into such an uproar. He started the video. It didn't take more than a minute and a half to get the picture. He turned it off and called Aguillero back in.

"You get your rocks off by watching one of your employees undress, Jorge? I don't need to see any more of this! Go wherever you're going with it."

"You still haven't figured it out? There's more to the show. Perhaps that will arouse your intellect. Watch the rest. If you still don't get it, I'll lay it out for you."

"You have no right..." His voice was shaking and his face was red. He felt flushed and was breathing fast.

"So, it upset you, I see."

"It isn't her act that upsets me, Jorge—it's you!" Markson snarled as he stood and got in his boss's face. "You take a beautiful, sensual performance and try to turn it into something tawdry. She told me about that club! It's in France and is one of the most respectable places in Europe. Government officials and VIPs from all over the world go there. It was an honor for her to be asked to perform."

There was silence for a moment as Aguillero let Markson simmer down. "She didn't show you the video, did she?" Aguillero asked finally.

"Actually, Jorge, I think she'd like to have a copy of it. She told me they didn't record regular performances. Again, though, that's ancient history. She did that while she was a postdoc, and it was her final performance."

Aguillero sniffed. "I think your GPS is broken and you've gone deaf."

Markson raised his eyebrows. "Excuse me?"

"Neither the location nor the timing is what you think.

This wasn't filmed in France, and she wasn't a postdoc. While you were doubling down on your disrespectful attitude at my house in December, your colleague was taking her clothes off for a roomful of lecherous gawkers in England. If you'd listened carefully, you'd have heard the announcer say so. Since you haven't seen the whole thing, you might want to continue—if only so you'll know what you're talking about if the subject comes up later?"

Markson sat in silence with his mouth open for a full fifteen seconds before trying to speak.

"You... you bastard!"

Aguillero nodded. "Know thine enemy—that's the saying, right? Well, you've decided to make me your enemy. I'd think a smart boy like you would at least want to know what I have. Call me back in when you're done."

Again, he left the room, closing the door behind him.

Markson scowled in the direction of the laptop. He hated to admit that there was even one thing Aguillero had gotten right, but it would be foolish not to know what was on the rest of the video. He clicked "play."

Aguillero waited patiently until Markson ripped open the door and ordered the department chairman back into his own office.

"OK, you son of a bitch, you've shown me what you've got. Now, how will that make us disembowel the paper?"

"You're not stupid, Lee. Hardheaded, arrogant, and disrespectful, yes, but not stupid. What do you expect would happen if I were to tell Dean Simpson that we have a public relations problem which needs to be addressed, and send her the link and the video? Suppose I tell her how disappointed I am that you didn't mention those disreputable things you knew about Clarke's character when you presented your glowing hiring recommendation?"

Markson held his tongue, afraid his emotions would react before his reason could get a grip on the full import of their boss's threat.

Again, Aguillero waited in calm silence while Markson imagined the subsequent conversations he and Katty would have with Dean Simpson and then the provost, and then the Human Resources Department. There was no upside to this.

Finally, Markson spoke up to ask, "Why the blackmail? Why not just take it to the administration right now?"

"Although it doesn't seem like it at the moment, Lee, I still see you as an asset to the department and the institute. I am even willing to tolerate Dr. Clarke if you keep her out of my way. What I am *not* willing to tolerate is that paper of yours. Your fanatic devotion to that Mexican misfit's delusions has cost us a friendship that was precious to us both, cost me my promotion to dean at LSU, and now it will take both you and Clarke down if you don't get your priorities right and put it aside. Either it goes, or you both go."

Shit, Markson thought.

Everything had just turned to shit.

Aguillero let him stew.

After a few awkward, silent minutes, Markson stood up. "I need to talk to Kat."

"Please do. For both of your sakes, I hope you can convince her to accept the situation."

Markson looked down, but he gave a slight nod as he walked out of Aguillero's inner office.

∞

As soon as Markson stepped into her office, Clarke stood up. "Lee, what's wrong? You're almost ashen. Are you OK?"

"No, damn it, I'm not OK. Right now, I'm pissed at everybody, including you. We need to talk. Right now."

She lifted her hands as if in surrender. "Speak to me. What did I do?"

"You did a full-frontal nudity strip show in front of a crowd during Christmas break, and didn't think to tell me about it?"

Her jaw dropped. "How did you find out about that?"

"Jorge has a fucking cell phone video of it in full color and sound! Kat, what were you thinking?"

She took a deep breath. "It was a charity show. I didn't think anyone in the States would ever hear about it. It wasn't supposed to be recorded."

"If it was a charity show, why were you so ashamed of it that you didn't tell me about it when we were chatting about how our vacations went?"

"I wasn't, and am not, *ashamed* of it. I was afraid you

wouldn't approve, and I didn't want to get into a big discussion about it."

Markson shook his head from side to side and blew a heavy breath out of his mouth. "Well, we're going to have that discussion right now."

"Why? What's this got to do with Jorge? What did he say to you?"

Markson explained that they were both over a barrel. Aguillero could take what he had to the administration right away. LAPI was a state school, and Louisiana was a politically conservative state. Clarke would be fired for her history of public nudity, and he'd be fired for not disclosing her past activity in his hiring recommendation. The publicity surrounding the warpship controversy would be thrown in as an aggravating factor. Yes, they could challenge it in court. They might even win, three to five years down the road. In the meantime, there was a risk that they might not be able to submit the paper because the institute would withdraw its permission. That could deprive them of the use of the data and analysis developed using LAPI resources, and those were essential content for the paper. Even if it got published, their reputations would be ruined, and their work discredited.

"Are you done?" she asked when he stopped speaking for a few seconds. She stood with her fists jammed against her waist and came around her desk until her angry red face was less than a foot from Markson's.

He stepped back. "Almost. I need you to work with me on

this, Kat. We can withdraw the request to submit the paper, indicating we need to make some refinements while we think through how to deal with it. We'll find a way. It's worth the wait. Maybe we can short-circuit the process—get Jorge charged with blackmail or something."

"No. We're going to submit it. I've had enough of this. Tell the son of a bitch that that show was a fundraiser for the benefit of needy children at Christmastime."

"Was it?"

Her face reddened, and she balled up her hands into fists as she leaned forward. "God damn you! Do you think I'm a liar and a slut?"

"No, Kat! God, no."

He reached out to her, but she smacked his hand away and turned aside.

He dropped his arms and took a less sympathetic tone as he continued, "Hey, look. I stood up for you in there. Your adult entertainment background isn't a problem for me, but your lack of concern for the impression it might make with the LAPI Board of Directors is. You are a beautiful performance artist, and they may be a bunch of self-righteous old farts, but they pay our salaries! At least if I'd known about it beforehand, I wouldn't have been so blindsided. I could have brought up it being a fundraiser as a defense, but now Jorge's probably not going to accept it as anything other than an excuse we made up together after he revealed the video."

Clarke started to head for Aguillero's office, but Markson

quickly put his hand on her arm. "Kat, do you think the paper's good?"

She turned and stood nose to nose with him again. "Damned good!"

"Do you think it will be accepted?"

She stepped back enough to gesture without hitting Markson. "If I didn't think it was good enough to be accepted, my name wouldn't be on it."

"If the paper's accepted, then Jorge's little game doesn't really matter, does it?"

"It matters to me! But... I get your point." She paused to take a breath. "Both of them, actually. I should have told you."

Markson stepped forward to embrace her, but she stepped back.

"I'm not in the mood for a hug. I want to hit somebody," she said, waving a fist at him.

"Maybe later. Before we make any knee-jerk decisions, let's see if we can talk him out of stooping to blackmail."

When Markson and Clarke showed up together, Aguillero admitted them immediately. He even offered coffee and tea, but they both declined. This wasn't going to be a friendly meeting.

Aguillero said, "Suit yourselves. Have you decided to make some modifications to that paper of yours?"

Markson looked at Clarke. She nodded to him to proceed.

"Not yet, Jorge. You don't have all of the facts, and we're hoping you might reconsider your strategy when you have the whole picture."

Aguillero laughed. "I've seen all the pictures I need to see! The only question is whether or not Dean Simpson gets them."

"Jorge, before we do something we can't recover from later, you need to know that Professor Clarke's performance in England was at a fundraiser for a children's Christmas charity. Please let her explain."

Aguillero put his hands over his face and then looked up. "This, I've got to hear."

Clarke put on her most respectful, professional demeanor and explained, "When I got back home to see my parents, I visited some of my old friends from the neighborhood. They have an annual fundraiser at Christmas to raise money to buy presents and clothing for needy children. It's sponsored by the burlesque theater associated with the town pub. I used to perform in the annual show before I left England, and they were aware of my final show as Cheshire Kat in France before I came to the States. They asked if I would be willing to do that show for the locals while I was there. It was for a good cause, and I agreed."

Aguillero shrugged. "Even if that's true, if that's supposed to excuse your participation in a pornographic performance as a member of our faculty, it doesn't. You can revise or withdraw the paper, or explain those 'special circumstances' to the dean after she's seen the video. She can make up her own mind."

Clarke glared at her boss. "This is demeaning and absurd."

Markson thought that everything was coming unraveled. Getting the paper published mattered more to him than his pride or Kat's. Aguillero was a prideful man. Maybe they could play into that.

"You opened our earlier conversation by telling me that no reputable journal would accept the paper," Markson cut in. "How about *Physical Review D*?"

Aguillero snorted. "Not a chance in the world."

"And if the paper is rejected, then no real harm is done?"

"We'll still be known as the institute that generated the rejected paper."

"But that will be on Katty and me, not on you."

"That's a risk I am not willing to take."

Markson looked toward Clarke and then back at Aguillero. "Even to avoid the risk of being charged with blackmail?"

"Blackmail?"

"Blackmail, extortion, whatever you want to call it. It's threatening to expose a secret or a disgrace in order to receive something in return. And it's a felony in Louisiana."

Aguillero took a deep breath. The thought of that hadn't occurred to him. He said, "I will not allow that paper to see the light of day with this institute's affiliation." But his voice wasn't as confident as it had been.

Markson picked up on that and used it. "So, you're not really sure they won't accept it. You were just blustering."

That pushed the button Markson had been hoping for.

"I don't bluster! That manuscript will never be accepted by *D-1* or any journal in its class!"

Markson turned back to Clarke and smiled before returning his attention to Aguillero. "Then, why not put your pictures aside and let the journal handle the problem? No blackmail, and no charges of blackmail."

Aguillero looked stunned, but recovered fast. "And how sure are you and your girlfriend here that the journal will accept it?"

Clarke stepped forward. "It seems disrespect runs both ways here, Professor Aguillero. My *colleague* and I are damned sure it will be accepted."

Markson nodded his agreement and then said to Aguillero, "I think I have a way to resolve this based on our conflicting perspectives, but I need a minute to discuss my proposal with Dr. Clarke. May we step outside?"

"Be my guest," Aguillero said as he swept his arm in the direction of the door.

When the pair returned, Markson began, "Jorge, I have tried my best to make amends for my disrespect at LSU, but I've clearly failed, and it's been unpleasant for us both. I am so confident that our paper will be accepted by a leading journal, that I will sign a binding agreement to resign from this faculty if it isn't. If you really believe what you've insisted about its rejection, you should jump at that. The paper gets rejected, you get rid of me, and you don't need to put yourself on the wrong side of the law."

Aguillero stared silently at Markson for fifteen seconds before he looked toward Clarke. "Only if she goes, too."

Markson started to speak, but Clarke interrupted him. "Without him, this place won't be worth staying at anyway. I'm in."

"One shot," Aguillero said.

"What do you mean?" Markson asked.

"You pick a major journal and submit your paper. If it's rejected, you resign. No second chances."

Markson shook his head and looked at Clarke.

"This is all bullshit," she said. "Do whatever you want."

Markson looked Aguillero in the eye. "If the paper is accepted, this ends, and you turn that video over to Dr. Clarke without keeping any copies, and the blackmail and the harassment end. We can't put that in any official agreement without revealing the video to the administration. Are you willing to write us a note to that effect right now? If so, we have a deal."

Aguillero hesitated and took a deep, audible breath. He stared at Markson, then Clarke, and then Markson again. Still without a word, he took a pad of lined paper from his desk drawer and wrote a short statement in longhand, then signed it.

"Will this do?" he said as he handed it to Markson.

The next day, Aguillero had explained to the Human Resources Department that the Alcubierre paper had become such a divisive issue within the faculty that the authors and the Physics and Astronomy Department had reached an agreement based on the journal reviewers' evaluations of the merits of the paper. HR approved the agreement he'd prepared, and they met in his office to complete the paperwork.

With the forced formality of a divorce mediation, Aguillero handed the papers to Markson. "Both of you sign all three copies. Each of you keep one and leave the other on my desk."

Markson signed and passed it to Clarke.

She picked up the pen, but turned to Aguillero before signing. "This is an outrage, but I'll sign it because I'm going to wipe my arse with it and rub it in your face when our paper is published."

Aguillero turned to Markson. "You see? Do you still think I'm wrong about her? You can submit your damned paper. I'm going outside. Your presence is fouling the air in here."

Using critiques from the reflector, they edited their manuscript to respond to concerns probably shared by potential reviewers. They chose *Physical Review D* for submission because it could expedite the review. It was one of the leading journals in the field. As soon as the manuscript was in its final form, Markson submitted it electronically.

Over lunch at Subway, Clarke complained to Markson, "It's been three weeks since we sent the bloody thing in."

"Even with expedited processing, *Physical Review D* isn't *Physical Review Letters*. It usually takes one to two months to get the first round of reviews back. Then, we'll have just fifteen days to answer. Let's enjoy our leisure while we have it."

When the initial reviews appeared in his email, Markson was perplexed. He forwarded them to Clarke. After she'd had time to read and absorb them, they went to the small conference room and took it over from a pair of graduate students who'd been practicing for their oral exams.

"Something's fishy here. Three highly negative reviews, all of them channeling Aguillero. If the comments we got online were as representative of the community as I think they were, I'd expect maybe one dogmatic negative review, but a strongly positive review would be at least as likely. What I really expected was three professional critiques that recommended publication conditional on some revisions, maybe one of which would be major."

Clarke scoffed and reached out to take Markson's hand in hers. "Lee, my love, you are so naïve. Jorge got to the editor. I wouldn't be surprised to find out that he was the one who leaked our paper on the reflector, just to have an excuse to fire us. I'll bet he *helped* the editor select three people he felt were the most qualified to review the paper, knowing they'd side with him. I wouldn't even put it past him to be one of the referees himself."

"Do you really think he's that unethical? He may be biased against us, but he knows he's biased. He'd recuse himself."

"Wanna bet?"

"We're not going to find out," Markson replied. "Peer reviewers are anonymous for good reason. It would be unethical for the editor to disclose them. Besides, if Jorge had gotten to him, he'd have rejected the paper outright, given these reviews. He didn't. He gave us fifteen days to revise it to meet their objections."

"OK, Mr. Do-It-By-The-Book. So, what do we do now? Do we tell Jorge?"

"We definitely don't tell him unless he asks. If he does ask, we tell him the truth. Meanwhile, with only fifteen days, we need to do some triage."

Triage meant dividing the reviewer's comments into three categories: things they could not fix with any feasible level of effort, things that were frivolous or trivial to fix, and things that could be fixed with some effort. The third category was the most important. It got priority.

They had conceptually solved the radiation problem already, so they started there.

"Shuttlecraft," she said, pointing a finger in the air when he suggested tackling this issue first.

"Bingo!"

"So, I assume we need to run some numbers, right?"

"Yep. I can do that."

"Good. In the meantime," Clarke said, "I'll see if I can find anything new in the literature that might help us respond to the negative energy and causality problems."

Markson grinned. "Deal!"

Using their EM observations, he estimated how close a warp-ship could come to a shielded landing station without damaging the station or its crew. The most optimistic answer was 35,000 kilometers, about the height of a geosynchronous orbit. A shuttlecraft could provide transport to the station at that distance. They needed four days for the calculations and to write their response.

The lack of causal connection between the interior and boundary of the warp bubble stumped them.

Clarke finally decided, "If there's a solution to getting information past the horizons in an Alcubierre warp bubble, it's hidden in new physics. I don't see any way that any form of signal processing could help."

Determining whether guidance commands could be preprogrammed into the warp field or delivered from outside the field could take years of concentrated effort. After three days, they accepted that the task was too difficult and they reassigned it to the first category: not frivolous and not readily solvable. Clarke's literature search and an additional three days of brainstorming about handling large amounts of negative energy came to the same dead-end.

With five days left, they spent a day and a half writing responses to the frivolous and trivial. "The frivia," as Clarke called it.

Markson was relieved. "At least we've gotten those out of the way."

Now, they had to return to the two unfixable elephants in the room—the energy problem and the GNC problem. These, they attacked along two lines of thought.

"We have overwhelming evidence that such a ship flew nearby, and therefore it must be possible. The fact that we don't know how it works does not mean it doesn't exist. It just demonstrates our ignorance," Clarke said. "Why isn't that enough?"

Markson nodded and stood up. "It ought to be, but it won't be. I think it's a good place to start, though. We ought to give that point a name." He looked down, stroking his chin.

She laughed. "Clarke's hypothesis?"

He smiled and looked up. "No, but the substance of your argument names itself. Your argument is that since the thing exists, it must be possible. Let's call it the 'existential argument.'"

"Boring!" she said with a frown.

He waved a finger in the air and nodded. "Perfect for a journal article!"

"You got any other ideas?"

"One, and it's *personal*."

"How so?"

"The same objection was made against my time travel proposal. Reviewers insisted that the Casimir effect could not produce negative energy that could actually be used. It was just a quantum accounting trick. The prototype and the billions of dollars in profits that CATSPAW made for Catalano Automated Trading put an end to that!" He pumped his fist for emphasis.

She smiled at his enthusiasm. "How do we apply that to the huge amounts of exotic matter the naysayers claim are needed for a warpship?"

"We point out that quantum approaches to creating negative energy in bulk have not been seriously explored. Beyond that, there may be solutions in some form of quantum gravity or string theory. There's no proof that it can't be done, and experience suggests that simply assuming something can't be done is unwise, at best. It was only a bit over a hundred years ago that determining the age of the sun based on astronomical and geological evidence was considered impossible because of energy considerations. It took $E=mc2$ and the idea of hydrogen fusion to resolve the problem."

She nodded. "I'm good with that."

Markson suggested they handle the GNC problem similarly since it hadn't been seriously investigated, either. "We'll point out that it's too difficult to solve in fifteen days. We know that modern digital signal processing allows faster data transmission than used to be possible. Our position is that we can't dogmatically assert what can't be done unless we've done the calculations and found that fundamental physical principles forbid it."

"And can we call that the 'experiential argument' since it's based on your experience?"

The idea charmed him. "Deal!"

The revised paper and cover letter addressing all of the points raised by each referee hit the editor's inbox at 4:45 PM on day fifteen.

∞

Markson saw the message from the editor as soon as he returned from an early lunch. He thought about asking his co-author to join him as he opened the message, but there'd been so much correspondence associated with the review process that he decided to make sure this wasn't just more administrivia before contacting her. The paper had already been revised twice in hopes of satisfying the three reviewers and the editor.

The message began by referring Markson to attachments containing the second round of comments from the reviewers. Two of the three reviewers had recommended rejection of the revised manuscript, suggesting it was wholly without merit and indicating that they did not want to see any further revisions. The third had complimented the authors on having successfully addressed the bow shock issue, but did not accept either their existential argument or their experiential argument for the energy and GNC issues. He recommended rejection of the paper, but indicated he would be receptive to one additional round of reviews if the other reviewers were so inclined.

Kat's going to have a field day with these comments, Markson thought. *She's going to see Jorge's fingerprints all over them.*

He shook his head in disgust and set them aside to read the decision of the editor:

"Dear Dr. Markson,

As you can see, all three referees are of the opinion that your paper, 'Broadband Electromagnetic Signals Coincident with a Gravitational Wave Signature Event,' does not meet the requirements for publication in

Physical Review D. As editor, I regret to inform you that I concur with their recommendations. If, after considering their reviews and comments, you are still of the opinion that this paper should be published, you may, of course, consider submitting it elsewhere.

Thank you for considering our journal."

"Shit," Markson said.

He forwarded the email to Clarke with the comment that they should get together later in the afternoon to decide where to go next.

When Clarke read the rejection, she didn't wait for later. She stormed down the hall to Markson's office. "Fuck them. Fuck them all! Let's publish the damned thing online."

Markson slowly turned his chair around. He'd been browsing some papers on *arXiv*. "Good afternoon to you, too."

"How can you be so calm? You know we're both going to be forced to resign, remember? Let's at least get our money's worth. How about *First Look Physics*?"

Markson thought for a moment. He inhaled deeply, then folded his hands in his lap. "What the hell? Why not *arXiv*?"

"Because *First Look Physics* is faster. They post immediately and then moderate by removing a paper if it doesn't meet their standards based on readers' responses. *arXiv* moderates first, and if their reviewers don't like it, we'll never see any responses."

Markson raised his eyebrows and tilted his head in thought for a moment. "Let's do both. *arXiv* has a lot more prestige, but I like being sure of getting immediate feedback."

Clarke smiled. "That's the spirit. Should we tell Jorge now or wait a while? Maybe it'll take a few days until he gets the news. Or maybe he knew before we did."

Markson looked to the side and frowned as he thought for a minute. "I still don't believe he had a direct hand in this, but just in case, let's get our *arXiv* paper ready to post first. We can shorten it for *First Look Physics* so the *arXiv* paper won't just be a reprint if they choose to publish. Remember, though, we should notify Jorge beforehand. That's just common professional courtesy."

"Still being Mr. Nice Guy, I see."

"Not really. Just protecting our reputations, Kat. We're the good guys here, and I want to keep it that way by not being a bastard."

"All you'll get by being a pussycat is smelly cat food."

"Would you like to work on the paper now, or do you need some more time for bitching?"

"No, I'm about bitched out for the moment. Where do we start?"

"Sit down," Markson said, indicating a chair next to his worktable. He took the chair across from her. "Do we need to make any changes before we post it? Since we don't have to please *Physical Review D*'s reviewers, do we want to go back to some of our original language?"

It took them about two hours to agree on the exact contents of the papers to be posted and nearly a week to edit them to the point where they were satisfied with every word and every equation in each.

"Let's post them," Clarke said.

"No, Kat. We've been through that. I'll forward the editor's letter to Jorge and ask whether we should meet with him or Human Resources to submit our resignations. As soon as we're off the payroll, I'll post the papers with us listed as unaffiliated co-authors, without a connection to LAPI."

"I'm not going to resign. Fuck 'em. They can sue me."

Markson had had enough. He stood up and walked over to her chair.

"They'll win. You signed an agreement that *we* proposed, and they can enforce it. Even without the agreement, your contract is renewable from year to year, and you don't have tenure, so you're not going to remain a faculty member at LAPI. Period."

Clark's voice broke when she asked, "Why are you taking his side?"

"I'm not, dammit, but we've still got choices to make! We can keep our word and leave like professionals with some semblance of dignity, or we can compound the problem by getting fired, which will communicate to the world that we can't be trusted. It will be hard enough to find a good research position as it is without creating a character issue."

"Shit! Shit! Shit!" She stood up, pushed him aside, and walked over by his desk to the trashcan, which she kicked completely across the room, scattering its contents throughout.

Markson knew she had a temper. He'd seen her angry before, but never like this. He stood by quietly, hoping the storm would subside.

She grabbed a tissue from the box on his desk and blew her nose before she began picking up trash off the floor and putting it back in the dented can.

"Sorry. I had to hit something. It was you or the rubbish bin."

"Are we OK?"

"Not really, but I guess it'll have to do," she said.

They had received summonses to Dr. Aguillero's office by the time Markson posted the manuscript to the internet. Aguillero had them sign their resignations and gave them separation instructions prepared by the Human Resources Office. He directed them to be out of the building by 5 PM.

Markson submitted both the papers they'd prepared at the instant he and Professor Katty Clarke became officially unemployed. The *First Look Physics* version appeared on the internet within minutes.

By the time Markson and Clarke had cleaned out what remained in their offices and packed their belongings into their cars, it was after 5 PM. Clarke suggested they get something to eat.

Markson agreed. "I feel like celebrating our freedom. Mansurs?"

"Not tonight."

"I'll treat."

Clarke grinned. "I will be delighted to accept your offer, but not now. I'd rather go to the café where we got lunch last week. Their internet access was reliable, and I want to have a look at the reception our paper is getting. Will you join me?"

"Let's do it."

They found a vacant booth. Markson plugged his computer into the power strip and connected to the Wi-Fi while Clarke got in line and ordered for both of them. By the time she called out for him to come help carry their trays, he'd accessed the *First Look Physics* home page.

"Back in the UK, we might call this high tea—except that they didn't have any cucumber sandwiches, love. Has anybody read our little treatise yet?" she asked as they put their meals down.

"I'm looking. Just got the page up."

She took half a chicken salad sandwich, walked around behind him, and looked over his shoulder.

He scrolled down the page and startled. "Wow, that can't be right—look at that!" He was pointing to the comment page counter.

"Bloody hell! 76 pages of comments already? What's it been, maybe four hours? Move over so I can sit beside you."

Once again, the comments fell into the usual two camps: Nobel Prize vs. junk science or worse. There were a few measured, thoughtful, and constructive responses, but all too many of them read like political campaign advertisements— *Our side is great; the other side is despicable.*

"What have we started?" Markson wondered aloud.

Neither of them had Twitter accounts, but that didn't stop #Markson, #Clarke, #Alcubierre, and #Warpship from trending on the platform. On Reddit, there was a subreddit devoted to their paper. And the digital frenzy soon erupted into the traditional media.

Within a week, Markson began to get requests for interviews and invitations to appear on talk shows. He turned down most of them, but couldn't resist when Willard Manchester asked him back for a second round.

"Why do they always ask you, love?" Clarke asked.

"You jealous?"

"A little bit, yeah. How come you get all the press?"

Markson laughed. "Beats me. You're more photogenic. Actually, I think it's because they already know me from when CATSPAW was in the news."

"Well, I could use a bit of exposure, love."

Markson smiled. "Exposure could become the issue if the tabloids start reporting on your career as a TV and nightclub performer."

"I'm not joking, and you shouldn't be, either. I'm still looking for a job, remember?"

Markson's smile faded. "You're right, Kat. I should have been more aware of that. Let me see what I can do."

A few days later, Dr. Katty Clarke was beginning to make the media rounds.

The initial public release of the work on *First Look Physics* had weakened their credibility with academic purists, and despite the notoriety of their *arXiv* paper—or perhaps because of it—neither of them had yet received serious job offers in the field of physics. Markson speculated that, until their work was published in a peer-reviewed journal, they would be considered fringe scientists who were too risky for a reputable academic institution. He knew from experience what that meant: exile from the profession. They couldn't let it stand.

"Are you willing to work with me to rewrite our paper for another journal?" Markson asked Clarke as they sat at his kitchen table sampling some cinnamon-rum ice cream; it had come from a local vendor which he favored because they created unique, homemade flavors.

"Seeing as how I'm unemployed at the moment, I think I can fit it in."

"Maybe we can fix that. Have you ever heard of NISTER, the National Institute for Spacetime Engineering Research?"

"No. God, what a horrible acronym. NISTER? What is it?"

"It's new. Actually, it *will* be new as soon as it's chartered. Based on our papers, it will pursue all aspects of superluminal spaceflight and time travel using sound extensions of relativistic physics, quantum theory, and cosmology. Interested?"

"And who is behind this endeavor?" she asked, her eyebrows knitted in a slight frown.

"Actually, I hope we are. I think we can pull it off. I'll fund it, and I'll hire the two of us as its management team. Then, we can gather a small cadre of the best people with open minds and get to work on figuring out what made that thing go."

She jumped up, shaking her head hard from side to side and waving her right arm at him sideways. "Oh no, you don't! I don't want your charity, Lee Markson! I can find a real job. I'm a PhD physicist, remember, and a good one." She spun around and stalked out, slamming the door behind her.

Markson sat back in his chair, speechless. *Where the hell did that come from?* Then, he erupted out of the chair and raced after her, catching up to her in his driveway.

She turned and glared at him. "Leave me alone!" she shouted, her hand on her hips and leaning forward.

He took a deep breath. "I drove, remember?"

"Take me home!"

Markson walked toward his car as though he was about to grant her wish, but then he leaned his backside against the front fender as he faced her.

"I don't want to take you home, Kat. You suggested the idea that I fund my own research, and now I'm going to do it. I can't do it alone. I don't know where you got the idea in your head that there's any charity involved. It's going to be damned frustrating work, and we're both going to earn every penny we take in salary to keep living like normal people."

She stood there alternately staring at Markson and wiping tears from her cheeks. He remained silent until she spoke.

"What do mean it was my idea?"

"Back when you were reaming me a new asshole for having a fortune and not using it to avoid working for Jorge, you told me I could have funded my own research laboratory. I didn't think I needed to, at the time. I said I was saving the money for a rainy day. I thought we could do the research through normal academic channels and save the money for a more needy cause. Well, things are different now. The storm is upon us. If you meant what you said back then, join me."

"What can I do? I don't know anything about business or administration or management, and my fields of expertise are signal processing and cosmology, not warp drives and quantum mechanical magic tricks."

Markson stepped away from the car and gently took her arm. "Let's go inside where it's comfortable and figure out what we each need to contribute to make this happen. You could start by suggesting a better acronym for our humble venture."

Her laughter led their way back to the kitchen, where she poured the Glenlivet and he refreshed the ice cream.

"Not exactly health food," she said as she lifted her glass toward him.

"Mental health food," he said as his glass touched hers with a sonorous clink.

"OK, now tell me how we're going to solve world hunger, or the equivalent in post-relativistic physics."

Markson snorted. "It's a good thing it *isn't* post-relativistic or we'd both be disqualified."

"You know what I mean, love. Post-Alcubierre physics sounds so... specific, and post-Aguillero physics sounds so petty."

"Post-ET physics, perhaps?"

"Right!" she sniffed.

Then, she got up and danced a little jig as she shouted, "Ooh—ooh—I've got it!"

"Saint Vitus Dance?"

"No, silly. The name! The Institute for Alcubierre Research and Technology."

"IART?"

"IFART. I intended to keep the 'F,'" she said, nearly drooling ice cream as she laughed.

Markson chuckled as he pointed at the chocolate stain that was growing on her shirt. When he recovered, he continued, "Anyway, we know what the top-priority research problems are: energy and GNC."

"What about radiation? Wasn't that also a major objection?"

Markson nodded. "But I think we covered that one in our papers. The ships just stay far enough away to protect the destination and use a shuttlecraft to land."

"Shuttlecraft. I still can't believe we're talking seriously. We sound like we're on *Star Trek*."

"The energy and GNC problems are serious enough to keep our institute busy for decades. We don't need to use its resources to attack a problem that can be avoided in practice until we've learned enough to make that practice possible."

"OK, but I still don't see where I fit in. If I'm going to collect a salary, especially from you, I intend to earn it. How? As I said, I don't have any relevant expertise."

Markson chuckled. "Neither do I."

She shot him a disbelieving look. "Bullshit."

"The ironic thing, Kat, for all of your honorable concern about you living on charity, is that you know as much about quantum mechanics and relativity as I do. And, by the way, I won't be paying your salary. Unless you change my mind, I will fund the institute as an independent entity. It will pay us both salaries which we will both more than earn. We can set up some sort of a board of trustees to govern it, but I do want us to maintain overall control."

"And how do we do the research?" she pressed. "How many people will we need to hire? Where will we get them?"

Markson thought those were good questions, so they discussed them. Over the next several days, they considered five different concepts for the operation of NISTER and, ultimately, one concept survived the give-and-take.

After one lengthy session, Clarke said, "What I think we're converging on is that we want to be sort of a privately funded National Science Foundation for superluminal spaceflight technology. Have I got that right?"

"Exactly. With the help of volunteer, outside reviewers, you and I have the expertise to review proposals and select those for funding that have a reasonable chance of advancing the science we're concerned about. We won't need a huge research staff with personnel offices and buildings and overhead. Just a couple of rooms, some computers, and an administrative support person or two. We can buy legal advice by the hour rather than hiring in-house counsel. It will still be challenging, but at least it will be practical."

Another product of these discussions was her more serious suggestion for the organization's name: The Foundation for Alcubierre-related Science, Technology, and Engineering Research: FASTER. When Markson asked why she'd added '-related' to Alcubierre, she mentioned that another FTL solution to Einstein's equations also existed, having been developed by someone named Jose Natario. It didn't get as much publicity, but she didn't want to exclude it from their mission statement. Markson liked the name immediately, and so FASTER it would be.

While FASTER was officially being established, they set up a temporary base of operations in Markson's study. The proximity to their new offices and the furnishings already in the study made the choice easy. They had a desk, a large table suitable for use as an oversized desk, two chairs, and a set of bookcases, plus network access and computer power sufficient for their short-term requirements. Additionally, it was comfortable, and the kitchen was only about fifteen feet away.

A few back-channel inquiries suggested several well-respected physics journals that might potentially take a chance on a warp drive paper, too. They selected *General Relativity and Gravitation* because Markson was acquainted with the editor and thought him to be more receptive to unconventional ideas than most others.

To avoid any legal issues with the use of data obtained from LAPI, they examined the original sources of the data they'd needed to make their arguments. They were pleased to find that, although they had processed most of it on LAPI computers using the database they'd assembled there, they'd built the LAPI archive by downloading files from publicly available sources. The institute could not, after all, prevent them from using any of the observations and analysis in their manuscript.

They rewrote it to match the journal's editorial guidelines and style, and then the familiar anticipation and tension of the review process began the instant Markson pressed "Send."

A few days after submitting to the journal, Markson received an acknowledgment from the editor that their paper had been forwarded to three referees who now had three weeks to return their comments. He realized this would be the perfect time to move FASTER from Markson's house to the new offices.

Markson foresaw a challenging effort. Neither he nor Kat had the knowledge to undertake the legal or financial preliminaries of setting up what they envisioned. Markson called on old friends and colleagues from his days at CAT. Henry Catalano, CAT's CEO, recommended a retired corporate CFO in New Orleans, and Makayla Birkwood, CAT's corporate counsel, had an attorney acquaintance in Baton Rouge who handled high-tech start-up companies.

Markson's experience from building CATSPAW was sufficient for the logistics of equipping the office space. In a few weeks, FASTER opened its offices at the Barringer Foreman Technology Park, which was only about a mile and a quarter north of Markson's house in Highland Park, and just behind the Barringer II shopping center in case they wanted a quick meal nearby.

With the lease signed and the utilities turned on, Markson and Clarke began moving in. The offices were furnished, but they would need additional computing power, so they ordered two large servers and an assortment of monitors, keyboards, mice, and storage devices.

Initially, there would be workstations for the two of them, and two more for staff as soon as anyone was hired. They designed the system's architecture so that additional workstations, storage, and processors could be added simply by plugging them into the local network and editing a few configuration files.

While they waited to hear back from the journal, Markson and Clarke continued to follow discussions of their work. Much of it was uninformed because sci-fi junkies, armageddonists, and conspiracy theorists had become prominent on so many of the social media sites where their work was trending. Even professional sites couldn't prevent the involvement of self-styled scientists who were untrained in general relativity and wanted to opine on the subject.

"If any of our referees are following this online, I hope the crap doesn't bias them against us," Markson said one day to Clarke.

"I just hope Jorge doesn't get to them again."

He sighed and shook his head. "I can see that not all of the conspiracy theorists I have to deal with are online."

She gave him a gentle jab in the chest.

∞

Two weeks later, Clarke asked, "Why haven't we heard anything? It's been three weeks."

"Twenty-two days, to be exact. Assuming the referees met their deadlines, and assuming that our paper is at the top of the editor's priority list, the editor still has to read their reviews, generate a preliminary decision and an accompanying punch list, and then assemble the package with identifying information stripped from the reviews. It's too early."

"You know, I could have stayed on the continent. Italy is very pleasant."

Markson grinned. "Would the referees' comments get to us any faster in Europe?"

Clarke stuck her tongue out at him.

"If you're looking for something to do while we're waiting," Markson offered, "we could develop ideas on how we're going to use FASTER to get some quantum mechanics types interested in our energy and horizon problems."

"Can I have a week's vacation, boss?" she asked in mock subjection.

"I'm not your boss. *We* are *our* boss. If you aren't putting me on and really need some time, take it."

She laughed. "You never know when to take me seriously."

"Got that right."

It was thirty-seven days before they received the initial evaluation from the editor—even Markson had begun to worry. When it appeared in the FASTER inbox, Clarke was playing golf. She saw it on her phone and called Markson to let him know she was leaving the course immediately.

"Come on over!" he said. "Bring a bottle of something. We'll either want to celebrate or drown our sorrows."

The message from the journal had four attachments. Three of them were reviewers' comments. They opened the fourth one first—the editor's cover letter.

The editor noted a significant divergence of opinion among the referees. Before he could accept the paper, the authors would have to meet the objections where the reviewers agreed. Where the reviewers disagreed, the authors would have to explain why they were making or not making revisions. A revised manuscript with responses to the specific concerns of each referee was due in fifteen days.

"Here we go again," Clarke said.

"That's true, but the editor's tone is a lot more encouraging. Let's look at the reviews and see what we have to do."

The individual reviews surprised them. Referee A was

a hardcore Aguillero clone who would never be satisfied. Unexpectedly, Referee B recommended that the paper be accepted with minor revisions that would require little effort. B explicitly mentioned and rebutted the core arguments made by Referee A, too. This was unusual. Reviewers didn't normally see each other's comments before submitting their own, but Markson surmised that B had thought through these concerns on his own and decided to preemptively dismiss them.

As Clarke finished reading B's review, she said to her co-author, "Although he doesn't call them by those names, he seems sold on your existential and experiential arguments."

Reviewer B also gave them a gift by citing several papers— unrefereed as of yet, but posted on *arXiv* by F. Loup and co-authors—that modified the Alcubierre metric. The modified metric lacked the GNC problem because its horizons didn't prevent access to parts of the warp bubble which needed to be controlled. It also required less negative energy than the original Alcubierre formulation. B included these points as grounds for his recommendation for acceptance because they supported Markson and Clarke's arguments that it might be possible to overcome the major objections with further research.

Markson printed the review from Referee C. "Let's see what's in the tie-breaker."

The third review was skeptical, but indicated a willingness to be convinced. Comparing it with B, Markson and Clarke noted that it asked for many of the same revisions which B had suggested. Comparing it with A, they saw it raised some of the same concerns.

"I don't see any point in responding specifically to A," Clarke said.

Markson agreed. "A has nothing unique that requires response. Responding to C will cover the issues raised by A, to the extent that they can be covered."

It helped that C had accepted their shuttlecraft solution to the radiation problem, but they couldn't duck the energy and GNC issues.

Any response that would satisfy C would satisfy B, so they accepted every suggestion that B alone or B and C had both made. Some of these would make the paper better, and they could live with the others. This was quick, would satisfy B, and go part of the way to convincing C of the paper's quality.

After that, the energy and GNC objections common to A and C had to be their main focus. Initially, they revisited the possibilities for new physics that had been discussed online, including the papers by F. Loup and co-authors. Could quantum gravity or a string theory-based unification of relativity and quantum mechanics lead to solutions to both the energy and GNC problems? The speculations were interesting but endless, and, most importantly, they were just speculations that were compounded in credibility by being in areas where neither Markson nor Clarke had any expertise. Reviewer A certainly wouldn't buy that, and neither would C.

Finally, Clarke said, "This is getting too complicated. We're overthinking this. What's the heart of our position?"

Markson looked down at the paper for a few seconds, and then back at her. "That we don't know enough to deal with these issues yet."

She pumped her fist. "Exactly. We need to say that!"

Markson shook his head. "We *did* say it. The only one of the three reviewers who bought it was B. You're never going to get that past A and C."

"Fuck A," Clarke said, punctuating her opinion with a vigorous one-finger salute. "Let's pretend we're lawyers. C is the jury, and our client is an alien spacecraft accused of having violated the laws of physics. We don't have to prove she didn't do it. All we need to do is convince our jury that there's reasonable doubt."

"She?"

"Ships and aircraft are generally referred to as 'she,' are they not?"

Markson laughed. "Touché."

They explicitly named and strengthened their existential and experiential arguments, and included a historical example where misplaced certainty about energy had delayed scientific research for half a century.

In 1912, geologist Alfred Wegener had noted the similarity in shape of the eastern and western sides of the Atlantic Ocean. He'd hypothesized that these had at one time been joined. He'd been met with the same hostility that the warpship concept was receiving because he hadn't been able to explain where the energy to rip continents apart could have come from. Nobody had been able to publish papers containing evidence that supported Wegener because of opposition from influential leaders in the field. It hadn't been until students of one of these leaders had changed his mind that papers on sea-floor spreading and continental drift had found acceptance. Now, Wegener's was the mainstream theory.

Markson and Clarke both proofread the revised manuscript and then set it aside to write responses to the reviewers and the editor. They explained each revision and provided rationales for rejecting the suggestions that they hadn't adopted. They thanked the reviewers and the editor for their contributions to improving the paper.

"There's one more thing I'd like to add, if you don't mind," Markson said when they'd finished their responses.

"What?"

"At the top of our cover letter, I'd like to insert a quotation."

"What is it?"

Markson typed the following:

"It ain't what you don't know that gets you in trouble. It's what you know for sure that ain't so. -- Mark Twain."

Six weeks later, Clarke began saying, "This is bad."

"I don't think so. I think the editor is fighting with Referee

A, who's being a pain in the ass," Markson countered, just as he did each time she brought up the concern.

"I hope your little quotation didn't piss off the editor," she said, not for the first time.

"More likely that it'll help him understand the real issue," Markson replied.

By the time the response came, they'd fully moved into the new FASTER office space. Markson saw it as soon as it hit the foundation's inbox, and he called Clarke to his desk. The title of the email was "Notification of Acceptance." But even without reading it, he could see that there were two attachments instead of the usual one, and he was curious.

In the first attachment, the editor explained that two of the three referees had recommended publication of the revised paper. Referee A remained adamantly opposed. The editor said that usually, in the face of such a strong opinion by a well-respected referee, he would have rejected the paper. In this case, he said, the other two referees were just as well-respected and the editor himself thought that the revised paper made a good case.

Markson made a fist, yelled "Yeah!", and stuck his tongue out at Clarke when they read:

"In particular, I have taken seriously the quotation you provided from Mark Twain. Sometimes, we can be too sure of ourselves for our own good."

The editor also explained that after he had notified
A that the paper was being accepted over his objection, A
had demanded the right to publish a comment stating his
objections to the paper. Such comments were not rare, but
his demand for simultaneous publication required an additional, accelerated review process before the comment could
be accepted. The comment was the second attachment that
Markson had wondered about. It was only seven pages long,
and they read it immediately. The editor had also offered them
an opportunity to submit a response to it, but indicated that
the response would also have to be reviewed and could further
delay publication.

Clarke gave a thumbs-up. "All things considered, I think
the worst is over. Should we write a response?"

Markson put his head down and hesitated for a moment
before looking up with a sigh. "Kat, I've had it. Enough! We've
beaten that horse to death. With LAPI, with journal reviewers
and editors, on the internet... Is there anything new we'd have
to add in a rebuttal?"

Clarke gave a slight laugh. "No, but I hate to let their bullshit go unanswered. It could diminish the reception of our
article by casual readers who haven't been party to the fracas."

"Why not just see what happens when the journal comes
out?"

Clarke took him by the hand. "You take a break. Let me
have a crack at it."

Markson shook his head. "I can't put up with another week

or two of this, and I don't want to delay publication, either. Enough."

"Give me two hours?"

"What for?"

"I can do it in two hours."

Markson startled. "Go for it."

One hundred and thirty-five minutes later, Clarke handed Markson a complete, properly formatted, first draft of their reply.

Markson broke into a huge grin. "You're fifteen minutes late!"

Another twenty minutes passed, during which they polished the text so that all that remained was to write a one-paragraph cover letter to go with it to the journal. They'd already addressed every one of the issues raised by the hostile comment in previous replies to reviewers and editors. Clarke's strategy had been simple and effective: cut and paste, format, and edit. The reply covered the ABCs—it was adequate, brief, and now completed.

That evening, they topped off their dinner at Mansurs with champagne and, of course, ice cream.

CHAPTER SEVEN

THE DOD

THE DEPARTMENT OF DEFENSE became concerned when the Markson-Clarke paper wasn't universally condemned or ignored. The small but enthusiastic group of relativistic physicists and cosmologists supporting it began to change some opinions, and so the DOD reacted. Professor Kesin Rao was one of many scientists dependent on DOD funding who was about to find out what their DOD research grant was going to cost them.

Rao represented Rhode Island State University in the LIGO Scientific Collaboration. His research focused on high-energy cosmological events. Much of it was funded by the AFOSR because it involved physics that might be applied to developing new sources of energy for military use, or new methods of detecting novel energy sources developed by an enemy.

"I guess one shouldn't look a gift horse in the mouth, as they say," he'd said when his department chairman had told him he would need to interrupt his work in the laboratory in order to meet later that day with an AFOSR grant administrator. "Are you going to be there?" he'd asked the chairman.

"No. He said he wants to meet with you alone in your office. He's writing the checks, so we'll do it his way," she'd replied.

Rao must have shown his irritation when the grant administrator—Dr. Blair Fredericks, whom Rao had never met—knocked on his door ten minutes late, because Fredericks took one look at him and immediately said, "I'm Blair Fredericks. Allow me to apologize. My plane was delayed coming in from D.C."

"No problem. It's happened to me," Rao replied, continuing to scowl. He pointed to a chair in front of his desk that was usually reserved for consultations with students. "I am very busy, though. Please sit down. Could we get right to the point?"

Fredericks took the seat, noticing that the wall behind Rao was bedecked with dozens of professional awards that included several for widely cited journal publications. He'd picked the right target. "Professor, I hope you'll understand why this couldn't be handled by telephone or email. It's a matter of national security and very sensitive. You may consider it classified if you like, but there won't be any documents associated with it."

Rao's scowl morphed into a quizzical grimace, and he leaned forward. "Isn't that rather unusual?"

Fredericks sat back, poker-faced, and folded his arms. "Actually, it is. The whole situation is unprecedented. We need your cooperation to assist in dampening rumors that threaten to reveal important work in fundamental physics, as it could have major military implications for our country. Can you help us with that?"

Professor Rao studied Fredericks for a moment. He understood he wasn't being asked a question. "What do you need from me?"

"I'm sure you've heard the rampant speculation generated by that paper in *General Relativity and Gravitation* claiming that the Earth is being visited by alien spacecraft—"

"That isn't exactly what the paper claimed," Rao interrupted him.

"Close enough. Our problem is that our military has a research program in advanced propulsion that could be compromised if the news and social media frenzy inspires *Wikileaks* or others to inquire too deeply. If they convince people that a warp drive is possible, their conspiracy theories may lead to exposure of what we're really doing with actually attainable physics."

"So, what can I do about it?"

"Your grant covers research on physics relevant to Markson and Clarke's paper. You could do your country a great service by having a very careful look at it and publishing a sharp, thorough rebuttal."

"Why me?"

"You're well-respected and you have expertise in the field. We're sure you'll want to do the right thing."

Rao thought he had already done the right thing. He'd been on the RISU team that had reviewed an earlier draft of the paper at the request of LAPI. His section of the RISU report had suggested that LAPI should permit the paper to be published after some significant revisions were made. The latest version of the paper had included most of those revisions.

"I read the paper. Suppose I didn't find anything fundamentally wrong with it?" Rao asked.

"If that were the case, Professor, I'd have serious questions about your competence. Several of the physicists who review our grant applications have told me that it is pure nonsense—pseudoscience."

"Are you saying my grant could be in jeopardy if I refuse this request or come to a conclusion you don't like?"

"Oh, not at all, Professor. At least, not directly. I'm just letting you know about the consensus among some of the other professionals in the field."

At home that night, while drowning his guilt in a third cocktail for what he would have to do the next day, Rao pondered the irony. Conspiracy theorists claimed Markson and Clarke were government agents whose paper was an attempt to suppress speculation about an illegal U.S. nuclear satellite. In actuality, government agents were attempting to suppress Markson and Clarke's paper. Rao understood what Dr. Fredericks had claimed, but he wondered what was really going on.

Variations on this meeting materialized in offices and laboratories throughout the relativistic physics community over the next several weeks. Within a few months, journal editors noted an eruption of manuscripts critiquing or openly attacking the Markson and Clarke paper. Peer reviewers saw these papers one at a time. They didn't notice that they all originated from authors who were highly dependent on DOD research grants. Or, if the editors made the connection, they took no action regarding it.

The DOD capitalized on the fact that these instigated critiques were, in fact, consistent with the opinions of many of the relevant experts. Many of the papers were published.

∞

"Why are we here?" Markson asked, indicating himself and Katty Clarke, who sat next to him at the table in Dean Simpson's conference room. "You fired us seven months ago, remember?"

Neither of them had much respect for anyone who'd been connected with their ouster from LAPI, but Markson had dissuaded Clarke from wearing her "Let Alcubierre Power It" T-shirt. Instead, they'd both selected neutral apparel, and showed up neat, clean, and informal.

Joanne Simpson was standing in front of her chair at the other side of the table with her arms folded across her chest. She scoffed and then smiled. "Technically, you resigned, but

I'll concede it was under duress. I apologize for that. We didn't have the whole story."

Simpson, as Dean of the College of Science, had invited Markson and Clarke to "a meeting regarding your controversial research." Professor Aguillero, as Chairman of the Department of Physics and Astronomy, sat beside her. He made a foul expression when she said that she hadn't had the whole story. A man and a woman who neither Markson nor Clarke had seen before also sat on their side of the table.

Clarke noticed that Simpson was wearing a dark blue woolen jacket with matching pants and a white blouse with a matching pearl necklace. Aguillero had on a new three-piece suit. His shirt had gold studs and cufflinks, each with a small diamond. The other man wore a gray suit that looked expensive, and the woman's outfit would have passed acceptably on Wall Street.

Clarke leaned over and whispered to Markson, "Something's up. They're dressed to the nines."

Simpson said, "I'd like you to meet Colonel Christopher Nilson from the Air Force Office of Scientific Research. Colonel Nilson is a PhD space physicist."

Nilson stood and reached across the table to shake hands with Markson and Clarke.

Markson immediately stood and reached across to accept the handshake. Clarke was slow to follow his lead. Her main reason for hesitating several seconds before extending her hand wasn't her dislike for all things military. She was instead taken aback by how much the two men looked alike even though the colonel was obviously older than Markson, perhaps by a decade or more. Identical in height, they had similar builds, although her colleague was a few pounds lighter. They also shared reddish brown hair, although the colonel's was short and neat while Markson's was longer and in need of a barber. They differed in another way, as well. Although in civilian clothes, Nilson wore his suit like a uniform: shirt, pants, and jacket appeared fresh from the cleaners, meticulously pressed and with every crease perfectly defined. Markson had never paid much attention to the finer points of dressing for success.

"With him is Louise Meier from the National Security Agency," Simpson continued before the three of them resumed their seats.

Meier was a striking woman. Her cream-white blazer covered a high-necked black blouse that called attention to the thin gold chain necklace holding an ornamental pendant with a single small white pearl. The necklace matched both the jacket and the blouse perfectly. Her straight blonde hair hung at least half a foot below her shoulders, and she pushed it aside before offering her hand. She was thin and almost as tall as Clarke, who stood at six feet. She was also pale, which gave an unnatural intensity to her dark, steel-blue eyes. Her arms and fingers seemed longer than they ought to be, according to the rest of her body.

The former faculty members felt uneasy as they completed the greeting ritual.

As soon as everyone was reseated, Simpson got to the point. "Colonel Nilson and Ms. Meier have made us aware of some data and analysis that lends a little credibility to what you've been saying in your papers and internet posts."

Aguillero snorted.

Simpson stopped and turned in his direction. "Are you OK, Dr. Aguillero?"

The formality got his attention. "Please excuse me. Something caught in my throat. Please... get on with it."

Simpson turned back to Markson and Clarke. "As I was about to say, they are offering to support your work with a grant that's large enough for you give the matter your full attention. Would you like to hear what they have to offer?"

Clarke gestured in the direction of the dean, to whom she spoke before Markson could decide how to respond. "I'll bet you mean they offered *you* a big grant if you rehire us," Clarke pointed out. "I doubt you're advocating funding for our independent foundation, FASTER. If you want us to pay any attention at all, cut the bullshit."

Simpson folded her arms and frowned.

Markson grinned and pointed at Clarke. "What she said."

Simpson unfolded her arms and placed her hands on the table in front of her as she leaned toward the couple. "*Of course*, the grant would be administered by the Physics Department—"

Markson interrupted with a question for Nilson. "Why LAPI? If you want us so badly, why not propose giving the grant to FASTER and cut out the middleman?"

Nilson sat back and looked Markson in the eye. "Because LAPI brings far more resources to the effort. A distinguished faculty in all of the right subject areas, an intimate relationship with LIGO Livingston, and a deep, powerful, information-processing infrastructure. It is also already cleared to do classified work, and many of the faculty already have clearances."

"Whoa." Markson raised his eyebrows. "Clearances?"

Maier answered his question. "Dr. Markson, our national security requires that anything related to this subject matter, including this meeting, be classified."

Nilson nodded and added, "Your work has enormous potential for human spaceflight. I have arranged temporary clearances for you and Dr. Clarke so that we can discuss some implications of that here today."

"Clearances *for this meeting*?" Clarke asked, her mouth agape.

"Yes. What we want to propose to you is classified."

She stood up. "I'm out of here!"

Markson touched her arm. "Hang on just a minute, Kat." He turned back to Nilson. "Are you going to tell us why you took down all of the gamma ray data?"

"I can do that as long as you understand that you can't reveal it without facing criminal charges."

"Suppose we don't want to hear anymore. Can we cut this off and leave?"

"Sure. We'd like to have you on our side. We're not your enemy."

Markson breathed deeply and hesitated. Finally, he turned to Clarke. "You can do what you want, Kat, but I want to know what's been going on. I'd like to stay long enough to get some answers."

Clarke shrugged while making a face, but she sat back down. "Don't mind me."

Nilson hesitated for a moment, considering whether this was the right time to address the issue Markson had just raised. He decided that satisfying Markson immediately might set a less adversarial tone for the meeting.

"We took the data down because it supported the speculation of some of our scientists that the event involved a faster-than-light alien spacecraft. That conclusion has huge national security implications. We couldn't find a credible excuse to sequester the conventional electromagnetic data which you used, just like our people did, to build a trajectory, but we could prevent the gamma ray data from being used as evidence of a bow wake."

Markson and Clarke both erupted, making it difficult for Nilson and the others to understand what either was saying.

Nilson intervened. "One at a time, please. I was answering Dr. Markson's question, so perhaps he could go first?" he suggested, looking in Clarke's direction.

She gave a dismissive wave.

"What you're telling us," Markson began, "is that the reason you suppressed the data we initially needed to convince our department that we should publish... is that we were right? Is that what you're saying?" Markson asked with a look of disbelief on his face.

"Not exactly. We didn't know at the time whether you were right or whether Professor Aguillero here, and those who've agreed with him, were correct, but we couldn't take the chance."

Clarke spoke up. "It sounds to me like you're pretty sure now. What changed your mind?"

"You did. Your paper with the Alcubierre signature in the gravitational wave data made a convincing case. I was surprised but gratified that you had as much trouble as you did publishing it. It also raises that enormous national security issue that we're hoping you'll help us address."

"What national security issue? Are you expecting an alien invasion or something?" Markson asked.

Clarke just rolled her eyes and looked at the ceiling while humming the theme from *The Twilight Zone.*

"We plan to study the technology," Nilson answered. "We don't want potential enemies undertaking the same research, so we have to discredit it. That's why neither the DOD nor the NSA have attempted to rebut the Russian accusations that the event was a malfunction in one of our satellites."

Maier nodded, signaling her agency's agreement.

"You're deliberately trying to discredit our work? Is he on your payroll?" Clarke asked, looking at Nilson while pointing at Aguillero.

Aguillero's face reddened. He jumped up, making a fist and pointing his extended finger to the heavens. "I am a man of honor! I do not take payment to tell lies. I am still not convinced that the Russians haven't got it right."

"And I am still not convinced that you weren't the one who leaked our reflector manuscript to the press." Clarke said as she sat back with her arms folded, looking him square in the eyes.

Aguillero leaned over the table and reached toward her, the tip of his finger coming inches from the tip of her nose. "If you weren't a woman, I would smack your face."

Markson stood up, grabbing Aguillero's arm. Aguillero yanked it out of Markson's grasp and glared at his former student, protégé and employee. Markson held Aguillero's gaze for just long enough to believe that his former mentor's indignation was genuine.

Nilson said, "I see that there's more going on here than I was aware of. I think we would all be better off if we dialed it back a bit."

"Do I really need to take this abuse?" Aguillero, still standing, asked Simpson.

Before she could answer, Nilson said, "Perhaps you could debrief Professor Aguillero later?"

Simpson nodded at Nilson and then turned back to Aguillero. "I asked you to this meeting because your department seemed the logical place to put the proposed program, but perhaps I should rethink that. We can discuss it later. I'll fill you in when we're done here."

Everyone understood Aguillero's tone even if they couldn't understand what he was mumbling on his way out.

Markson addressed Nilson: "So, what, exactly, do you want with us?"

"We'd like to see how far any present or feasible new technology can take this. If it is even remotely practical, we would like you to help us develop a small prototype just like you did with CATSPAW. LAPI's mission to use interdisciplinary emerging technology to develop practical applications fits our goal exactly. This project is the perfect combination of cutting-edge physics and incredibly futuristic engineering."

"But we couldn't publish. We couldn't even rebut the crap that detractors like Professor Aguillero have been spreading." Markson indicated the door with his thumb. "That's what you meant by 'helping you address the national security issue.'"

"Yes," Nilson admitted.

"And you'd expect us to shut down FASTER?"

"Of course. It's becoming part of the threat."

"You're so full of shit," Clarke said.

Markson just shook his head.

An awkward eight seconds of silence preceded Simpson's next remark, which was addressed to Markson and Clarke when it came. "There's a magnificent opportunity here."

"For you, maybe," Clarke replied. She turned from Simpson to Nilson. "We have to shut down our own foundation and work for you, and then we won't be able to publish. I probably won't even be allowed to participate in the research, right?"

"Possibly not."

Markson looked concerned and sounded puzzled as he glanced at Clarke and then the colonel. "Wait. What am I missing here? Why not?"

"She's a British national, Dr. Markson," Nilson responded. "It could be difficult to get her the required clearance."

Markson frowned. "Didn't you just tell us that you got both of us clearance for this meeting?"

"Yes, but it is a temporary, secret clearance for an extremely limited purpose. A permanent clearance higher than Top Secret would be required for the work, and that's much harder to justify."

Markson stood up. "I'm sure you can buy yourselves a couple of competent physicists who don't mind working in a coalmine where they never see the light of day, but I don't think that's for us. For the moment, I may have to fund FASTER myself, but at least we can publish our results so that others can build on them."

Clarke rose. "What he said."

"Wait, please," the colonel said as he gestured for them to return to their seats. "I think we can work something out. You don't have all of the information you need to make such an important decision."

Markson stopped, but he didn't sit down. "I'm a data-driven guy. Make your case."

"Dean Simpson, may we have the room?" Nilson asked.

The request startled the dean. "You want me to leave?"

"Just briefly while we discuss some personnel matters

covered by the *Privacy Act*. Only Ms. Meier and I need to be involved in this part of the discussion."

"OK. I'll be across the hall when you need me."

∞

As soon as Simpson left, Nilson got up and came around to sit next to Markson. Maier picked up her black steel briefcase and placed it by the chair at the end of the table closest to Clarke before she sat down.

She motioned Clarke to move to the adjacent seat, saying, "Dr. Clarke, I have something to show you."

Clarke looked at her colleague. He shrugged. He didn't see any reason for her not to have a look at their show-and-tell presentation, although he was curious about the special attention being paid to Clarke.

As soon as Clarke was seated next to Maier, Nilson changed the tone of the meeting. This was clearly Nilson's show, and his expression was no longer collegial.

"Dr. Markson, Dr. Clarke, this isn't an academic exercise. The Department of Defense can reward or punish people at levels which the Department of Physics never imagined. Ms. Maier has prepared a small example for Dr. Clarke. If necessary, we can discuss others afterward."

Maier stood up and bent over to pick up the briefcase, which she placed on the table in front of Clarke. She dialed in the combination and removed a fat, legal-sized folder from the locked briefcase, which she then set aside. She opened the folder on the table in front of Clarke. "You might want to look at these before they're posted anonymously on the internet."

Clarke looked bored as she glanced down, but then her gaze grew more intense. In a few seconds, she set the images aside and picked up the pages of text that had been offered. "Cunt! Where did you get these? You have no right—"

"Kat, what's in there?" Markson interrupted.

The woman, who was still standing, looked down at Clarke, who remained seated. "Would you like to show him, or should we just keep this between us?"

Clarke looked at Markson. Then, she picked up the papers and waved them at him. "These wonderful leaders of the free world have the pictures of me starkers on the British TV show and exotic dancing in England. The same stuff Jorge black-mailed us with. Actually, I'm OK with that," she said pointedly, looking to Maier. "I look good, it's already available to the public, and it's nothing I'm the least ashamed of." She turned back to Markson. "What pisses me off is that they have a list of pornographic websites they claim I frequent! To the extent any of it is true, it's nobody's fucking business but my own."

When Markson moved to approach Maier, Nilson took him by the shoulder. Markson ripped himself free of Nilson's grip, knocking over his chair as he stood up. He'd taken the woman by the lapels and jammed her up against the nearby wall hard enough to rattle the artwork on it by the time the colonel recovered, but Nilson was quick enough to separate them before either Markson or Meier could escalate the encounter. Markson was both impressed and frightened that, even while she was being manhandled by him, Maier had never let go of Clarke, whose arm she had taken hold of when Clarke had risen to join the fray.

"Thank you for giving us more leverage against you, Dr. Markson. You have just assaulted a federal official. That's a felony," the woman said as she released Clarke and straightened her collar before returning to her seat.

Nilson sighed and shook his head. "I'm sure you've heard the phrase 'the carrot and the stick,' Dr. Markson. Dr. Clarke, do they say that in the UK?"

"Ja, Herr Colonel. *Wir sagen das.*"

Nilson took off his suit jacket and hung it over the back of an adjacent chair before he sat back down. "Funny, Dr. Clarke. Look, you two, you made us show you a piece of the stick to get you to take this seriously. It will be much more pleasant for all of us if we can stay with the carrots. We can offer both of you prestigious academic positions with large salaries if you will join our project, Dr. Markson. We may even be able to work our way around Dr. Clarke's clearance problem if she'd like to assist you."

"Fuck you," the two physicists said in unison. They looked at each other in response to the echo, and laughed.

For more than an hour, the government officials alternated threats and rewards. They described the stark conditions Markson and Clarke could face in a federal penitentiary if they were convicted of assaulting a federal officer. They promised them both GS-15 senior scientist positions with the DOD. They threatened to audit Markson's tax returns for the year when he'd become wealthy at CAT, and then offered him a senior executive service position at DARPA. They threatened to revoke Clarke's green card and deport her, but then offered her a full professorship at the Naval Post Graduate School.

Finally, both sides realized this was not going to end with a voluntary agreement.

Clarke summed it up: "You can take your carrots and your sticks, and shove them up your asses."

The colonel stood up and retrieved his coat. "Have it your way. This meeting may be over, but you will soon find out what happens to people who put their personal egos before the national security of the United States."

PART III

THE DOD

CHAPTER EIGHT

WASHINGTON

SECRETARY OF DEFENSE (SECDEF) William Kinnon
welcomed Attorney General (AG) Frederick Knowles and the
recently appointed Deputy General Counsel of the Air Force,
Rhea Cartwright, into his office in the Pentagon. Cartwright
was representing the Air Force in their discussion of "the
Markson problem."

The day before, the SECDEF, the AG, and the Secretary
of the Air Force had all met with the President to brief him
on the disinformation campaign which the DOD had been
waging against the idea that a faster-than-light spacecraft
had been detected as it flew past Earth. They'd explained that
they believed any attempt by potential adversaries to develop
such technology would pose a serious threat to U.S. national

security, and the largest contribution to achievement of radical new capabilities had always been the belief that they could be accomplished. It was essential to continue to reinforce those enemies' confidence in the dogma of conventional physics that faster than light travel was impossible.

Meanwhile, it was the intention of the DOD to find a way to convince or, if necessary, force Lee Markson to join a DARPA project focused on exploring the technology and possibly building a small prototype. The President had given them the go-ahead, just as long as their methods would be legal and not require any direct action on his part.

Kinnon liked to spread out. His desk by the window lacked the real estate he wanted when he was working, so he used it largely for teleconferences and when meeting with people he wanted to keep at a formal distance. His files and research materials were usually piled on the conference table in the middle of the room; he treated this table like the oversized desk he had always wanted, but never convinced any of his employers to buy. It was not an ideal setting for this kind of meeting, but he cleared half of the table and the three of them sat down.

Cartwright had left a meeting at Vandenberg AFB in California, late in the afternoon of the day before, so that she could fly back to Washington in response to her boss's phone call ordering her immediate return. Even with the military transport direct from Vandenberg to Andrews AFB in Washington, she hadn't arrived at the Pentagon until after 1 AM. Her boss, the Secretary of the Air Force, had given her a lengthy explanation of the day's scheduled meeting and her instructions. However, a shower and fresh clothing couldn't conceal what running on three hours sleep and a quart of coffee was doing to her concentration.

Cartwright was concerned as she pointed out, "The Secretary told me that I'm to help you find a legal way that we can convince or coerce a Dr. Leland Markson to lead the scientific team on a DARPA project headed up by an AFOSR Colonel named Christopher Nilson. He said it has something to do with faster-than-light technology that will give whoever gets it first an insurmountable predominance of military power. I wasn't functioning at full speed and, honestly, a lot of the information went over my head. Before we get started on the legal possibilities, can we review exactly what we're doing and who the players are?"

Her request seemed reasonable to Kinnon, so he and the AG summarized their meeting with the President, closing with, "The bottom line is that we need to accomplish two things: first, discredit Markson and his entourage; second, recruit him, willing or not, to help us develop this technology."

She had some questions.

"Why Markson? It seems like an awful lot of effort and at least a little political risk to go after this one guy. Surely, there are other physicists who are just as smart. Some of them probably already work for us at the AFOSR. I'm told Colonel Nilson himself is no slouch. He's heading up the project you want to put Markson on at DARPA, and he's already got some sharp people working for him."

Kinnon spoke in a monotone, like he was reciting a list of groceries. These were just the facts. "Markson is the only person in the world who has actually built and demonstrated a machine that uses anything related to this technology. He knew enough about both the science and engineering of it to modify them and make a practical time machine. Everybody else believed it was impossible, and they ridiculed him for suggesting it. Now, he's rich and smug, and the so-called 'experts' have egg on their faces. The Alcubierre theory he adapted to his CATSPAW device is behind the technology these aliens are using to travel the galaxy. Who else besides Markson would you want to lead the effort?"

"But we could train someone—"

"That takes time. Eventually, the bad guys are going to figure out Markson was right—especially if he's on the loose and banging his drum about it. Whoever gets the technology first is the winner. There is no second-place trophy."

"What makes it so critical?"

"Two things. First, an FTL weapon is inherently unde-tectable. No radar could see it coming in. Stealth isn't required—it's built into the physics. You'd have nothing on any detection system, and suddenly—BLAM!—you'd be toast. Second, you don't even need to put a warhead on it. One of the objections to using the technology for spaceflight is that the superluminal bow wave in front of what Markson calls a 'warpship' contains so much energy that, as the ship decelerates at the destination, it vaporizes the destination.

In fact, a low flight over enemy territory could sterilize a whole corridor."

She pondered that for a moment. "I assume somebody has offered him some incentives?" she finally asked.

"Oh, yeah. He's too rich to care about monetary incentives, but we offered him the opportunity to lead the research program. He initially seemed interested, but then he refused because the research and results would be classified. He wants to publish everything. He insists it's necessary for the progress of the science, but I don't doubt the Nobel Prize has something to do with it. That insistence on publishing is what makes his mere presence in the public eye so dangerous."

The AG, who had been sitting passively and listening to the conversation, brought up the other side of the equation. "There was a meeting at LAPI between Colonel Nilson and an NSA operative named Louise Maier, with Markson and his professional partner and girlfriend, Katty Clarke. The government folks offered both of the physicists excellent jobs, but were turned down rudely and unprofessionally for the reasons Will just explained. Maier felt they had no choice, so she showed Clarke some background research the NSA had done. It seems Clarke likes to perform naked in so-called 'gentlemen's clubs' and enjoys porn on the internet. Markson took offense and slammed Maier up against a wall. God knows what would have happened if Nilson hadn't intervened to defend her."

"So, he assaulted a government official. You can arrest him. Doesn't that get him off the street?"

"Temporarily, at best. It's a minor charge, and with his money, he would instantly post bail and use the arrest as another reason to attack those who are critical of his work."

"Besides," Kinnon interjected, "it wouldn't do anything to get him into our custody or encourage him to work with us rather than against us."

Cartwright sat back, hands clasped across her chest, and thought for a minute before addressing her ideas to Kinnon. "Mr. Secretary, I think we can get him into our custody. I have no idea how to get him to like it."

"It will be enough if we can legally give him orders to do the research. The main thing in our favor is that he really wants to do the work. He's fascinated by it. He just doesn't want to do it *for us*. If we can get him into it, maybe he'll come around."

She folded her arms together, still sitting back. "The President could exercise his emergency powers since the state of emergency he declared is still in effect. He could commission Markson as an officer in the Air Force under 10 USC 603(a)."

"But Markson doesn't have to accept the commission," the AG said.

"And the President told us not to involve him," Kinnon reminded Knowles.

Cartwright stood up and walked around the room. She put her arms on top of her head for a few seconds and stared out the window, then clasped her hands together at her waist and turned to the men still sitting at the table. "If this is as big a national security concern as you've said, then we don't have to be nice about it."

The men looked at each other and then back at her.

"Of course not," Kinnon said.

"If an envelope addressed to him with the return address of the Secretary of the Air Force was hand-delivered, signature required, would he sign for it and read it?"

It was Kinnon's turn to think for a moment. "I don't know."

"Suppose that envelope was the fourth or fifth of a sequence containing offers or veiled threats, all of them carefully drafted to appear innocuous if revealed to the public, but calculated to irritate the hell out of him?"

"Then, based on his history with us, he'd probably refuse it or throw it away."

"Good. We can use that." She turned to the AG. "Have you got an indictment against him on the assault charge?"

"Not yet."

"How quickly can you get it?"

"Couple of days, at least. Maybe a week."

"And can you hold up service on the arrest warrant until you're ready to take other actions following the arrest?"

"Assuming it's not more than a few months."

"That's more than enough time."

Kinnon grinned at her. "What have you got up your sleeve?"

"Suppose our office sends him a few of these missives and waits until the courier, who'll be one of our people, notes that

Markson's response to these deliveries has become hostile enough to make it likely he'll ignore the next one."

When she didn't continue, Kinnon said, "And...?"

"And then the Secretary of the Air Force appoints Leland Markson an Air Force warrant officer (W-1) under the authority of 10 USC 603(a), and sends him, in the same kind of envelope, a copy of the warrant—along with orders for him to report to the nearest Air Force base within 24 hours for in-processing."

"Why would you send him the warrant?" the AG asked.

"The Secretary's warrant that appoints him an officer, not the arrest warrant," she responded.

"Won't work. Your service doesn't have warrant officers," Kinnon said.

"You're half-right, Mr. Secretary. We haven't had them for decades, but that's by our choice, not any act of Congress, and we are free to revive that rank if we choose to do so. Now might be a good time to revisit that possibility."

Kinnon broke into a huge smile. "I see where you're going with this. If he's home, but refuses to sign for the package when it's handed to him, the courier can leave it on the doorstep and it will be legal service whether he reads it or not."

"Exactly!" she said, returning the smile.

"And why do I need the arrest warrant?" the AG asked.

"Technically, the Air Force can't arrest Markson until he's already in their custody, because the warrant appointing him doesn't go into effect until he reports for duty. It's one of those catch-22 law school problems."

"So, I have him arrested... then what?"

"He has a custody hearing in federal court. You ask the court to release him into the custody of the Department of the Air Force for determination of his status as an Air Force warrant officer who appears to be AWOL because of his failure to report in accordance with orders issued and served upon him. I will have someone there to provide copies of the warrant of appointment, the orders, and the certificate of service to the court, the DOJ prosecutors, and Markson's attorney. The DOJ will not object."

The AG nodded and shrugged his shoulders. "OK by me."

Kinnon continued to smile. "Remind me never to get on your bad side."

The banging on the front door was loud, persistent, and annoying. It was 2 AM, and it took Markson nearly a minute to wend his way up the hallway from his bedroom in the right rear corner of the house to the foyer near the left side at the front. By the time he got there, the intruders—who claimed to be U.S. marshals—were threatening to break down the door.

An armed man in a marshal's uniform and two stocky men in suits pushed their way in as Markson opened it in his pajamas and bare feet. One of the suits waved a badge in some sort of wallet, motioning too fast for the physicist to read it. All he could tell was that the credential was shiny, goldish, and had what looked like an eagle in the middle of it.

"Doctor Leland Markson, you are under arrest. Place your hands on top of your head and turn around."

The man with the badge put it back in his pocket as Markson complied. He placed the physicist's arms behind his back and secured them with handcuffs, while the others ransacked the house and placed evidence tape on his computer and file cabinet. The prisoner wasn't permitted access to his cell phone, which they'd sequestered along with his computer.

An hour later, Markson, along with everything they had seized relating to the controversial waveform observed by LIGO, was deposited in an unidentified location that looked much like a prison. About thirty hours later, he found himself standing in handcuffs beside yet another marshal, positioned in front of a federal judge in a tiny courtroom that looked nothing like the elegant ones seen on television.

The judge sat behind a desk on a slightly elevated platform. There was no gallery or jury box. A clerk of court sat at a table at floor level, directly in front of the judge, and facing in the same direction as him. There were two government attorneys sitting at a table and facing the judge, and they were positioned on the left side of the aisle running from the door at the rear to the clerk's table. One of them represented the Department of Justice and the other was from the Air Force.

The DOJ attorney told Markson and the judge that the third government attorney, who was standing at a similar table on the right side of the room, was a federal public defender with a high-level security clearance; they were requesting that he be appointed to represent Markson during the proceedings. The proceedings themselves were a detention hearing to determine whether or not to have Markson held in custody until he could be arraigned a week or two later on a federal indictment that accused him of assaulting a federal officer.

"Your Honor, I would like to be represented by my own attorney," Markson protested. "I can afford to hire one I can trust rather than someone provided by the same people who have forcibly brought me here in secret."

The DOJ and USAF attorneys told the judge that the proceedings were urgent and involved sensitive, compartmentalized information. They said that even if Markson could find an attorney who could pass the security screening for the necessary clearance, the background investigation would take six to ten weeks—which was not acceptable under the special circumstances of the case.

Shit, Markson thought. *It's not about any assault. It's about the alien spacecraft. Bastards.*

The judge appointed the public defender to represent Markson for the purposes of the current hearing and said he would decide whether to let Markson hire his own counsel once he'd heard the arguments of counsel. He directed the marshal to remove Markson's handcuffs and asked Markson to take the empty seat next to his attorney at the defense table. When the DOJ attorney assured the court that the marshal had the necessary clearance, the judge allowed him to remain in the rear of the room next to the door.

As soon as he was appointed, the public defender objected to the entire proceeding on the grounds that the only justification which the DOJ had presented for holding Markson at all was a minor assault charge having no connection to national security. "This belongs in a normal U.S. District Court," he finished, "not here in classified proceedings which are closed to the public."

Markson was pleasantly surprised that his attorney seemed ready to make some genuine effort to represent him.

His spirits perked up further when the judge turned to the DOJ attorney and said, "I don't see that this court has jurisdiction. There's nothing about a simple assault that threatens our national security, and even if there is some connection, I can't see how it would justify detaining this man without bond. And if he is released, what have you accomplished? You don't need the classified material until trial, and this is just a detention hearing. This court is closed and classified because it is meant to deal with terrorists and spies. Are you accusing the defendant of being a terrorist or a spy?"

"No, Your Honor, but if I may explain, the assault was directly related to a national security situation that could be even more significant than a terrorist attack. We are prepared to present the details to the court at this time. They relate directly to the preferred detention option."

"Well, I've got to hear this," the judge said. "What's so special about this matter that a normal court can't handle it?"

The DOJ attorney told the court that Markson had assaulted NSA Agent Louise Meier and Air Force Colonel Chris Nilson during a classified meeting at LAPI, the purpose of the meeting having been to convince Markson and Clarke to stop publicly revealing the passage of an FTL spacecraft. That knowledge, if it fell into the hands of the Russians or the Chinese, posed a major risk to national security, given that it could enable them to get the technology before it was developed in the U.S. He pointed out that Markson's total hostility toward cooperation with the government of the U.S. made it essential that he be detained without access to any means of communicating with the public.

"So, you just want to keep him quiet? Why not simply get a court order?"

Markson's attorney leaned over toward his client while looking at the judge. "May we have a minute, Your Honor?"

The judge nodded.

After some whispering, the public defender said, "Your Honor, my client says that although he will appeal any gag order issued against him, he will obey it as long as it is in force."

The judge looked toward the DOJ advocate. "Tell me why that isn't good enough."

"It isn't good enough for two reasons. First, there's no guarantee Markson will keep his promise. Once the information is released, no amount of punishment for violating the order can repair the damage. Second, any hearings on the matter are likely to involve highly classified information, requiring appellate judges with the same clearances this court has. That's not practical, and there'd be an enormous temptation to cut corners."

Markson's public defender began to respond, but the judge raised his hand. "I think I need to hear what the national security issue is so I have some context for evaluating what's been said so far. Once I know what we're dealing with, I'll be better prepared to hear additional arguments on the detention issue."

Now, it was the Air Force attorney who addressed the court. He explained that the classified material discussed at the LAPI meeting was evidence collected by the DOD. Markson wanted to publish it in support of his claim that the September event involved the effects of a spacecraft flying by Earth at close range, at seven times the speed of light.

"I thought that was impossible. Defense, do you agree that this is what's at issue here?"

The public defender spoke briefly with Markson before saying, "That's not the whole issue, but my client agrees that the event was caused by such a warpship. He would like to present his side of the story."

"I'll give you a chance at the appropriate time, Counselor, but I want to get the rest of the Department of Defense's position in my head first."

The DOD made its case that the threat of the nation's enemies developing faster-than-light travel first would be a national security catastrophe, and that Markson's cooperation with the DOD was essential to preventing it from happening.

As Markson's attorney tried to rebut the government attorneys with Markson's assistance, it became clear to the court that the DOD and Markson did not disagree on the physics and the data. The dispute was far less technical: the DOD wanted to conceal and discredit the physics that Markson wanted to publish. The DOD saw the possibility of reverse-engineering the technology as significant, and Markson did not. The DOD saw that possibility as a major threat to the survival of the U.S. as a world power, and Markson did not.

After many rounds of back and forth between the two sides, the judge had had enough. "The choice you've all left me with is difficult but clear. The relevant facts are not in dispute. If, as the government claims, those facts present an imminent threat to U.S. national security, this court has jurisdiction and the government's request for detention should be granted. If, as the defendant contends, there is not a current or serious threat to our national security, this matter should be referred immediately to the U.S. District Court having jurisdiction over the assault. Unfortunately, Mr. Markson, your beliefs and behavior, including the alleged assault—as reported here by the government and generally conceded by you to have been accurately reported—do not give me confidence enough to take your word over that of the trained national security experts cited by the government during their arguments."

Markson's attorney stood up. "Your Honor, I object to this court making a ruling on the basis of expert testimony, which has been presented as hearsay that we've had no opportunity to challenge through cross-examination."

The judge shook his head. "Nice try, Counselor, but you know as well as I do that this isn't a trial, and guilt or innocence isn't being decided. This proceeding is only a detention hearing at which hearsay is widely permitted." He asked the DOJ attorney what the DOJ was requesting.

"Under these circumstances, we would normally be asking that Markson be detained indefinitely without bail as a matter of extreme national security. In this case, there is an additional factor that suggests a different custody arrangement. We would like Your Honor to release Mr. Markson into the custody of the U.S. Air Force immediately after this hearing. He was appointed as a warrant officer by the Secretary of the Air Force and failed to report for duty as ordered. He is away without leave—AWOL, as it is commonly called."

Markson looked at his attorney and then at the DOJ attorney. "What the fuck?"

The judge banged his gavel.

"Your Honor, may I be heard?" Markson asked without waiting for his public defender to intervene.

"If you want to be heard in this court, Mr. Markson, you'll watch your language."

Markson took a deep breath and addressed the court. "I'm sorry, Your Honor, but I don't know what he's talking about. I'm not an officer in any military service. Taking orders to kill people without mercy and without question isn't my thing."

The DOJ attorney said, "Your Honor, my Air Force colleague can explain this to both you and the defendant."

With the court's permission, the Air Force attorney explained that the Secretary of the Air Force had issued a warrant appointing Leland Markson as a Warrant Officer (W-1) and issued him orders to report to nearby Keesler AFB for processing into the service. To support the claim, he presented two documents to the court clerk. The first was a copy of the warrant issued and signed by the Secretary of the Air Force at the direction of the Secretary of Defense, under the emergency powers provided in 10 US. 603(a), and enabled by the President's previous declaration of a national emergency related to the event in the sky over the Indian Ocean. The second document was a copy of the orders issued to Markson to report within 24 hours to Keesler AFB—which was the closest base to Markson's residence—for in-processing and the receipt of further orders. He provided copies to the court and, with the court's permission, to Markson and his attorney.

"These are copies. Where are the originals?" the judge asked.

The attorney handed another piece of paper to the clerk, who handed it to the judge. "This receipt says the originals were delivered to Mr. Markson's house by courier the day before he was arrested. It says Markson refused to accept delivery and that the envelope containing the documents was left on his doorstep with his knowledge. That constitutes legal service of the documents."

"May we have a minute?" Markson's attorney asked.

The court took a brief recess so that the pair could confer in private. It was a short conversation.

"Did you receive these documents?" the attorney asked.

"I don't know! Some courier asked me to sign for an envelope from the DOD. They've been hassling me with bribes and threats almost daily, and I've gotten fed up with it. I refused to sign and slammed the door in his face."

"That's not good. Is it possible he left it by the door when you refused to sign?"

"I don't know... I certainly didn't go looking for it."

"So, he's probably telling the truth about the documents being served to you."

Markson looked down and sighed. "I guess."

When the hearing resumed, the judge had one more question for the Air Force attorney. "And I presume he didn't show up within 24 hours at Keesler?"

"That's correct, Your Honor," the Air Force advocate said.

The judge looked in the direction of the defense table. "Do you have any questions for the witness, Counselor?"

The attorney looked at Markson and shrugged. Markson looked down and shook his head.

"No, Your Honor," the public defender said.

"In that case," the judge said, "I am granting the government's motion. Leland Markson, you are hereby released from the custody of the Department of Justice into the custody of the U.S. Air Force. The marshal will escort you accordingly.

This court is adjourned."

Markson's public defender shook his head and wished Markson well. Shortly after that, Markson was on his way to Keesler AFB.

∞

The following morning, an Air Force military police officer escorted a handcuffed Markson to a small conference room where the Air Force attorney who'd been his adversary the day before was seated at a table with four chairs. The other three chairs were unoccupied.

"I don't think the handcuffs were necessary, airman. Please unhook him and then wait outside."

"Yes, sir," the airman said to the civilian, who was clearly in charge.

When the enlisted man had closed the door, the attorney invited Markson to sit down. "I know this has been unsettling. After I explain what's happening and what your options are, you will have a choice to make. Before you make that choice, I will give you all the legal background you'll need to make a well-informed decision. Because this is classified on a need-to-know basis and I don't have a need to know all of the factual information you will require, someone else will provide that shortly. Once you have the full information, then you'll choose."

"What is it that I'm supposed to be choosing?"

"Whether or not to accept your appointment as an Air Force warrant officer."

"Done. I reject it. May I go now?"

"No. They tell me you're a data-driven guy. You don't have enough information to make that decision for yourself—yet."

"I have all of the information I need. I'm out of here," Markson said as he stood up and turned toward the door.

"You know, as a warrant officer, you would outrank that airman waiting outside, but he's better trained than you will ever be in hand-to-hand combat. You're a speck taller and a couple of pounds heavier, but I'm willing to bet you won't get three feet past that door if you open it."

Markson turned back to the table and sat down. "But I'm free to reject your bond of servitude after I watch your dog-and-pony show?"

"We will no longer have any grounds to keep you in our custody."

Marson took a deep breath and scowled, but then he let out the breath with a loud sigh and resignedly waved a hand. "I'm all ears."

The attorney explained that the Secretary of the Air Force had the authority to appoint civilians to the military rank of Warrant Officer-1 (W-1) in times of emergency. Warrant officers ranked above all non-commissioned officers (NCOs), but below all commissioned officers. They were generally individuals with special technical skills in high demand and short supply, and were usually assigned to special units or special assignments in regular units where their unique expertise was essential; furthermore, these were usually not direct combat roles. Markson's unique position as the world's current expert on the Alcubierre metric and its possibilities for propelling a faster-than-light spacecraft fit that concept perfectly.

"And they can force me to do that?" Markson asked.

"No. If you want to accept the appointment, one of our NCOs, with no sidearms or handcuffs this time, will assist you with what we call 'in-processing' and you'll sign a lot of forms, be fingerprinted, and get sworn in. If you choose not to accept the appointment, we will notify the court that the Air Force releases you back to the custody of the U.S. Marshal's Service, and it will be up to the federal civilian courts as to what happens thereafter, but we'll be out of your hair."

"Why would I possibly want to give up working as a free man in one of the most interesting research establishments in the world, on a problem of literally earthshaking importance of my own choosing, and where I can freely publish my results and maybe even, who knows, win a Nobel Prize... in order to work on what I am ordered to do, in secret, in a second-rate military lab, with no chance to publish?"

The attorney sat back in his chair. "I'm not the one who can answer most of those concerns, but I can tell you that if you accept the appointment, it is limited by law to two years or whenever the declaration of emergency ends, whichever comes first. This is not a lifetime or career engagement. Think of it as a temporary career detour in the service of your country."

"Any more legal stuff you want to feed me?"

"Not unless you have questions," the attorney said.

Markson shook his head, so the attorney picked up his briefcase and stood up. Markson also rose, but the attorney gestured for him to sit back down.

"I doubt you'll see me again," the attorney told him, "but now you'll have the opportunity to ask those '*why would I want to do this?*' questions of someone with the clearance to have answers. Listen to them carefully before you decide, so that you can choose wisely. Good luck!"

After the door closed, Markson could hear the attorney saying something to the airman outside, but he couldn't hear it well enough to eavesdrop.

A minute or two later, the airman opened the door, stepped in, and put a bottle of water on the table in front of Markson. "He asked me to get this for you, sir. He said the person you need to speak with should be here in about ten minutes."

"Can't I just go now? I have no intention of enlisting in the Air Force."

"That's above my pay grade, sir," the airman said before leaving the room and closing the door behind him.

Three minutes later, the door opened again and a woman stepped in, closed it behind her, and took the seat across the table from Markson. Markson didn't know how to react. It was Louise Maier, the woman from the National Security Agency whom he had manhandled at LAPI in defense of Katty Clarke. The primary alleged victim of his alleged assault on a federal officer. The woman who, in effect, had called Clarke a whore.

What the hell is she doing here?

Clearly, he was about to find out.

"Dr. Markson, you have a simple binary choice to make in the next half hour. You can accept your appointment by the Secretary of the Air Force and become Mr. Markson, Warrant Officer W-1, USAF, or reject it and remain Dr. Markson, under indictment by the U.S. Department of Justice. I'm here to give a firm, factual basis for your decision. It won't take long, and when I'm finished, you will have to decide. Is that clear?"

"Why you?"

"Because I am one of the few people who have all of the information you need and am already involved in this project. By the way, everything we say here is Top Secret. You have a temporary clearance for this meeting. Shall we begin?"

Markson waved his hand for her to proceed. *It's not like I have a choice.*

"The last time we were together, Colonel Nilson mentioned the carrot and the stick. Here are the carrots: If you accept the position being offered to you, all of the federal charges against you will be dropped and any potential charges against Dr. Clarke will be taken off the table. You will be assigned to a secret laboratory that is already staffed with top-echelon scientists and engineers who are working on determining how a warpship could be built, including pursuit of some of the research paths you have been unsuccessfully advocating as priorities—"

"Like what?" he blurted out.

"Like quantum mechanics in highly curved spacetimes, for example." She noted both his silence and the subtle widening of his eyes before she continued. "You would be the leader of the scientific and engineering aspects of the program. By law, your appointment will expire when the President's declaration of emergency is rescinded or when two years passes, whichever comes first, and you will then be free to return to the private sector with all of the knowledge you have obtained during your tenure as an officer."

"And I can publish what I've learned?"

"Be serious. Of course not."

"Then it's no good to me."

"That's for you to decide, but even if you decline this offer, you will not be publishing anything related to building a warpship. That whole area of research is being classified as we speak, just as atomic energy research was during World War II."

"That is so stupid!"

"I'm not going to debate that with you. I'm just presenting the facts as they are. Would you like to hear about the sticks?"

"Let me guess. If I don't play ball, you'll put me in jail and continue to slut-shame Katty like you're already doing. What else have you got?"

"For starters, Dr. Clarke injected herself into your assault on me, so she could face the same charges you're facing."

"You bitch!"

"Oh, I'm just getting started. We'll shut down FASTER by classifying everything it is doing and, as soon as Dr. Clarke is unemployed, or maybe even before based on her lack of character, we'll see that her visa to stay in the U.S. is revoked. When she gets out of jail, she'll be put on the first plane back to England."

Markson's face reddened as he took a deep breath. "So, I join your team, or you'll go after her, is that it?"

"Just one more thing. When your friend Huntsman told you what he'd seen in the high-energy data before it was classified, we were monitoring that call. When he saw it, it wasn't classified, but when he told you about it, it was. We'll make sure he's charged with that."

"Goddamned fucking Nazis. You're just Goddamned fucking Nazis!"

"We're just American patriots, Dr. Markson, but we do play hardball to protect this country. Here are your options: Join our team and do the kind of research you've dreamed of, or reject the opportunity and destroy yourself and your two best friends. Your choice."

"If I sign up, you'll leave them both alone?"

"No charges will be filed against either of them, and our social media operatives will lose all interest in Dr. Clarke's salacious pastimes."

"What about FASTER?"

"As long as it doesn't violate the national security directives or reveal classified information, it can continue to operate unobstructed. Surely, there will be areas on the periphery of the core science that will be unclassified and yet of interest to

FASTER, and also of interest to you once you have completed your tour of duty. Those avenues of research and your related findings, of course, could be published."

Markson breathed deeply again. "What do I have to do to accept your offer?"

"One of the base's administrative personnel will walk you through in-processing and provide you with sealed orders and transportation to your assigned post. You will open the orders when you are on the plane, and follow them. Their substance is what we have already discussed, but even I am not privy to the details."

"What about my house? Who's going to take care of that? My finances?"

"We will make those arrangements. One of the papers you will sign during in-processing will provide for a company the Air Force employs to act as your agent in those matters. As soon as your tour of duty is complete, the agency will be terminated."

"How will I let people know I've signed on with you?"

"That will be classified. Make a list of who you'd like notified. Keep it small. *Very small*. We'll see if we can get them cleared to have that information."

"I don't like that."

"You have two options, and I never suggested you'd like either of them. Sign on, or not. You do the research you love while many of your friends wonder where you went, or you and your two closest friends go to jail. Now, you must choose.

Shall I call a sergeant with the paperwork, or a marshal to take you into custody?"

CHAPTER NINE

THE COLLABORATOR

MARKSON HAD LOST COUNT, but thought it had been about ten days since his arrest when he arrived at what appeared to be his ultimate destination, somewhere in what looked like the Appalachian Mountains. He was escorted immediately to the director's office by a military policeman.

As Markson stood in front of Nilson's desk, the office appeared smaller than what he would have imagined for a colonel commanding a classified research facility. Nilson's desk faced the entrance, and behind him, on a credenza, were some pictures of a woman and several children. Probably his family. There were also half a dozen books between bookends, the end on the right being shaped like the nose of a missile with the end on the left being the tail—the books constituting its body. Above the credenza on the wall was a gallery of framed commendations, autographed pictures of military celebrities, and pictures of Nilson at various Air Force installations. In the center of the array, the largest frame of the bunch displayed a diploma. Christopher Nilson had earned a PhD in physics at Cal Tech. Like the conference room, the office had no windows.

As project director, Nilson, stood and extended his hand to welcome the newcomer. Markson didn't respond to the gesture, and Nilson resumed his seat without responding to the slight.

Nilson had worn civilian apparel at LAPI. Here, Markson had expected a blue uniform and a chest full of ribbons and medals. Except for the silver eagles on his shoulders, though, what the man wore made him look more like an army private than a senior officer in the Air Force. It was an ugly orange and brown camouflage outfit that Markson had seen referred to in the movies as "BDUs," whatever that meant.

"It's good to have you on our team, Mr. Markson. I see they haven't found you a uniform yet," Nilson said.

Markson took a deep breath and thought for a moment before speaking. "You act like everything's normal—like I'm just some new recruit reporting for duty. Well, I'm not. I signed those papers because your partner Louise Maier made it clear that if I didn't, then she would see to it that two of my best friends would have their lives destroyed along with mine. I'm a prisoner here no matter what the paperwork says. Let's not pretend otherwise."

Nilson looked baffled. "How did Maier get involved? She's NSA, not Air Force."

"Didn't you put her up to it?"

Nilson asked Markson to wait in his outer office. As soon as his administrative assistant had closed the door behind them, Nilson picked up the phone. Ninety minutes or so later, he summoned Markson back in.

"I still don't know how she got involved," Nilson told him, "but I believe you. I got my wrists slapped royally for asking the question. I was told that whatever inducements may or may not have been involved, your signature accepting the appointment was valid and binding. I am under direct orders from the Secretary of the Air Force to treat you as an Air Force Warrant Officer (W-1), so let's get that out of the way."

"What does that mean, exactly?" Markson asked.

Nilson pointed at him. "When you came in, I addressed you as Mr. Markson."

"I thought you were just being rude."

Nilson shook his head. "It wasn't meant personally. I did that to make a point which you need to remember. Like it or not, you have accepted an appointment by the Secretary of the Air Force as a military officer, a warrant officer under my command. The appropriate mode of address to a male warrant officer is 'Mister' even if the officer holds a doctorate. However, as long as your conduct reflects your continued awareness of that relationship, it is my intent to forego the rigors of military courtesy and give you the kind of personal courtesy appropriate to you as a professional scientist in an elite research institution. We can skip the uniform, but civilian clothes notwithstanding, you are still a military officer under my command. Are we clear on that, Mr. Markson?"

Markson drew himself up as ramrod straight as he could, snapped his heels together, and raised his right hand to his forehead. "Crystal clear, sir!"

Nilson laughed and shook his head. "You can skip the faux salute, Dr. Markson; it looks more Marx Brothers than martial."

Markson was installed in a one-room "VIP apartment" in what he later learned was called "the research building" and directed each day to a conference room for what the government called "in-briefings" by people he was told would be scientists "on his team."

In order to explain what he expected Markson's initial attitude to be, Nilson told the team that Markson was working involuntarily in the interest of U.S. national security under orders from the Secretary of the Air Force, but he didn't mention the details or Markson's military affiliation.

"Dr. Markson should be treated with the same respect as any other senior scientist on this project. I hope the work will prove sufficiently fascinating that eventually coercion will no longer be required, and part of your job is to make him feel like a revered colleague rather than a conscript."

At first, Markson refused to engage much with the government's research people. *They can bring me here by force and compel me to sit in this chair,* he mused, *but they can't make me think.* He found satisfaction in paying little attention to the first three of eight planned familiarization briefings that took place in a windowless rectangular room with a large screen and lectern at one end. *Just show up and pretend to play their game.*

The dull, institutional tan of the walls and the coarse dark carpet added to the miasma of the environment. A table the same shape as the room, but about half its length and width, left space around its sides for a dozen or so chairs. He was given the seat at the end of the table directly facing the screen. His "team" occupied the seats at the sides, and they took turns stepping up to the lectern to present their pieces of the show.

He resisted the temptation to show his contempt by not showering or changing clothes. *They'd tell Nilson and he'd probably force me to take supervised showers and wear a uniform.*

After a day and a half of PowerPoint presentations, he felt proud that he still didn't know much of what the AFOSR and DARPA were up to, and relieved that he didn't care. He just wanted out.

The afternoon briefing that came fourth in the sequence complicated things. It was the first one that addressed physics he hadn't seen before. The DOD had brought quantum mechanics to bear on the energy problem. This was an approach he and Clarke had sought unsuccessfully to convince LAPI to allow them to explore. It irritated him more than he cared to admit that it intrigued him more than he cared to admit.

Finally, he rationalized giving the presentation his full attention. *If they're going to make me a prisoner, at least I can get something in return by picking their brains.*

After the final in-briefing, Markson was assigned a workspace in a secure laboratory where employees sat in cubicles. From the seven primary research efforts he'd been briefed on, he was asked to select one of three to join as the task leader. He decided that the navigation task was the only one where he had sufficient skills in both the mathematics and the physics to lead, and it interested him.

Markson's in-processing and familiarization had been handled by subordinates—mostly civilian scientists and administrators. His choice of assignments was handled personally by Nilson, who a week later called him into his office. The civilian administrative assistant immediately knocked on the door to Nilson's inner office and ushered Markson in, closing the door behind him.

"Dr. Markson, they've told me that you asked some good questions during the briefings and even made a suggestion or two. Your choice of task was thoughtful, and it's clear you are taking this seriously. Your cooperation has alleviated the need for any further unpleasantness, and I hope that we may eventually be able to find some positive incentives to recruit Dr. Clarke to assist you."

Markson scoffed and made a stink-face. "You have a knack for saying exactly the wrong thing. You've just reminded me why I hate being here even if the work is exactly what I'd want to be doing if I were free to choose it. For that, I think I'll take the rest of the day off." He rose and turned to leave.

"Markson, wait. You have my word; we'll leave her alone."

Markson turned back slowly, stepped forward and leaned across the desk, eye to eye with Nilson. "Why the hell should I believe anything you say?"

"Because I've already protected her from the Departments of Defense, Justice, and State. I talked them out of shutting down FASTER as a security risk and cutting off her funding. The AG thought he could win some brownie points with the President by charging her with attempted assault on a federal officer because of that unfortunate LAPI session, and then asking State to revoke her green card based on the criminal charges. The SECDEF got wind of it and asked my opinion. We put a stop to it so fast that they didn't even generate any paperwork."

"That wasn't supposed to happen! We had a deal!"

Nilson leaned forward. "And I am enforcing it, despite the DOJ and NSA having other ideas."

"Why? What do you care?"

"The Air Force I have served in for several decades may have its faults, but lack of honor isn't one of them. Besides, I want you, and eventually her, voluntarily involved in the project, not here as people in bondage. I won't go near her again, and neither will anyone else. I think as you get into it that you'll make that transition. When you do, then you'll want her on your team. When you're ready, you can offer her the job."

Markson was surprised to find himself considering the possibility that Nilson had a hidden streak of humanity. As much as he despised power and hierarchies, perhaps a good person could use them to do good things. He was getting uncomfortably close to recognizing that.

"Fat chance that's ever going to happen. And it's your team, Colonel Klink, not mine."

"Colonel Klink was an idiot. I'm not. As soon as I think I can trust you, you will be the project's scientific director."

Markson reluctantly admitted to himself that Colonel Nilson was not an idiot. Evil, perhaps, but not stupid. He also recognized that he couldn't defeat the massed weight of the DOD head-on. He would have to take a different approach.

"If you're serious about that, you can begin by getting me internet access," he said after a pause.

"Until I am confident that you understand and will respect the highly classified nature of our work, I won't take the risk that you would use that access to reveal what we are doing."

"You want me to lead the science team? I need to be able to access the literature and discuss the physics with my colleagues elsewhere."

Nilson smiled. "I like you, Markson. You may not think much of me, but I hope that will change. We're a lot alike in more than just appearance. Here's what I can do for you now. I'll get you read-only access to *arXiv* and other selected sites. If there are particular sites you need, give me a list."

"How can you provide read-only access? To perform searches and click on links, the communication with the websites will have to be two-way."

Nilson cocked his head to the side. "Let's just say that there'll be some kick-ass artificial intelligence between your desktop and the internet."

Markson thought about that briefly before responding. Perhaps he could find a way around their software once he logged on. "Something's better than nothing, I guess. What about interactions with colleagues?"

"If you need to ask questions of colleagues elsewhere, you can pass them through some of the other physicists on the project who have the necessary clearances and understand what can be said and what can't."

"I suppose that will have to do."

"For now, yes."

As Markson turned to leave, he noticed that one of the reasons the office had seemed unexpectedly small was that there were bookcases against all of the walls except for the one behind the desk. Bookcases full of books. Books that appeared to have been in recent use.

He must not underestimate this man.

When he got back to his desk, he mulled over his interview. He thought the colonel appeared genuinely convinced that he would eventually decide to cooperate. Perhaps he could build on that conviction and make Nilson complacent. When the restrictions placed on his activities and limits on his access to resources were relaxed, he might then be able to contact someone on the outside to let them know what had happened.

∞

Weeks later, Markson's plan seemed to be working, but it had produced an unanticipated side effect. As Nilson became more comfortable with Markson and less threatened by his potential for rebellion, Markson became more appreciative of the potential of the project and more sympathetic to Nilson. The path to altering the mindset of the government to his benefit had become a two-way street. He liked what he was doing, and so he had to keep reminding himself that he wasn't there by choice.

He decided to try an experiment to see what the limits were when it came to what he could get away with. He set up an appointment with the colonel.

"Come in, Lee, what do you need?" Nilson greeted him with a cordial smile when Markson knocked at the open door.

"You once told me that if I wanted Katty Clarke on the project, I could hire her," Markson said with a poker-face.

"You're not the scientific director yet, Lee. I trust you more, but not completely. But if you want me to make her an offer, just say the word."

"Not until I'm the boss, Colonel, but I would like very much to know where she is and how she's doing."

Nilson sat back in his chair with his hands clasped in front of him. He frowned.

"What's the matter?" Markson asked.

The colonel sat up and grinned. "I said before that you and I are alike. If I were in your position, even if I loved the work here, I'd try to get a message to my girlfriend and partner. You wouldn't by chance be trying to get me to do your reconnaissance for you, would you?"

Markson knew better than to bluff. A lie here would destroy the progress he'd been making in the trust-building department. He laughed and deliberately exaggerated his smile. "Damn." He paused. "You also said you're not an idiot. You were right about that, too. Can't blame me for trying."

"No, I can't. I'd have been suspicious if you hadn't made a move sometime soon. Anything else I can do for you?"

He shook his head. "No, that about covers it."

Markson got deeper into the project as the months passed, and soon there were days when he didn't think at all about the outside. He mused about what he'd do differently if he were the scientific director. He was the group's expert on all things relating to gravitational waves, and the more experienced of the only two people who could do calculations using the equations of general relativity. While others in the group attacked the energy and radiation problems, Markson led the research attempting to overcome the GNC problem by using several of the papers which had been brought to his attention by referees of his and Clarke's journal manuscripts; they served as starting points to deal with the causality limitations imposed by relativistic horizons inside the Alcubierre warp bubble. In case that failed, he assisted the other person capable of performing the calculations in examining whether the "gravitational slingshot" maneuver used by NASA to steer and accelerate deep space probes would work on a warp bubble moving faster than light.

He soon earned Nilson's trust to the point where he was given a regular two-room apartment in the dormitory building; it faced the research building across an open space, within sight of a few VIP parking places at the research building and a thirty-foot wide strip of grass that people called "the park," between the paved parking and the dorm.

He could spend his non-working hours reading or watching whatever TV channels the facility's cable connection provided, and then just walk across the park to his office. It was his only real opportunity to get a look at his surroundings. He had a picture badge with a chip that let him in and out of the dorm and the research building, and it also gave him access to his work area. Anyplace else was still off-limits, his badge not programmed to give him access elsewhere. He was delighted when he was finally given unsupervised access to the cafeteria and the commissary, at least, so that he didn't need an escort to eat or purchase some deodorant. He was almost beginning to feel like a normal person.

One night, he dreamed he had taken Colonel Nilson's place as the project manager. He was even wearing an Air Force uniform with a star on the shoulder—not just a warrant officer's bar or even a colonel's eagle, but a star. *General Lee Markson, fancy that.*

And Katty Clarke wore the uniform of a staff sergeant, and shuffled in and out of his office receiving and obeying his orders. "Yes, sir, General, sir."

He awoke in a sweat. He had to get out of there to save his soul.

$$\infty$$

First on his agenda was to get a message to someone on the outside who might be able to free him through the legal system. Getting a message past the virtual security walls might be easier than getting himself past the physical ones. Henry Catalano was familiar with the legal system and also had contacts in the military who might be able to confirm whatever information Markson could smuggle out. It was worth a shot to try.

Nilson's level of trust hadn't progressed to the point where this was going to be easy. Markson's internet access was keystroke-monitored and effectively one-way inbound. That meant he'd have to get access through another user's account, which would require some luck. Everyone in the facility had high-level security clearance, and the information-security training to go with it. There weren't going to be any passwords taped to monitors.

Markson's lab was windowless, with ingress and egress requiring an access card, but once you were inside, it was open-format. There were fourteen people including himself in his unit, set up in four rows of four workstations, with two of them vacant. The desks were identical, with a computer having no commercial manufacturer's markings, a detached keyboard, and a twenty-four-inch monitor. Next to each desk was a freestanding bookcase that was three feet tall and just as wide. A set of computer manuals and a set of DARPA policy manuals occupied the bottom shelf of each bookcase. The remaining two shelves varied from being empty to overstuffed, depending on the occupant of the workstation. Visitors were never allowed inside. Only those individuals assigned to the project and their immediate supervisors could enter. Markson had even heard that Colonel Nilson had personally denied a four-star general's request for an exception to the rule.

As he disciplined himself to be more observant, Markson took particular notice of one of the data analysis technicians, Viktor Rakov. The man was a stocky Russian who he put at about forty, give or take a couple of years, with a ruddy complexion and short black hair that looked like the barber had cropped it by putting a bowl over his head. His cubicle was one row over from Markson's. On rare occasions, Rakov would leave his system logged in when he went to the restroom.

That was a breach of protocol, but nobody seemed to make anything of it since there were other persons with clearances who sat nearby with a direct view of the workstation. They would make it virtually impossible for an unauthorized person to gain access in the three to five minutes it took Rakov to relieve himself. It wasn't enough time to help Markson, but it was a place to start. Markson was encouraged, and enlarged his personal surveillance pattern to observe whenever someone took a bathroom break.

He was even more encouraged to find that Rakov wasn't alone. A physicist whose office was in an alcove attached to the open area, Irina Ivanova, also left her console online when she went to the restroom. It took him a while to find out because her seat was only visible from one workstation that everyone passed on the way to the bathroom. The restroom itself was a single, unisex facility—the only one available without someone having to scan out of the restricted area and then scan back in.

Markson timed some bathroom breaks to get a glimpse of her monitor by approaching the toilet as she was returning to her office space. She was quick, usually away from her desk for less than four minutes.

He needed to find out what she was working on in order to justify an opportunity to consult with her. Her portion of his in-briefing had been limited to discussing unpublished Russian data she had which reinforced his and Clarke's analysis of the event. Her workstation's more isolated location, and some non-standard equipment he could see as he passed her alcove on the way to the bathroom, suggested that there was more to her work than what she had included in the briefing.

Soon, he got a break. The facility's cafeteria didn't look like much, but it had a complete hot meal line, a sandwich and salad bar, and vending machines for drinks and snacks. The décor, however, was pure military industrial. Some six-foot by three-foot steel tables with four matching steel-and-black plastic chairs per table. The walls needed cleaning and the floor had cracked tiles. Like everything else except the commissary, it had no windows. Its main redeeming feature was that it was one of the few places in the compound where socializing wouldn't be seen as a suspicious activity.

One day, Markson noted Rakov and Ivanova eating lunch together. He walked over and said hello.

Ivanova rose and stood smiling warmly as she extended her hand. "Dr. Markson, I am honored. I have wanted to get better acquainted for some time, but given the unfortunate circumstances that brought you here against your will, I didn't know how you'd react. I was hoping you would take the initiative. Thank you. I have been following discussions of your work closely on the internet. You and Dr. Clarke were very badly treated. You may have to wait fifty years, but you will eventually be recognized for one of the most important discoveries in twenty-first century physics." After they shook hands, she pointed to the chair across the table from them. "Please, join us."

Ivanova was tall for a Russian woman—just a couple of inches shorter than Markson—and thin, perhaps 135 pounds, he guessed. She wore a tasteful but relaxed, open-necked, long-sleeved blue cotton blouse that tucked into loose-fitting black trousers. She looked... comfortable.

Markson accepted their invitation. "The honor is mine, Dr. Ivanova, and thank you for the kind words," Markson said with some sincerity. "I have been looking at some unpublished

EMP data from Russian satellites. It doesn't surprise me that they didn't release all of it. Are you familiar with it?"

"I am the one who provided it to you, Dr. Markson. My pleasure."

Markson nodded in acknowledgment. The revelation prompted him to ask about her background. Before emigrating to the U.S., she'd been a full professor at Moscow State University, where she'd chaired the Department of Physics. Rakov had been one of her graduate students and had emigrated with her without finishing his PhD. Her specialty was electromagnetic pulses. Before coming to the DOD, she had been a professor at Stanford University.

Markson liked how clearly she spoke without the verbal static like "uhs" and "ums" that he found to be so frequent and so distracting in others. Her English was excellent. Only slightly accented and much better than his limited knowledge of Russian, which he thought he'd better keep to himself for now. Given her experience, he was sure she must be in her sixties, but it didn't show. The dark red hair that she wore short and somewhat unkempt didn't have a trace of gray. Her skin had a rugged look, but more the kind that you'd see on people who spent a lot of time outdoors rather than the elderly—it was tanned, rather than pale.

He turned to her colleague. "And is it permitted to ask what you do, Dr. Rakov?"

"I am Mister Rakov, Dr. Markson. Please, call me Viktor. My work is need-to-know, but involves data analysis. I left

Moscow before completing my dissertation. I was afraid if I missed opportunity to accompany Professor Ivanova, I might never go to U.S.A. I am child of Mother Russia, Dr. Markson, but also son of American dream." Rakov, unlike his mentor, still retained his accent.

With additional prompting from Markson and an approving nod from Ivanova, the Russian revealed that his specialty was digital signal processing. Markson wondered who was better at it—him or Katty?

"Call me Lee, please, Viktor. I'm glad you both came. Dr. Ivanova, are you the one to ask if I have any questions about the Russian sensors or data?"

"Of course. The official channels are so, how you say, constipated? We should work together. Please call me Irina."

"Thank you, Irina." Markson smiled.

He'd made new friends and taken a deep professional interest in a new specialty: Russian surveillance satellite data. He wondered how they were accessing it, and whether the Russian government knew what they were doing.

Markson didn't want to be obviously cultivating a relationship with his new friends, so he limited his contacts for the next two weeks to "accidental" meetings at lunchtime. Since the cafeteria was open from 7 AM until 7 PM, he could take lunch at the same time as they did on some days and not on others. These lunchtime discussions were limited to socializing—to building trust on a personal level. He did observe that when his Russian colleagues went to lunch, they logged out of their computers, unlike their practice of leaving themselves logged in when they went to the bathroom.

After several lunches with them, he was ready to tighten their relationship and focus it. He began with simple questions about the type and purpose of the sensors that provided the data he'd received from Ivanova. She asked Nilson to allow him to correspond with her over the facility's internal LAN so that they could exchange files electronically. The colonel agreed, since the request involved no external access which could compromise security.

As soon as Markson's clearance upgrade was confirmed, more complex questions about the signal processing algorithms had him sitting in a chair pulled up beside Rakov's desk while the data specialist explained what his software did. When Viktor used the restroom, Markson observed that Viktor didn't log out of the network and left him sitting there unattended.

Even so, Markson felt he was under constant, careful observation. Whenever he got up to stretch his legs or use the bathroom, he felt that several of his fellow workers were watching him. They didn't seem to take much notice of other workers in the lab—just him. Sometimes, several of them would be talking and would stop as soon as they noticed he might be listening. He was supposed to be leading the scientific effort and needed to be aware of what was going on in the unit—yet, it was him they didn't seem to trust. If he was going to become a true insider, it would have to begin with the Russians.

Eventually, he devised a line of inquiry that brought him to Ivanova's workspace. To precisely assess the power consumption, size, and weight of the alien craft, he wanted data with a level of accuracy and precision that wasn't available in the current archive. It had to be Russian data because he already had access to observations made by the U.S. and its allies, and there was no hope of getting anything from the Chinese. He asked Irina whether such information existed and whether she could get it. He made sure the question was sufficiently complex that she needed him at her side while she sought the answers and downloaded the data.

At first glance, her workstation differed little from the others, but the differences, however subtle, were significant. She had two keyboards. One was a high-end, standard American one like you could buy in Office Depot or on Amazon. The other was in the Cyrillic alphabet used for the Russian language. She had a forty-inch monitor that she kept on the floor in the corner, except when it was in use. When Markson asked about it, she would only say that it was for "special projects." He wondered what could be more special than what he'd already been shanghaied to work on.

Ivanova had one set of high-precision optical and microwave measurements that she'd not previously provided because she hadn't realized that Markson needed them. "Here are the ones we used to develop an initial trajectory for the source," she told him.

"We?"

"As soon as the event occurred, AFOSR was asked to examine it. It looked a lot like somebody had set off a nuke in space, but there were some strange things about it. The Pentagon didn't want to make any accusations that could reveal details of our surveillance capabilities unless we could prove something that would make it worth the risk."

"I'd like to know more about that. Their analysis might help tie down some of those details Nilson wants me to determine."

"All that I can tell you is that, with regard to the data I just gave you, I snatched it as soon as it appeared in the Russian database, and I had Viktor run it through his QC software and pass it on to the colonel."

"So, you all worked for the AFOSR?"

"Yes, until we came to believe we were probably dealing with an alien technology. Then, our AFOSR working group was transferred to DARPA and a full-scale project was established."

"May I ask when the project was set up?"

Ivanova smiled. "While you were fighting with your institute for the right to merely discuss a faster-than-light spacecraft, we were setting up a laboratory to build one."

"You knew about the Alcubierre signature?"

"Oh, no. That was all yours!" She tilted her rimless, wire-framed glasses to the top of her head and pointed upward to her left before sweeping her arm to the right, watching its progress as if following an object in the sky. Leaving her arm pointed upward at the end of its trajectory, she turned her head to look Markson in the eye. "We just knew from the trajectory and the existence of the EM bow wake that the thing was super-luminal." She dropped her arm. "The wonderful thing you've brought to the party is understanding the fundamental physics of how they did it."

Markson couldn't resist reaching out to touch her hand. "You have no idea how much that means to me. Just to hear someone say it. Someone who thinks it matters." He lifted his hand and turned away as his eyes moistened. He was becoming too fond of this woman whom he had to keep under surveillance if she was going to be his ticket to contact with the outside world.

Markson was a bit disconcerted at how quickly Irina returned the first time she left him alone at her desk. She'd stood without saying anything and walked toward the bath-room. He hadn't timed her, but all he'd done after she'd disap-peared around the corner was to get up from his chair and begin a closer inspection of her computer and its peripherals when he noticed her from a distance—already watching him leaning over her keyboard. He hoped she hadn't seen him touching it.

The moment he saw her, he called out, "Irina, I'm glad you're back. What's this here?" He pointed at some symbols near where his head had been. "I can't read it, even up close."

She quickened her steps as she approached and seemed uncertain—perhaps suspicious? It was not a good sign. "That's still in Russian. I only translated the relevant parts. Your eyes are not what's failing you. You seem to have forgotten your Russian."

Markson felt his face flush. Of course, they would have done a complete background check. How naïve to think he could have concealed his familiarity with the language.

"Your Cyrillic font isn't anything like the one in my textbook. It looks like a cross between Klingon and Orc," he said, trying to buy time to work his way out of appearing to have tried to deceive her.

"Klingon, I know. What is this 'Orc?'"

"It's a language from *The Lord of the Rings.*"

"A novel about the Tsar of Saturn, perhaps?"

Markson broke into laughter. He loved her wry sense of humor. Often, he couldn't tell whether she was speaking seriously or seriously putting him on. Either way, though, the conversation gave him an idea.

"It would help me and take some of the workload off of you if I could relearn enough Russian to read some of the files myself," he said.

"You want me to teach you? Is that what you're asking?"

Markson explained that he wasn't looking for anything like formal lessons—just the opportunity to look over her shoulder as she translated things for him. He suggested that she might print out something easy in Russian for him to try on his own in order for her to check his progress. She seemed to take the request at face value because their relationship did not change as a result of her questions.

The next time she left her desk, there was an observer, but Markson didn't let the moment go to waste. He timed her.

She was out of his sight, and he out of hers, for less than three minutes. That wasn't going to be enough time.

He couldn't help it that their mutual admiration was becoming genuine mutual friendship. They shared a deep disrespect for government bureaucracy and a love for the science. Once, she told Markson, "Physics isn't my job. It is my hope and my art." He began making tea for the two of them when they were working together. Sometimes, he would bring some kind of sweet treat, or she would bring a Russian dessert concoction he wasn't acquainted with.

Eventually, she couldn't resist showing off how she'd found a way into the Russian defense-information network. She could send requests for data by spoofing the accounts of scientists or military officers with the necessary clearances. When the recipient attached data or provided a link in a message and clicked "reply," the message appeared to go to the spoofed source in Russia. It actually wound up in a special account on Ivanova's workstation.

"Of course," she said, "this is all being done in Russian and you're not proficient enough to follow it exactly, but I think it's cool!"

"I think it's damned clever, even if I can't read most of it yet." His Russian was getting better faster than he let on, but he didn't need to telegraph the fact.

When he put all of the pieces together, he saw a way to get a message out. If he could have access to her console for about five minutes—unobserved—he could use her special account and spoofing software to send a message to Catalano through an account outside the DARPA firewall. The DARPA security software wouldn't see it because Ivanova had designed her malware to disguise the traffic as sensor data so that Russian security wouldn't catch it. He selected Catalano rather than Clarke because more than half a year had passed, and he was still not free. Catalano, a retired colonel, had connections inside the DOD which might enable him to be more effective.

The challenge, of course, was how to arrange being alone and unobserved for at least five minutes at Ivanova's workstation.

∞

A target of opportunity appeared when the one person within view of Ivanova's workplace took their annual leave the week before Christmas. Markson wasn't going to wait any longer. He'd already been captive for more than six months, so he decided to take a big risk. If he got caught, he'd lose all of the trust he had built with Nilson and forfeit Irina as a friend. Several weeks earlier, in preparation for carrying out this part of his plan, he'd purchased a fast-acting laxative at the PX. He'd selected a cashier who he'd doubted knew him and paid cash. The first irrevocable step toward getting the five minutes he needed with Ivanova away from her computer would be to put the laxative into the tea he brought them when they worked together. He would treat both cups the same. The reaction had to be the same for both of them or she and security would suspect something immediately.

This turned out to be more wrenching than he'd expected. He was genuinely fond of Ivanova. He enjoyed her enthusiasm and her brilliance, as well as her sense of humor. He liked the way she bent the rules in order to do what made sense so that she could complete a task. Despite her relative antiquity compared to his youth, he also found her attractive. She laughed a lot and peppered her conversations with large, sweeping gestures. Her clothing was always neat and professional, yet loose and comfortable. She refused to get bifocals and had the habit of turning her rimless, wire-framed glasses up onto the top of her head to get them out of the way when she wanted to see something at less than arm's length.

They had grown close enough to begin sharing a number of office rituals—like their morning tea. As he put the laxative into the cups, he knew it was necessary if he was going to obtain his freedom, but he couldn't escape the disconcerting feeling that it was an act of betrayal.

Several hours later, though, he wondered when she would start feeling its effect. He was feeling it already. He had to hope he could hold out until she went to the restroom. He was beginning to worry, but she finally got up and rushed around the corner.

He took her seat and brought up the Cyrillic keyboard, and then he logged into her special account. *Thirty seconds.*

He activated the spoofing package, found the target account, and was able to log into that successfully after remembering to switch back to the English keyboard on the second try. *Another seventy-five seconds.*

He opened the mail program and created a new message addressed to Henry Catalano. *Thirty seconds more.*

A minute later, he'd finished typing the body of the message and signed it.

He clicked "Send" and began erasing his tracks by logging out. *Fifteen seconds.*

It took about three quarters of a minute to cleanly shut down the spoofing software and log out of her special account, and a final thirty seconds to erase all remaining traces of what he'd done.

Fifteen seconds under five minutes. He'd figured it right— she hadn't returned yet.

Now, he needed her back fast or he was going to have a more embarrassing laundry problem than the small one he'd planned. He hurried to the restroom and knocked.

"In a minute," she said.

"I need to get in there now," he said, a bit louder than usual.

She came out two minutes later.

"Excuse me," he said, brushing her shoulder as he pushed past her. The delay had been perfect for his credibility, but it would take work to salvage his briefs and trousers. He decided to make the best of it.

He stopped by her desk as soon as he left the bathroom. "I'm sorry I was so rude back there. I really had to go bad. I hope you don't mind if I take a quick break. I need to take care of something back at my apartment."

Ivanova looked up and broke out laughing. "Didn't quite make it?"

Markson tried to look as embarrassed as possible. Although he couldn't see the back of them, he thought the light-colored cotton trousers he'd worn that morning must be presenting a convincing picture. "I'm afraid the damage may be serious and I need to repair it. I think there was something wrong with our tea this morning. I'm going now."

"Again?" she teased.

He couldn't suppress a wry smile. "Not that way," he said.

While Markson took a shower and washed his pants, Henry Catalano was in his office opening what appeared to be an email from the New York Air National Guard. When he opened the message, though, the text claimed a different origin. Much to his astonishment, the message purported to be a distress call from Lee Markson.

Catalano didn't know quite what to do. If the message was legitimate, the last thing he'd want to do was alert the DOD that Markson had gotten a message to him. On the other hand, if it was a hoax, then the DOD needed to be made aware that one of their accounts had been hacked. Some investigation was in order before he decided on a course of action.

He hadn't kept current on the warpship controversy. Although he enjoyed following Huntsman and Markson's careers as friends and former employees, he wasn't deeply into the science unless he could make money with it. Still, a few hours on the internet led him to suspect the message was genuine.

He noticed that Markson had stopped responding to the avalanche of attacks on his work, his integrity, and his sanity. Just as intriguing, he'd stopped responding to attacks on Katty Clarke, who Catalano suspected had a closer relationship with Markson than that of mere co-author. Markson wasn't the docile type. He was highly vocal and had now gone suddenly silent. Not a good sign.

Catalano's suspicion turned to certainty when he ran across a rant by Clarke on the internet, charging that the DOD has done something to Markson. She described bribery and black-mail attempts which she claimed they'd been subjected to at a classified meeting at LAPI.

If this is true, she's risking jail time by revealing classified information. Either way, she's concerned enough to take chances, Catalano thought.

He read her post closely, looking for details. She named names. One of them leaped out. *Colonel Nilson. Same name and rank as the guy the message says is holding Markson.*

Catalano figured that whoever had sent the message knew about that meeting and had access to restricted DOD mail servers. It was either Markson or a highly professional, state-sponsored intruder. *There is no reason such an intruder would send this message to the CEO of an investment firm like me*, he thought. *The only thing that makes sense is that it came from Lee.* His next step was to decide what to do about it.

He needed to get the message to someone who would act vigorously, but who wouldn't hand him up if caught. Although past the normal retirement age, he was still a colonel in the Air Force Reserve who could be called to active duty and court-martialed. He picked up the phone to call his close friend and confidant, Ken Huntsman, but hung up before he completed dialing. His personal ties to the NASA associate administrator would make both of them obvious targets for criminal investigations relating to the unauthorized disclosure of secure DOD communications.

"This is a challenge," he said aloud to himself. "If I trust someone enough to tell them about this and trust that they'll care enough to carry through on it, they're bound to be close enough to me to make me a target if anything goes wrong—even if they hold their tongue."

He looked around the room, reread the message and the internet posts, and contemplated his options until an inspiration materialized. A few minutes' reflection had been sufficient. He copied the message to a file that he edited to delete who had received it and where it had originated. He then copied the redacted file to an empty thumb drive and called in his Chief Information Officer.

"Suppose, hypothetically," he began, "I had a file I wanted to send to someone, but I wanted to be sure that it couldn't be traced back to me. Not even by the NSA. Could that be done?"

"May I ask what's in the file?"

"No."

"It may make a difference. Is it text? Pictures? Was it done on a word processor?"

"That matters?"

"Pictures and word processor files contain metadata that could be traceable."

"Assume it's just text from an email."

The CIO thought for a minute. "The surest and easiest way would be to print it on a public printer and send them the hard copy anonymously. You'd have to wear gloves to avoid leaving fingerprints."

"Could I scan the printout to a CD and have a courier deliver the CD anonymously?"

"Use a public scanner that burns CDs, but if they trace it back to that scanner, they might find you because you'll have to pay for the service somehow. The courier is another weak link."

Catalano smiled. "Thank you. You've given me exactly what I needed to know."

That evening, Catalano printed the edited file and went to an Office Depot in a part of town that was far removed from his own wealthy neighborhood. He told the floor salesman he was interested in buying a scanner system to make CDs for his church. "We don't really have much money, and we need something easy to use. I'm sort of computer illiterate."

"I have just the thing," the salesman said. He showed Catalano several pieces of equipment.

"Can you demonstrate it?"

The salesman connected the floor model computer and scanner together, and scanned one of their advertising brochures. Catalano nodded his approval. "Sure looks simple. Can I try to make a CD? I'd like to see if I can do it myself."

The salesman was reluctant. Catalano insisted, but promised to pay full-price for the demonstrator equipment and a box of blank CDs if he succeeded. In a minute or two, he had the disk he wanted.

"Sold," he told the salesman.

"Would you like our extended warranty?"

"I won't be needing that," Catalano said as he paid the astonished salesman $575.49 for the equipment in cash.

The manager at the Goodwill donation center was delighted to have what looked like an almost new scanner show up overnight. It had no packaging material, but the manuals were there. It might bring fifty or sixty dollars.

The local street gang a few blocks away was pleased to find the abandoned computer which they could sell. They weren't pleased when the pawn shop told them that the hard drive had been removed and it was worthless.

The waste management driver never noticed as the refuse truck's compactor crushed a carefully discarded hard drive.

The CD had cost Catalano almost $600. It was worth every penny, he thought as his gloved hands slipped it into the prepaid shipping sleeve. The return address was blank. The first line of the "ship to" address said "Dr. Katty Clarke."

CHAPTER TEN

THE POLITICIAN

WHEN MARKSON FAILED TO SHOW UP for work at FASTER the day after he was arrested, Clarke left a voicemail and an email for him. That afternoon, news reports said he'd been arrested on felony charges of assaulting a federal officer but had then been released, so two days later when Clarke had still received no responses, she contacted the local missing persons bureau, who took a report but didn't appear concerned.

When a "For Rent" sign appeared on his lawn two weeks after that, she looked up the real estate company's website and noticed that the only contact information on their website was the same phone number that appeared on the sign in Markson's yard. She called them, but they refused to provide any information about the identity or whereabouts of the property owner—whom she knew to be Markson, but whom they claimed wished to remain anonymous. They also refused to provide any information about who owned their company.

Based on Nilson's threats during the meeting at LAPI, she suspected the Air Force of foul play and immediately filed a *Freedom of Information Act* request. In just a week, faster than light speed by bureaucratic standards, their response denied any information regarding the person of Lee Markson, whom they said did not appear in any database of DOD personnel, either civilian or military. She got a similar response shortly thereafter from the Department of Justice, which insisted that a federal court had released Markson although they provided no details.

Exhausted by months of fruitless pleading and scolding on social media, she was nearly ready to give up. His disappearance had become old news, explained away by hundreds of posts and even a few reputable media stories speculating that he'd fled the country in order to avoid trial on the charges he was facing. Many of the internet posts were from self-styled "patriotic" fringe groups convinced that Markson's warship proposal was part of a conspiracy to cover up Chinese or Russian nuclear weapons in space.

The message on the mysterious CD re-energized her. It was short, but there was enough that she felt confident from its style and content that it wasn't a hoax. Suddenly, she had a weapon.

"Now, what the fuck do I do with it?" she asked aloud as she stood in her FASTER office with the disk in her hand. She sighed, took a deep breath, and sat down at her desk to begin to make some notes:

Social media has been ineffective so far.

When the DOD finds out about this message, they'll take action. Whatever they do, it won't be good for me. I need to delay that as long as possible.

FASTER is probably under surveillance.

I need help from someone I can trust who has inside government contacts.

I'll need to take some risks.

She decided to continue working on this from home just in case FASTER was being bugged. She didn't believe the government would really go that far, but felt better being sure. The more difficult decision had to do with involving people who had the resources she needed, but whom she hadn't approached before because they'd discouraged Markson from pursuing attempts to get the DOD data or challenging DARPA in any way. She wasn't sure they'd be interested, and also wasn't completely confident that they wouldn't inform the DOD about the message, but they were her only realistic remaining option. With her notes in hand and her plan in mind, she headed home.

At her apartment, Katty Clarke typed "Catalano Automated Trading" into DuckDuckGo and clicked on one of the returned links. This was personal, and she wanted it kept separate from FASTER in case it attracted the wrong kind of attention. From the CAT homepage, she clicked on "Contact Us." The message she posted said:

> *"I need to reach Mr. Catalano regarding the whereabouts of Dr. Lee Markson. The matter is urgent."*

At the bottom of the message, she left her full name, her cell phone number, and her email address. The automated system acknowledged receipt of her message.

When two days had passed with no response, she invested several hours online and was rewarded with Henry Catalano's private office phone number. She called it. His secretary said he wasn't available—each of the fourteen times she called.

The fifteenth time, she tried an experiment. *Perhaps he works late*, she thought. *Later than his secretary*. She called the number shortly after 7 PM.

"Catalano," the voice on the line said.

"Katty Clarke here," she said. "Lee Markson's been kidnapped by the government, and I think you can help set him free."

Catalano hadn't expected her to track *him* down after she got his package. That complicated things. He was too vulnerable and had to stay completely out of it. He couldn't risk letting on that he knew anything about the message from Markson.

"Ms. Clarke, is it? What makes you think Lee has been taken by the government?"

"It's Dr. Clarke, but call me Katty. From an anonymous source, I received a message from Lee that said he was being held by DARPA. He said they had arrested him in order to force him to work on one of their research projects. I checked. Anything like that would be highly illegal."

"Assuming you can trust your anonymous source, what do you think I could do about it, Dr. Clarke?"

"You have contacts at the Department of Defense. You owe Lee. He made a fortune for you. Just poke around. Find out where they're keeping him and who's in charge. Anything I can use to spring him."

Catalano had to be careful. How could he put her off without discouraging her from pursuing the matter aggressively?

He scoffed. "You have no idea. In the first place, most everything DARPA does is classified. 'Poking around' classified installations and documents could get me court-martialed with long-term housing in a federal prison. Second, I don't owe Lee anything. Yes, I made a bundle from his work, but he was fully and completely compensated for that work—for which I, by the way, paid at considerable risk because the work was highly speculative."

"So, you're just going to let him die in captivity?" she demanded.

He could hear her anger as she shouted into the phone, her voice cracking. He couldn't blame her, but he dared not let her know that. He forced a calm, neutral tone.

"If the government wanted him badly enough to go to all the trouble of illegally taking him into custody to work on a secret project, they're going to take good care of him. He's a valuable asset. He won't be dying anytime soon unless he tries to escape. Your intention to 'spring him' could be the thing that gets him killed."

That thought hadn't occurred to Clarke.

"Anything else?" Catalano asked.

"You're not going to help, are you," she said. It wasn't a question.

"I'm not going to mess around with DARPA—no, ma'am."

"Thank you for your time." She slammed the handset into the cradle. "Arsehole."

She did not expect to find plan B to be as easy as it turned out to be. Plan B was contacting Lee's mentor at CAT, Kenneth Huntsman, who was now an associate administrator at NASA. His phone number and email address were listed in the public directory of senior NASA officials. She left a message on his voicemail and sent a similar message to his email:

"I need to speak with you regarding Lee Markson. The matter is urgent."

Huntsman saw the messages when he returned from Christmas leave. He was intrigued, but decided to return her call from home. It was unlikely to be official business, and he didn't want the conversation to become subject to the *Public Records Act*. He was aware of the controversy over their paper, and wasn't sure what she might be trying to get him into. He wasn't even sure his new correspondent was actually Katty Clarke. He'd approach this with caution.

He called early that evening and asked what he could do for her. She told him about the secret message.

"I called Henry Catalano," she continued, "but the bastard blew me off like it was nothing. Didn't give a shit that the guy who made a fortune for him has been kidnapped or worse. You're Lee's last hope, Dr. Huntsman. If you don't care enough to help, who will?"

"What could I do that you can't do yourself? Have you called the FBI? They handle kidnappings."

"You don't get it!" she shouted. "None of you get it! It's the damned *government* that's taken him! The FBI is on their team, not his!"

"Do you have any proof?"

She filled him in on what had happened before the kidnapping and told him about the recent message. Huntsman had been following the saga online and immediately understood the significance of what she claimed had happened... if it was true. But he needed time to verify her identity, assess her credibility, and plan a course of action.

He told her the problem was that, unlike Catalano, he had no access to the inner workings of the DOD, and certainly not to the clandestine world of DARPA. What he knew about the AFOSR was limited to a few unclassified projects that overlapped the NASA mission.

"I don't see how I can help. If I think of anything, I'll call you back."

Before doing anything else, Huntsman called Henry Catalano. Clarke's description of Catalano's response to her inquiry didn't sound like the man he knew. Surely, Catalano would want to assist, and he did have an inside line to the DOD.

"Ken, I can't get involved. I and anyone I've been talking with about it will be the first targets of the DOD investigation into who might have been involved in assisting him if you do get him out. That won't do anyone any good. I hope you and Dr. Clarke can spring him, but the farther you two stay from me, the better. Good luck!" was what his former boss told him.

Clarke was delighted when Huntsman called again two days later. She hadn't really expected him to get involved. His expressed intent to call her back after he'd time to think had struck her as more of a bureaucratic brush-off than a serious commitment.

"Dr. Clarke, I reviewed your papers in detail and followed the discussions on *First Look Physics*, *arXiv*, and social media, looking more closely than I did before. I think you and Lee are right, just like Lee was when he published his thesis. We made a fortune off of that, and I wouldn't bet against him again. I'd like to help, but we need to keep this between us, and under no circumstances should you contact me at my office."

Huntsman declined her request for him to try to get information about Markson's whereabouts through the DOD. "I don't have any useful connection with the Defense Department," he told her. "I have another idea, however. I can't make any commitment and I don't want to discuss it on the phone. Can you come to Washington tomorrow?"

She told Huntsman that, since she was all that was holding FASTER together, it would be difficult, and she was reluctant to accept his paying her way. He also didn't want to pay her fare, but not because of the expense, which he could readily afford.

"As soon as your name is connected with my credit card and an airline ticket," he pointed out, "snoops in the government might connect some dots we'd rather keep separated. Perhaps I can come down there. Is your schedule free tomorrow?"

"I'll make it free. Thank you."

"Good. Let me check my schedule and see if I can make some arrangements. I'll get back to you in a few minutes."

While she waited, she wondered. She wasn't used to government officials being so responsive. *Maybe there's nothing wrong with them as people. Maybe it's just the job,* she thought. Did he have some kind of ulterior motive? Something personal?

When Huntsman called back with his proposal, he had her full attention.

"Dr. Clarke? Ken Huntsman here. I'm going to make you the same offer I made Lee ten years ago. I'll fly down tomorrow and take you to lunch at Mansurs. No corporate jet this time, though, so I won't be in until after noon. Could you meet me there around 1 PM?"

"Wow, thanks! I know where it is. Lee took me there. It's the best."

When she arrived at the restaurant, the maître d' was expecting her. He directed her to a discreet, out-of-the-way table in a dining room that had no windows. It was rarely used in the daytime because customers preferred the ambiance of at least some natural lighting. There sat a tall, athletic-looking man with loosely combed sandy brown hair who was reading something from his phone. She liked what she saw and smiled. He looked up and immediately smiled back.

The man stood as she approached. "Dr. Clarke?" he asked.

"Dr. Huntsman, I presume? Call me Katty," she responded.

He extended his hand. "I'm Ken. I'm pleased to meet you, Katty. Please join me."

From the large size and the décor of the room, she assumed this was tailored for group meetings. The vacant mini bar near the door reinforced her impression.

The NASA associate administrator was not what she'd expected. Despite the suit, he didn't look like a bureaucrat. He had the complexion of someone who spent a lot of time outdoors.

His voice was husky and slightly deeper than average. He spoke rapidly and clearly—more like a celebrity newscaster than a boring Washington executive. She was glad she'd worn her conservative white blouse and full-length black wool skirt. She wouldn't look out of place sitting with him in a high-class place like Mansurs.

As soon as they were in their chairs, a waiter in a long-sleeved, white dress shirt, black tie, and black chest-to-knees apron appeared with menus. Huntsman ordered iced tea. She ordered her tea hot. The waiter said he would return shortly and left them to select their meals.

Clarke looked around again, noting the dark gray carpet. The only thing brightening the room besides the lanterns were the tangerine tablecloths and matching napkins. "Don't take this the wrong way, but I sense we're sitting in the dark on purpose."

He nodded. "Actually, the important thing is to be alone. This time of day, the only place in the restaurant unlikely to have someone sitting at the next table is in this room. This has to remain strictly between the two of us, Katty. Unless I can rely on you to keep it that way at least for now, we don't have anything to talk about."

Huntsman thought she looked startled. She hesitated and stuttered, "S-sure. Sure."

"You sound uncertain. Are you really sure?"

"I'm sure. You just caught me by surprise. I had to think about it for a second. We did just meet, you know," she said in her normal voice and cadence.

"Good! I like that."

They turned their attention to the menus.

Huntsman smiled as he remembered his first lunch with Lee Markson at Mansurs. "You know, the day I met Lee for the first time, I brought him here. I'd never been here before, and the waiter recommended the cedar-roasted redfish. It was delicious. I think I'll have that again."

Clarke laughed. "What did Lee have?"

"Steak."

"It figures. I like to avoid red meat, but in honor of the occasion, I'll have the same cut he usually orders when we come here. Your meeting with him seems to have turned out well. I hope this one with me does, too."

Huntsman was still grinning when the waiter returned. They placed their orders and waited until they were alone before Huntsman revealed what he was considering. "When I was up on the hill as a NASA Congressional Fellow, I got to know a few congressmen quite well. These are people whose districts have NASA facilities or aerospace companies with connections to military or civilian space programs. As an associate administrator at NASA, I've had the opportunity to strengthen most of those relationships, and we're talking about folks who've been there long enough to have clout. Do you see any downside to my making a few discrete inquiries?"

"God, Ken. I thought angels had wings. The Air Force could crush me like a bug if they have a mind to, but Congress has muscle," she said.

"Don't get your hopes up, Katty. I need to feel my way around a bit and see who I can approach with the full story. If I spill the beans to the wrong person, we could be in deep shit. It might even make them push Lee further inside the black ops inner sanctum."

"Black ops?"

"The super-secret stuff they do that's off-budget and sometimes in violation of U.S. or international law."

"You're scaring me."

"You ought to be scared. I'm surprised they haven't gone after FASTER and your immigration status."

Clarke startled, and she stared at Huntsman wide-eyed and open-mouthed. She'd been so worried about Lee that she hadn't considered the possibility that threats to her person still existed. "Isn't my green card supposed to be permanent?" she asked.

"Things aren't always what they're supposed to be when you're dealing with national security, but if they haven't bothered you yet, you're probably OK for now."

She threw her hands up in the air. "Now, I'm more worried than ever. Why did you mention it if I'm OK for now?"

"I'm just letting you know why I'm planning to do this slowly and with great caution. If the right person is available, this could work—but it has to be the right person, and I can't even be sure such a person exists among my congressional contacts. If not, I'm going to make sure I don't make things worse. That's what I'm getting at."

Clarke took a deep breath in through her nose and exhaled through her lips.

"You do yoga?"

Clarke made a face. "What? How'd you know?"

"The deep breath exhaled through the mouth. They teach that in yoga and meditation classes. It can be very relaxing."

"So they say, but I don't think it works very well. I'm not very relaxed. Now, I understand why you wanted to keep this meeting secret."

Huntsman reached over and put his hand on hers. "It's OK. We're going to get Lee back. You're not alone in this anymore."

He spent most of the rest of the afternoon with her at her home in the Northgate Apartments about a mile and a half north of her former office at LAPI. It brought back memories. He had sold Lee Markson on joining CAT to build CATSPAW in a similar apartment in the same building. Markson had kept his place remarkably neat for a male postdoc. It amused him to find that Markson's partner in this adventure was as idiosyncratic as Markson was. She'd left her place cluttered and somewhat disorganized even when it must have seemed likely that a high-ranking out-of-town visitor might be her guest.

Huntsman wanted to get as much detail from her as he could and make copies of any documents that he thought might help him make their case on Capitol Hill. They sat down side by side at the coffee table, which she cleared by tossing the piles of magazines and reprints over onto the sofa.

She went to her bedroom and came back with a single, large folder. "Everything I have that has anything to do with this is here."

Instead of looking at the folder immediately, he stared at the two-foot by three-foot, high-definition color photograph on the wall opposite the sofa. The background check he'd done on her after her initial contact with his office had turned up one challenge to her credibility that he'd have to be prepared to address if asked about it.

"Not everything, Katty," Huntsman said as he pointed at the expensively framed portrait of her dancing nude in a nightclub. "I hope you'll understand why I have to ask this, but I will need to be able to deal with it if it comes up—"

She completed his thought. "You're talking about public nudity."

"Yeah. That won't play well with American politicians. They may be total hypocrites, but they're all prudish as hell in public. I need to know at least two things—was any of it illegal, even the slightest bit, and are you still doing it?"

"No and no, Ken. I danced for the joy of it, audiences loved it, and it paid some bills. It was not only completely legal, but culturally accepted in the countries where I performed. That said, except for a children's charity fundraiser in England that the government folks were trying to blackmail us over, I haven't performed since I left Virgo. That's why I love that picture. It's from a show I was invited to give at the finest club in France. It was my best performance as an entertainer."

"So, it's not something you want to do again in the fore-seeable future."

She scoffed. "What I want to do again is dance for Lee in the privacy of our home. Would that be too much to ask?"

"Let me see what I can do to make that happen," Huntsman said.

As soon as he got back to Washington, Huntsman found reasons to go to the Capitol on NASA business. He arrived early and left late. He spent breakfast, lunch, and dinner with members of Congress whom he knew well and considered friends. One at a time, or in twos or threes. Recalling good times and discussing space research policy unofficially so that they could let their hair down. No cameras. No spin.

It took over a month before he'd satisfied himself that the person he thought most desirable could be trusted and might be convinced to help. The man was ideal for the task. As an undergraduate, he had majored in physics with a minor in economics, and then he'd earned post-graduate degrees in law, finance, and international relations. He was smart enough to understand quickly what Huntsman had to say. Moreover, he chaired the House Committee on Science, Space and Technology. At hearings where Huntsman had been present as a NASA associate administrator, the chairman had mentioned how big a fan he was of science fiction and spaceflight. It was the perfect committee and the right mindset.

From his personal landline at home, Huntsman placed a call to the office of the Honorable Alberto Reyes, a congressman from the great state of Texas. "Hi, Al. It's Ken. Can we meet somewhere to talk?"

∞

Huntsman was a big fan of business lunches. They gave him a chance to get out of the office without disrupting his time for relaxing at home in the evening. Congressman Reyes' family had decided not to relocate from Texas to DC. He was often too busy to take time off for lunch and preferred a leisurely late meal at a quality restaurant to a long evening alone at his apartment on 8th Street. They compromised and did it the congressman's way.

At Erika's, reservations were mandatory. Upon entering, diners followed a red carpet leading past the coatroom that was staffed in heavy weather to relieve patrons of wet outer clothing and umbrellas, and over to a dark, reddish-brown lectern. At the lectern, a maître d' wearing a tuxedo verified the reservation and then led diners to their particular seats.

Huntsman reserved a small, well-lit table where they weren't likely to be overheard, but would be visible enough to avoid the impression that they were meeting in secret.

Reyes arrived ten minutes after Huntsman. He was a heavy-set man several inches shorter than Huntsman with short, curly black hair and a ruddy complexion that was partly concealed under a large and bushy black mustache. His goatee contrasted with the rest of his facial hair because it was more gray than black. Although he wore a jacket, it was only because the restaurant required it. Beneath the jacket, his shirt collar was unbuttoned, held in place only by a loose string tie.

The red and brown theme at the entrance also dominated the interior of the restaurant. The carpet was dark brown, the curtains dark red, and the ceiling patterned in medium brown and dark red geometrical patterns. Despite the dark colors, the room was well-lit by the chandeliers and the reflectivity of the flesh-colored walls adorned with brightly colored oil paintings in dark, reddish-brown frames.

Reyes nodded his approval of the arrangements as he took his seat. Immediately, a waiter approached with a wine list, a beverage list, and their menus, which were all bound in real leather—reddish-brown, of course.

"Separate checks, please," Reyes said.

The waiter, who appeared to be in his late 50s or early 60s, asked what they would like to drink. Huntsman ordered decaf while Reyes asked for a craft beer. Huntsman asked the waiter if they could order immediately so that they wouldn't be disturbed later.

"Certainly, sir."

The waiter recited the evening's specials and then stood silently while they studied the choices and made their selections. The two men waited until he left before commencing their conversation.

Noting that Huntsman also had an open collar and had loosened his tie, Reyes said, "I gather that this is not official business." His voice rose at the end as if asking a question.

"Not yet. I'm hoping you'll help me make it official business."

Reyes raised his dark, bushy eyebrows. "Is this your agenda or the agency's?"

Huntsman breathed in before speaking. "I have a long-time friend and colleague who I have reason to believe was shanghaied by the DOD, probably the Air Force, and put to work for DARPA against his will—"

Reyes arched his back slightly and interjected, "Why?"

Huntsman put his hands on the table, leaned forward, and lowered his voice even though nobody was within earshot. "His research at LAPI had serious national security implications. The DOD instigated a series of attacks on his work to discredit it. When the social media discussions of his papers continued to generate expanding public discussions, he disappeared just after he and his co-author rejected bribes and threats intended to get them to withdraw their papers and secretly continue the same research for DARPA."

Huntsman sat back, cocked his head to the side slightly, and waited for the reaction. It took a few seconds.

When Reyes spoke, he wasn't smiling. "That's a serious damned charge, Ken. If you want me to wade in, you'd better have the evidence to back it up. What's this about? It's not that alien spaceship thing, is it?"

Huntsman raised his eyebrows and crossed his arms. "That's exactly what it is."

"Hey, look, I'm as big a fan of science fiction as anyone. 'Warp factor five, Mr. Scott,' and all that, but most of the experts say it's impossible. What do you think you know that the rest of the world doesn't?"

Huntsman explained in layman's terms how Miguel Alcubierre had discovered a solution to the Einstein field equations that allowed for faster-than-light travel. He reminded Reyes that Lee Markson had gained notoriety and become quite wealthy by adapting those equations to build a practical time-reversal device which Catalano Automated Trading had used to invest in the stock market until Congress had shut it down.

Reyes grinned. "I remember that. The SEC was fit to be tied when the former AG said there was no law against using a time machine for investments. The press was all over us to fix the loophole. I never saw the House act so fast, and the Senate passed our bill by acclimation in an hour. That was about how long it took thereafter to get the President's signature on it. So, this spaceship guy is the same one you hired at CAT to develop CATSPAW?"

Huntsman smiled and nodded for emphasis. "Yep." Then, he sat back and raised his right pointer finger in the air like a living exclamation point. "I got the idea for CATSPAW when I saw his time-reversal paper in *arXiv*. Only a few people were taking it seriously, but he was right, and the few of us with the vision to see that made a fortune."

Reyes was quiet for a moment, but then he frowned and said, "I've been following that matter on the internet. Didn't he get arrested and flee the country?"

"I don't think he fled the country at all. I think the Department of Defense has him."

Reyes looked skeptical. "What makes you think that?"

Huntsman leaned forward again, this time pointing his finger directly at the congressman. "I think he's right about the faster-than-light idea. I also think the DOD knows he's right. I think they wanted to silence him in public while hoping he could build them some sort of practical warp-technology device."

Reyes exhaled audibly, sat up, and pushed back from the table a bit. "Well, that's a hell of a story. Do you have anything to support it?"

Huntsman reviewed the evidence presented in Markson and Clarke's papers, and added his own impressions of the ensuing online debates and journal rebuttals. He gave Reyes a copy of the anonymous communication that appeared to be from Markson and explained why it was credible.

The congressman was a quick-study. He grilled Huntsman about the objections to the physics and the allegations that, even if the physics was correct, the construction or use of such a vehicle would not be feasible. Fortunately, Clarke had thoroughly briefed Huntsman. And as a physicist himself who'd managed cutting edge R&D projects for NASA, Huntsman had, with some effort, developed an adequate understanding of each of these issues. He had little trouble responding to questions about them in language that Reyes could follow.

After several hours, the congressman was convinced that the Markson-Clarke papers were sound, and that the DOD probably had Markson in custody. "It's too bad there's no *direct* connection to the DOD, though. It's all circumstantial," he said.

"Ah, but there is! I didn't get to that. Dr. Clarke found out that Markson's house in Baton Rouge is being rented out by a real estate company that keeps its ownership and clients secret. I had a PI check on Markson's finances. The real estate company is paying all of his insurance, taxes, and utility payments related to the property. He has no outstanding loans and there have been no charges on any of his credit cards since he disappeared, except for ongoing subscriptions—and all those bills are being paid by a corporation that seems to have no business purpose, but is reported to be a cover for military and CIA money-laundering operations designed to cover black ops. Turns out that the mystery company is the owner of the real estate company."

"No shit!"

"Yep."

"Well, that ices it—but why didn't they take Clarke?"

Huntsman opened his arms, palms facing Reyes as if to say, *"Isn't it obvious?"*, but he didn't say that. Instead, he said, "She's a British national. That could risk engaging the British government." When Reyes didn't act like that was sufficient, he added, "Also, her background is more in data analysis and cosmology, whereas what they need is engineering physics, and that's Markson's strong point. From their point of view, she's probably more trouble than she's worth. Instead, they've just tried to discredit and marginalize her."

Reyes nodded again. "You started out by saying you want to make this official business. What do you have in mind?"

Huntsman leaned forward. "NASA should be jumping all over this. We've spent billions looking for signs of extraterrestrial life. We've spent hundreds of millions on numerous programs directed at exploring advanced propulsion systems. We even ran small laboratory experiments with the Alcubierre metric at Johnson Space Center, although nothing came of them. Now, along comes evidence that ET exists and has an Alcubierre warpship, and suddenly the agency goes silent? Damn, Al, I sure wish my congressman would look into that. And if the DOD is deliberately discrediting scientists who they don't like, and kidnapping others who they need, doesn't the Congress have some oversight responsibility regarding possible violations of the law?"

"You want me to open hearings?"

Huntsman nodded rapidly. "I think it's the only way anyone's going to get the DOD's attention. Nobody else has the clout."

The congressman picked up his napkin and wiped his mouth. "Let me talk to the members of the Committee on Science, Space and Technology. As chairman, I think it's the right venue. If the members are alright with it, I'm inclined to give it a go."

"Thank you," Huntsman said as they stood to leave.

Reyes extended his hand. "Thank you for the information. I think I can put it to good use."

CHAPTER ELEVEN

THE CONGRESS

THE NEXT DAY, Reyes called the committee's ranking member, James Diggs of Ohio. He opened the conversation with, "I've just heard the damnedest thing I've heard in years. Come on over to my office. I want to tell you about it. I think you'll find it interesting."

When the ranking member arrived, Reyes greeted him with a handshake and a glass of Kentucky bourbon before he led him to a comfortable, white leather easy chair by the bookshelves that constituted the wall to the left of his desk. Reyes took the bigger, dark brown upholstered chair that would have faced the adjacent side of a small square table in front of them, had there been a table there, but there wasn't—just a comfortable place to extend their feet while they talked. Nothing in the space between them. No documents to review. This needed to be as much a friendly, social occasion as a business meeting.

In many ways, the two men were as different as two people could be. Reyes wore his light blue, button-down shirt with the collar unbuttoned and the neck open, secured only by a string tie with an ornamental clasp made of Central American silver and carved turquoise. Even on the floor of the House of Representatives, he often dressed this way. Diggs wore a brown suede business suit with a matching shirt and tie. This was as informal as he ever got.

Reyes told Diggs what Huntsman had said and asked the former criminal prosecutor what he thought. Diggs didn't hesitate.

"Those are some serious charges. Are you considering holding a hearing?"

"Well, either the charges are false and Huntsman should pay a price for farting around with us, or they're true, and the DOD should pay a price for doing an end-run around the Constitution. Either way, a hearing or series of hearings should settle the matter."

It took Reyes about twenty minutes to convince the ranking member that at least one hearing should be called, and another hour and two refills on the whiskey for the man to support opening a full, bi-partisan investigation.

Twenty-six days later, the chairman's staff had gathered the necessary documents and prepared a proposed witness list for planning purposes.

In closed-door sessions with the full committee over the next two months, the members agreed to subpoena Huntsman. From his testimony, they'd decide whether or not further proceedings were necessary. If the investigation continued, then the witness list and agenda could be informed by Huntsman's testimony.

Representative Serrano wanted to close the first hearing to the public because she was concerned it might cause wild speculation and possible public hysteria. "In Florida, we already have a bunch of space nuts picketing the Kennedy Space Center. If it looks like we're taking them seriously, their number will probably triple, and that could begin to interfere with operations there and at the Cape."

"My experience has been that covering things up only makes them worse. I understand your concern, but I don't think conducting secret hearings will help," the chairman responded.

She looked anxious. "Is there any way we can keep this off the front page?"

"That, we can do. I'll schedule Huntsman after the mid-morning break on a day when we usually hold administrative status briefings. It'll look like a routine review of NASA projects in his directorate."

"I hope that's sufficient," she said.

The chairman set a date and the committee issued a subpoena from the House of Representatives to Dr. Kenneth Huntsman,

Associate Administrator of the Science Mission Directorate of the National Aeronautics and Space Administration.

Following standard procedure, the summons was served on Huntsman through the NASA General Counsel's Office. The general counsel assigned a senior attorney, Elaine Hansen, to assist Huntsman with his testimony. Hansen was a tall, attractive brunette with more than twenty years' experience in the executive branch on Capitol Hill.

"Do you have any idea what this is about?" she asked Huntsman.

"Could be any number of things. Did the subpoena ask me to bring any documents? That might give us a clue."

"Nothing. It is rather unusual for a summons not to specify the subject matter. They usually want you to be prepared. Is there any possibility it's a criminal investigation?"

"No! What, are you worried I've committed a crime?"

"No, but this is unusual. Perhaps someone on your staff may be under investigation?"

"I don't think so."

"I'll contact the committee counsel. Perhaps she can tell me something."

Several hours later, Hansen called Huntsman. "The committee counsel says it's about some NASA satellite data relating to gravitational waves. Does that mean anything to you?"

"Yeah. It's a physics thing. Somebody influential probably wants to know why we aren't funding their pet project. I can handle it."

"OK, good, because it's Greek to me. I was a poli-sci major. As usual, though, I'll be sitting right beside you at the hearing in case you need any legal guidance on NASA policy and procedures."

∞

A slight echo sounded when Chairman Reyes banged the gavel as the members of the committee took their seats and staff members finished putting their briefing packages in front of them. "The House Committee on Science, Space and Technology will come to order."

For this meeting, Reyes had chosen one of the smaller hearing rooms in the Capitol. It was often used for closed, classified briefings that excluded the press and spectators. There were no windows and no second-story gallery. The room had a faint smell of old leather and old wood. Seating for observers resembled what could be found in a courtroom rather than a theater. The chairs were not designed for comfort. This was not the venue the committee would use when it intended to put on a show. Depending on what happened next, that might come later.

That day, there was little media interest aside from a few reporters from NASA and Aerospace-themed publications for what appeared, based on its position on the schedule, to be a routine inquiry by a committee into the activities of one of the federal agencies under its jurisdiction. The agenda item was titled "Administrative Oversight of the Scope of NASA Science Mission Directorate Research." Spectators were few, mostly including tourists who were happy to see how their government worked and unconcerned with the specific subject matter. The chairman hoped to keep it that way for as long as possible.

The commotion in the room faded as people resumed their seats after the mid-morning break. Huntsman took the center chair at the table reserved for witnesses. Hansen sat beside him, leaving the other five chairs there empty.

Huntsman wore his "congressional testimony uniform"—a dark gray suit with a sparkling white shirt, starched but without buttons on the collar, and a dark, monochrome blue tie. Hansen had also dressed for the show.

They were familiar with the process. As associate administrator, Huntsman had testified before this committee on several occasions. There was, though, a critical difference this time. While officially speaking for his agency, he had a personal agenda he hadn't disclosed to Hansen.

Reyes introduced Huntsman, reciting his credentials and favorably commenting on his testimony before the committee on previous occasions; then, he stacked his welcoming notes neatly and put them aside. He picked up another sheaf of papers, placed it on the table in front of him, and turned to the issue at hand.

"Dr. Huntsman, I presume you are aware of the papers published by Drs. Leland Markson and Katty Clarke at the

Louisiana Advanced Projects Institute, which suggest that a faster-than-light spaceship of some sort flew through our solar system about three years ago, and also aware of the public controversy surrounding those papers?"

The muted conversations among the tourists in the gallery stopped.

"I am."

"Have you read those papers?"

"I have."

"Have you read the commentary pro-and-con by various physicists concerning the validity of those papers?"

"I have."

"Does NASA have a position on the validity of their claims?"

As the chairman waited with his hands clasped on the table in front of him, Hansen leaned over and whispered something to Huntsman. He shook his head and whispered something back. She waved a finger at Huntsman, who pushed her arm aside and continued shaking his head. Finally, she sat back and, with a resigned look on her face, waved her hand at her client, who then answered the question.

"Mr. Chairman, at this time, NASA does not have a position on the validity of these claims."

"Why not?"

After additional whispered discussion with Hansen, he answered, "It is beyond the scope of any of our funded projects."

"Do you think that's smart, Dr. Huntsman?"

Brushing aside Hansen's effort to provide legal guidance, he raised his voice, "No, sir, I don't."

After a brief discussion on what such a task would cost and how it could fit within NASA's program management structure, the chairman yielded the floor to the ranking member, Mr. Diggs.

Diggs was dressed for the cameras his staff had ensured would be waiting outside in the hallway. His dark blue suit accentuated a gleaming white shirt. The white handkerchief in his pocket highlighted the formality of the suit, and when he spoke, he had a strong voice with just a trace of an urban accent—from Cleveland's inner city, perhaps. His pace was measured, deliberate.

"Dr. Huntsman, you said NASA has no opinion on the validity of Markson and Clarke's claims, is that correct?"

"Yes."

"Let me ask you this. Do you personally, as a professional physicist working on the cutting edge of space research, have an opinion on the matter?"

Huntsman sat up straighter and pulled his jacket closed. "Yes, sir, I do."

"Would share it with us, please?"

Hansen whispered to Huntsman, taking him by the arm when he tried to turn away.

He pulled his arm free and responded to her aloud. "He asked my opinion, not the agency's, and I'm going to give it to him."

The congressman leaned forward a little. "Excuse me?"

Huntsman extended his hands. "Excuse me, Congressman. I was explaining to my counsel that your subpoena requires me to answer your question and to tell the truth. Is that right?"

"You bet it is, Dr. Huntsman," Diggs said, pointing his right index finger to the ceiling while glowering at the NASA attorney.

The associate administrator spoke in a sharp, crisp, rapid cadence. "In my professional opinion, Markson and Clarke have made a compelling case that the gravitational wave signatures they've detected are the wake of an Alcubierre warpship. For the signals to be as strong as they were requires that the ship be inside the orbit of the moon."

An eruption of shutter clicking and a few photo flashes accompanied an undertone of indistinct conversation coming from the gallery. The chairman vigorously gaveled the meeting back to order.

"May I continue, Mr. Chairman?" the congressman asked.

"Proceed."

"Dr. Huntsman, many papers published in the peer-reviewed literature debunk this alien starship hypothesis. How do you explain that?"

With a cold stare, Huntsman preempted any effort by Hansen to intervene. "I have examined those papers and observed that many of them are funded in whole or in part by grants from the Department of Defense. Informally, I have made some personal inquiries. I have reason to believe that the

DOD has made a deliberate and concerted effort to discredit this work."

Diggs' time was expiring. He asked Reyes for permission to extend for three additional minutes. The chairman declined in order to assure each member an equal opportunity to participate. The floor was given to South Florida Congresswoman, Ileana Serano.

Serano looked young for her fifty years. Her dark blonde hair was frequently mistaken for brown, and that day she wore a plain blue business dress. Her only adornment was a single gold ring worn as an earring in her left ear. Her voice was feminine—pitched just a speck higher than the men's, but firm and penetrating as she began, "Well, I think I know what Mr. Diggs was about to ask. Why would the DOD want to suppress this? What evidence do you have to support such an accusation?"

This was the question Huntsman had been waiting for. He sat up and leaned forward. "In addition to my private inquiries directed to some of the authors of those papers Congressman Diggs asked about, I was made privy to a message Dr. Clarke received through an anonymous source. The message appears to be from Dr. Markson, and says that he is being held against his will at a DARPA facility where he is being compelled to work on the development of warp technology for the Air Force."

Several reporters ran from the room, cell phones to their faces. Tourists began texting madly or turned to family members with excited gestures and quizzical looks. *"Did he say what I thought he said, Martha?"*

The chairman banged the gavel, but the chatter continued. Reporters who'd just left the room began returning, and a camera crew from a local news station in Congressman Diggs' district started to enter from the hallway. Reyes ordered the camera crew out and threatened to close the meeting to the press and public. It took him four minutes to quell the commotion.

When he finally reestablished control, he said slowly and evenly to the gallery, "When I said I will close this hearing, it was not a threat; it is a promise. You will behave, or you will be gone."

As the hearing resumed, Serano asked why Huntsman believed the message to be genuine. He responded, "There are several indicators that tell me the message is from Lee Markson, who I believe is being held as he asserts in the message."

He explained how the letter mentioned specific people and placed them in contexts that only he and Clarke and the people mentioned would know. "I understood how serious this is," Huntsman continued. "I asked Dr. Clarke if she still had the envelope that it was sent in. She did. I had someone check it out. It had been mailed pre-paid from New Jersey and there were no fingerprints on the envelope or its contents. She lives in Louisiana. From her demeanor and concern, I could tell it frightened her. It made no sense for it to be some falsification on her part."

He next noted that the events mentioned in the letter precisely fit the timing of Markson's disappearance from the public discussions of his work. From vigorous advocacy to sudden silence, as if a switch had been thrown.

"Although I realize it is subjective," Huntsman went on, "I worked very closely with Lee on the CATSPAW project. I know how he thinks and how he talks and how he writes. The words in the message are written in Lee Markson's unique voice. His vocabulary. His style. Factual information wrapped concisely around a bit of wit and a flash of controlled anger. I don't know how he got it to her, but that message was from Lee Markson," he said, with emphasis on the words *that* and *Lee Markson*.

Representative Serano had one final question: "Is there any other way we can verify the authenticity of that message?"

"Yes," Huntsman answered as he slapped the table in front of him. "Subpoena the Director of DARPA and ask him. Make DARPA produce Markson and ask *him*."

After the hearing was concluded, the committee members discussed the matter with their staffs and exchanged some emails. The chairman took a poll. The consensus was that Huntsman's suggestion to subpoena someone from DARPA was appropriate.

The DOD responded to the committee's informal inquiry by insisting that the work of DARPA was too highly classified for them to present it in such a hearing, even though the members held clearances. The DOD would fight such a subpoena. Rather than engage in a long legal battle, the committee accepted the DOD's counterproposal to have a senior official from the Air Force Office of Scientific Research testify instead.

The chairman scheduled one of the largest hearing rooms in the Capitol, but not a seat was vacant. The members sat behind a table with fifteen seats centered around the chairman's position. The part of the table facing the witnesses and gallery was hidden by dull red fabric. The fabric concealed a wooden strip that prevented any embarrassing tumble of pens or papers from in front of a congressman and limited the view a camera might have of what lay on the table.

The witness table faced the members. It could accommodate seven people at most and was not as high off the floor as the members' perches, designed in this fashion so that the committee could look down on the witnesses and gallery. Some people found a metaphor in this.

The gallery of VIPs, reporters, and some citizens lucky enough to get admission sat in curved rows behind the witnesses, as in a theater. Political theater, in this case. Television lights and cameras cluttered what otherwise would have been side aisles, so anyone entering or leaving had to use the center aisle and work their way across those who sat between their seat and the center of the row.

"I have a few announcements," the chairman said after he'd called the hearing to order.

He presented the schedule and advised everyone that some matters before the committee could require discussion of classified material, in which case the hearing would be temporarily closed to the public. He ended with a caution: "I realize there's a possibility that the testimony presented here may at times be surprising or controversial. That gives all the more reason that the proceedings be conducted in a professional, orderly manner. Anyone causing a disruption will be removed...." He paused just a moment and then continued, "By force, if necessary."

A young, long-haired reporter near the back stood, raised his hand, and called, "Mr. Chairman?"

"This is not a news conference. I'm not going to take questions."

"If you close the hearing, when—"

"Sit down, sir. If you don't sit down, you will be removed," the chairman said without raising his voice, but gesturing for emphasis.

The reporter scowled and shook his head, but he sat down.

Reyes introduced the DOD witness, Colonel David Maine, Vice Commander of the Air Force Research Laboratory, and noted that Maine was accompanied by a DOD attorney, Donald Wolfson, to assist him with legal and security classification issues. Colonel Maine stood six-foot-one as he raised his hand to take the oath. He had a runner's body, probably not weighing more than 160 pounds without the load of medals on his chest. Prematurely gray and wearing titanium eyeglasses with small, round lenses, he looked more like a college professor than a warrior until you noticed how he stood ramrod straight and that his gray hair had not a single strand out of place.

As usual, Reyes straightened his welcoming notes, put them aside, and spread a new sheaf of papers in front of him before he began the questioning.

"Colonel Maine, the committee staff has made you aware of our concerns about certain allegations regarding DOD activities that relate to the papers published by Dr. Lee Markson and Dr. Katty Clarke, as pertaining to faster-than-light travel. Correct?"

"Yes, sir."

"And, in particular, you are aware of the testimony of Dr. Kenneth Huntsman indicating his belief that you have Lee Markson involuntarily working on a related DOD project at a DARPA facility?"

"I am aware that he made that claim, yes, sir."

"Is that claim true, Colonel?"

The DOD attorney leaned over and whispered to Maine, who nodded in agreement before answering, "Any discussion of personnel working on classified DARPA research projects would also be classified. I can neither confirm nor deny his allegations in an open hearing."

The chairman shuffled through his notes and neatly re-stacked them several times as he rephrased and modified his question, but the answer never varied. Reyes found it necessary to cast a cautionary glance at the gallery from time to time as murmurs of dissatisfaction became audible. He shared their frustration, but was not going to let the hearing get out of his control.

Finally, he had to accept that, even under subpoena, the witness wasn't going to answer the question—at least not unless he closed the hearing. Reyes didn't want to do that so early in the day.

"Alright," Reyes said. "Let's try something else. Are you familiar with the science in the Markson and Clarke papers?"

"No, sir. I am not an expert in general relativity. My technical background is in nuclear weapons."

The remainder of the chairman's allotted time was equally unproductive. He passed the floor to Congressman Diggs.

"You say you are not a relativistic physicist?" Diggs asked.

"That's correct. I have a PhD in nuclear physics from MIT and am an expert in nuclear weapons technology."

Diggs threw up his hands. "Unless you are admitting that the Russians are right about you folks illegally blowing up a nuke in orbit, you have nothing to contribute to this discussion. Why are you here?"

It was an indictment rather than a question. Diggs looked around to confirm it had had the impact he wanted, and then continued.

"Our agreement with the DOD specified the testimony of someone familiar with the project we are investigating. Is your appearance just a sham to duck our subpoena? We can fix that, you know."

Maine looked startled. He leaned over to speak with his attorney while keeping his eyes on the committee. Wolfson whispered something to Maine. He whispered something back, to which the attorney shook his head, and then he sat up and addressed Congressman Diggs.

"Sir, I am completely familiar with any relevant projects and can answer any questions that do not require access to classified materials."

"Are there physicists working on projects within the scope of our summons?"

The DOD attorney and Maine leaned toward each other and whispered before Maine responded, "Any discussion of such personnel working on classified DARPA research projects would be classified."

Diggs tried several times more, but then decided it was hopeless. "Mr. Chairman, this witness is of no value. Unless we are prepared to go into a closed session, I yield the remainder of my time."

"Thank you, Mr. Diggs. I hope we haven't reached that point yet. Ms. Serano, you may proceed."

"Thank you, Mr. Chairman. Colonel, without disclosing which specific personnel may be working on projects within the scope of our subpoena or their specialties, can you tell us this: are there any professional personnel of any kind on these projects who have been compelled to participate against their will?"

Maine said he didn't understand the question and asked her to repeat it more slowly. She paused while giving him a knowing stare, and then said, "Without disclosing... which specific personnel... may be working... on projects... within the scope of our subpoena... or their specialties... can you tell us... are there any... professional personnel... of any kind... on these projects... who have been... compelled to participate... against their will? "

Murmuring and a few snickers sounded in the gallery while Maine held a lengthy confidential discussion with Wolfson.

"Do you need a recess to discuss this?" the chairman asked.

The attorney shook his head and Maine answered, "No, Mr. Chairman. The Department of Defense categorically denies that any of our military or civilian researchers are being coerced."

"Then, how do you account for the message from Dr. Markson?"

"*Allegedly* from Dr. Markson, Congressman. Other than Dr. Huntsman's personal opinion, there is no evidence that it is authentic."

"Are you saying Dr. Huntsman is a liar?"

"Not necessarily."

"What, then? Delusional?"

Maine shook his head. "He's probably just the victim of a well-executed hoax."

"So, even though you won't deny that Dr. Markson is working on your project, you will state today under oath that he is not being coerced—is that correct?"

"Any discussion of personnel working on classified DARPA research projects is classified. I can neither confirm nor deny such allegations in an open hearing."

Follow-up questions from Representatives Ito and Roberts were no more productive than previous inquiries, and Chairman Reyes recessed the hearing to enter a closed session. Everyone who did not have at least a top-secret clearance and a need to know the information to be discussed was excused, and the doors to the conference room were closed and guarded. The committee members on the panel, Colonel Maine, and his attorney remained in their places. Even the committee staff members were excused, with the exception of two who had clearances.

As soon as he had been assured that the room was secure, Chairman Reyes called the hearing to order again and, after reminding Maine that he was still under oath, began questioning the witness.

"Colonel Maine, will you now answer my question? Is Dr. Lee Markson involuntarily working on a related DOD project at a DARPA facility?"

Maine and his attorney conferred for less than five seconds before he said, "No, sir, he is not."

"Have you checked the personnel rosters of every DARPA facility?"

Maine looked confused. "No, sir. I haven't checked any personnel rosters. The ones for highly classified programs like the one mentioned in your subpoena are classified. I didn't have a need-to-know."

Reyes erupted, "Didn't have a need-to-know? The reason we brought you here was to investigate the allegations that your people have illegally impressed an American scientist into involuntary servitude on one of your projects, and you didn't think a look at the project's personnel roster might be relevant?"

"No, sir. It isn't necessary."

Reyes took a deep breath and then another as he deliberately composed himself. "Then, Colonel, how can you say under oath that Dr. Markson isn't working in such a facility?"

Maine again spoke privately with his attorney before responding. "I know he isn't because it would be illegal, and as a matter of policy, we don't break the law."

Reyes leaned forward. "Then, please tell me why an Air Force-funded contractor is renting out Dr. Markson's house in Baton Rouge and paying his personal expenses? If he voluntarily accepted a position with them, such shenanigans wouldn't be necessary."

There were whispers and murmurs around the room as Maine conferred with his counsel before answering, "I have no knowledge of any such arrangements."

Reyes sat back, folded his arms tight across his chest, and shook his head from side to side with a scowl. Diggs and Serano looked at each other as Diggs rolled his eyes toward the ceiling.

"Yeah," Serano said in a whisper.

David Maine was not the witness they needed. They needed someone from DARPA, from within the specific project, and not an administrator from the AFOSR. Reyes adjourned the hearing and ordered the committee staff to follow up on the subpoena they'd issued to the DOD to produce Lee Markson. They could argue that national security precluded his testimony, but they couldn't refuse to produce him.

In September, following the usual summer recess, the committee reconvened, but it wasn't because the DOD had honored the subpoena.

CHAPTER TWELVE

THE ESCAPE

THREE MONTHS HAD PASSED since he'd sent his message to Catalano, and nothing had happened. It seemed like the only way he was going to get out was to do it himself. There was no point in his attempting an escape until he had a plan, however. It would have to cover how to get off the grounds of the facility and also how to remain at large long enough to achieve the goals of the plan—which were still vague. What should his top priority be when he got out? What was essential to accomplish before he was recaptured, if that should happen?

Developing the plan required working backward since his goals would determine what needed to be done and constrain what he needed to take with him when he left.

He rejected trying to meet in person with Clarke, Huntsman, or even Catalano. It would take too much time and resources to travel that far before he was caught. The government would have every surveillance device in their arsenal supporting the manhunt for him.

He thought about locating a local network TV station and calling a news conference, but there was a risk they wouldn't believe he was really Lee Markson. If they reported him to the police as a crackpot, the DOD would be there within minutes and all would be for naught.

His best hope would be to get internet access as quickly as possible and contact one or two trusted individuals. Then, if he was still free, he could place posts on popular science discussion websites like Reddit. This limited goal simplified the logistics of his escape. He could travel light; he'd wear the most comfortable clothes he had that would be suitable for hiking and take along one set of business casual outer clothing in earth colors, a bottle of water, and some trail mix in his backpack. He'd wear his watch, and in his pockets he'd only carry his wallet and government ID. Because the DOD hadn't permitted him to keep his credit cards, he'd need some cash. Even so, it wouldn't be easy.

All personal communications devices—including laptops, tablets, and cell phones—were forbidden in the compound, so he had no way of obtaining one, legal or otherwise, to take along. He'd have to find an internet café or library with public internet access. There was nothing like that in the immediate vicinity of the facility, which was isolated in the mountains from what he could see—probably somewhere within 20 miles of Oak Ridge, Tennessee, as best as he could determine from fragments of conversation among others working there. Colonel Nilson would not tell him where he was.

While eating lunch with the Russians late one morning, he asked Ivanova where she lived.

Rakov looked up at her. She glanced at him and then looked Markson in the eye. "You have a top-secret clearance, my new friend, but you do not have a need-to-know."

Markson had anticipated the possibility that she wouldn't give him any useful information, but not the candor of her response. "Your home address is classified?" he asked.

She nodded with a wry smile. "For you, unfortunately, it is. Colonel Nilson was quite emphatic. Is that how you say it—*emphatic*?"

Markson knew better than to inquire further.

So, getting out was only the first insurmountable obstacle. Once outside the fence, he would have to conceal himself in order to avoid capture, and without knowing where he was or where he was going, he'd need to determine the direction in which to go, find transportation, find a location to access the internet, and stay free long enough to use it for half an hour.

By spring, almost a year had passed and Markson had free run of the DARPA compound—at least to the extent that anyone did. He could wander between the dormitory building where he was housed and the research building, including the adjacent parking lots. He could visit the cafeteria and the commissary. Within the research building, he was badged to access several major work areas. About the only thing he could see outside the security fence was an employee parking lot that terminated a road erupting from a forested mountainside. None of this seemed to be of much use.

The compound itself was roughly rectangular and surrounded by a double row of chain-link fences sixteen feet high, each topped by razor wire. The fifteen-foot space between the fences was illuminated and monitored by cameras around the clock. Signs on the fences warned that deadly force was authorized against trespassers and that automated systems were in place to deliver such force.

The only opening in the fence was where the single, small, paved road leading from the complex passed through the heavily guarded gate. Each morning, workers who were allowed to bring their cars into the compound would present their badges to be admitted, and each evening, they would have to present them again before the sentry would open the electronically controlled gate to let them out. Workers who were on foot—because they had parked in the lot outside the fence—had to pass through the two doors of the guard house next to the gate, one door being on the exterior side of the fence and one on the interior. Inside, between these two doors, another armed sentry checked each person's identification against a list of persons authorized to enter the facility. The list was updated daily. The ID check was repeated when workers left the facility.

Markson was sure he was on the list—with a notice in big bold letters, probably red ones: *"Restricted to the facility. Egress not authorized."*

He considered escape methods he'd seen in movies: tunneling out, building a glider and flying out, and hiding in a supply truck as it left the compound. Of these, the only one remotely practical was the truck.

For several months, he recorded every service vehicle he saw leaving. He noted the procedures the sentries used when checking the credentials of the drivers and any passengers before opening the gate for their exit. A sentry always did a visual inspection of the vehicle, including its interior. Sometimes, apparently at random, they pulled a truck aside and conducted a detailed search.

He noticed that, except for a refrigerated food truck that restocked the cafeteria and an infrequent step van that restocked the commissary, everything with a closed compartment large enough for him went to the research loading dock, where a crew transferred the inbound or outbound cargo. In all cases, the vehicle was never unattended when unlocked. This idea wasn't going to work.

Desperation led him to reconsider an option he had rejected when he'd first begun thinking about hiding in a vehicle: someone's private car. Although most of the employee parking was located outside the fence, there were several small lots reserved for senior scientists, high-ranking managers, the handicapped, and VIP guests—all inside the facility's perimeter. All of these lots were in plain sight from various buildings' windows, and many of them were in sight of the guards at the compound's entrance. He didn't see how he could break into someone's car to open the trunk and hide without being seen, even though one of the VIP lots was next to the research building in which he worked and in sight of his apartment.

With the same thoroughness he had devoted to observing commercial traffic out of the compound, he made notes on the daily ebb and flow of employees.

A few weeks were sufficient for him to recognize the opportunities and threats. Some workers stayed late. By the time they left, the offices and compound were nearly vacant. He might be able to get into a late stayer's trunk without being seen if he was extremely careful and very lucky. Unfortunately, the guards were much more likely to search a lone vehicle leaving at an odd hour than one leaving at the normal hour.

Still... What the hell? he thought. *If they catch me, what are they going to do, hold me captive?*

Now, all he had to do was wait.

One evening in late September selected itself, and he was ready to go. From his dorm, he noticed a car parked in the VIP lot by the research building. It was hard to see because there was a heavy rain coming down, accompanied by light fog. It was windy, there was lightning nearby, and the temperature was in the upper 40s. The guards were less likely to want to stand outside under these circumstances, and the low visibility

and noise accompanying the storm would reduce the likelihood that he'd be seen or heard.

"Perfect day to go for a pleasant little ride," he said aloud
as he looked out the window at the gloom.

He went to his closet and grabbed the clothing and backpack
he'd prepared months ago for the occasion, dressed as warmly as
his plans permitted, and set out as if he was returning to the office.

When he reached the research building, he looked around.
Seeing nobody, he approached the parked car and took out a
small tool which he planned to use to jimmy the trunk. The
car was an early 1990s-vintage Chevrolet Caprice which didn't
appear well-maintained.

Might as well try the door. Maybe the guy was in a hurry.

When the handle yielded to his pull, he put the tool away
and opened the door gently to avoid any sound from the hinges.
He leaned in and popped the trunk release, then stepped back
and closed the door as gently as he had opened it. At the rear
of the car, he carefully lifted the trunk lid. It was empty except
for a roadside emergency kit and some jumper cables.

Excellent.

The mat on the bottom was damp, probably from some
leaking rain, but certainly not wet enough to dissuade him.
He climbed in and pulled the trunk closed.

By the time half an hour had passed, he was sure he hadn't
been observed. After two hours passed, he began to worry.

It was becoming uncomfortably warm to be huddled in the
confined space, and he unbuttoned his outer jacket. Suppose

the car had been left there because it had broken down, or its owner had gone on official travel in a government car? He had water and snacks in his go-kit, but that didn't reduce the tension.

"I knew this was too good to be true," he muttered.

He was awakened by the sound of the engine starting. He looked at his watch. 11:30 PM. He listened carefully as the car backed out and turned. If it was still thundering, he didn't hear it, but the rain was still falling. Then, he heard voices.

"Good evening, Dr. Pritchard. Late night, huh?"

Probably the sentry speaking, Markson guessed. The name 'Pritchard' sounded familiar—maybe a manager in one of the other laboratories in his building?

"Yeah," Pritchard said. "They had me on a damned teleconference with one of our people inside the Chinese space agency. I'm tired, and the wife's pissed. At least the rain's slacked off a bit. I hate driving at night in bad weather."

"I hear you. Have a nice evening, what's left of it."

Markson heard the gate rolling back and then felt the car accelerate.

Half an hour later, it came to a stop, and after a minute or so, Markson heard the driver get out and close the door. Thirty seconds or so after that, he heard another door close—one that sounded like the front door of a residence. He waited ten more minutes before cracking open the trunk just enough to see outside.

It was dark. The rain had tapered off, but the fog had thickened, and the residential streets weren't well lit. At the far end of the street, he thought he saw a wooded area that might conceal him long enough for him to get his bearings. As quietly as he could, he got out and closed the trunk.

By the time he had walked uphill two blocks to the trees surrounding the small development, he was sweating and overheated. He hadn't expected it to feel like this late on an autumn night: he was a boater, not a mountain climber. He relieved himself in the woods before attempting any reconnaissance.

While taking care to stay in the shadows, Markson searched the edges of the development, hoping to locate a sign or a business that could tell him where he was and where the closest likely access to the internet would be found. It was after 3 AM when he found a small pile of rubbish someone had dumped, or perhaps it had fallen out of a pickup truck alongside the edge of the road bordering the woods. There was a section of the *Oakridger* newspaper, and several advertisements addressed to someone in Oliver Springs, TN.

My guess, Markson thought, *is that Dr. Pritchard was kind enough to give me a lift to a dormitory suburb of Oak Ridge.*

In another hour, Markson had done a bit more reconnoitering and the fog had lifted. There was only one main road in and out of the development. In one direction, light reflected from the clouds. In the other, darkness. He headed toward the light, still keeping off the road. He figured they wouldn't be looking for him yet—they wouldn't notice he was gone until he didn't show up for work—but he saw no advantage to taking unnecessary chances.

It was dawn by the time he got to town. The woods ended against a four-lane highway. Across the highway, he could see a variety of commercial and public buildings. Now, he had to come out into the open. He shaved and changed out of his hiking clothes. He put on the business casual clothes he'd packed and stashed the remains of his kit under a bush in case he had to come back for it later.

Next, to find a place with public internet access. "I'll just walk into town and ask," he said to himself.

Directly across the highway from the woods stood a rustic, two-story wooden building with an open porch surrounding the second floor. The earth colors of the porch were punctuated above and also just to the left of the entrance, on the ground floor below by a large white sign that was bordered in red with modern red script: *Ruby's Diner - The 'Doesn't Matter to Me' place to eat.* He was hungry anyway, and he might not have to ask where he was since it could be printed on the menu.

In short order, he was delighted to be eating buckwheat pancakes with a scoop of ice cream at 400 Main Street, Oliver Springs, Tennessee.

A friendly conversation with the waitress informed him that the Oliver Springs Library was less than half a mile away. "Just follow the railroad tracks next to the restaurant," she said. "The library used to be the Oliver Springs Depot. It opens at 9."

Markson ate slowly and left a large tip.

The walk was less than a quarter of a mile. The town had an interesting mixture of nineteenth century architecture. There were red brick buildings that looked like they'd once housed factories mingled with wooden structures that could have been residences, but weren't. Many had historical plaques in front, always with white block letters on a matte green background. It appeared that this little place in the Appalachian boondocks had once been a thriving mining community. The police department on the other side of the tracks was the only thing that seemed anachronistic with its bright white SUVs parked neatly in a row beside the old building. Beyond the police department, Markson passed the water department, also across the tracks, and arrived at the library on his side.

The building was wooden from top to bottom except for the asphalt shingles on the roof, and everything was brown except for the several shades of beige used to outline the windows and doors. Like Ruby's Diner, it had a porch, although it was on the first floor. The windows were double hung with six panes top and bottom—typical of the period. The small green sign at the base of the lamp post at the edge of the sidewalk by the road said, "Oliver Springs Depot 1896." On the lawn to the left of the walkway leading into the library, there was a much larger green sign on posts in an eight-foot by four-foot flowerbox with small American flags, one in each corner of the box. The sign read: *Oliver Springs PUBLIC LIBRARY & ARCHIVES.*

As soon as he entered, he saw the public computers. He tried to log on to one of them, but a pop-up message told him that access required a library card.

He hurried to the front desk. "How can I get a library card?" he asked the librarian.

"Are you a resident of Oliver Springs?

"No, I'm just visiting. Can I get a temporary card?"

"I'll need to copy your ID. I can have a card for you when we open tomorrow."

"I'm sorry, but that won't do," Markson said. He dug into his pocket and pulled out the DARPA badge he had been hoping no one would see. *Thank God I didn't throw it away*. He presented it to the librarian. "This is a national security matter. I need access to the internet immediately to get a message to a NASA Associate Administrator."

The librarian scrutinized his badge.

Shit. I hope she doesn't watch Willard Manchester. If she recognizes me, this could go south in a hurry, he thought.

"Do you have any other ID?" she asked.

He handed her his driver's license. She copied the driver's license, wrote something on a form which she required him to sign, and then she took his mug shot. Two minutes later, he had what he needed. She kept his license as security. As he turned away from her desk, he let out a deep sigh that might have been audible, had anyone been paying attention. He hadn't realized he'd been holding his breath.

As soon as he was logged in, he sent emails to Clarke,

Huntsman, and Catalano. Next, he quickly went to *First Look Physics* and *arXiv* to post comments to the threads about their papers, and then he did the same thing on the similar thread on Reddit. He stopped briefly to glance around the room, then got up and looked out a nearby window. Seeing nothing unusual, and certainly no sign of pursuit, he went back online.

A quick search revealed the stalled congressional hearings about the warp signature. Using information from the committee's website, he next sent emails to the chairman and ranking minority member. Although he felt he was taking a risk by staying in the library too long, he found websites where he could provide news tips to the television networks. He posted messages to ABC, NBC, CBS, FOX, and CNN before he logged off, hurried back to the front desk, and exchanged the temporary library card for his driver's license.

He'd just stepped onto the library's porch when he saw the man with the sidearm at the end of the walkway.

Within seconds, the man had checked something on his phone and begun walking briskly in Markson's direction. The look on his face said, "Gotcha!"

"Shit," Markson said as he turned left to make a run for any nearby wooded area. If only he could get into the trees, he might be able to evade this guy.

The armed man was faster and the trees much too far away, however, and Markson quickly realized that he couldn't escape.

He stopped, turned, and said to him, "You're too late. I've already contacted the congressional committee and the news media."

The man produced a document and a badge. "Dr. Lee Markson, I have been directed by the Speaker of the House of Representatives to present you with this subpoena and escort you to Washington, D.C. to testify before the House Committee on Science, Space and Technology. Will you come with me voluntarily?"

"You're not from the Department of Defense?"

"No, sir. I am a United States Marshal."

Markson was wary. Everything had happened so fast, but he knew that the man who'd arrested him at his home had been a U.S. Marshal.

"Why should I believe you?" he asked. "It's quite a coincidence that you appeared here in the middle of nowhere on the very day I escaped from the DOD concentration camp up the road."

The marshal held out his badge and the document again. "Dr. Markson, I really don't want to have to use force. Please look closely at the badge and the subpoena."

Markson examined the items. They looked genuine enough. "So, how did you find me?"

"I was directed to the lab by the committee chairman. I was going to serve the subpoena on the lab director, but the place was swarming with security forces scouring the woods nearby. When they told me that you weren't at the facility, I took a guess that they weren't technically lying because you had escaped. I figured you'd head for the nearest public place with internet capability, so I did the same."

Markson laughed and held out his hand to the lawman. "I am delighted to meet you, Marshal. I have a strong urge to visit the Capitol. Lead the way."

CHAPTER THIRTEEN

THE CONGRESS AGAIN

THE DOD INSISTED that the afternoon session be closed, and this time the chairman didn't object. Reyes wanted this witness to be uninhibited by restrictions on the content of his testimony. Over the objections of the DOD, the witness was Lee Markson.

The hearing would be held in the same room where the committee had questioned Huntsman. During their open morning session, a U.S. Marshal had described how he'd taken Markson into custody in the parking lot of a public library just a dozen miles from a classified DARPA facility. His tale of

Markson's initial attempt to flee, followed by his eager surrender when told that the marshal had been sent by Congress and not the DOD, confirmed Huntsman's testimony that Markson had been held against his will. Now, everyone wanted to hear the story from Markson himself.

Outside the Capitol, more than two hundred protesters carried signs and shouted slogans expressing their ire that Markson's testimony would be closed. Some of them wore "Let Alcubierre Power It" T-shirts. News media, themselves angry about being excluded, made the morning testimony and the afternoon protests their lead stories. Reyes told reporters that the committee would release a redacted version of the proceedings, which satisfied nobody.

While the protesters protested and the reporters reported, attorneys from the Department of Justice and the Department of Defense informed Reyes that Lee Markson was still under federal indictment for assaulting a federal official and faced additional military charges for leaving his post at DARPA without permission. After consulting with House General Counsel, the chairman informed the government attorneys that there was no legal bar to the committee issuing a subpoena to a person under indictment and that the hearing would proceed as planned. He denied their requests for access to Markson to take him into custody and that he be handcuffed during his testimony that afternoon.

"At the moment, Counsel, this witness is in the custody of the U.S. Congress, and we have advised him of his right to retain his own lawyer to respond to your demands in an appropriate venue. I see serious *habeas corpus* issues here that we are not going to attempt to resolve at this hearing. Perhaps by the time we release him from his subpoena, the appropriate federal court will resolve the matter."

Meanwhile, Makayla Birkwood had been stunned when she'd gotten Markson's phone call at 9 AM. She was the corporate counsel for Catalano Automated Trading, the high-speed automated investment company for which Markson had developed the CATSPAW device. Markson believed she may have kept them all out of jail when the Securities and Exchange Commission and the U.S. Attorney for the Southern District of New York had been investigating them for alleged securities fraud.

"Makayla—help! I'm in trouble, and I need a lawyer who I can trust without question and who knows how to handle the feds, and I need them today," had been Markson's opening words.

He'd explained the situation and waved off her disclaimers that she wasn't a criminal lawyer. The SEC worked with the DOJ on the securities fraud accusations, and here it was the DOD working with the DOJ. Different players, but the same game.

"Please, Makayla," he'd said. "I really need you. If Henry will cut you loose, at least until this hearing is over, I'll make it worth your while."

She'd called him back shortly. "Mr. Catalano is not only willing to let me take leave, he's adamant that he pick up the tab. He muttered something about another opportunity to do the right thing. You've got yourself an attorney."

By 10:15 AM, the CAT corporate jet was en route to Washington D.C.

They had little time to prepare for the hearing. As soon as Birkwood arrived at the Capitol, she was escorted to the staff office where the committee had been keeping Markson away from the press and those who wished to make him their prisoner again.

Markson was relieved when one of Reyes' aides opened the door and escorted Birkwood in. She didn't appear to have changed. In her early fifties now, she seemed as wiry and athletic as she had when he'd last seen her seven years ago at CAT. She ran forward and took him into her arms. Markson wasn't a big hugger, but this one he returned with heartfelt enthusiasm.

"Still a fan of big earrings and understated necklaces, I see," he said as he stepped back, delighted at the sight of the first familiar and friendly face he'd seen in many months.

The jewelry was typical of the way she could adapt a well-tailored designer dress to a formal, high-level business meeting or a party.

"I didn't have time to go home and change," she said, "but Henry sent you this."

She was holding a business suit in Markson's size, complete with a matching shirt and tie. Markson laughed and shed a tear. The one didn't cause the other.

Markson and Birkwood had barely entered the hearing room when a DOD attorney rose from the seat next to the center of the witness table to object to Birkwood's presence, arguing that she didn't have the requisite security clearance. She told Markson to take the center seat at the table as she stood at the lectern to address the issue. Speaking with few gestures and vocal emphasis, but some speed, she reminded the committee that the DOD had given both Markson and Clarke temporary clearances at the meeting at LAPI when it had fitted the DOD's convenience.

"That's different. That was a private meeting, off the record. This is a congressional hearing," the government attorney said as Markson glared up at him from the adjacent chair.

Birkwood slowed her pace and took a more calculated tone as she made a quarter-turn to look across her shoulder at the DOD advocate. "Oh, really? Perhaps, you know, you've forgotten that committee witnesses' attorneys are routinely cleared to advise their clients as they testify."

As Birkwood and the government attorney engaged in their arguments, Reyes had to remind them both to address their remarks to the committee and not to each other. Birkwood knew from her experience with the SEC when to dial it back. When the government attorney countered that the instances Birkwood had cited didn't involve the complex technical details of classified projects, Reyes pointed out that she would not be privy to the testimony of anyone other than her client and that the details of the science were not expected to be part of Markson's testimony for the current hearing. When the government persisted, the chairman had had enough.

"You're the one who demanded that the hearing be closed, Counsel!" Reyes said. "Now, you have two choices: you can issue Ms. Birkwood a temporary clearance for this hearing, or I can open the hearing and restrict the questioning to unclassified matters. Keep in mind, disreputable or criminal behavior on the part of DOD personnel can't be classified just to cover it up."

Before swearing in Markson, Reyes wanted to resolve another matter regarding his legal representation. As with the previous witnesses, Reyes asked Markson to confirm that he was familiar with the purpose of the proceedings and also advised him of his right to consult with his attorney. Additionally, he advised Markson that the DOD had made the attorney who'd sought to eject Birkwood available to consult with him on certain issues.

Markson was livid. "Mr. Chairman, I want to be clear about this. That woman represents the DOD, not me. She just tried to deprive me of my own lawyer. I did not request her presence. I will be speaking for myself, not the DOD, at this hearing."

"I understand your position, Dr. Markson, but you are still subject to the jurisdiction of the department, and they are entitled to have one of their attorneys present to advise you on legal and national security matters. I would caution you and Ms. Birkwood to at least listen to what she may have to say. I'm sure you wouldn't want to inadvertently violate the law or put our country at risk," the chairman said.

Markson began to rise from his seat, but Birkwood put her hand on his lower arm with more than a trace of a squeeze. When he saw the look on her face, he sat back.

She turned from Markson to Reyes. "Of course not, Mr. Chairman. Please have her speak with me, and I will advise the witness."

In order to preserve the privacy of her conversations with her client, Birkwood insisted that the Air Force attorney be seated at one end of the table while they took the other. Grudgingly, the attorney moved to the right end. Birkwood and Markson rose and moved to the left.

"Is that satisfactory, Ms. Birkwood?" the chairman asked.

"Yes, Mr. Chairman, thank you," she replied.

"In that case, let's proceed."

Reyes swore in Markson and introduced him. The introduction prepared by committee staff with the assistance of Ken Huntsman and Katty Clarke was thorough, accurate, and impressive.

Preliminaries complete, Reyes got right to the point. "Dr. Markson, I'm going to begin with what may be the most important question you will be asked. Did the Department of Defense coerce you, in any way, to undertake the work you have been doing for them?"

"Yes, sir. They tried to bribe me and Dr. Clarke. When that didn't work, they threatened us both. When that failed, they had me arrested and impressed into the Air Force, and told me that if I didn't cooperate, they'd take further action against us both. Yes, I'd say I was coerced."

The chairman asked Markson to walk them through the details. Markson explained how he and Dr. Clarke had been presented with the "carrot and the stick" by Colonel Nilson and Louise Meier at LAPI.

When Reyes asked what Markson meant by being "impressed into the Air Force," Markson started with the not-so-coincidental appearance of an Air Force attorney at the detention hearing following his arrest, with an order appointing him as a warrant officer in the Air Force.

"They used my alleged Air Force officer status as grounds to have the court release me into their custody. They took me to Keesler Air Force Base, where that woman, Louise Maier from the NSA, told me that if I didn't sign the papers accepting the appointment, they would file additional charges against me, Katty Clarke, and Ken Huntsman, as well as accelerate their character assassination of Katty on social media. I couldn't let that happen, so I signed—but it sure wasn't voluntary."

Reyes turned and said to the aide behind him, "Remind me to ask Secretary Kinnon about that when we get him in here." He then turned the floor over to the ranking member, Mr. Diggs, to continue the questioning.

"It seems that their 'carrots' were pretty generous, Dr. Markson. Why would either of you reject the opportunity to work on something you obviously enjoy and earn more money than most people ever hope to earn?" Congressman Diggs asked, his hands spread as if in invitation for a credible answer.

"Because the work was going to be classified. We couldn't publish it. Scientists don't do basic research for the money. If you want to make money, you go into the industry. Make things you can sell. Basic research is about expanding human knowledge. If you don't publish what you learn, it's useless. It's like they said about the doomsday machine in *Dr. Strangelove*: the whole point of it is lost if you keep it secret. That's why publication is so crucial to a scientist's career."

Representative Serano wanted to know more about the threats to Dr. Clarke. Markson refused to provide specifics of the personally embarrassing material he had mentioned in his testimony.

"You realize you are under subpoena, Dr. Markson?"

"Yes, ma'am. I realize that. I also realize that the level of detail you are demanding would be of no assistance to your investigation, but could be of great embarrassment to Dr. Clarke. It would be unconscionable for me to provide that testimony."

"Well, I think it would be useful for this committee—"

At this point, the chairman interrupted, "As you know, Ms. Serano, I don't believe we need to get into that here. Dr. Clarke has been assisting the committee staff in preparing for the scientific aspects of Dr. Markson's testimony. If you think the matter is essential for some purpose, we can discuss it with her, off the record."

Markson's heart raced. He'd been taken directly from the library to a hotel near the Capitol, where congressional staff had provided him with background material in preparation for his testimony. He hadn't been allowed to contact Clarke or anyone else except his attorney. He was excited that she was well and had been involved in the investigation.

After a fifteen-minute recess, it was Representative Ito's turn.

"Dr. Markson, at the DARPA facility, how many people were working on this project?"

The DOD attorney asked permission to confer with Birkwood. "That's a personnel issue. It's classified and not germane to anything before the committee. He shouldn't answer that," she told her.

Birkwood advised her client that the hearing was closed and that everyone in the room had clearance. Since the matter was not SCI, he could answer.

Markson nodded at Birkwood and turned toward Ito. "I don't have the full picture, but at my location, I saw about two dozen and corresponded with maybe a dozen more who were located elsewhere."

"Where were they located?"

"I asked. They wouldn't tell me."

"Were any of these other people coerced?"

"Not to my knowledge."

"So, there were less than fifty people working on the project?"

"I can't say that. I only had contact with about forty, but I heard mention that the NSA, the AFOSR, and the Naval

Research Laboratory were all contributing to the work. I don't know the extent of their efforts or who was really in charge."

Ito concluded his questioning by exploring the management structure at the DARPA facility where Markson had been held.

The chairman recognized the Honorable William Roberts of Alabama, who spoke with a slow, pleasant southern drawl. "Dr. Markson, let me expand beyond that a bit. What would you say was the project's probability of success?"

"Zero," Markson said, ignoring another attempt by the DOD attorney to convince Birkwood to advise him not to answer.

The congressman appeared to be taken aback. "I expected you might say it was not good, but why zero?"

"There are three things that weigh against any progress being made, given their approach. First, the necessary physics relating to both the energy and the GNC problems is completely unknown."

"Let me interrupt you for a moment, Dr. Markson. I saw those terms, energy and GNC, in our briefing materials, but I must admit I didn't have time to study them thoroughly. Could you explain what those terms mean in language suitable for us history majors?"

Markson laughed. By now, he was used to the questions, and so he began with his elevator speech on the energy issue. "The problem is simple in concept. The kind of spaceship we're talking about requires exotic matter that acts like it has negative mass—a sort of repulsive gravity—but nobody knows how to make it and many physicists believe it can't be made at all. Those of us who are convinced by the observations that someone or something has done it have a long road ahead of us in discovering how."

Roberts nodded. "OK. That wasn't so bad. What about that GNC thing?"

"This one isn't simple even in concept," Markson admitted. "The problem here is that the warp bubble carrying the ship, which allows it to go faster than light, has regions in it where space and time are so distorted that no information can pass through them. We call these 'horizons.' To change the course or speed of the bubble, the crew would have to tell all of the parts of the bubble how to change their shape by reconfiguring the exotic matter. Unfortunately, the information about the changed configuration could not pass through any of these horizons, so parts of the bubble beyond them would not be controllable. At best, you couldn't reliably steer the bubble. At worst, the attempt to change its shape could destabilize the bubble and collapse it, destroying the ship."

"But you think these aliens, if that's what they are, know how to do that?"

"I can't be sure. I'm certain we saw such a bubble fly by, but we didn't see any sign of active maneuvering as it passed. Maybe they use passive navigation like superluminal gravitational slingshots, or maybe they've figured out some form of active navigation that doesn't require passing information across the horizons. Either way, it's far beyond any physics we know now. That's why I think reverse-engineering one of these ships quickly is a pipe dream."

"So, you were about to tell us what you think is required?"

"Yes. It's pure, basic research that will probably take decades, and a broader range of insights and approaches than a government crash program like this can accommodate. That was my first point. Second, the secrecy is extremely counterproductive and totally unnecessary. It prevents the cross-fertilization of ideas that enables ideas to build on each other. The more difficult the problem, the more essential it is to broaden the base of inquiry. Finally, the project is focused on building a device. As I just noted, it is incredibly premature to even be thinking about such a thing. First, we need to understand the physics. Only then can we begin to work on the engineering."

The chairman noted the expiration of Roberts' allotted time and glanced at the outsized Rolex on his right wrist. He announced that the committee would reconvene again in a closed session the next day.

As the members began packing up their notes, Markson stood to be recognized. "Mr. Chairman."

"Yes, Dr. Markson?"

"May I make a request, please?"

"What is it, Dr. Markson?"

"I didn't realize Dr. Clarke was assisting the committee. Would it be possible for me to see her this evening, perhaps over dinner? I would like to get caught up on what's been happening out in the real world while I've been isolated."

Reyes looked left and right, but the other members were already gone or on their way out. He turned back to their star witness. "As soon as you have completed your testimony, you will be released from our subpoena. If we accomplish nothing else through these hearings, we would hope you will be free to go about your business unmolested at that point, but that may be in the hands of the federal courts and your capable attorney."

Markson spoke again, but his microphone had been shut off and everyone in the room was rising to leave. *Crap*, he thought. *Not free yet. On the bright side, at least I can get a decent meal tonight.*

∞

Immediately after Huntsman's congressional testimony, he and Clarke had begun making the rounds of the radio and TV talk shows and various internet venues. Huntsman had soon backed off, though. The Administrator of NASA had suggested that these appearances were inappropriate for a NASA associate administrator, and Huntsman reluctantly had to agree. Clarke, however, was under no such constraints, and for the first time had begun to feel that she could do something that might make a difference.

Clarke was a natural for television. She was an attractive woman, articulate and poised, with an excellent stage presence honed by hundreds of appearances in adult entertainment venues, some with rowdy audiences. She'd quickly learned to handle or deflect questions that focused on her extracurricular activities and keep conversations focused on the flight of an alien warpship near Earth, as well as the DOD's underhanded efforts to suppress and discredit that amazing discovery. She always managed to bring the end of an interview around to the question, "What happened to Lee Markson?"

When he reappeared, she initially declined the dozens of invitations for guest appearances on major news programs in order to focus on helping the committee prepare for his testimony. When she learned that the DOD and now the DOJ were continuing their efforts to sequester and coerce him, however, she reconsidered that plan. She'd seen firsthand how vicious public opinion could be when used against someone. Perhaps she could turn the tables.

She called Willard Manchester, of whom Lee had spoken highly, and asked if she could have a twenty-minute segment that evening.

He was delighted, but hesitant. "It's almost noon. It'll be difficult to give you that much time on such short notice."

"Even if I'm willing to talk about nudity?"

"Be at the studio at 7:15 PM for makeup."

Manchester knew how to build ratings. With short commercial spots all day until an hour before showtime on his network, Manchester hyped the upcoming "tell-all" appearance of Katty Clarke, the notorious physics professor with the inside story on the disappearance of Lee Markson and a willingness to "reveal all." Then, he placed her last in his line-up so that viewers would have to watch the whole show to avoid missing her segment.

"Our final guest this evening is a physicist and former LAPI professor who's been deeply involved in the controversy surrounding the alleged visit near Earth of an alien starship, and also the disappearance of my former guest, Lee Markson. Please welcome Doctor Katty Clarke."

Clarke entered from stage left with a huge theatrical smile and waved to the applauding audience in the same fashion she'd perfected as an exotic dancer. She'd carefully selected a white blouse with a deep V-neck revealing as much cleavage as she thought she could get away with without appearing unprofessional. Her skirt was the red one that Aguillero found so offensive. She wanted the largest audience she could get, and she knew how to get it.

Her judgment was vindicated when the studio audience roared their applause, which was punctuated by a few whistles and even one loud, "GO, KAT!"

She didn't care if the reaction seemed sexist. She had exactly what she wanted: the audience's full attention. Her wave and big smile were genuine as she reveled in the thought that, all around the country, people were probably on their cell phones texting friends, "Hey, turn on Willard Manchester. That scientist lady who used to be a stripper is on!"

The set was larger and more open than those she'd experienced previously. Lights of all shapes and sizes hung from railings along the ceiling and others protruded from poles at the sides. Three huge cameras on wheels, each with its own camera-man pushing it around, occupied more of the stage than she ever would have guessed from watching the program on the tube. She was surprised that the program's Washington-at-night backdrop, which appeared on the screen behind the set, was not inserted into the picture electronically or painted onto a large sheet at the back of the stage. It was projected against a screen as wide as the stage and extending upward from the floor at least eighteen feet.

Unlike the set, which was larger than life, Markson had been right when he'd told her how short Manchester appeared in person compared to how he looked on television. The thing that struck her, though, was the way he dressed. Here he was, a prime-time TV host, but instead of wearing a fine suit and designer tie, he wore a plain white dress shirt with green pinstripes, the neck unbuttoned, with a dark, blue-patterned tie that wasn't even pulled tight. The geek-chic look was capped by the heavy black suspenders draped over his shoulders to hold up his navy-blue trousers.

If anybody was going to invite physicists to be guest stars on a popular talk show, he'd be the one, she mused as she strolled across the stage and took her seat next to Manchester. The contrast was perfect.

"Thank you for joining us tonight, Dr. Clarke."

"Thank you for having me," she said as she took the initia-tive by reaching out to shake his hand, even while maintaining eye contact with the camera and audience.

Manchester let go of her hand and picked up some papers from his table. "The Attorney General just released a copy of the indictment charging Lee Markson with assaulting a federal officer. He said this federal crime is the reason they arrested Dr. Markson, not his work on the alien spaceship theory. The AG said they simply used his being in custody as an opportunity to assist the Secretary of Defense, who was concerned about it. Does all that have anything to do with your willingness to appear on my show this evening?"

"Of course! It's bullshit!" she replied in anger, tossing her hair to the side for emphasis.

Manchester made a mock horror face. "Well, I'm glad we're on cable."

"Don't mind me. It's just that I'm so pissed that they keep persecuting Lee even after their game is over," she said with a wave of both hands. "Their big secret, which never was a secret, is out." Here, she turned from addressing Manchester to face the camera. "The Russians know about the warpship. So do the Chinese. Even the faculty wimps who were too timid to let us publish our original paper know better now."

She turned back toward the host. "What's the point? It's just plain mean. That's all it is."

He nodded. "I can see how you might feel that way, but he did slug a woman from the NSA, didn't he? Shouldn't he pay for that?"

She tapped her chest emphatically with her finger. "I was there. He didn't slug her!" She put her hand on her lap and then raised it again, pointing it at the camera positioned directly in front of the audience. "He should have, though. She was threatening me in a most disgusting manner, and he came to my defense! All he did was try to pull her away from me. He held her against a wall for a second."

"She was threatening you?"

Clarke raised her hand to eye level and rubbed her thumb and first two fingers together in the universal symbol for money and greed. "She and that Air Force colonel tried to bribe us with jobs and titles." She turned toward the camera again. "When that didn't work, they threatened us with criminal prosecution and public humiliation."

"Can you be more specific about the threats?" Manchester asked.

"She had pictures of me performing nude on British TV and a show I did at a respectable, high-class gentlemen's club in France and repeated as a charity performance in England. At least those were legitimate. The thing that got my goat was when she showed me a list of pornographic websites she claimed I'd frequented and said they would be posted on the internet."

"You're saying Lee Markson was provoked?"

Her eyes got big, and she pulled her head back. "He bloody well was!" She turned again toward the camera and the audience, and leaned forward. "Suppose some clownette from the spy shop said she was going to post accusations that your lover was a porn addict on the internet—how would you react?"

"I'd probably slug her," Manchester admitted, "but I want to follow up. Are you and Markson lovers? And what's with the nudity?"

Before she could begin to answer, Manchester turned to the camera. "Those questions and more when we return."

During the break, Clarke told Manchester she would answer his questions honestly and in full *if* he kept it brief, so that they could come back to the issue of the DOJ and the DOD's bad faith in their continued pursuit of charges against Markson. She was giving him a ratings bonanza, and she expected him to keep his end of the bargain and give her a pulpit.

"Deal!" he said. Realizing that the studio audience had overheard the whole conversation, he addressed them: "I always keep my word, right?"

The standing-room-only crowd gave a louder and longer round of applause than Manchester had expected. He couldn't be sure whether it was to validate his character or to encourage Dr. Clarke, but either way, he'd take it. He acknowledged the audience with a nod, and with a nod to Clarke, he resumed as the "On Air" light illuminated.

"Welcome back to *The Willard Manchester Show*. Our guest tonight is Dr. Katty Clarke. Dr. Clarke, what is your personal relationship to Lee Markson?"

"We're a couple. Not engaged, but we sometimes share a bed. He's precious to me."

"Do you have any plans for marriage?"

"Right now, my plans are for putting an end to this absurd, make-weight prosecution."

Manchester paused for a few seconds. "I think that is important, and I want to come back to it as we close out our interview this evening, but I would like to clear the air about something our viewers are going to want to know."

She rolled her eyes and shook her head. "I know what's coming. I said I'd answer it. Ask your questions."

"You did appear nude on British TV, and you did strip in clubs in France and the UK, correct?"

"Yes, to both questions."

"Why?"

"The TV show was *How to Look Good Naked*, a reality show designed to boost women's confidence about their bodies. When I was in college, I tried out as a contestant because, as a teen, I'd had trouble getting dates. I was too smart and seemed to scare men off. I thought I was pretty, but since I couldn't get a date, I began to doubt my body image. The show encouraged me to accept my appearance. I was nude in the final episode because I'd come to realize that I am beautiful and worth looking at."

"I can't deny that!" Manchester said, shaking his head from side to side with a suggestive smile.

She returned the smile innocently. "Shortly after the show aired, I got an offer to perform at a local club. I didn't know anything about adult entertainment, but the money would be a welcome addition to my scholarship, which barely paid my tuition. One of the regular performers took pity on me and taught me some basics. The audience liked it, and I found their applause a satisfying reinforcement of my positive body image. As I got better at performing, offers came from farther away and paychecks grew correspondingly. It was both pleasant and profitable. That's why I kept doing it."

"But you don't do it anymore?"

"No. I planned to stop after I began my postdoc at Virgo, but I was invited to do a show by a well-known and well-respected club in France. My performance there was widely reported. When Aberto heard about it—"

"Aberto?"

"The Italian cosmologist who hired me as his postdoc on the Virgo project. He was furious—almost fired me. I learned my lesson."

"You told me there was one show you did after that which was being used against you."

She repeated what she'd told Markson and Aguillero about being recruited by old friends to do her French show again for the English Christmas fundraiser.

"Someone in the audience recorded the whole set on their phone and sent it to Professor Aguillero. I'm sorry it happened, but I am not sorry I did the show. The children needed the toys and clothing, and I enjoyed the opportunity to dance again."

"Dr. Clarke, I admire your courage and willingness to share all that with us. Now, I'm going to keep my part of the bargain. What did you want us to know about the government's behavior toward Lee Markson?"

Clarke summarized her case in verbal bullets, which she embellished with big sweeping gestures throughout:

"Lee and I discovered evidence that a faster-than-light spacecraft had flown close by the Earth. The fact that it's possible to go faster than light and the existence of an alien civilization that built the ship—either fact, by itself, would be world-shaking.

"The discovery was rightly controversial, but the DOD believed it was true. Instead of joining the physics community in the research, they tried to suppress the evidence.

"When we published our evidence and analysis, they used financial pressure to solicit unfavorable reviews and comments, and suppress favorable commentary.

"They called us into a meeting at LAPI to try to buy our cooperation in their fraud. We would have to 'admit' our papers were false while working on a classified project based on those same papers. They made the institute offer us our old jobs back. They offered us government jobs. When we refused, they threatened Lee and me both with legal and financial disaster.

"When that threat didn't work, they accused me of frequenting porn sites, saying they'd publish that information on the web along with my TV and nightclub videos. When Lee had enough and rose to my defense, they used it as an excuse to charge him with a violent federal crime—even though nobody was injured, and they had provoked his reaction in the first place. It was just an excuse to arrest him a little while later.

"They hauled him off to a high-tech work camp rather than jail and made him work on their project. They *enslaved* him. That shows their real purpose.

"Finally, when Congress blew the whistle on their despicable game, instead of apologizing, they doubled-down and told the committee chairman that they plan to continue this sham prosecution."

"And what should they be doing instead?" Manchester asked when she'd finished.

"Drop the charges against Lee. Issue apologies to him, me, and all of those physicists they intimidated into publishing misinformation or withholding supportive papers. Pay the two of us back salaries for our time away from LAPI. That's what they should do."

"Well, there you have it, ladies and gentlemen. We have run out of time today, Dr. Clarke, but I hope we can have you back sometime in the future, perhaps after this all gets worked out. So long for now! This is Willard Manchester, and you have been watching *The Willard Manchester Show*."

After the director gave the "cut" sign, Manchester turned to Clarke. "That was a sincere invitation, Katty. For you and Lee both."

∞

Birkwood brought Markson a clean shirt and tie just in time. Breakfast had to be limited to toast and coffee because Reyes kicked off the next day's session two hours earlier than usual. He wanted to wind up Markson's testimony before lunch so that they could move on to grilling the DOD in the afternoon. Two things remained to be discussed with Markson: should the research be secret, and should it be managed by DARPA? With those questions in mind, Reyes asked Diggs to begin.

That day, Diggs was wearing his wire-rimmed glasses rather than the slightly nerdy plastic frames he often wore in less formal settings. He was also taking a more oratorical tone than he'd previously taken in the hearings. "Dr. Markson, you do understand that there are serious national security concerns if potential adversaries get this technology before we do?"

"I don't believe such concerns are well-considered, Congressman."

"So, you're perfectly OK with, say, the Chinese having a warp drive and us not having one?"

Birkwood leaned over for a brief conference with her client before he said, "No, sir, but that's not going to happen. And even if it did, it wouldn't be a national security issue in any meaningful sense of the word."

"How can you be so confident that we're going to get it first if we don't maintain secrecy?"

"Because I'm totally confident that nobody's going to 'get it first' *regardless* of whether or not we maintain secrecy." Markson went on to explain that the problem was so difficult that it would take many decades, perhaps a century or more, to reach the point where a small-scale demonstration device could be built—and that it would require an international effort to do even that. "We, as humans, will have to do it together or we won't be able to do it at all," he finished.

As Reyes passed the floor to Representative Serano, he was concerned that she might bring up the specifics of the DOD threats against Katty Clarke which he had cut off the day before. She wore the bright red jacket and black blouse combination she often put on for television appearances. There were cameras by the dozens just outside the hearing room, and a salacious scandal would make for great ratings. As it happened, however, she merely followed up on the second half of Markson's assertion about the lack of any necessity for secrecy.

"You said that it wouldn't be harmful to our national security if a foreign power got the technology before we did. Why not?"

"The real question is, why would it? You don't need a warp drive to nuke New York or London or Beijing or Moscow. Sadly, we are quite prepared to do that right now. We don't know much, but everything we do know about these warpships tells us that they're worse than useless for short trips. The bow shock would require that they keep 30,000 kilometers or more away from anything they pass over or near. If one were launched from enemy territory toward us, it would sterilize the entire ground track under its trajectory from there to here."

"You don't think it could be used as a weapon?"

"It will be an essential weapon if we ever get into a war with the aliens who built the ship we observed, but they're already ahead of us. We don't need to try to keep it secret from them. They're the ones with the secrets. For Earthbound warfare, a warship would be prohibitively expensive and generate huge amounts of collateral damage without providing any militarily significant advantage."

"Would you declassify the whole program?"

"Yes, ma'am. If there's any national security issue at all, it's the extremely remote possibility that these aliens may indeed visit us someday. Lacking warp technology would put us at an extreme disadvantage. The fastest way for human beings to protect this planet is to work together to understand the physics well enough so that we can deal with that eventuality. It won't be us against the Chinese. It will be us and the Chinese against ET. That's the true national security interest."

By the time Ito and Roberts had finished exploring the secrecy issue, the tone of the questioning suggested that the sensibilities of the committee were leaning toward Markson's view of the situation. Reyes decided the time had come to address his second topic for the day.

"Dr. Markson, putting aside for the moment the question of secrecy, how should we manage this research? Is DARPA the right place for it? If not, where?"

"If you want to build a warpship, the place to start is not by asking a military applied research institution to build a warpship. It's by asking the physics community to study the basic physics of superluminal systems and negative energy phenomena. You have to know how to make cement before you can build a concrete fortress."

"Why shouldn't the research be focused on the end product?"

"Because that narrows your options prematurely. Instead of that fortress, consider a large office building. Before the Civil War, the tallest buildings were limited in height by the strength and weight of masonry. With the development of inexpensive processes for the production of steel and the invention of steel-reinforced concrete, real skyscrapers could be built. If the goal in 1830 had been to build a fifty-story building, the research would have been assigned to architects and stonemasons when what was really needed was the work of chemists and metallurgists. Do you see what I'm saying?"

"So, how would you do what you're suggesting in practice?"

"Declassify and decentralize the program. Put the government funding in a single agency like NASA or the National Science Foundation. Have them conduct the work through grants to universities and laboratories—including DOD laboratories when merited. The grants would be issued based on peer-reviewed proposals, and limited in scope and length. That's what Dr. Clarke and I were planning to do with our foundation."

"Mr. Chairman, may I ask the witness a question?" Ms. Serano inquired. The chairman nodded. "Dr. Markson, wouldn't it be helpful for the government to have some sort of an institute to focus the effort? Something like the National

Centers for Disease Control or the National Center for Atmospheric Research?"

"Again, that's one of our objectives for FASTER, the foundation I created along with the help of Dr. Clarke. It could be very effective if the right person were in charge."

"You mean someone like you?"

"I never thought I'd hear myself say it, Congresswoman, but in the last two years, I've learned a few things. So, yes. Someone like me."

During lunch, the chairman met in his office with the ranking member and the SECDEF. Before Secretary Kinnon arrived, Reyes cleared all of the books and papers from the top of his old-fashioned, dark brown desk, except for a copy of the Constitution and a newspaper from his hometown, which he placed face-up so that the headline would be readable by anyone who stood or sat facing him: *Kidnapped Scientist's Freedom Threatened Again.*

The brown and white easy chairs that usually hosted Diggs' and Reyes' private meetings had migrated with the assistance of one of Reyes' interns. The white chair was behind the work-table near the wall, and was occupied by a large box of reports. The brown one was immediately to the left of Reyes' desk and adjacent to the small credenza, holding the lamp which illuminated the front left side of the desk. There was just enough room remaining on it to hold three photographs of Reyes' family and, on occasion, a glass of spirits for a high-ranking guest. That day, it held bourbon.

The chair usually used by an intern assisting Reyes in his office was reserved for Kinnon. Reyes was angry, so it was nothing plush and comfortable, but he also wasn't rude, so the Secretary would not be asked to stand. Instead, he would be seated in close proximity to both congressmen, with the chairman in front of him and the ranking member almost directly to his right.

As soon as Diggs arrived and was seated, Kinnon was invited into the office. He had not been kept waiting. Both Reyes and Diggs understood how to use time well.

"Mr. Secretary, this won't take long. Is it still your intention to have the Department of Justice prosecute Dr. Markson after this hearing?"

Kinnon didn't hesitate. "Yes, Mr. Chairman. He assaulted two government officials, one of them a woman, escaped from lawful custody, and, although he hasn't been charged with it, placed our national security in grave danger. Turning him loose to run free without consequences for his actions would be irresponsible."

"It seems you didn't feel that way when you had the Secretary of the Air Force exercise his emergency powers to appoint him as a warrant officer in the Air Force—that was your idea, wasn't it?"

Kinnon looked the chairman in the eye. "We gave him an opportunity to atone for his behavior by serving his country—an opportunity he wasted."

"You mean he wasted it by coming to testify at these hearings?"

"By breaking an agreement he voluntarily signed, leaving his post, and failing to complete his tour of duty in performing research essential to our national security. By going AWOL. That's what I mean."

"And you intend to court-martial him for that?"

"That's up to his commanding officer, but I'd expect his commander to do that."

"And it doesn't make any difference to you that his signature accepting the Secretary's warrant was coerced?"

"So he says. I don't know anything about that, but he should have brought it up through his chain of command."

Reyes had sat back with his arms folded, scowling as Kinnon spoke. Now, he leaned forward and placed his hands on the desk. "I have two documents here that should make it clear to you why you should not continue to hold Dr. Markson beyond this hearing. One of them is legal and the other is practical. Which one would you like to talk about first?"

Kinnon sat up straight and leaned forward. He waved his hand at the two items on the desk. "Mr. Chairman, I can see them both. The Constitution authorizes us to deal with Markson in accordance with the law, which we have done. He was, and still is, under federal indictment and facing charges for leaving his post without permission. The newspaper is political, not practical. With all due respect, sir, I will not put this country in jeopardy just because doing the proper thing is currently unpopular."

Diggs joined the conversation. "Mr. Secretary, if I were Dr. Markson's attorney, I'd have him back on the street in a heartbeat, and I'm sure he can afford higher-powered representation than me. Have you ever heard of *habeas corpus*?"

"I'm well-familiar with it, Congressman. Everything was done with due process. *Habeas* only applies when there have been no hearings, no due process. We followed all the rules."

Diggs chuckled. "Well, let's see. You hauled him off to a secret court in the middle of the night. Refused to let him contact an attorney of his choice and, over his objections, gave him someone who worked for you—"

Kinnon interrupted, "He worked for the DOJ and the federal court, not me—"

Diggs interrupted in turn, "Well, excuse me. I stand corrected. This public defender worked for your partner in this charade, the Attorney General, right? He certainly didn't work for Markson, right? You're not going to win this one when you take it to court, Mr. Secretary. Why not end it now, before you make yourself and the Administration look worse than you do already?"

"Mr. Chairman, Mr. Diggs... the General Counsel and the Attorney General tell me that we are on sound legal ground. I'm not going to overrule their legal expertise for political convenience, that headline on your desk notwithstanding. May I go now? You've subpoenaed me to testify tomorrow, and I'm sure you expect me to be well-prepared."

Reyes looked at Diggs, who shrugged and raised his eyebrows. Then he answered, "We will resume this conversation tomorrow, Mr. Secretary, when you are under oath."

When Kinnon was gone, Reyes told Diggs he thought the SECDEF had just made a huge mistake. Diggs nodded, finished off his remaining swallow of bourbon, and headed for his office. Reyes' intern had a sandwich ready for the chairman, who had a few preparations to make before attending additional meetings.

After lunch, the committee informally spent another hour alone with Markson in the conference room before thanking him for his testimony and releasing him from their subpoena. When he left the room, Markson was immediately taken into custody by a U.S. Marshal.

Makayla Birkwood went directly to the Federal District Courthouse to file the *habeas corpus* motion she'd prepared just in case this happened.

∞

The remaining witnesses on the committee's agenda were Colonel Chris Nilson, Director of the DARPA warship project, and William Kinnon, the Secretary of Defense. The colonel would lead off the afternoon's proceedings.

Nilson wore the expected dress uniform for his congressional testimony, complete with nearly a dozen rows of colorful ribbons on the left breast of his jacket, each of them announcing one of his many noteworthy accomplishments to those who know the code. A DOD staff attorney sat by his side.

Chairman Reyes began by asking Nilson to describe the meeting at LAPI which had resulted in the incident involving Markson's alleged altercation with Louise Meier from the NSA. Reyes was surprised but pleased that Nilson's version didn't differ in substance from the way Markson and Clarke had described it. The tone and details were different, but Nilson's account contained the same essential events in about the same order.

"OK, now tell us how he came to be working for you at that DARPA facility," the chairman continued.

Nilson conferred for a few seconds with his DOD attorney before responding, "I was notified by a sealed dispatch from the office of the Secretary of the Air Force that Markson had accepted an appointment as a Warrant Officer (W-1) under the Secretary's emergency powers, and that he was under orders to report to me."

"Didn't that strike you as a remarkable turn of events, given your previous confrontation with Markson?"

"I wasn't as surprised as you might think, Mr. Chairman. The core of that confrontation was not the fact that Markson didn't want to do the research—it was only that he insisted the work be unclassified so that he could publish it. I was hoping someone more persuasive than me had found a way for him to get past that."

The chairman folded his arms, leaned back, and frowned. "So, nothing seemed out of the ordinary. He just strolled into your office like any other new recruit reporting for duty?"

"No. When he arrived, he was escorted by a military policeman. That was definitely odd. I welcomed him, but he didn't
appreciate the welcome. It was obvious he didn't want to be
there, but I had my orders, the warrant appointing him was
signed by him and valid on its face, and he had his orders, so
we worked out accommodations."

Reyes made some notes that he handed to his aide and
then looked up at the witness again. "Colonel Nilson, I am
gratified by your candor thus far. Perhaps we can shorten this
proceeding somewhat. Are you familiar with the testimony
that Lee Markson gave to this committee over the past two
days?"

"Yes, Mr. Chairman. Your staff provided me with tran-
scripts to review during lunch so that I could prepare to answer
your questions about it."

"With regard to things about which you have personal
knowledge, is any part of his testimony false or misleading?"

"Yes, sir."

"And what would that be?"

"His assertion that his confinement and assignment to my
command was illegal."

"So, he was lying about that?"

Nilson shook his head. "No, Mr. Chairman. He really
believes it, but he's not a lawyer."

"Are you?"

"No, sir, but my chain of command assures me that everything was done in accordance with the law."

Reyes shuffled through some papers in front of him and then neatly restacked them. "Except for his legal opinion about his captivity, would you agree that his testimony is an accurate narration of your relationship with him?"

Nilson thought for a moment and leaned toward his DOD attorney. They whispered, and then he nodded and faced the panel. "There may be some differences in detail, dates, or things like that, but nothing substantive."

"Thank you again for your candor, Colonel." The chairman looked to his left. "Mr. Diggs, you have three minutes."

Representative Diggs leaned forward and took a less congenial tone. "Are you aware that Lee Markson was led away from this building in handcuffs just before this hearing resumed this afternoon?"

Nilson sat straight up and looked startled. He glanced toward the attorney beside him, who shook her head and turned her palms up as if to say, *"I don't have a clue."*

He turned back to face Mr. Diggs. "No, sir!"

"Were you aware that the DOJ and the DOD intend to continue prosecuting Markson for his supposed assault on Ms. Meier and have added charges of being AWOL because he finally declined your continued hospitality?"

"I knew that was a possibility, Congressman Diggs, but I didn't expect him to be taken into custody before the hearing was over."

"Do you think that's fair?"

"That's not for me to say, sir."

Diggs leaned further forward, pointed his right index finger skyward, and raised his voice. "You have a subpoena from this committee that directs you to answer our questions, Colonel Nilson!" He pointed his finger at the witness. "Do *you* think it's *fair*?"

The USAF attorney put her hand on Nilson's arm before he could respond. Their gestures and whispered discussion grew vigorous and loud enough that the chairman interrupted.

"Do you need a recess, Colonel Nilson?"

"We're almost done, Mr. Chairman," the attorney responded.

"I'm ready to answer the question," Nilson said, ignoring the attorney's attempt to continue their private discussion."

"Please do."

"Before I answer, I want to be absolutely sure I understand your question. You are asking for my personal opinion, and not that of the Air Force or the Department of Defense, is that correct?"

"That is correct. The DOD made its official position crystal clear off the record during the lunch break. I want to know what you, as a person who has answered our questions thus far with more integrity than we've had reason to expect, think of that position."

Again, the USAF attorney took Nilson's arm, but this time, he pulled it away. "Sir, I am ashamed of the way we treated Dr. Markson and Dr. Clarke at the institute. I was disgusted by Ms. Meier's crude attempt to blackmail Dr. Clarke, but we were both following orders. The filing of charges in order to take Dr. Markson into custody may have been legally sound, but it was never fair. At least back then, they had a national security justification. Now that the information is public, that justification no longer exists."

"And his impressment into the Air Force?"

"I don't know whether it was legal or not. I'm not a lawyer, and I still believe it was in the national interest to do it, but it was not something of which I, as an officer in the U.S. Air Force, am proud."

Even though the hearing was closed and there were no reporters or gallery attendees in the room, there were congressional aides and a few representatives who weren't members of the committee, and there was enough commotion that the chairman had to rap his gavel to return the room to order before asking Diggs if he was finished.

"I have one more question, Mr. Chairman. Colonel Nilson, who gave you your orders?"

"I was told they came down my chain of command directly from the Secretary of Defense."

There was no objection when Reyes asked for unanimous consent to recess the remainder of the proceedings for the day in order to prepare to examine the next witness first thing in the morning. The next witness would be Secretary of Defense William Kinnon.

∞

The lead story on the major networks' evening news was the day's testimony and the re-arrest of Lee Markson. The President summoned AG Knowles and SECDEF Kinnon to the Oval Office. When they entered, they found him sitting not behind the chief executive's dark brown antique wooden desk, but on one of the two plush, upholstered beige sofas by the coffee table in the center of the room.

He motioned them to the identical sofa at the other side of the table. "I thought you boys might be a bit more comfortable here. Those straight-backed old wooden chairs by the desk were made kinda hard on purpose. Helps people get to the point. I'm not in a hurry here. We gotta get this right."

The two cabinet members had come from their offices on zero notice and wore their plain day-to-day business suits rather than something more attuned to a meeting with the President. The President himself wore a black suit with a vest, a white shirt, and a black tie with a white power stripe. The seating may have been informal and friendly, but it didn't require a presidential seal in the rug to know who the top dog in this cozy kennel was.

"I just cancelled the national emergency I declared because of that alien spaceship, and now one of you boys is going to tell me why we're still holding that Markson fella."

Knowles looked at Kinnon. He didn't say a word, but his awkward, unexpected silence and blank expression said, "*Hey, pal, it was your idea.*"

Finally, the SECDEF said, "Mr. President, Markson physically assaulted an NSA employee, a woman, and then went AWOL from his assigned station as an Air Force warrant officer. If we don't hold him accountable, at least on the indictment, the courts will lose faith in our ability to keep our word in such matters, and the public will think it's OK to assault federal officers."

The President sat looking Kinnon in the eye for several seconds before he turned his attention to the Attorney General. "What do you think, Fred?"

"Mr. President, I filed the charges and ordered the arrests at Will's request. Unless he can give me a good reason, I don't have any grounds to ask the court to dismiss the indictments."

The President leaned back and covered his face with both hands for a moment before asking, "Did either of you see the interview Willard Manchester did with that young woman who wrote the papers with Markson?"

Neither of them had.

"I hope you at least heard what Colonel Nilson had to say this afternoon..."

"Mr. President," Secretary Kinnon said, "I'm going to address that with him—"

"No, Will, you're not. As I was about to say before I, uh, was interrupted, I've taken calls this afternoon from nineteen Senators and five senior members of the House—from both parties—who are not on that committee, and turned away forty-two calls... more from less senior members. Every one of them wants both of your heads on a platter."

Kinnon and Knowles exchanged glances.

"Let me talk to them, Mr. President," Kinnon began. "Let me explain our problem."

The President leaned forward and looked the SECDEF in the eye. "Our problem, Will, is that the DOD is on the wrong side of this." He paused for a moment. "No. *Our* problem is that *my administration* is on the wrong side of this... and *your* problem is how you are going to fix it."

Kinnon looked mystified. "I don't understand, Mr. President... You authorized Markson's arrest and detention for good reason. Are you now directing me to release him? How can we be assured he'll show up for trial? He's wealthy and famous. For all we know, he could head for some country that doesn't have an extradition treaty with us."

The President shook his head. "Fred, I don't think Will here gets the concept. Explain it to him."

"The President is asking us to consider dropping both the indictment and the military charges altogether, Will. I concur," the AG told Kinnon.

"What? Why?" Kinnon was stunned.

The AG glanced toward the President.

"White House mail is running twenty-to-one against us and, uh, that's happening in the inbox of every member of both houses of Congress," the President said.

"So, we're just going to cave to public opinion? That's so unlike you!" Kinnon persisted.

The President glowered at the SECDEF. "We're not caving

to anything, but we're not going to ignore it, either!" He turned to the AG. "Fred, what do we have to do to kill this thing?"

The AG explained that since an indictment had been issued, a federal court would have to approve dropping those charges. He suggested going back to the same court that had approved the arrest warrant and transfer of custody to the DOD. He said he could file an emergency motion to dismiss the charges that evening and have a hearing set for first thing in the morning.

"Will we have any problem getting that motion granted?" the President asked.

"Not if the DOD supports it. The Secretary of the Air Force can direct Markson's commander to abandon any planned court-martial. In federal court, we can cite Nilson's testimony as new information under oath that changed our understanding of the circumstances under which the events occurred," the AG responded.

Kinnon looked chastened. "Does my job depend on this?"

The President nodded. "It does."

Kinnon shook his head, bewildered.

"Here's the thing, Will," the President said in a softer tome. "You've got to stop thinking about this like a lawyer. You've gotten too attached to the idea that because he got physical defending his girlfriend's honor and rejected your hospitality, he ought to be made to pay. When you took the oath as my Secretary of Defense, you, uh, put on a different kind of hat. This job is inherently political. If we don't put this behind us right now, then the people will see to it next year that I lose my job. When I lose my job, then, um, you lose yours. Do you understand?"

Kinnon took a deep breath and nodded. The light had finally penetrated the fog. He turned to the AG. "Do you need me to sign anything? I won't be able to come to court unless the committee releases me from its subpoena. I'm scheduled to testify tomorrow."

Knowles proposed that they draft a formal request from the DOD to the AG, asking that the charges against Lee Markson be dismissed, and attach it to the motion. Kinnon agreed, and the President concurred.

The President had another instruction for Kinnon: "As soon as the motion to dismiss is filed tonight, notify Markson's attorney and release Markson on his own recognizance. Don't officially tell him that the charges will be dropped until the court grants the motion—just, uh, that he's free to go for now. Tomorrow, start your testimony by telling the committee how pleased you are to announce that Lee Markson has been released... that all military charges have been dropped, and that you have requested that the AG ask the court to dismiss the remaining federal charges.

"And, Fred," the President continued, "as soon as the court grants the motion, notify me and Will. I'd like him to be able to relay that to the committee during his testimony as soon as it happens."

"Yes, Mr. President," they said simultaneously.

As the two cabinet officers turned to leave, the President asked Kinnon to remain for a moment. After the AG closed the door behind him, the President spoke. "If there are any reprisals against Colonel Nilson, I will have your immediate resignation. Is that understood?"

"Crystal clear, Mr. President. You have my full support. If I may go now, I need to get Fred the paperwork to get Markson out of detention in time to make the 11 PM news."

The President broke into a big smile and patted Kinnon on the shoulder. "That's the spirit, Will. I knew I could count on you!"

∞

SECDEF Kinnon sat next to the DOD legal advisor as Chairman Reyes rapped his gavel and introduced them. The Secretary was prepared for the cameras he knew would follow his every step after he testified. His suit was top of the line, dark gray with wide-spaced, thin white pinstripes. The tailored white shirt, silver cuff links, and black tie with its slanting white stripes made a statement .

The chairman noted for the record that the hearing was closed. He reminded Kinnon that he was under oath and then granted the SECDEF's request to make a brief opening statement before proceeding with his testimony. Kinnon sat rigidly as he spoke.

The committee members were startled and delighted when Kinnon announced that Lee Markson had been released from confinement late the previous night, that Kinnon had ordered the military charges dropped, and that he had asked the Attorney General to request a dismissal of all other federal charges pending against Markson. A flurry of side conversations between the members and some of their staffers revealed that none of them had been notified by the government and that Markson had not contacted any of them. Moreover, in a city notorious for news leaks, the story had not been made public.

Reyes gaveled the hearing back to order. Then, with his arms folded in front of him on the table, and in his most deliberate, carefully modulated cadence, asked, "Mr. Secretary, why didn't you notify me last night, and why haven't we heard this in the media?"

The SECDEF explained that he'd intended to release Markson early the previous evening and notify both the committee and the press in advance. "Unfortunately," he continued, "the paperwork took much longer than expected. They needed a court order before the detention center would release him. It was after 3 AM by the time that happened."

"My phone works at 3 AM, Mr. Secretary."

"The night was almost over, Mr. Chairman, and I decided to wait because Markson asked that we not make his release public until the morning. He wanted to have his first few hours of freedom in peace before the press descended on him. The President agreed. He said we owed Markson that much. I apologize if it was the wrong thing to do."

"We can discuss that later in my office, Mr. Secretary," the chairman said, before returning to the planned agenda.

In response to the usual preliminary questions, Kinnon said that he understood why he had been called to testify and that he had read the testimony of previous witnesses.

"Mr. Secretary, do you now admit that Dr. Markson was taken by your department against his will and forced into service on a project designed to explore and develop this alien technology?"

Kinnon conferred briefly with the DOD attorney before answering. "Yes, sir."

"And by what authority did you do that?"

"We had direct authorization from the President and the concurrence of the Attorney General and the General Counsel of the Air Force, Mr. Chairman."

The chairman turned to a staffer seated behind the committee table and, in a voice intended to be heard throughout the room, said, "Would you see to it that the witness, the President, the AG, and the General Counsel are provided with copies of the United States Constitution?" Then, he addressed Kinnon again.

"Alright. Let's assume that you were acting in good faith when you had Markson shanghaied. Based on the testimony we have received so far, it seems to have been both unnecessary and counterproductive."

The DOD attorney leaned toward Kinnon, but Kinnon waved his hand as if to say, *"I've got this one,"* and looked Reyes in the eye. "Mr. Chairman, I object to the term 'shanghaied.' Dr. Markson was legally detained by the Department of Justice because he was under a federal felony indictment. The court legally transferred him to our custody in accordance with a warrant appointing Dr. Markson as a warrant officer (W-1) in the Air Force under Article 10, Section 603(a) of the United States Code."

The chairman didn't blink. "Mr. Secretary, even if your department acted in good faith, it does not appear to this committee to have acted ethically. Call it 'detained,' 'arrested,' 'impressed,' or whatever euphemism you want to paint over it, but he was shanghaied. Now, I want to know whether you still believe such extreme action was justified."

Kinnon presented the arguments that had convinced the President and the AG to authorize taking Markson. He reinforced those points using classified documentation provided to the committee. He closed with, "We really didn't have much choice, given Dr. Markson's irrational and dangerous disregard for our national security."

"So, tell me again why you were so accommodating as to free him just in time for your testimony this morning?" Reyes asked.

"As I said before, the circumstances have changed since the matter has become public. Confining him is no longer essential to our national security."

"Of course, it wouldn't have anything to do with political pressure resulting from the overwhelming tide of public opinion, would it?" Kinnon started to speak, but the chairman cut him off. "You don't need to answer that, Mr. Secretary."

Even Kinnon couldn't resist a tiny smile. He admired watching a political master at work even if, at the moment, he himself happened to be on the wrong end of the stick.

The chairman reserved the remainder of his time and passed the floor to the ranking member, Mr. Diggs.

"Mr. Secretary, I applaud your initial efforts to get Dr. Markson and Dr. Clarke to join your project voluntarily. That's the way it should have been handled." Diggs paused, and then he pointed his right index finger in the air. "But, sir, in my state, government officials do not use pornographic pictures to blackmail our constituents or their loved ones into involuntary servitude. Whatever were you thinking?"

Kinnon paused and spoke with his attorney before answering. "I was unaware of that at the time, and I apologize for it. Colonel Nilson and Ms. Meier were instructed to use all possible legal incentives to recruit Markson and Clarke. I'll admit the directions could have been more specific. Even so, they exercised poor judgment. We'll address that to ensure it doesn't happen again."

When Kinnon kept repeating the same responses to further questions about the impressment, Diggs changed the subject. He asked for the SECDEF's opinion of Markson's assertion that the secretive, in-house DOD approach to solving the technical problem was ineffective and had only delayed the nation's ability to understand and eventually acquire the alien technology.

Kinnon dismissed the argument as being derived from a naïve, internationalist attitude common among academics. "That same argument could have been made when we set up the Manhattan Project," he pointed out. "Ever since World War II, we've kept a step or two ahead of our enemies by maintaining scientific superiority. Markson's concern about threats from the aliens is irrelevant. If they come, their technology will totally outclass ours, no matter what we do. The Chinese and the Russians aren't a hypothetical threat. They are powerful adversaries who have spent fortunes on espionage in order to steal our technology. It would be plain stupid to just open the door and give away the store on the warp drive thing."

Congresswoman Serano was about to begin her questioning when a messenger handed a small slip of paper to the Secretary, who asked permission from the chairman for an immediate ten-minute recess, which was granted.

When the session resumed, Kinnon said, "Mr. Chairman, before Congresswoman Serano begins her questioning, I have news I believe will be of interest to the committee. May I proceed?"

"The floor is yours, Mr. Secretary."

Kinnon announced that the motion to dismiss the indictments against Lee Markson had been granted and that there were now no federal charges pending against him. Reyes nodded his approval while Digges exclaimed "Alright!" Serrano gave a thumbs-up as the remaining members of the committee whispered amongst themselves until Reyes banged the gavel and Kinnon resumed his announcement.

He told the committee that they had been unable to contact Markson to notify him and were going ahead with the public release of the information in hopes that Markson would get the good news more quickly from the news coverage than if they withheld it until they could locate him.

On behalf of the committee, Reyes thanked Kinnon for having "done the right thing" and then resumed the normal order of business.

Serano took up Markson's point that there was no military value to faster-than-light travel at distances as short as those we have on Earth, and that it couldn't be used anyway because of the collateral damage from the bow shock. "Was he wrong?" she asked.

"Dr. Markson may be an excellent physicist, but his testimony shows his ignorance of military matters," the SECDEF responded.

"How could such a spacecraft be used as a terrestrial weapon?"

"Without going into detail, even in this closed hearing, consider an orbital platform with the capability to launch not spaceships, but small faster-than-light drones. There are two ways these could be used. With a thermonuclear payload, they could hit a target with zero warning. More significantly, there is a non-nuclear option, again with complete surprise. The 'collateral damage' Dr. Markson mentioned could be the payload of an otherwise unarmed superluminal drone. There would be no need to violate the treaty against nuclear weapons in space."

Serano raised another issue. "Dr. Markson told us that it could be fifty years or more until we know enough about the physics to build any sort of device, peaceful or otherwise. What is the DOD's position?"

"I am not in a position to agree with that, Ms. Serano."

"What is your best estimate? Twenty years? Ten?"

"It could be. We won't know until we try."

"Mr. Secretary, forgive me for being frank, but when you answered us about military applications, it sounded like you knew what you were talking about. Now, it sounds like you don't. Does your department have any substantial scientific data or analysis that tells us that Dr. Markson's assessment of the difficulty of the research involved here is incorrect?"

Kinnon frowned. He hadn't expected the question and hadn't prepared for it. He conferred with the attorney before answering, "No, ma'am."

Chairman Reyes rapped the gavel. "I think this is a good place to break for lunch."

The hearing recessed. The SECDEF and the members of the committee returned to their respective offices, where their staffs had arranged for their meals and briefing papers to be ready for them so that they could spend the break preparing for the afternoon session.

When the hearing resumed, it was Representative Ito's turn.

"Mr. Secretary, you summarily dismissed the threat from the aliens. Dr. Markson cited that threat as justification for the need to accelerate the research through an open international effort. Why doesn't that concern you?"

"I don't accept Dr. Markson's premise that the research will proceed more rapidly in the open market, so to speak. The atomic bomb, guided missile technology, radar—all were developed within secret military projects. Fifty years later, our satellites are still being launched by vehicles derived from military programs. The supposed efficiency of open, unclassified research is a myth."

Ito leaned forward. "If I recall, Mr. Secretary, all of the fundamental physics necessary for a nuclear weapon had been done by 1939, much of it by the Germans. What the Manhattan Project accomplished was the nuclear engineering. Similarly, Maxwell published the equations for radio waves before a practical radio was invented. Marconi did the early engineering. And the Russian Tsiolkovsky was the father of rocket science, was he not? In the case of our nuclear missiles, I believe they were designed by German rocket scientists we captured after World War II. Dr. Markson says we're not ready to undertake faster-than-light engineering yet and that the science itself is best done openly. It seems to me you're proving his point."

Congressman Ito and then Congressman Roberts continued to pummel the Secretary. They challenged his responses to Markson's suggestion that the project be turned over to a civilian agency, as had been done with the space program. That discussion finally ended with the following exchange initiated by Roberts' final question:

"Mr. Secretary, for all the time we've spent on the subject, it seems that your total objection to turning this research over to NASA, for example, rests on two arguments. First, you claim that the subject is a military and national security concern which should remain covert, and second, that you've already invested in it heavily—so, why reinvent the wheel? Have I got that right?"

"I believe that captures the sense of my position, yes."

"So, if we don't accept your military rationale for keeping everything under wraps, then it all boils down to a turf war, correct?"

"No, sir! For the sake of our nation, I hope you will not direct us to declassify this work, but even if you do, duplication of the resources we have created to perform the research would be costly and unnecessary."

"Again, let me reminisce. Wasn't that what the military said about the space program when President Eisenhower created NASA? That worked out rather well, don't you think?"

As soon as Reyes adjourned the meeting, he headed out through the back of the hearing room to avoid the reporters who'd gathered out front and were badgering Secretary Kinnon. Serano and Diggs had also headed for the reporters. Before long, the DOD, NASA, and a dozen major defense and aerospace contractors were competing for various pieces of what promised to be a large and lucrative basic science initiative.

CHAPTER FOURTEEN

THE AFTERMATH

IN THE WEEKS FOLLOWING the hearings, Reyes and Diggs met privately with Markson, Huntsman, and Nilson—both individually and as a group—in order to explore options for organizing the government's warp drive research. As expected, Nilson continued to advocate for placing the program within the Department of Defense, preferably in DARPA or the Air Force Office of Scientific Research (AFOSR).

One evening as they ate dinner in an out-of-the-way Washington, D.C. restaurant, the three physicists were bemoaning what they saw as the unproductive and time-consuming nature of the committee's attempts to produce a politically acceptable way to structure funding and the priority-setting for the research.

Markson had had enough. "We aren't getting anywhere," he said, "but it's just as much our fault as theirs."

"What do you mean?" Huntsman asked.

Markson looked at his boss and mentor from CAT. "You try to impress the politicians with how well NASA has done in the past with government programs, and what you say is true, but you don't dare admit that another path could be better this time. That might raise questions and issues you'd rather not bring to their attention."

The associate administrator's face reddened. "That's not fair, Lee. NASA's track record is directly relevant to its competence to lead this program. I don't see you complaining about Chris's advocacy for the DOD."

"Aw, come on," Nilson said. "Lee's been complaining about us both. At least we've actually been working on the problem while you took a bye."

"Stop it!" Markson demanded.

Startled by Markson's outburst, Nilson and Huntsman stared at him.

He put his hands on the table and spoke in a slow, quiet manner. "The fact is that all three of us have been pushing our own organization so that we can be in charge. I'm just as guilty as you are, pushing for a private foundation to run it. And, deep down, all three of us know this is now bigger than any of us. Why have the politicians been talking behind closed doors to us without involving the academic community or the private companies? Heck, they wouldn't even let me bring Katty into the conversation. Ken, you're one of the nation's experts in research funding. Why are we so privileged?"

Huntsman thought for a moment. "Because we have credibility. The politicians need us to justify their spending to their constituents."

Markson looked to Nilson. "You know he's right. That's why the DOD has so many bases in places that, without coincidence, are in the districts of powerful congressmen. Have I got that correct?"

"Guilty as charged," Nilson admitted. "You sound like you have something in mind. Out with it."

Markson paused and took a deep breath. "If we can figure out how to use this technology, it could save the human species. Right now, the Earth is a single point of failure for us. Even if we colonize the solar system, the sun will eventually go nova. Warp technology opens the galaxy to us. We have to get this right for the human species, not for NASA or the DOD or FASTER or the U.S. I think the three of us should combine our influence and credibility, and jointly present Chairman Reyes and Mr. Diggs with a proposal that we can all back—and sell them on how it will make them heroes in the history books and winners in the next election."

Nilson and Huntsman looked at each other.

Nilson spoke up. "Whatever happened to the Lee Markson who didn't give a crap about politics or hierarchies or, dare I say it, leadership?"

"I was wondering that myself," Huntsman said with a grin.

"You two were my teachers. I didn't always appreciate the way you did it—especially you, Chris—but teachers you both were, nonetheless. Don't complain if I learned something."

Huntsman looked at Nilson. "You game?"

"Let's give it a shot," the colonel agreed.

They had many days of discussion already behind them, so it did not take long for the trio to create an acceptable plan.

With Diggs' approval, Reyes convened the full committee to consider the proposal their three experts jointly recommended. After receiving testimony from academic and commercial organizations, the committee turned the proposal into legislation, which then passed the House and Senate with little debate. Just four months after Markson's congressional testimony, the President signed into law a bill creating the National Institute for Spacetime Engineering Research (NISTER).

When she first heard it on the news, Clarke thought the name was hysterical. "I see you convinced them to use that gross acronym you proposed when you threw the foundation idea at me."

Markson laughed with her. "It wasn't my idea this time. I wouldn't let them have FASTER because we're keeping that. Ken proposed NISTER with no prompting from me. I guess great minds just think alike."

"You could have given them IFART. I would have let them have that," she said with a giggle.

Markson shook his head. "At least they structured it well. Let's go get some ice cream to celebrate."

NISTER would be managed by a "NISTER Consortium" of eight universities along with NASA, the DOD, and the LIGO Laboratory, each organization having one trustee on the board. One of the universities would host NISTER and its consortium. That school's trustee would be chairperson of NISTER's Board of Trustees. The board would appoint a Director of NISTER and a Deputy Director of NISTER. The NISTER Consortium was modeled on the management structure of Virgo, and it was a compromise that everyone liked.

To bring NISTER into existence, the university members were to be selected competitively based on criteria developed by the three government trustee organizations, but with input from "recognized experts." Nobody was astonished to find that these experts included Markson and Clarke. But while the pair would assist the government in designing the selection criteria, they declined to participate in reviewing proposals or selecting the winning schools. They wanted to retain the option of being part of one of the university teams competing for a position in the consortium.

When Markson returned to Baton Rouge, Dean Simpson asked him to rejoin LAPI as a full professor and lead their efforts to become the NISTER host institution—with the expectation that, if they won, he would be NISTER's first director. He asked for a couple of days to consider it.

He was tempted. He wanted to be in charge, to be able to

direct the research down pathways he believed would have the most chances of success, but that also gave him pause. Success would require prolonged, stable focus and funding. When the space shuttle had been proposed, the DOD had agreed to transfer many of their heavy launch operations from their own expendable vehicles to NASA's "space truck." As soon as the first major shuttle accident had occurred, that decision had been reversed.

What happens if there's a national security scare relating to the aliens or to speculations about our Earthly foes getting a bit ahead in the research?

He realized that government money was never secure, and that not even the Director of NISTER could guarantee stable funding and purpose. The only way to do that would be for Markson to use his own money. If he wanted to assure that public, open research would always have an advocate that could back up their rhetoric with resources, he would have to protect and preserve FASTER.

He would stay at the foundation.

When Markson met with Simpson again, she was easily convinced to give his former position as a tenured associate professor to Clarke, who would then become the institute's liaison to both NISTER and FASTER. When she asked him if he'd decided to accept her offer of a full professorship to lead the NISTER effort, he told her he knew someone who was better qualified.

Dean Simpson raised her eyebrows. "Who do you have in mind?"

All she could get out of him was, "I'll let you know as soon as I've talked him into it."

Ken Huntsman was curious when Markson asked him to fly down from D.C. for lunch at Mansurs, with Markson picking up both the airfare and the meal. Markson reserved what by now had become their "recruiting table" at the restaurant—the one where Huntsman had begun recruiting him for CATSPAW and where he'd treated Clarke when she'd recruited him into the effort to rescue Markson from the DOD.

The maître d' led Huntsman to the table, and Markson stood as they approached. "Long time, no see!" he said with a broad smile.

They shook hands as the maître d' left, and Huntsman asked, "Can we eat before the sales pitch? I didn't eat on the flight and I'm hungry."

Markson laughed as they took their seats. "Is it that obvious?"

"You think? All expenses paid? This restaurant? This table? It has to be a proposal of some kind, and it better not be accompanied by a ring."

Markson smiled and looked down, then laughed a little. "You're not my type! Let's eat."

A waiter appeared before they'd completely taken their seats. As soon as they settled in, he presented Markson with the wine and beverage list. "May I interest you in one of our fine house wines?"

"No, thank you, I'm driving today. Your coffee is always superb. I'll have a cup of that."

"Very good, sir." Turning, he presented the list to Huntsman. "And how about you, sir?"

"Actually, I'll have a glass of your best brandy, please."

"Oh, very good, sir! Here are your menus. Our luncheon special today is roast lamb with a yogurt-garlic sauce and asparagus. I'll be right back with your drinks."

As the waiter headed toward the kitchen, Markson asked, "Are you going to have your favorite cedar-roasted redfish today?"

Huntsman got a wicked grin on his face. "Since you're buying, my friend, I think I'm going to have the filet mignon."

Markson raised his eyebrows and nodded. "In that case, I'll have the redfish!"

The waiter returned with a carafe of brandy and a chilled snifter into which he poured it, as well as a small coffee pot from which Markson could fill and refill the cup with the Mansurs logo on it. "May I take your orders?"

Huntsman ordered his steak and Markson his fish. As they waited for their meals, the pair caught up on what each other had been doing.

Markson wasn't prepared when Huntsman asked, "When are you and Kat going to get married? You two are a perfect match."

The younger man stumbled through some gibberish about being too busy so far to have thought about it and not being quite ready to think about it now. Mercifully, the food arrived in time to mitigate any further embarrassment for either of them.

The cuisine was Mansurs' usual: insufferably delicious. Amid a repeat of the mirth attending to selecting their main courses, the pair consulted the dessert menu and decided that nothing fancier than a small dish of vanilla ice cream was required for dessert. On the other hand, they hadn't yet discussed what Lee had called the meeting to discuss, so instead of ice cream, they each ordered a large French pastry and a non-alcoholic chocolate grasshopper mocha. That should give them enough time for their conversation.

Huntsman took a bite of pastry. "OK. Now, I'm ready for business. What's this all about?"

Markson related his conversation with Dean Simpson. "Ken, I think it's critical that NISTER get off to a good start. You're the only person I know who can ensure that happens. I'd like to recommend you for the NISTER professorship."

Huntsman looked puzzled. "When you testified in Congress, you said someone like you should lead it. You're perfect for the job. If you've turned it down, you must see a problem with it. What makes you think I'd want it? I'm not even qualified. I don't know anything about faster-than-light physics."

Markson nodded. "All that seems to make sense, so I understand where you're coming from, but I've got a different perspective. Hear me out."

"Oh, I intend to. I'm curious, and besides, I owe you at least that for the free lunch."

Markson laughed. "Let's take it piece by piece. In the first place, I learned a little bit about management from you and Henry at CAT, and I'm learning on the job at FASTER, but I don't have anywhere near the skills or experience necessary to handle a big, public organization funded with tax money and subject to the political winds. You do, and that's more important to the success of NISTER's first director than his or her knowledge of warp mechanics. You've been successfully managing a NASA research directorate for several years, and learned enough about FTL physics to sell it to a major congressional committee and blow the lid off a government cover-up. You're the one who's perfect, not me."

Huntsman raised his eyebrows and frowned a little, arms crossed in front of him. "Maybe, but you can learn. You'll need those same skills at FASTER, and that hasn't stopped you from accepting the lead there. Wouldn't you rather manage the big show than a small sideshow?"

"Ken, the truth is, I still don't trust the government. Once the next election takes place, the winners could reconsider. Maybe they'll decide Nilson was right after all, or even that the whole thing is junk science like Aguillero said. FASTER may be small, but it has one major advantage—it's privately funded. By me. And Katty and I control it. If NISTER goes under and the tide turns against the work, we'll still be there as a lifeboat. I won't risk letting that go."

Huntsman sat with his arms still folded, still contemplating the situation. Markson broke the awkwardness of the long silence by excusing himself to go to the restroom. When he returned, Huntsman was sitting up with his hands on the table.

As soon as Markson was back in his seat, Huntsman said, "Lee, I haven't told anyone this yet, so please keep it to yourself. I'm planning to retire from NASA at the end of the year. I have more money than God, but the clock is running, and I want to spend some of it while I still can. I don't want another job."

Now, it was Markson's turn to sit and ponder things silently. He slouched to one side with his hands clasped in his lap. After half a minute, he sat up. "OK. In one way, that's consistent with my proposal. You were planning to leave NASA anyway. I'll tell you what: I think I can sell the dean on a fixed-term appointment... say, five years. My concern is getting things off on the right foot. Your credentials should give our proposal a leg up in the competition for LAPI to be the host institution. If they succeed, you'll be Chairman of the Board of the NISTER Consortium and, I hope, Director of NISTER. Your five years will set its direction and tone for decades to come, and then you can walk off into the sunset."

Another long silence. Huntsman took a deep breath and sighed. "Shit. There's something deeply attractive about the opportunity, but so much can happen in five years. There are things I want to do, places I want to see, people I want to visit. I don't want to be tied down by a commitment like that. It's too big a slice out of the rest of my life."

Markson looked Huntsman in the eye. "Would you give me three years?"

"Could you sell it to the dean?"

Markson grinned. "Probably, if I take her to lunch."

∞

As the allegations from the congressional hearings accumulated, beginning with Huntsman's testimony before the winter break and ending with the DOD's testimony following Markson's, JoAnne Simpson felt more and more used. Aguillero had taken advantage of being Chairman of the Physics and Astronomy Department to convince her that the work done by Markson and Clarke had no value. She'd almost gotten comfortable with the unusual way Aguillero had handled the situation when Nilson and Maier had shown up at her office to tell her that Aguillero had it all wrong.

They'd told her they could fix it all up if she just set up a meeting. Now, she'd found out on national television that the meeting had been a shameful attempt, probably illegal, to shut down and classify potentially Nobel Prize-winning research that had been going on in Aguillero's Physics Department in the College of Science, of which she was dean, before he'd talked her into effectively letting him fire the people doing it.

Her father had always told her, "Don't get mad. Get even." She felt mad. It was time to get even.

The president of the institute and the dean recognized that any institution which could recruit both Markson and Clarke to their proposal team had a significant competitive advantage. LAPI had its close association with LIGO and a faculty with the expertise and experience to put together a winning proposal—if they could recruit the two scientists they had treated so badly. For Simpson, it would be a pleasure to watch the department chairman make them the offers she had in mind. *He* was going to convince Markson to return to the institute as a full professor and lead the team preparing their proposal to host NISTER. *He* was going to promote Clarke to Markson's old position—tenured associate research professor. Clarke would be part of the proposal team, as well. *And he will smile with an abiding sincerity while doing it.* The dean called the Physics Department chairman to her office.

Aguillero made it clear that the prospect of Katty Clarke as a tenured professor in his department was unacceptable. "She is unqualified both academically and morally for a senior faculty position." He would not budge, adding, "There isn't room for both of us in the Department of Physics and Astronomy."

He said this more than once during his heated conversation with the dean. She was certain he didn't care that he was putting LAPI's chances for winning the NASA contract at risk.

Simpson wanted to fire Aguillero, but he had tenure, and firing him would require both good cause and a great deal of time-consuming administrative bureaucracy. It would be easier just to remove him from his position as the department chairman. She believed that she had adequate cause, but it pained her deeply to use it as a threat. It felt too much like the way they had treated Markson and Clarke. Unfortunately, the circumstances left her no choice.

"Jorge, I have kept this conversation professional and collegial, but this is going to happen whether you like it or not. If you can't find a way to put your emotions aside and accept Dr. Clarke as your departmental liaison to the institute in our proposal, I will replace you with someone who can put the interest of this school first."

Aguillero stood up and approached her, and he shook his finger in the air between them. "I am a tenured full professor and department chairman at this institute, and we have rules! I will see you in court if need be. You are not going to make that whore of a 'just-recently-got-her-PhD' assistant professor, who we previously reprimanded for insubordination, a tenured associate professor in my department! Period."

The dean sighed, turned, and stepped away from Aguillero. When she turned back to him, her voice was deliberate and measured. "I have spoken with others in the department. You pressured our faculty to disapprove submission of what may be a Nobel Prize-winning manuscript. You suggested that their promotions or research funding might be at risk if they supported publication of the paper."

Aguillero looked startled, then defiant. "There's nothing improper about letting my employees know their actions have consequences if they don't hold their colleagues to the highest standards!"

"Among *our* highest standards, Dr. Aguillero, are those of independent judgment and freedom from intimidation. You violated those standards, and that is grounds for removal of a department chairmanship. And lobbying referees and editors of peer-reviewed papers to reject a paper because you disapprove of it is just plain unethical, not to mention embarrassing to the institute. You could be fired for that."

"Nonsense! I did nothing of the kind. Even if you think you can prove I did something improper, it will not do you any good. My lawyer will tie you up in court for months. If you need that little strumpet for your RFP, stick her in a special program with Markson. They deserve each other. They've got no respect for authority. Let's see how Markson likes it when she won't follow his rules."

"Ask your lawyer what happens to your pension if you are fired. You have until close of business today to send me your approval for Clarke's appointment or your resignation as department chairman."

Aguillero started to speak, but she cut him off and pointed to the door. "Out!"

That afternoon, Aguillero announced his retirement from LAPI, effective immediately. The next morning, the dean appointed Dr. Zhao Ming as the Acting Chairman of the Department of Physics and Astronomy after he told her he wasn't interested in taking on the position in the long-term because it would interfere with his research. She tasked him with providing her some recommendations for a permanent replacement within two weeks. It was a severe challenge, but one which he was willing to accept in order to get back to doing quantum mechanics full-time as quickly as possible.

The dean's timeline wouldn't support a nationwide search, so she limited it to the institute. Several of the Physics Department's faculty were interested in the position. The least expected and most interesting candidate for Ming to consider was someone whose primary research expertise was in mathematics rather than physics. Dr. Shanta Jelani wanted to focus on physics full-time and was willing to accept the administrative burden as chairman of the department as her price of admission.

Ming knew Jelani by reputation and from their service together on the panel that had reviewed Markson and Clarke's papers. He was impressed by the recommendations she received from both Lee Markson and Katty Clarke, the only physicists who knew her work well enough to evaluate her competence in the field. He asked her in for an interview.

When she arrived, Ming was sitting at Aguillero's former desk, which was bare except for the computer and its accessories. Aguillero had cleared all of his possessions from it, the credenza, and the walls when he'd departed. Ming wasn't planning to reside in the space for more than a few weeks, so he wasn't repopulating it with stuff of his own.

"Please have a seat, Professor Jelani. I'd offer you coffee, but the Keurig machine was Jorge's. It's probably in Argentina by now. I'll get right to the point. What makes a well-established senior mathematician with less formal background in physics than some of our junior faculty, and none in astronomy, think she ought to be Chairperson of the Department of Physics and Astronomy?"

Jelani had come well-prepared. "We are hoping to become the national focus of research in faster-than-light travel. What are the top two theoretical obstacles that our former colleagues, whom we treated so badly, faced in making a case for their interpretation of the observations of the event?"

Ming was expecting a sales pitch, not an oral exam in physics. "Well, they brushed off the radiation issue, so it would have to be energy and the horizon problem that prevents control of the vehicle."

"Exactly," she said. "And what two branches of physics are likely to lead to useful approaches to those problems?"

Ming wrinkled his brow and his lips to match. He was intrigued and even a little charmed by her surprising approach, but he didn't quite see where she was going with it. "Quantum mechanics and general relativity."

Now, she raised her eyebrows and opened her eyes wide. "And who is the department's expert on quantum mechanics?"

"I am," he said with well-earned pride.

"Right! And who had been this department's expert on the mathematics of general relativity?"

Ming laughed out loud and bowed slightly. "And you want to solve our problems full-time?"

She nodded. "I have some ideas. I'm wondering if there are topologies in four-dimensional or higher dimensional spaces, like in string theory, that might allow for tunneling through the horizons or creating and collecting negative energy. I even think we might have a productive collaboration on some of these approaches. We could try to make some progress together on quantum gravity. That's an opportunity I'll never see again."

Ming was awed, but he still had a remaining concern. "I would be delighted to have you as a member of our department full-time, Dr. Jelani, but shouldn't the department chairman come from within the department? Do you think you can be accepted as a physicist rather than as an interloper from the Mathematics Department?"

She folded her arms. "You know, when we were reviewing the Markson-Clarke paper, nobody except Aguillero ever questioned my physics credentials or membership in the department, and he only resorted to that when you and I crossed him. It wasn't a problem then, and unless you know something I don't, it isn't now."

Ming nodded. "I'll let you know, Shanta."

Simpson accepted Ming's recommendation to transfer Professor Shanta Jelani to full-time in the Department of Physics and Astronomy and appoint her as the department chairman.

∞

Jelani's first priority was to rehire Markson. Assuming she could sell him on the idea, he could help her persuade Clarke. She called him at home that evening.

"Hi, Lee! It's Shanta. I'm glad I caught you. I have a proposal for you."

Markson caught the brightness in her voice. He'd been expecting a call from the LAPI administration, but was pleasantly surprised to hear from Katty's close friend and one of the few faculty colleagues who had supported them during the battle over publication.

"Shanta! It's a pleasure to hear from you. What's up?"

"I don't know whether you've heard, but Jorge quit. I've got the job now, and I'd like to have the opportunity to talk you into rejoining my faculty in a very senior position. If you can spare an hour to meet with me, we have a lot to talk about."

Markson was sure he knew what she had in mind and he didn't intend to return to LAPI, but he had an agenda of his own to pitch and was glad to have a friendly ear on the inside. "Would one o'clock work for you?"

"See you in the departmental office at one!"

Markson arrived several minutes early, but the departmental secretary immediately ushered him into Jelani's inner office. The place looked different. Aguillero had used to brew the coffee. Jelani had it catered. Two urns, robust and decaf, plus a pitcher of hot water accompanied by a variety-box of tea bags, all sat on a wheeled cart that also hosted two kinds of Danish, some donuts, and some "everything" bagels with a tub of cream cheese. Folk art from India and Africa adorned the space where Aguillero's Keurig machine had resided.

Jelani got up from her desk and pointed to the refreshment cart. "I wasn't sure what you liked, so I had them bring a little bit of each. I don't think we're going to want to be disturbed. Grab yourself something. Let's sit at the table." She had nothing in her hand as she approached. No paperwork. No notepad.

Markson poured himself a cup of coffee and sat down. He noticed that she'd rearranged the chairs, two on each side so that no one appeared to have preferred seating.

She took the chair directly across from him. "No snack?" she asked.

"Just had lunch."

Unlike his meetings with Aguillero, Markson was attired more formally than the department chairman this time. No jacket—he hadn't gone that far—but he wore black wool dress slacks with a pastel green business shirt and matching tie. Jelani noticed the silver cuff links and tie pin immediately.

"You didn't dress up just for me, did you?"

Being the chairman of the department hadn't toned down her love of bright colors and soft fabrics. The subdued appearance of women's academic business attire wasn't to her liking, and she was draped in blues and purples with tasteful, delicate gold highlights.

"I could ask the same. What can I do for you?" Markson asked.

"I know you told Dean Simpson 'no,' but I'm hoping I can convince you to join our faculty again, Lee. I know the institute doesn't deserve your respect—not right now—but I think perhaps we can earn it back again if you'll give us the chance. I'm planning to make it worth your while."

Markson was curious about how they planned to build the consortium if they were to lead it. Before he declined the offer, he wanted to hear the details. That would provide a basis on which to judge whether or not to propose Huntsman as an alternative. "I'm always open to new data."

The ironic significance of those precise words addressed to the department chairman did not escape her.

"In your congressional testimony, you said you thought any government effort in this area should be managed by a civilian institution run by somebody like you. Do you still believe that?"

"I do."

"Good. I'm glad to hear you say that, because I agree with it. How would you like a chance to make it happen?"

"How?"

She leaned forward, elbows on the table. "We are going to compete to be the lead university for the NISTER Consortium. If we win, one of our faculty will probably be appointed the Director of NISTER."

Markson sat back. "And you want me on your team."

"I want you to lead our team and be the first director of NISTER."

At Markson's insistence, Jelani explained in detail the rough plans they currently had for the organization of the consortium and the institute. "Of course, as soon as you are on board," she continued, "you can take your red pencil to them. I also plan to hire Dr. Clarke into your old position, and her input will also be welcome. Once you become director, she'll become the department's liaison since it wouldn't be appropriate for the director to hold both positions."

Markson nodded. "It's generally a good beginning. It needs some fine-tuning, but the essence is there."

"So, you'll do it?"

"I have a better idea."

She looked confused. "Excuse me?"

"Actually, I know someone who's better qualified for the position. If I we convince him to take the position, it will give you a stronger proposal and give NISTER a stronger start."

"Who? Why?"

"Ken Huntsman. Because he knows enough of the right kind of physics to compete with anybody—except for me or Kat—and he knows more about navigating federal bureaucracies than the two of us together will ever know. The folks evaluating the proposals are government folks who are skeptical of the ability of academics to manage their money and keep them out of political trouble. I'm certainly not a person who leaves that impression—at least not the keeping-out-of-trouble part."

"So, you want your old position back, but with a promotion to full professor, of course?"

"No. Kat earned it. Tenured research associate professor, just like I had. She can work her way up to full professor in due time."

"What do you want?"

"Me? I'm going to be rowing the lifeboat."

"Lifeboat?"

"FASTER. I want to keep it alive for two reasons. First, to fund research that's too far out of the box for even enlightened organizations like NISTER, and second, to be there if or when the political wind turns against NISTER and its mission. Nothing lasts forever, and especially things built on a wave of public ire about something the public doesn't actually understand and can't relate to as soon as it's out of the headlines."

"Have you discussed this with Dr. Huntsman?"

Markson repeated the conversation he'd had with Huntsman, including Huntsman's unwillingness to stay in the job for the long-run.

Jelani found that a serious concern. "I'll have to insist he sign a binding three-year commitment," she told him.

"I'm sure he'll be OK with that."

"And as you've noted, you and Dr. Clarke are the world's experts on warp science. Everything I envision for the future of NISTER under our leadership depends on having that level of expertise in-house. Unless Dr. Clarke rejoins us full-time, Dr. Huntsman won't be sufficient to carry the weight. She was treated like dirt by Jorge and, to a lesser extent, even by Dean

Simpson. If I were her, I wouldn't be inclined to give LAPI another chance. Can you make it happen?"

Markson put his chin in his hand, elbow on the table for a few seconds, and then sat up with a blank expression. "I don't know. Let me see what I can do. I'll get back to you as soon as I can. When do you need to know?"

"Clock's running on the proposal submission date. I'd like to know that Huntsman and Clarke are both on board within 72 hours. Remember—no Clarke, no Huntsman."

Markson realized that, given his earlier conversations with Huntsman, getting the written agreement to the three-year commitment would be nothing more than a formality. Convincing Clarke to return to LAPI would be a challenge no matter how sweet the offer was. The discussion could get heated, and he wanted to make sure that the heat stayed on the professional side of their lives rather than their bringing it home. The most comfortable venue for her would be her office at FASTER.

As he approached the four parking spaces reserved for FASTER at the Barringer-Foreman Technology Park, he saw cars in two of the spaces next to his usual spot. He'd hoped to catch Clarke alone after hours, when their only employee, a jack-of-all-trades "Office Manager" named Marissa, had left for the day. Their offices were cubicles, and the only private area was their conference room, which he thought had the wrong ambiance for their conversation.

He parked and entered the orange, one-story building. The technology park architecture resembled a strip mall more than an office building. Each company had its own entrance to what was structurally similar to a large, commercial rental storage unit or small warehouse. The difference was that the walls, floors, and ceilings were finished, and each unit, though otherwise empty, offered a bathroom and complete utilities. Markson and Clarke had reduced costs and retained flexibility by using seventy-eight-inch-tall movable partitions to partition the fifty-foot by forty-foot floor plan into individual offices, the smallest of which housed their servers. There was also a conference area separated from the rest of the space by fixed, floor-to-ceiling soundproof walls.

When Markson came in, Marissa was in the small reception area at the entrance, seated in front of a file cabinet next to several piles of files she'd stacked on the floor. "Hey, you're working late. What's the occasion?"

"Hi, Lee! Katty asked me to see if we could arrange the paper files in the same way the electronic files are organized. It'll make it easier to find corresponding items when we're dealing with both."

"Cool. You think you'll be much longer? I'd hate for you to miss dinner on our account."

"Bill's ordering pizza for the kids. I'll probably be another hour or so."

Markson didn't want to wait until he and Clarke were too tired to deal with what he had to resolve. It was already late in the day.

He went to Clarke. "Hi, Kat. We need to talk, and I'd like to do it here rather than in the conference room. Do you mind if I let Marissa take off now? She can finish the files tomorrow."

Clarke shrugged. "Sure. What's up?"

"I'll tell you in a minute!" Markson stepped back into the reception area to release Marissa—who, having overheard their conversation, was already collecting her purse and sweater. When he returned, he sat down at her worktable and asked her to bring her chair from behind her desk and join him. "I have a proposition I want to run by you."

As he'd feared, she was hostile to the idea from the beginning. He'd hoped the fact that Shanta Jelani had been her friend and confidante while she and Markson had battled Aguillero would be enough to make Clarke receptive, but realistically, he knew her well enough not to expect that attitude to materialize.

"The last time we were there, the dean tried to bribe us, and then they threatened to paint me as a whore on social media, remember?"

Markson had expected the hostility, but not the intensity. "Kat, please don't go there. The threats came from the government people, not Dean Simpson. Shanta says JoAnne wants to do the right thing. She's giving the good guys a lot of latitude to make amends. That's what I want to discuss with you."

"They were going to publicly humiliate me, and now you want me to go work for them again?"

"Kat, I don't think she knew about the threats. That's why they made her and Aguillero leave the room—so they could deny it all later."

"Well, she can't deny the bribes."

"Look, Kat, we were both treated badly. I was on your side, remember? And I admit that the LAPI administration was responsible for a lot of it, but they can't take the blame for everything that happened. If we can't get past that, we're all going to miss out on an extraordinary opportunity."

"Let's cut to the chase," she began. "They want to submit a proposal against the RFP for membership in the governing body of an institute designed to study superluminal propulsion and related sciences, with LAPI as the lead school, and they want to feature us as the PIs. Do I have that right?"

"That was their original idea," Markson said.

"Their *original* idea? They have a new idea?"

"Yes. Actually, I talked them into it. And you're an essential part of it."

"OK. I'm listening." She was leaning back in her chair, arms folded across her chest and with a scowl on her face that said, *"I don't give a shit what you're going to say, you're never going to get me back in that unforgivable place."*

Now comes the explosion, Markson thought. And then he told her, "The Department of Physics and Astronomy is creating a new, tenured full professorship dedicated to leading the

NISTER Consortium if their proposal is accepted. That professor will almost certainly be the Director of NISTER when it is established."

"And that's you, of course," she said, spreading her hands with a bored tone and expression.

"No. There's someone better qualified whom I've recommended to Shanta. She's agreed with my reasoning and will sell it to Dean Simpson. I'd like you to support it. May I explain it to you?"

"What are you going to do? Go back to your old position?"

"I'd like *you* to take that position, Kat. She's going to offer it to you, including tenure. That's why Jorge quit. By accepting her offer, you can stick it to him."

She had no intention of letting Markson know she felt a pang of joy at the thought of such targeted revenge, but she raised her eyebrows briefly and pondered the idea for a moment before resuming her arms-folded frown.

"And what will you be doing?" she asked.

"I'm going to stay here. We need to keep FASTER as a lifeboat in case the political winds change in a few years. NISTER will be largely government-funded. It could go away as rapidly as it came to be."

She jumped up and leaned across the desk toward him. "You bastard! You want me to take a middling position at LAPI while you stay here and run the show? I never did believe that whole 'equal partners' thing. I'm not your goddamned pawn who you can just push around the board as you choose!"

He reached over to take her hand.

"Don't you touch me!" She stepped back and began to come out from behind her desk.

"Kat, wait! I haven't told you who's going to run NISTER and how you fit in! You're not being pushed aside. You're the lynchpin that ties everything together."

She shook her head, but she did stop and turn to face him. "Some lynchpin. Were you planning to get my opinion before you pushed me into place?"

Markson, who had stood when she had, sat down and asked her to do the same. She hesitated, but then she took her seat.

"That's exactly what I am doing now. Nobody has been hired yet. No proposal has been submitted yet. No universities have been selected yet. NISTER could be established by others, and we will have missed our opportunity to influence its direction and structure. And, if you accept, you will be working with friends and supporters in depth. Will you let me tell you what I got Shanta to accept?"

"Why didn't you talk to me first?"

"Because she called me before I had everything settled in my mind. She was on an incredibly tight timeline and offered me the full professorship. I had to turn it down and sell her on my recommendation for who should get the next offer instead. She accepted my suggestion if, *and only if*, you'll agree assume my former position. The very next thing I did was come back here to talk to you and explain it. I'm not trying to diminish your influence, Kat—I'm trying to grow it."

"I liked you better when you were Mr. Fuck-the-Establishment, sticking it to Jorge. Now, all of a sudden, you want to be a kingmaker... or is it being king that you have your sights on?"

"My disrespect for the establishment sure paid off well, didn't it? I had to be rescued by Congress."

"What's your point?"

"Look, I've learned a bit and grown up a bit, Kat, and one of the things I've learned is that it's better to be wearing a crown, to use your metaphor, than to be wearing handcuffs. We have leverage now that we'll probably never see again. Let's use it to get what *we* want, for a change."

Clarke squirmed in her chair. She readjusted her position twice, then sat up and looked Markson in the eye. "OK, so who is more qualified than you are to run NISTER?"

"Ken."

Clarke liked Huntsman, and they both owed him for his part in ending the government kidnapping and cover-up, but she was surprised. "He's a physicist, but has no special expertise in warp mechanics. Won't he be a weakness as PI in our proposal?"

"Actually, he'll probably be our greatest strength. Nobody has any expertise in warp mechanics except you and me, and I'm not going to be a PI in anyone's proposal. That's why you joining the team is so critical. The other deciding factor will be how the consortium and NISTER will be managed. I have zero experience when it comes to managing a large government agency and its interactions with politicians. Ken's been a NASA associate administrator who was highly instrumental in getting political support for the investigations of the DOD misconduct and for the establishment of NISTER under civilian auspices. Between his cachet as an administrator with a decent knowledge of faster-than-light technology, and your mastery of the field as a resource, which he can draw on daily, we have a winner."

"And how do I fit in after we win?"

"I led the warpship research for LAPI before. You'll lead it now from the same position I had. In addition to that, you'll remain on the board of FASTER. You can continue the research you're doing here at LAPI, too. If NISTER doesn't fund it, FASTER will. We're not subject to the same conflict-of-interest rules as government agencies. It's private money."

The anger was gone, and she was beginning to be intrigued. "So, tell me about this 'lynchpin' thing again."

Markson explained that, in her position in the LAPI Physics Department, she would be the scientific liaison of the department to both NISTER and FASTER, the two sources most likely to be funding most of their research in the area. She would exert a strong influence on the direction that research would take and also on faculty appointments in the area.

She shook her head as she gathered her thoughts. "Shit. I can't believe I'm saying this, but I'll do it. Just keep Dean Simpson away from me."

Markson broke into a wide grin, nodded in appreciation, and added, "You'll have to address the issue of the dean with your department chairperson."

Markson sat with Clarke in his FASTER office as he keyed Huntsman's home number into the speakerphone. Huntsman lived in the suburbs of Maryland, a short commute from NASA Headquarters on E Street SW in Washington, D.C. He scrupulously avoided using government property for private business, especially when it came to anything involving money—like anticipated job offers.

Clarke recognized Huntsman's voice. "Hi, Lee, what's up?"

"I thought you'd like to know that Shanta Jelani, who has taken over the chairmanship of the Physics and Astronomy Department from Jorge Aguillero, likes the idea we discussed of your leading the LAPI proposal for NISTER and becoming the first Chairman of the Board of the NISTER Consortium, assuming LAPI is selected for that responsibility. She's willing to offer you a tenured full professorship dedicated to that responsibility. There are two conditions she's attached to it."

"Good so far," the NASA associate administrator responded. "What are the conditions?"

Markson explained that when he'd told Jelani of Huntsman's reluctance to remain in the post for a prolonged period, she'd been concerned. "I told her that you were agreeable to three years. She wants that commitment in writing."

"I can do that," he said. "What's the other condition?"

"Katty Clarke. Shanta said that unless Kat would join the team, there'd be no deal."

"I'll bet that's going to be a tough sell!" Huntsman laughed.

"It was," Clarke chimed in.

"Hi, Kat! I didn't know you were on the line. It sounds like Shanta knows what she's doing. Assuming this goes through as planned, will you be up for some golf when I get settled down there?"

Clarke laughed and stuck her tongue out at Markson. "Shanta plays, too. Too bad we can't get sailor-boy here to join us."

"Yeah, I know. I tried."

Markson sat shaking his head. "What was it Mark Twain said? 'A good walk spoiled'?"

Clarke and Huntsman laughed, and then Huntsman said, "We have a deal. Is that what you two wanted to hear?"

"Yes!" the pair said in unison.

In less than twenty-four hours, both Ken Huntsman and Katty Clarke were under contract as tenured faculty members of the institute's Department of Physics and Astronomy.

When it became public that Markson had declined to lead the anticipated LAPI NISTER proposal effort in order to preserve his leadership of FASTER, he began receiving hundreds of postal letters and nearly a thousand email messages per week, many of them seeking jobs and some asking for grants. Initially, he tried to read and respond to each one, but the volume was unmanageable. He eventually had to establish an automated reply process. If he didn't recognize the sender of an email message, the recipient received the following response:

> *Due to the volume of correspondence we are receiving, it is not possible to reply personally to your message. Your interest in FASTER is appreciated. Please consult our website for information about our organization, including how to apply for employment or funding.*

The word 'website' in the response was a link. Most postal correspondents received a similar response, except the URL was provided.

One message caught his attention, however. It was from Henry Catalano... except that it wasn't. The return address was Catalano's corporate email at CAT, but the message was from Irina Ivanova. She'd captioned it with the title: "I have to go."

It was a brilliant double-entendre. It, along with the method of transmission, let Markson know that she'd figured out how he'd gotten his message out from DARPA, but it also accurately stated her current concern. Ivanova wanted out of DARPA, and she wanted Markson to recommend her for a senior faculty position in the Department of Physics and Astronomy at LAPI. And she wanted to bring Rakov along as her student.

Markson would have reached for the phone on his desk and immediately dialed the number Ivanova included in her message, but she'd said not to call before 8 PM. Given Clarke's initial reaction to the offers from the institute, he decided not to tell her about this until he found out more from the Russian. He liked Ivanova personally and respected her professionally, although he wasn't sure how she would fit into LAPI's current plans. Rakov was talented enough to give Clarke some competition in the signal-processing arena. Clarke would probably consider each of them as both an enemy and potential rival. That was a hornet's nest not to be disturbed prematurely.

"You seem distracted," Clarke said as they ate dinner in Markson's kitchen.

He was looking down at the table and didn't answer right away.

She picked up a paper napkin from the holder on the table and waved it in front of his face. "Lee?"

He looked up. "What?"

"You seem distracted. What are you thinking about?"

Markson didn't want to say. He was irritated that he had to wait to talk with Ivanova, and also irritated that waiting irritated him. Additionally, he was irritated that he couldn't figure out a good way to call her while being out of earshot of his ever-present significant other. "Nothing. Just some administrative correspondence I received at work today." It was almost true.

"Can I help?"

"Actually, you can... I need some time to respond to some of the inquiries we've been getting that are specifically addressed to me. I'd like to get a few of them out of the way tonight. Could you do the dishes while I go into the office for about an hour?

I think that should be enough time for me to get caught up on the ones with deadlines."

"You sure you don't want me to come with you?"

"These are things I have to respond to personally, so you'd just be looking over my shoulder while I read and type, and we'd both have to come home to a sink full of dirty china. If you'll do them tonight, I'll do them tomorrow. Deal?"

She shrugged her shoulders. "Sure."

He was at his desk by 7:55 PM, and immediately dialed the number from the email. It rang just twice before the familiar voice said, "*Dobray vecher*, Dr. Markson, *kak delah?*"

Markson laughed out loud. "Good evening to you, Dr. Ivanova! I'm doing just fine. How 'bout yourself?"

He could hear her laughter on the other end. "I see you still understand a bit of Russian. Nonetheless, I think we probably should continue in English, yes?"

"*Da*," he agreed. "I'm intrigued by your inquiry, Irena. I'd like to know why you two want to leave DARPA and what you have in mind specifically. That will help me to figure out whether I can be of any help."

She explained that she had some ideas she wanted to explore relating to the warpship problem that weren't in line with the DARPA approach, and if they panned out, she wanted to be able to publish them. In addition, she felt Rakov had more than qualified for his doctoral degree, but there was no way for him to earn the credential from inside the invisible world of SCI-rated research.

"We have to go," she said with a snicker.

"Yeah. Sorry about the tea."

"You're the one who ended up with the laundry problem! Actually, I admired your ingenuity when I figured out what you'd done. That's another reason we want out. We came to this wonderful country because things like what they did to you aren't supposed to happen. We could have stayed in Moscow if that was the kind of place we wanted to inhabit."

Within about forty-five minutes, Markson had a good feel for their motives and capabilities. Both of them could be strong assets to LAPI's faster-than-light effort if the right positions and the resources to support them could be found.

"Irina, I can't make any promises, but I am optimistic. Let me talk with some people. I'll get back to you in maybe a week or so."

"*Spaciba. Da svidania menya droog.*"

"*Pahzhaloosta.* I'll be in touch!"

Over the next several days, Markson found ways to sound out Jelani, Huntsman, and Clarke about the directions LAPI and NISTER were planning to take with the civilian side of the FTL research, but without disclosing his own agenda. He could see several possible ways they could be brought on board, and to the benefit of all concerned.

Markson felt it was critical to avoid antagonizing Clarke any more than was necessary. He knew she wouldn't respond favorably to hiring either of the Russians in any capacity because of their close association with the DOD, and he needed her on board regarding both of them before he approached Jelani or Simpson. That meant he had to have everything lined up in order to approach her.

He searched the internet for everything available on the professional accomplishments of Ivanova and Rakov, also checking to see whether or not either had any scandals or issues that could come back to bite him if he recommended them for a position. He remembered how Aguillero had reacted to finding out that Clarke had done nude television and performed as a stripper.

His extensive background check confirmed his expectation that both of them were "clean as a whistle" and highly competent as scientists. "Time to light the fuse, but not here," he said aloud as he shut down his browser. Again, he decided to make his approach at the friendliest professional venue.

While Kat now had offices at both LAPI and FASTER, and spent most of her time on her full-time position at the institute, she made a point of being at the foundation for at least an hour every afternoon. Promotion and apology notwithstanding, she wasn't comfortable at LAPI yet.

When she arrived at 4:45 PM the next day, they exchanged the usual greetings and she went to her office. He let her settle in and begin reading her mail before he stuck his head in the door. "Got a minute?"

She looked up and pushed the keyboard back. "Sure. What's up?"

"How's your Russian?"

"I took German and French. That's why I went to Italy for my postdoc. Does this have anything to do with those Russians at DARPA you told me about?"

Markson covered his anxiety by forcing his face to look cheery. "Actually, it does. They both want to leave the dark side and come out into the light. I think we can use them."

"And you want us to hire them?"

That alternative hadn't occurred to Markson. It wasn't the best option, and they probably wouldn't accept it, but it might be useful to see how she felt about that before breaching his own proposal. "That's a possibility."

"Why?"

He spent nearly half an hour telling her about their experience, expertise, and accomplishments. He reminded Kat of what he'd told her soon after he'd been released from DARPA— that Ivanova had disapproved of the government's conduct and volunteered that he and Clarke should win the Nobel.

"I don't know," she said after a while. "I can understand the practical side of taking advantage of what they know, but it has the same kind of smell as when your country built its space program on that Nazi, Wernher von Braun."

"Kat, Irena is no Nazi. Neither is Viktor. That's not right. You don't know them. I do. They're good, decent people!"

Both Clarke and Markson himself were startled at the intensity of his response.

She raised her arms in a defensive posture. "Fine. Hire them if it means so much to you. Just keep them out of my way."

"You *can* see how they could contribute a lot to our program, right?" he asked.

"Yes, yes. They can be useful. I just don't want to have to deal with them. It would be a constant reminder of what they put us through."

Markson took a deep breath. "They didn't put us through anything, Kat. More than that, they disapproved of what we went through. Putting them in the same boat with Nilson just because they worked for him makes no more sense than putting *us* in the same category as Jorge just because we worked for him."

"OK, OK. You win. Why are you still hammering at this?"

He took another deep breath. "Because I'd like for us to recommend that Shanta hire Irena as a faculty member and admit Viktor as a student."

Clarke shook her head from side to side in disbelief, and then she sniffed and looked up. "No fucking way!"

"You agreed that they have a lot to offer."

"No."

"She was, and probably still is, the DOD's top expert in the field."

"I don't give a shit. They're evil."

Markson walked around her desk and spun her chair around to face him, getting in her face. "No, Kat, they're not. They were on our side from the beginning. I can understand why they may remind you of the evil things done to us, but *they weren't the ones who did anything wrong.*"

He stepped back as she sat stunned. Her eyes moistened and he realized he had pushed too hard.

He walked back around to the front of her desk as her eyes began to tear up. "I'm sorry, Kat, but it's frustrating that you almost lumped Shanta in with Jorge as a reason for refusing her offer to rejoin the faculty. Please don't make that mistake again. Please. These are two good people who we need on our team. You and Ken helped me escape from DARPA. Can't we help them do the same?"

She put her head on her desk and hid her face. He sat down and put his hand on her arm as she took several deep breaths. Finally, she looked up. "I just hate them all so much that I lost track of the details. What do you want me to do?"

He explained why he wanted them to recommend a tenured full professorship for Ivanova. She, like Markson, had a background in relativistic physics and electrical engineering. She had worked on signals intelligence and, like Clarke, on digital signal processing. She'd led those who figured out the trajectory from the EM data for the DOD. She'd held senior faculty positions in several countries, and anything less than a tenured full professorship would be a demotion.

"So, you want her to outrank me?" Clarke sat with her eyes wide, head cocked to the side.

"It's not what I want, and it won't last forever. She earned it the same way you will, and in a lot less time than it took her. Besides, as a NISTER liaison and FASTER trustee, you'll be reviewing her grant proposals whichever way they go. And she'll be reporting to Shanta just like you, so for practical purposes, that makes you equals."

Clarke breathed in deeply. "What about Rakov?"

Markson explained that Rakov had been Ivanova's PhD student and had completed "all but dissertation" when he'd accompanied her to the U.S. They would ask Shanta to admit him as a student in the department with Ivanova as his thesis advisor. He'd work on a topic related to the FTL project.

"How will he be funded? A NISTER grant?"

"My personal opinion is that the most effective use of him as a resource would be to give him a research assistantship funded by NISTER and have him work directly for you."

Markson waited for the explosion. It didn't come.

Instead, Kat sighed, shook her head, placed her wrists on the edge of her desk, and wiggled her fingers before looking up. "Do I have any say in this?"

"Of course. He could work for Irena, but I think you and he would be a marvelous team. After you've met him, if you don't want him as your assistant, fine. But please, don't lock him out without a hearing because of who he worked for in the past."

"So, why me?"

"Because his expertise is in signal processing, just like you, and he may already be as good at it as you are. Separately, either one of you is formidable. You can learn from each other, and then nobody will be able to touch either of you. If the two of you team up with the quantum physics folks, you may even be able to attack that horizon problem with some sort of quantum signal processing. Meanwhile, you can look for any sign of previous events in archived electromagnetic data from satellites, as well as ground-based telescopes and radar stations. Suppose you could get some trajectories and figure out where they come from? The opportunities are mind-boggling."

"So, I can say 'no' to Rakov working for me if I want?"

"Yes. Yes. It's your call. If you don't want him as a resource, we'll have to get him a research fellowship, but that can be arranged. There is one thing you'll have to do in any case, however."

She grimaced. "Like I couldn't see that coming. What?"

"You are the department's expert on signal processing, and that's the subject of his thesis. Ivanova will be his primary advisor because of their history together, but I'm sure the department will insist that you be his second referee."

"May I interview him?"

"If you're OK with us—and I do mean us—recommending them to Shanta, I'm sure she'll want to interview them before making a final decision. When they come down for that, we can set up a separate interview for Rakov with you."

"God, Lee, you should sell timeshares. I can't believe you talked me into this. Let's do it."

The next morning, Clarke scheduled an appointment with Markson and Jelani for that afternoon in Jelani's office. It took less than twenty minutes for Jelani to ask Markson to invite the two Russians to Baton Rouge.

Two weeks and a ton of paperwork later, Irena Ivanova had a faculty contract with LAPI, Rakov was a registered PhD student, and Clarke had a new graduate research assistant.

Rakov had aced his interview with the skeptical Katty Clarke. When she'd asked what he thought he could contribute, he'd said he thought he had a way to detect the optical signature of previous events if they existed. When she'd asked how, he'd been hesitant to tell her without a commitment that he'd get the assistantship. After more negotiation, he'd tendered a possible example without telling her how he'd found it. He'd also showed her the data and his analysis.

"Damn!" she'd said. "You've got a job."

EPILOGUE

ONCE HE'D SETTLED IN at LAPI, Rakov gave Clarke the key to his success in finding evidence of a prior instance of an FTL vehicle's wake. The key was the wake's unique signature: opposing tracks leading away from a flash. The Russian had developed a signal processing algorithm tuned to isolating such signatures even when deep inside the noise. It worked with any image, radio, or IR, visible on up through gamma rays. Sources could be planetary probes, surveillance satellites, Earth-orbiting telescopes, or terrestrial telescopes.

Clarke was impressed by his work and intended for them to build on it together for his dissertation. Recognizing that mass application of the technique and its offspring—as the two improved it—would require analyzing terabytes of data which was stored on a large server cluster and processed on a supercomputer, she asked Rakov how he'd found an instance without such a database.

"I have mentor with access to secret Russian and Soviet archive. One flash recorded as possible U.S. test of nuclear weapon in space later discarded by Russian analysts as faulty sensor. I apply algorithm to all sensors recorded for that time;

it identifies many of them as positive. NASA, European, and Japanese observations also passed test."

"Can we use the data? Isn't it classified or something?"

"All data but Russian and Soviet was public. Russian data is classified by Russia, not USA, and Soviet Union no longer exists. Unless you plan to visit Moscow, who will prosecute us?"

"Viktor, I didn't like you before I met you, but I am liking you more and more every day. Don't tell Lee, but I'm glad he browbeat me into hiring you."

"What is this 'browbeat'?"

Clarke laughed. "Ask your thesis advisor. I think she will be able to translate it for you."

One of the first grants approved and funded by NISTER was used to purchase additional storage and processors for the LAPI supercomputing center for the exclusive use of the FTL research group. An additional grant paid for Ivanova's salary and those of her student assistants; they'd acquire every unclassified record from satellite and ground-based electromagnetic imaging systems over the frequency range from 30 MHz to gamma rays. Within eighteen months, the system was up and running, using the powerful new Rakov-Clarke "Warp Burst Detection" algorithm that won Rakov his doctorate on a large but as yet incomplete set of data.

Within two years, the data archive was complete and had been processed in its entirety. LAPI found two previous examples in addition to the one Rakov had identified on his own. The DOD shared an additional instance they'd identified in classified data, although they wouldn't release the raw data from which they'd found it.

Ivanova kept Rakov at LAPI by offering him a FASTER-funded postdoctoral fellowship to work with her on trajectory analysis. She wanted to know where these hypervelocity visitors to the solar system were going. Were they all from the same place? All going to the same place? The observations they'd discovered seemed only marginally usable for such an investigation, but the questions were so Earth-shaking that it seemed necessary to take the shot.

Four years after the establishment of NISTER, there'd been enough peer-reviewed papers regarding FTL space travel using various proposed warp technologies, all published in reputable journals, that the subject had become at least marginally acceptable within the physics establishment, and *The First International Conference on Faster-than-Light Physics* was convened in Rome, Italy.

The FTL group from LAPI was heavily represented because they were the leaders in the field. Rakov presented a paper by him and Clarke titled "Improved Algorithm for Identifying Warp Bubble Signatures in EM Image Data" which described the latest version of their software. A paper by Ivanova and Rakov called "Identifying and Tracking Warp Bubbles Using Observations of Opportunity" described how the events captured by the algorithm were used to generate possible flight trajectories of the bubbles. Rakov presented the paper even though he was the second author because Ivanova elected not to attend.

"Half the staff is going. Somebody has to stay home and mind the store. I'll go to the next one," she'd insisted.

The LAPI group wasn't the only one attending from the U.S. FASTER was represented by Markson, who presented a paper co-authored with Jelani: "The Effect of Warp Bubble Configuration on the Radiation Problem in FTL Travel." It explored the possibility of reducing the internal and external radiation attending the moving bubble by altering the shape of spacetime slightly and without any new physics. The possibility was quite small.

Even the DOD attended. Colonel Christopher Nilson, still running the warp project at DARPA, presented an unclassified paper titled "Terrestrial Military Implications of FTL Technology." He argued that the knowledge gained in the intervening years between the congressional hearings and the conference supported the notion that the technology could be weaponized for cost-effective use on and near the Earth.

In response to a question from the audience, he said, "I am not advocating it. I would oppose it if it became feasible. I am only pointing out the possibility so that processes can be put into place nationally and internationally to deal with it before it becomes a reality."

As they waited in the airport to return to the U.S. from Rome, Jelani huddled with Markson and the others from the institute. She'd been toying with an idea for months, and a paper by an author from the People's Republic of China seemed to have made significant progress along similar lines. They discussed it until their flight's boarding call was announced.

Clarke picked up her luggage and headed for the gate.

Jelani grabbed her bags and strode along beside Clarke. "I'd like to work with you on that. Can we set aside a little money to get Zhao Ming involved since it involves quantum mechanics? Besides, he speaks Chinese and can actually talk with the guy—whose name I don't remember because I can't even pronounce it."

Markson caught up and made them a trio. "I heard that. If we find that NISTER can't do it, think I can manage some FASTER funding."

Jelani took Markson by the arm, stopped, and turned to face him. "You should, Lee. It's possible your testimony to Congress was unduly pessimistic."

THE END?

ACRONYMS

ACRONYM	DEFINITION	NOTES
AFOSR	Air Force Office of Scientific Research	
AG	Attorney General	
CAT	Catalano Automated Trading	Fictitious - see Ch. 1
CATSPAW	Casimir Alcubierre Temporal Signal Propagation Anomaly Waveguide	Fictitious - see Ch. 3
CEO	Chief Executive Officer	
CIO	Chief Information Officer	
CNN	Cable News Network	
DARPA	Defense Advanced Research Projects Agency	
DOD	Department of Defense	
DOJ	Department of Justice	
EM	Electromagnetic	

EMP	Electromagnetic pulse	
EOF	Empirical orthogonal function	
FASTER	Foundation for Alcubierre-related Science, Technology and Engineering Research	Fictitious – See Ch. 6
FOIA	Freedom of Information Act	
FTL	Faster than light	
IFART	Institute for Alcubierre Research and Technology	Fictitious – See Ch. 6
GNC	Guidance, navigation, and control	
GW	Gravitational wave	
IR	Infrared	
KAGRA	Kamioka Gravitational Wave Detector	
LAN	Local Area Network	
LAPI	Louisiana Advanced Projects Institute	Fictitious - See Ch. 1
LHO	LIGO Hanford Observatory	

LIGO	Laser Interferometer Gravitational Wave Observatory	
LLO	LIGO Livingston Observatory	
LSC	LIGO Scientific Collaboration	
LSU	Louisiana State University	
NCO	Non-commisioned Officer	
NISTER	National Institute for Spacetime Engineering Research	Fictitious - See Ch. 14
NGC	New General Catalog	
NSA	National Security Agency	
NSF	National Science Foundation	
POTUS	President of the United States	
QC	Quality control	
RISU	Rhode Island State University	Fictitious – See Ch. 5
SCI	Sensitive compartmentalized information	

SEC	Securities and Exchange Commission	
SECDEF	Secretary of Defense	
SIGINT	Signals Intelligence	
TAN	Transient Astronomy Network	
TOA	Time of arrival	
UHF	Ultrahigh frequency	
USAF	United States Air Force	
UTC	Coordinated Universal Time	
UV	Ultraviolet	
VHF	Very high frequency	

ACKNOWLEDGMENTS

WHEN I FIRST BEGAN TO WRITE FICTION, my author friend David Stewart got me started with a short story workshop he led, and he helped me develop good habits that have served me well.

I am indebted to Professor JoLee Passerini, the students in her Creative Writing class, and the members of the Writers' Haven at Eastern Florida State College, particularly Kenny Reynolds and Taylor Keene. They joined my wife Liz in convincing me to accept the challenge of National Novel Writing Month in 2016. Once I made the commitment, they inspired me, taught me, and challenged me to do it well. This encouragement, helpful advice, and valuable assistance were essential for turning a vague idea I had in 2011 into over a hundred pages of fiction, a complete first draft except for the opening scene, by the end of the month.

Peter L.W. Brathwaite, a long-time friend and colleague who served his country well as a congressional staff member, answered quite a few questions I had about the scenes involving congressmen and congressional hearings. Thanks, Pete!

In the fall of 2018, I sent a beta version to some friends and professional colleagues. Among them were Paul D'Agostino,

Lee McLamb, Wynn Rostek, and Tim Wilfong, who all provided encouragement and suggestions which I found reassuring and deeply appreciated.

Three beta responses deserve special attention. Nicolas Arnaud of the Virgo Experiment at the European Gravitational Observatory in Italy was kind enough to review the science and the administrative aspects of gravitational wave observations as portrayed in the novel. His comments reassured me that I hadn't badly botched anything in the science and told me what I needed to fix on the administrative side. Thank you, Dr. Arnaud!

Long-time friend Ellie Hilton was working on her own novel, so we agreed to swap critiques. She provided a thorough, detailed analysis, including several pages of commentary and suggestions plus handwritten page-by-page annotations on her copy of the manuscript. She identified areas of concern in the development of several characters and in the presentation of the scientific concepts for lay readers, enabling me to address these issues effectively.

Finally, our son Martin sent his comments as a series of email messages as he read the story. When I compiled them, they added up to seventeen single-spaced pages of pure gold. He had no hesitation about telling Dad when "the movie isn't playing." He identified many of the same issues that Ellie Hilton had noted and added valuable additional insights based on his training in psychology and social work. In particular, he identified a subconscious factor, the Dunning-Krugar effect, that explained my having presented the scientific material at an inappropriate level for a general audience in the first two chapters of that early draft. This helped me to avoid it later. He also pointed out specific passages and concepts that he found especially effective and entertaining, which encouraged me to keep working hard.

Thank you, Ellie and Martin!

This book was inspired by a lecture called "Warp Mechanics 101" delivered in 2011 at a *DARPA 100 Year Starship Symposium* in Orlando, Florida by Dr. Harold "Sonny" White, the Advanced Propulsion Theme Lead for NASA at the Johnson Space Center. He was kind enough to send me copies of his charts on the Alcubierre metric shortly after the lecture.

Dr. White's lecture was based on the solution to Einstein's field equations developed by Miguel Alcubierre, on which this entire *Alcubierre Metric Connection* series is based. The world in general and I in particular are deeply indebted to Dr. Alcubierre for his curiosity, open-mindedness, and ingenuity.

My editor, Jennifer Collins, provided detailed guidance where there were opportunities for improvement. She also let me know what was well-written. Both services were priceless, and I much appreciate them.

My cover designer, Dave Leahey, and my interior designer, Victoria Wolf, made this book look good. Thank you both! I also appreciate the proofreading by Luna Imprints Author Services.

ABOUT THE AUTHOR

FRANK MERCERET is an atmospheric physicist and criminal lawyer turned author and public speaker who loves his family, and writing fiction, poetry, and drama. When he isn't writing, he also enjoys golf, amateur radio, and making music on the ukulele.

The story behind Lee Markson and Ken Huntsman developing the CATSPAW technology mentioned in *Wake Turbulence* is told in full in the first book in the Alcubierre Metric Connection Series, *CATSPAW*, available on Amazon at: https://www.amazon.com/dp/B097KSYD4C (eBook) or https://www.amazon.com/dp/1737185806 (paperback).

If you enjoyed *Wake Turbulence*, please review it on Amazon. For the latest on the Alcubierre Metric Connection, visit frankmerceretauthor.com.

You may also want to have a look at *First Verses*, the poetry chapbook Frank wrote for his family, on Amazon at https://www.amazon.com/dp/165515415X (paperback only).

Made in the USA
Middletown, DE
09 May 2022

65536701R00314